Praise for *All That's Left Unsaid*

'An unforgettable debut, utterly compelling from start to finish. Original. Heartbreaking. Gripping. I just loved it'
Liane Moriarty

'An urgent story that commands an audience.
All That's Left Unsaid is a gripping and unflinching narrative that is as heart-wrenching as it is unputdownable'
Karin Slaughter

'A shocking, deeply moving and truly special debut. Savage and heart-breaking, *All That's Left Unsaid* tackles some hugely important issues, yet is also a richly crafted mystery, a story that is both impossible to put down and impossible to forget'
Chris Whitaker, *We Begin at the End*

'A story of great grief and even greater love, this beautiful and powerful book will break you open and change you inside'
Alice Pung OAM, *One Hundred Days*

'A stunning debut, an unputdownable mystery combined with a profoundly moving family drama about the ways we hurt and hide from those we love most – and how we mend and strengthen those lifelong bonds. It blew me away'
Angie Kim, *Miracle Creek*

'Tracey Lien's story pulls you back twenty years, then pushes you, heartbroken and stunned, into today's bright light.
All That's Left Unsaid is honest, aching, and filled with beauty. It will transport you'
Julia Phillips, *Disappearing Earth*

'One of the most profoundly affecting novels I've ever read, *All That's Left Unsaid* is a wrenching, propulsive story . . . [and] is for anyone who has ever been told they are the lucky ones'
Katie Gutierrez, *More Than You'll Ever Know*

Tracey Lien is the author of the debut novel *All That's Left Unsaid*. Born and raised in South Western Sydney, Australia, she earned her MFA at the University of Kansas and was previously a reporter for the *Los Angeles Times*. She lives in Brooklyn, New York.

ALL THAT'S LEFT UNSAID

TRACEY LIEN

ONE PLACE. MANY STORIES

HQ
An imprint of HarperCollins*Publishers* Ltd
1 London Bridge Street
London SE1 9GF

www.harpercollins.co.uk

HarperCollins*Publishers*
1st Floor, Watermarque Building, Ringsend Road
Dublin 4, Ireland

This edition 2022

1
First published in Great Britain by
HQ, an imprint of HarperCollins*Publishers* Ltd 2022

First published in Australia by
HQ, an imprint of HarperCollins*Publishers* Australia Pty Limited 2022

Copyright © Tracey Lien 2022

Tracey Lien asserts the moral right to be identified as the author of this work. A catalogue
record for this book is available from the British Library.

ISBN: HB: 978-0-00-851189-0
TPB: 978-0-00-851190-6
ANZ: 978-0-00-854707-3

MIX
Paper from
responsible sources
FSC™ C007454

This book is produced from independently certified FSC™ paper
to ensure responsible forest management.

For more information visit: www.harpercollins.co.uk/green

This book is set in 11/15.5 pt. Bembo by Type-it AS, Norway

Printed and Bound in the UK using 100% Renewable Electricity at
CPI Group (UK) Ltd, Croydon, CR0 4YY

For my parents

Chapter 1

The circumstances of Denny Tran's death were so violent that most people in Cabramatta were too spooked to attend his funeral. At least that's how it seemed to his big sister, Ky. The funeral hall had been all but empty—her dead seventeen-year-old brother lay in the glossy closed casket; her parents and a few relatives knelt next to a blown-up photo of a grinning Denny; and a Buddhist monk chanted prayers in exchange for lunch.

The only non-family in attendance were Denny's high school teachers, who huddled together big-eyed and confused by the lack of seating and eulogies. At the wake, they stood in the doorway to her family's narrow townhouse, still holding the flowers and signed cards they'd brought to the funeral (no one had told them that Vietnamese families take cash), and waved at Ky like they were getting a waiter's attention.

"Hi, Ky!" Mr. Dickson said in a voice that was too cheerful for the occasion, his mouth stretched wide in what appeared to be an effort to correctly pronounce her name. He'd always called her Kai, even though she'd corrected him in year eight when she sat in his math class four times a week. "*Keeee,*" she'd said, her voice small, "like a key that unlocks a door." Maybe it was amnesia, but every time he read the class roster, she became Kai again, and after a third correction, she gave up. Kee. Kai. Whatever.

"Hey," Ky said, rushing to clear a spot on the coffee table for the flowers.

She could feel the teachers' eyes scan her parents' living room, identifying everything that was familiar to them (Panasonic television, years-old McDonald's Happy Meal toys on top of the VCR, Ky's framed university degree, photos of Denny winning Highest Academic Achievement four years in a row), and everything that was unfamiliar (the ancestral altar that featured black-and-white photos of her unsmiling dead grandparents, a bright red calendar hanging above the television reminding them that 1996 was the year of the rat, a doorway full of shoes). The other teachers, whom Ky recognized as Ms. Faulkner and Ms. Buck, continued to study the room, smiling at Ky's younger cousins, one of whom grimaced in response.

"Are your parents around?" Mr. Dickson asked.

"Mum's in the kitchen."

Her mother had stayed up the night before hand-rolling more than a hundred buns for the wake. Ky helped stamp the tops of the buns with a spot of red food coloring but expressed skepticism about her family needing to prepare so much food. Because even though she'd been away from Cabramatta for four years, she knew how this town worked: If a family suffered a "good" death—the kind that happened to old people, the kind that everyone was prepared for—the Asians in town showed up with family members in tow, gifting envelopes stuffed with cash. But if it was a "bad" death—the kind caused by terrible luck, where children or gangs or heroin were involved—everyone was suddenly too busy, was out of town, or hadn't heard the news. Her own parents had pulled a similar move on friends and acquaintances before, claiming that they were tied up with work when really they were superstitious about bad luck rubbing off with proximity.

"This is different," her mother had said after Ky questioned who would eat all the food they were making. She refused to look Ky in the eye when she spoke. She refused to acknowledge that Denny had suffered a bad death, the worst kind, a nightmare that stole her words and silenced her family. She refused to stop moving, as though afraid the truth would catch up to her if she slowed for even a moment.

Ky had made a show of dropping the stamp onto the kitchen counter. "*How* is this different?" she said, trying to draw her mother's eyes back to her, trying to get someone—anyone—in the family to look her straight in the face and talk about her brother.

"Because he is my son!" her mother said, slamming the dough back onto the counter so hard it looked like her body was ready to collapse into itself.

Ky had restrained herself from saying more. She'd bitten her tongue as thoughts tumbled through her head. Of neighbors not showing up to the funeral. Of her parents' coworkers— who usually demanded wedding invitations from people they hardly knew—conveniently being too busy to swing by to pay their respects. Of their playing games of mah-jongg with one another, eating boiled peanuts while gossiping about the good boy, the smart boy, the painfully unlucky boy who was in the wrong place at the wrong time. She saw them shaking their heads as they spoke of how the world wasn't what it used to be, how ruthless people had become, how indiscriminate luck was in a town like Cabramatta, in a country as confounding as Australia. And it made her angry. Ky alternated between clenching her jaw and grinding her teeth when she thought of what people might be saying about her brother, because what the hell did they know? Bad luck was meaningless, defeatist. Bad luck was throwing your hands up before you'd even tried—it was a footnote, something that happened to *other* people. Bad luck made Ky want to loosen her strained jaw and scream at her absent neighbors. But she knew that even if she tried, no noise would come out. She could only ever fantasize; she could never really be heard.

People would come, Ky's mother said again, her thick hands pushing and grabbing and twisting the dough as though her love for her children was measured by her sweat and exertion—how much food she made, how springy the buns were once steamed. They would come for her son, she repeated, and it would be embarrassing not to have enough food at the wake, and the family couldn't afford to be embarrassed anymore.

Ky wanted her mother to be right. Denny deserved a crowd. More than a crowd, he deserved the presence of every person he would have met had his life not ended so soon. In the days leading up to the funeral, Ky caught herself daydreaming about hundreds, no, thousands of strangers making pilgrimages to Cabramatta for her brother. In her imagination, they crowded into her parents' driveway, spilled out onto the sidewalk, filled the neighboring streets, and shouted about how badly they wished they'd known him. But even though the daydreams were her own creation, she kept losing control of them, her mind allowing Minnie, whom she hadn't seen in years, not since they'd had the worst fight of her life, to appear and shift the focus to Ky. Collectively, the imagined pilgrims would turn on Ky, demanding to know where she'd been, why she wasn't there for Denny in the end, how she could be so selfish as to abandon her baby brother like that. Fantasy Ky would freeze, her daydream tongue getting fat and useless in her parched daydream mouth, until she forced herself to snap out of it.

Back in the living room, Mr. Dickson stared at Ky, expecting her to show him to the kitchen. Ky stared back—she usually knew what she was meant to do, what was socially appropriate, but she was slow to act. Sometimes she felt like she was watching TV instead of occupying her own body. And right now the thought of having to translate Mr. Dickson's condolences to her parents—not to mention the awkward, stilted conversation that would follow—made her want to excuse herself and make a run for it, out of the house, down the street, in any direction, breaking the sound barrier, eventually escaping her own skin.

"They're busy right now," Ky said, not exactly lying. Her mother remained in a cooking frenzy. The last time she saw her father, about thirty minutes earlier, he was in his funerary black slacks and white shirt—barely discernible from his regular work clothes as a bank teller—lying straight on Denny's single mattress. "Plus, their English isn't great."

"I would still like to—"

"Here, have some food," Ky said. "Mum spent ages making these, so she'd be happy if you ate it."

She piled buns and noodles onto paper plates for the teachers, her armpits growing sweaty enough that she could feel them squeak under her white button-down, her rimless eyeglasses sliding down the broad bridge of her nose. Her family rarely hosted guests, and white guests other than the Avon lady were the rarest of all. Ky could remember only one other occasion when a white person had visited: When he was eight, Denny had befriended a freckly orange-haired boy who once came over to play G.I. Joes. Ky's mother, suspicious of white people—convinced that they might steal—made him stay outside the house. Denny and his friend played in the doorway, with Denny sitting inside, the white boy sitting outside. Ky, who was thirteen at the time, told her mother that she was pretty sure this wasn't normal, and that even though she herself had no white friends, she was willing to vouch that Freckles wasn't a thief.

"They don't seem to mind," her mother said, poking her head from the kitchen to watch the two boys go to war with their figurines.

But Freckles must have told his mother, and she must have minded, because he never came by again.

Minnie, who back then was over at Ky's house every day after school, had said that Ky's mother was onto something. "White people *are* thieves," she said between blowing huge bubbles of grape-flavored Hubba Bubba gum. "Captain Cook! Christopher Columbus! The *French*! White peeps are OG thieves to the max, man."

"What are you talking about?" Ky said.

Minnie theatrically smacked her own forehead, rolling her

ALL THAT'S LEFT UNSAID

eyes as far back as they'd go. "God, Ky, they've stolen your faculties, too."

"My what?"

"Your mum's not crazy, man . . ."—Minnie cocked a finger gun at Ky—"she's smart."

While it irritated Ky that Minnie always seemed to take her mother's side, she secretly appreciated how normal her friend made her feel. When Ky later recounted stories of her parents to her white friends in university, they made no attempts to reassure her that her family was like every other refugee family, that their values and actions were typical of immigrants from Vietnam. Instead, they observed that her mother sounded paranoid, that she might benefit from talking to a therapist. And whenever Ky brushed up against their judgment, she was reminded that the act of sharing her family's stories was a kind of betrayal, a way of setting her parents up to fail in the eyes of outsiders, a way of inviting such outsiders—who had no grasp of what her parents had been through or how deep their love was for their children or that Viets just did things differently—to laugh *at,* and not *with,* her. During those times, Ky missed Minnie most.

"So, how long are you back?" Mr. Dickson said, twisting a clump of noodles with his plastic fork like it was spaghetti. His eyes moved between Ky's face and the TV screen behind her, where a news anchor showed a graphic of the growing hole in the ozone layer.

"I'm sorry?" Ky said, snapping back to the room.

"They were talking about how bad that hole was in the eighties," Mr. Dickson said, angling his chin at the screen.

"Can't believe we've made it to the nineties and they still haven't figured it out."

Ky turned to the screen, where the news anchor had cut to coverage of the impending bushfire season.

"Uh," she said, straightening her back because she didn't know what else to do. "Right."

"Anyway, I was saying," Mr. Dickson said after clearing his throat of noodles and returning his attention to Ky, "how long are you back?"

Ky was surprised that he knew that she no longer lived in Sydney. But of course Denny had told his teachers; he'd been wide-eyed about her move to Melbourne for university, about her internship with the *Herald Sun,* her first printed bylines. He'd even asked if he could live with her, just for a bit, so that he could know what life was like outside of Cabramatta. She'd said they could talk about it on her next trip home. She hadn't expected that trip to be for his funeral.

"I took a week off, but work said I could take more if I need it."

"I'm sure your parents are glad to have you back," said Ms. Buck. Her hair was still as strawberry blond as Ky remembered, but her freckles appeared to have joined forces over the years, forming large islands of light brown on her otherwise milky skin. "I just can't imagine going through this tragedy. It's just . . . so devastating. I'm sure it means a lot to them to have you home."

Ms. Faulkner nodded, but her lips remained firmly pressed together, her eyes bloodshot, tears pooling at the edges.

Ky suddenly felt self-conscious about the dryness of her

own eyes. She hadn't cried during the funeral. Neither had her parents.

You know what they're thinking, right? said a voice in Ky's head. There was something about being back in Cabramatta that brought Minnie into Ky's every thought, every conversation. She couldn't remember a Cabramatta without Minnie, and her friend's voice always appeared when she least expected it. *They reckon you don't care.*

That's not true, Ky thought.

Yeah, it is. They think you're a stoic Asian with no feelings and you're drawing on your Confucius values.

What are you even—

You know, the one where Con-fu-cius say, crying is for bay-bee.

Ky desperately wanted to explain to the teachers that just because her family didn't cry didn't mean they didn't care. In fact, there were so many signs that they cared, so many ways to tell that they hurt—the fog that had appeared and refused to leave her mother's eyes since she learned that Denny had died; her father's silence, not because he didn't want to speak, but because he clearly couldn't find the words anymore; the clenched jaw and endless sweating and dead-end fantasies and imagined conversations with friends who weren't even here. The Tran family cared. They'd just been hollowed out.

No one asked.

What?

You know, Ky, you don't have to explain shit to these teachers. They didn't ask, and it's none of their business.

But—

Just stop it.

9

"So what comes next?" Mr. Dickson said, still mindlessly twisting his fork.

"I don't know if there's anything else after the wake," Ky said, finally returning to the real world, responding to real questions.

"Have you . . ." he said, glancing at Ms. Faulkner and Ms. Buck before returning to his noodles, "heard anything else? About what happened?"

Ky noticed Ms. Buck shifting her weight to her other foot; Ms. Faulkner chewed her bottom lip as she looked down at her own plate of noodles. None of the teachers met Ky's eyes.

The facts, which Ky had gotten secondhand from her parents, were patchy, and recalling them made her skin turn cold as she continued to sweat. From her mother, she'd learned that Denny had gone to Lucky 8, a banquet-style seafood restaurant, after attending the traditional December year-twelve formal. It was the first and only time Ky's parents had allowed Denny out with friends at night—a reward for doing so well in school—and it came only after months of begging, with assurances from Denny's best friend, Eddie Ho, that they just wanted an excuse to prolong an evening of formal wear. Denny had even roped in Ky to help him make his case.

"Come on, Mum," Ky had told her mother over the phone weeks before the formal. "It's Lucky 8. People get married there. Plus, *I* got to go to an after-party when I had my formal."

"You did?"

Ky paused, thought about whether she'd actually told her mother about the party she'd attended all those years ago.

"Yes," she said, crossing her fingers. "It'll be fine! He's

basically an adult, he's a good kid who's never ever gotten into trouble, and it's Lucky 8!"

"But Cabramatta is not like when you lived here," her mother said in Vietnamese. "It's changed. The people are different from what you remember, it's—"

"Stop stressing so much and just let him go. You're gonna stunt his growth if you keep smothering him."

From her father, Ky learned that the formal itself went off without a hitch. Denny won the title "Most Likely to Succeed," which came with a sash that he tucked into the breast pocket of a borrowed suit. He used a disposable camera to take photos with friends, with the teachers of Cabramatta High, of the crusty and over-fried dinner served at the RSL club. And then they walked to Lucky 8, a restaurant known for having a wedding singer perform even when there wasn't a wedding; a restaurant that had six tanks filled with live fish and lobsters and king crabs; a restaurant reserved for celebration and hope and new beginnings.

What happened next, according to both her mother *and* her father, was bad luck. It wasn't the glib kind of bad luck that accompanies a stubbed toe or stolen hubcaps, but the kind of bad luck that shimmies across rooftops looking for a family to curse, for a child to steal. Ky had asked her parents what the police had told them, but instead of sharing what else they knew, they simply shook their heads, their eyes swollen and red, their lips forming the words *Bad luck, bad luck*. Ky had wanted to yell at them then, too, but when she opened her mouth—silence.

"I don't know," Ky said, finally locking eyes with Mr.

Dickson. "We haven't heard anything from the police since the incident."

"Well," Mr. Dickson said, pausing the twirling of his plastic fork, "if there's anything we can do, any way we can help, just say the word."

Jack shit, Minnie said in Ky's head.

"Thanks," Ky said, speaking over the imagined voice that continued in the background.

Mr. Dickson nodded while chewing. Ms. Buck rested a hand on Ky's shoulder; it took everything for Ky to not squirm away. Ms. Faulkner looked like she was about to cry.

Inaudible to anyone but Ky, Minnie continued: *But I tell you what— Ky, as a Good Big Sister, will do more than jack shit! She will take matters into her own hands, won't you, Ky? She will redeem herself for failing her brother! She will step up for the first time in her pathetic do-good, rule-following gimp of a life! Because those dipstick cops won't do shit! Because they'll just write us off as troubled FOBs with FOB troubles! Because if we can't speak up when one of our own is beaten to death, then what the fuck is wrong with us? Because, because, because!*

When Ky's parents called to tell her that Denny had been stomped to death in Lucky 8, she didn't answer because she wasn't home. When they tried her at work, she didn't answer because she was on deadline—she had been assigned a human-interest story on a couple living in their car who had just won the lottery. When her parents left a message with the newspaper's front desk, Ky never got it because Becca Smith, the receptionist, said she couldn't understand them through their thick accents.

"I think a Chinese man called for you," she said. "He gave

me a number, but honestly, it was hard to understand him, so I didn't write it down."

"Oh, thanks." Ky looked around, hoping that someone else was listening in on the conversation, someone who could validate her feelings, assure her that, yes, the encounter, like so many of Ky's previous interactions with Becca Smith, was objectively off-putting, and that Ky's response—to feel unsteady, as though someone had kicked the back of her office chair—was not only normal but appropriate, more than appropriate, maybe even too generous. She didn't catch anyone's eye. It was just between her and the perpetually sunny receptionist. "I guess I'll check my Rolodex for Chinese Man and call him back."

"Great! I'll leave you to it!" Becca Smith said, tapping her acrylic nails on Ky's cubicle divider, her smile stiff, as though she had detected but not fully processed Ky's sarcasm.

Ky didn't immediately listen to the voice messages her parents left on any of her phones. It would be something dumb, because it always was: Denny wanted to go on a school camp—was that safe? Denny wanted to drop physics in year eleven—would he still be able to become a doctor without it? Denny needed to travel for a debating tournament—was that legitimate? Did teenagers lie about these things so they could do drugs instead?

When it came to Denny, who was five years younger than Ky, it was as if her parents had lost the ability to parent, forgotten that they'd done it once before, panicked at the prospect of having to do it again. The Trans clung to the old country and the belief that boys were more valuable than girls. After all, boys carried on the family name and were traditionally the breadwinners. Even the best of girls eventually married and joined someone else's family. Ky also suspected that, with Denny, her family felt they had a fresh start. Denny was born in Australia, after the family had settled in Cabramatta. Ky was their trial-and-error baby, brought from Vietnam, toilet-trained in a Malaysian refugee camp, and sent to English as a Second Language classes from kindergarten through year two. Her parents doubted whether Ky would succeed, feeling she was too much like them. Denny represented an untainted opportunity, one where they wouldn't have to make compromises. Which, she understood, was why they were so precious with him, so unable to make decisions without worrying that they were jeopardizing their only son's future.

Ky had resented Denny when he was first born, but she remembered the moment her heart thawed: Denny, still wearing a nappy, squatted beside a six-year-old Ky as she colored in the flags of all the countries participating in the 1980 Summer Olympics in Moscow. Ky had warned Denny not to touch her colored pencils or to put his sticky fingers on her worksheet. So Denny planted himself beside her, elbows on knees, chubby chin in his hands. He watched her quietly, the scratch of pencil on paper the only sound in the family living room, when all of a sudden she heard the sloppy wet sound of a juicy fart. When Ky whipped her head from her worksheet, Denny's mouth was a circle, his eyes enormous. Before she could accuse him of being a big dumb baby who pooped in his pants, the toddler said, in the same cadence as the people they'd seen in Ajax Spray 'n' Wipe commercials, "Oh no!" And something inside Ky—the walls that she had erected to keep her from liking the baby brother that her parents loved so much more—collapsed. She laughed and laughed, and she couldn't stop, and her stomach muscles hurt from it, and she was gasping for air. And then Denny started rolling on the floor laughing, too, and the rolling made his butt squish into the wet poop, which made the scent radiate from his nappy, which made Ky gag, but she couldn't stop laughing, and she swore it smelled so bad she could taste it, but she couldn't close her mouth because she had to keep laughing.

Back in her Melbourne apartment, after she'd picked up a pizza and a six-pack of Tooheys New because she wanted to train herself to be like her colleagues, who didn't flush beet red after two sips, she played all the voice messages.

In the first three, her father, who spoke to her only in Vietnamese, said to call him back as soon as possible, that this was urgent. In the fourth, he said something had happened to Denny. In the fifth, that Denny had been killed, that they were organizing the funeral, that she had to fly back as soon as possible. His voice never broke; she never heard tears. She rewound the tape, replayed the messages from the start so many times that the words became meaningless. She wondered whether she even understood Vietnamese anymore—whether she was so rusty that she had simply misheard, that by *killed,* her father actually meant "graduated early because he was that smart, and why couldn't you have been as smart as your little brother?" She considered a scenario where her brother was being bullied at school. Maybe her parents were worried, and she was being called home to stand up for him, to slap or smack his bullies, to demand that the school protect its brightest student.

"How do you *not* get the shit kicked out of you, man?" Ky had asked Denny a year earlier when he took home first place again across all subjects except PE. Ky was home for a weekend to celebrate Tết. Their mother had put them to work scrubbing and squeegeeing the ground-floor windows so that their townhouse would be sparkling for the Lunar New Year.

"I don't think people get beat up for being nerds these days," he'd said.

"Yeah, right."

"Well, *you* didn't get beaten up when you were in school."

"That was different," Ky said as she picked dried bug spatter off the windowpane.

"How?"

Minnie, Ky had wanted to say. In year two, when a group of white girls had pulled back the corners of their eyes every time they passed Ky, Minnie had threatened to shave the ringleader's head. For a whole month, every time they saw the blondies at the canteen or during assembly, Minnie would pantomime head shaving. Once she even mimed shaving her eyebrows, which made the lead blondie cry. That was Minnie at eight. By the time they reached high school, Minnie was a walking DO NOT DISTURB sign that shielded Ky from having her hair pulled, her ankles tripped, her seat spat on.

"I dunno," Ky said. "I guess I just stayed out of people's way."

"Same," said Denny, removing his rimless eyeglasses from his nose. He'd picked out a pair similar to Ky's because he'd heard her say that rimless eyeglasses were sophisticated and made people look more mature. Ky thought they made him look like a child tax accountant. He held his glasses by the temples and tried squeegeeing them. "I just don't rub it in."

"What do you mean?"

16

"Like . . ."—Denny raised his eyeglasses to the light, made a face upon seeing that they were now even dirtier than before— "there are other nerds that get beaten up, but it's not because they're nerds. It's because they go out of their way to make everyone else feel dumb."

Ky felt a phantom shove against her back. She knew Denny wasn't calling her out—it wasn't in his nature—but he might as well have been.

"That's very mature of you," Ky said, swallowing hard. "Also . . ."—she cocked her head at Denny's grimy glasses— "that's gross."

"I know, I thought maybe the squeegee would work—"

In her Melbourne apartment, Ky hugged her phone's answering machine to her chest, no longer questioning her comprehension of Vietnamese. She called her father, peppered him with questions: What happened? How did it happen? Who was with him? What did they know? Her father had told her to just come home—they could talk about it later. She sat for a while as the cheese on her pizza congealed. When it resembled a Frisbee more than food, she threw it out and was struck with the urge to clean. She fished through her laundry basket for dirty underwear, filled her bathroom sink with water and Cold Power, and submerged her clothes, shaking her hands under the surface to create bubbles. She took off her own rimless glasses—the ones she bought because she thought they made her look mature, worthy of being taken seriously—and rubbed them with alcohol wipes. She needed to shower, too. As she stood naked in the tub, water pounding her back, she was overcome by a need to scrub the tub. She squatted down low, sponge in hand, rubbing creamy globs of tile cleaner into the bathtub and tiled walls, then used her arms as an extension of the showerhead: the water hit her shoulders, ran down her arms, and dribbled off her fingers in the directions she pointed.

Her mother had taught her to clean the air of germs using a steam bath of vinegar. She had never explained the specifics, though, so Ky poured a liter of vinegar into her teakettle, turned on the stove, and waited for it to boil. As her apartment took on the aroma of sweaty feet, she simultaneously felt she couldn't breathe and like she was being turned inside out. There was so much that she wanted to say—to Denny, to her parents, to anyone who would listen. Apologies, explanations, painful observations that she knew revealed volumes of truth. The words in her head rushed to arrange themselves, colliding and falling in a panic, and in her desperate attempt to speak, she found that all her body would permit her to do was gasp. Each time she opened her mouth, air, then not enough air, over and over again, until the room fell dark and everything went quiet, and it was just her, alone, hiccupping through cries that didn't sound like her own, blanketed by steamy, sour air.

Chapter 2

No one in the Tran household was allowed to sleep past eight in the morning. Even on Sundays, when Ky still lived with her parents, she was startled awake by her father's Vietnamese variety shows—the latest *Paris by Night* on VHS featuring Khanh Ly's morose songs longing for a prewar Saigon—or by her mother smacking a feather duster handle against her door.

The day after Denny's wake, the Tran house was quiet. Ky checked her watch: eight-thirty. Outside she heard cars whooshing, magpies singing. Her pager showed nothing from work; she almost leapt out of bed, panicked that it had malfunctioned and she'd missed an assignment. It was only after putting on a sock that she remembered she was off for the week. And then she remembered why.

Falling back into bed, Ky looked around her room, unchanged from when she lived there. The walls covered with posters of *Edward Scissorhands* and Boyz II Men, the stick-on earrings that she'd stuck to her window, the secondhand Cabbage Patch Kid sitting on her dresser. The doll was bought at St. Vinnies when Ky was eight years old; her mother had been so worried about used toys carrying skin diseases that she'd bleached it, turning the brown-haired, beige-skinned doll albino. Ky had redrawn the doll's features using a permanent marker and colored its hair with orange and pink highlighters. She'd taken it to school because that's what the blondies did, and preemptively announced that her Cabbage Patch doll looked the way it did because it was possessed, because it was evil on the inside, and that made it cooler than regular dolls. The popular girls, whose mothers put their hair in super-high ponytails so that their blond locks fanned out the tops of their heads like fountains, didn't buy that it was cooler, but they did buy that it was evil. During lunchtime they made Ky and her doll chase after them. They would squeal, genuine panic on their faces when Ky got close. Minnie, who had already become Ky's best friend, had refused to join in, choosing instead to lie on the cold metal playground benches, staring at the overhanging gum trees while picking the dirt from under her fingernails.

"You make yourself a try-hard when you do that," she said, straightening her back, her nose in the air, when Ky returned from chasing the popular girls.

"I do not!"

"Do too."

"Swear to god I don't."

"You *literally* try too hard to be their friend, which makes you a try-hard."

"So what?"

"So they don't even want to be your friend!"

"You're just jealous because you don't have a Cabbage Patch Kid," Ky said. She believed herself to be right—Minnie's mother never got her anything, not even secondhand, not even when everyone, even poor kids, had a Cabbage Patch Kid. But she suspected that Minnie was right, too, because playing with the popular girls didn't feel good. They laughed and shrieked and hollered at Ky as she got closer to them—all signs that everyone else was having a great time. But as Ky pushed against the limits of her athleticism, arms and legs flailing, hair sticking to her sweaty face, Cabbage Patch doll flopping in the air, she felt constantly on the brink of tears.

"I'm not jealous," Minnie had said, arms crossed over her chest.

"Then why are you being so *weird*?" Ky said, mirroring Minnie with her own crossed arms.

"Don't you think it's unfair that they always make you the monster? Why can't they be the monster? Why do you always have to chase them?"

"Um, because my Cabbage Patch Kid is evil?"

"But it's *not. You* made that up. And they made you chase them even before you got a stupid Cabbage Patch Kid."

"It's not stupid!" Ky said. She gripped her doll tighter out of indignation, but also from the discomfort that Minnie had stirred. Because, although she didn't know it at the time, her subconscious had been keeping a ledger of how powerless and ugly the blondies (and, to be honest, the brunetties, the redheadies, and the curlies) made her feel. In each interaction with them, no matter how small, she detected a fundamental injustice, an innate advantage that they had over her and people who looked like her. Why did they never get in trouble for doing things that made her feel rotten? Why was she never allowed to win? Why *did* they want to play with her only

21

when she agreed to be the monster, with or without a Cabbage Patch Kid?

"Fine," Minnie said, throwing herself back on the metal bench. "It's not stupid, but *they're* stupid and I hate them."

"Agreed," Ky said. She had never thought to hate the blondies, but in that moment, she was willing to try it on to see how it felt. Holding her bleached Cabbage Patch Kid against her hip like it was a real baby, she asked Minnie what they should play instead. Minnie reached into her pocket and pulled out a looped piece of yarn. She weaved her fingers through it, forming a cat's cradle.

"Wanna play strings?" she said. "I invented it myself."

Back in her childhood bedroom, the aged Cabbage Patch doll now stared back at a grown-up Ky, its eyes smudged and lopsided.

Ky dragged herself out of bed and stumbled down the hall, surprised by how easily she slipped into the movements and habits that seemed to come with the house. In Melbourne, she had trained herself to be an adult—to wake up early without complaint, do her own laundry and dishes, walk gently so that her footsteps wouldn't bother the neighbors downstairs. But all her progress vanished in a puff whenever she returned to Cabramatta.

"I thought you said moving out had changed you," Denny said on her last visit home six months earlier.

On that trip, Ky had just had another fight with her mother, stomped through the house, slammed a door, and screamed into a pillow. Instead of forming proper sentences, she grunted whenever her mother asked her a question, and defaulted to

"I dunno" whenever her father asked her why she was groaning like a dying water buffalo.

"I *have* changed," Ky said as she walked with her brother to pick up a loaf of Tip Top from the corner store. The street where her family lived was unchanged from when she was a child—cars still drove too fast, fresh laundry still hung from cramped apartment balconies, and the closer she got to Cabramatta's tiny but dense downtown, the more loud-talking, visor-wearing, tightly permed Vietnamese aunties she encountered on the sidewalk. "You don't get it; when I'm in Melbourne, I'm so independent and responsible. I have an actual feather duster that I use to dust my shelves."

Denny raised both brows.

"The problem is *her*," Ky said, meaning their mother.

"Yeah," Denny conceded.

They passed a woman old enough to be their grandmother pushing a cart filled with jars of preserved lemons. Ky smiled as they crossed paths. The woman looked at Ky as though Ky had farted.

"Tough crowd," Ky whispered.

"She probably thinks you want to rob her."

"For her lemons?"

"Times have changed, sis."

"*What* times?"

Denny shrugged.

"Anyway," he said, pushing his glasses back up his nose, "you were saying that Mum's the problem."

"I can't explain it," Ky said, pushing up her own glasses,

too. "It's like she won't let me be an adult. It's, like, whenever I make any progress, she has to cut me down."

"Mums are just protective of daughters. And she's an Asian mum, which makes her more . . . more . . ."

"Crazy?"

"Intense."

"I'm twenty-two and she makes me feel like I'm thirteen."

"You act like you're thirteen."

"Denny!"

Her brother raised both hands in surrender. With his floppy, center-parted hair and too-large Michael Jordan T-shirt—a hideous bright red Nike knock-off that printed the athlete's face across the torso and sleeve so that one of his eyeballs was creased under the armpit—Ky couldn't help but think that Denny looked thirteen. It seemed the only thing puberty had done for him was make his body longer and his voice perpetually cracked.

"I read something in *Woman's Day* about that," he said.

"Why are you reading *Woman's Day*?"

"It was the only thing they had at the doctor's office. Anyway, it was about why mums and their daughters always fight."

"Because mums are jerks and daughters don't like having jerks for mums?"

"Nah. The article said it's because mums don't want their daughters to repeat their mistakes, so they're extra critical about everything. But daughters just want their mums' approval, so when their mums are critical, they get pissed off. Like you do."

"Whatever," Ky had said, annoyed that her little brother was summing up one of her biggest life problems with an article from *Woman's Day*. "And don't even pretend like you understand, because you don't."

"What?" Denny said, taken aback.

"There's a lot of pressure being the oldest and a girl, okay?" Ky said, suddenly walking faster, her feet matching the beat of her heart. Denny swung his legs farther with each step to keep up.

"Okay," he said.

"You wouldn't get it."

"But what if I did—"

"You were born perfect," Ky said, cutting her brother off, "and you can do no wrong, and you're gonna become a doctor or whatever just like Mum and Dad want, and you don't feel the pressure because you're just, like, that's your default setting. You naturally do everything right already . . ."—they were both now power walking—"but for me, it's like I'm moving against the current, and Mum keeps crashing into me, reminding me of how I've come up short and how disappointing I am, and she just . . . she never gives me any credit, and doesn't seem to care that I'm a fully formed person who has her own life and is on her own path and just wants a friggin' break, you know?"

"I know."

"*Sure* you do," Ky said, rolling her eyes.

Denny went quiet for the rest of their walk. At one point, he placed a hand on his sister's shoulder and gave it a pat that lingered just long enough to be awkward. He pulled his hand back, like he was unsure whether he should have done two pats to make it less weird.

Remembering the way Denny had looked at her—the weak smile that said, *I get it, I really do*—she now stopped outside his bedroom. A part of her expected to see her brother asleep in bed or studying at his desk. Instead, she saw her father, fully dressed in his bank teller clothes, his short salt-and-pepper hair pomaded flat against his head, his body straight and still, like a Chinese vampire, lying on Denny's perfectly made-up bed.

"Dad?" Ky said in English.

Her father's body momentarily seized, like he'd been caught doing something he wasn't meant to be doing. He cleared his throat, relaxed, but didn't move.

"Are you—" She eyed his pin-striped pants, of which he owned about a dozen pairs. Her father's wardrobe was like Superman's, filled with the same button-downs from Big W and slacks that Ky's mother altered to fit his skeletal frame. Even with his pants taken up and his sleeves brought in, Australian clothing still looked too big on him.

"What is it?" he said in Vietnamese, suddenly upright.

While Ky had never learned to talk to her mother without devolving into her teenage self, she'd never learned to talk to her father at all. So little did he speak that Ky had long assumed he had nothing to say to her, had zero interest in her life, wanted to be anywhere but here. So the thought of asking him a direct question or showing him that she cared came unnaturally, if it came at all. In the end, she settled on asking whether he was going to work.

"Oh," he said, smoothing down a gray cowlick. "Yes. I am." He looked around Denny's immaculate bedroom as though unsure of how he ended up there.

Ky stared at her father, waiting for him to say more. She oscillated between wanting to hear from him and being afraid of what he might say. Questions clawed at the back of her throat: Why had he been sleeping in Denny's bed the past few nights? When would he be ready to talk about what happened to Denny and divulge everything the police had shared? Was he okay? Was there anything she could do to help? As much as she wanted answers, though, she was afraid of the burden with which they came. Because what would happen if he told her that he *wasn't* okay? And what would happen if he said there was nothing she could do? And what would happen if he was truly vulnerable and broken and she crumpled under the weight of his grief? If the Tran family had been the kind Ky regularly saw on TV, she imagined that they might huddle together, hold one another, and tell themselves they would get through this as a family. Instead, they'd become pros at avoiding one another, never quite existing on the same plane at the same time, struggling to reach one another.

Her father stuck his hands into his trouser pockets, pulled them out, fidgeted with the seam of his shirt. It irritated Ky to see that he looked as uncomfortable talking to her as she felt talking to him.

"When things like this happen, the police write up a report about it, right?" he finally said, steadfast in his Vietnamese, even as Ky kept responding in English.

"You mean, a police report?"

"Yes. The police would have a report about what happened to Denny. Is that right?"

"Hold on," Ky said. "Didn't you talk to the police?"

"Yes, they told us about Denny," her father said, hands still fidgeting, eyes focused on a speck on the floorboard.

27

"But you didn't ask them for a report?"

"No."

"Are you bloody serious?"

Her father's eyes immediately shot from the floor to Ky, his facial expression a warning. Ky swallowed but stopped short of apologizing.

"They didn't offer us anything," he said, his eyes returning to the ground. "Your English is good. Can you go get it?"

"Dad—" Ky began, doing her best to suppress the teenage tantrum that was fighting to break the surface. She'd never liked being the family translator. Even as a kid, she felt embarrassed every time her parents called on her to read government mail or school newsletters, or asked her to get on the phone with Medicare. Initially, her source of embarrassment was that her parents—two grown adults—were so bad at English. A believer that people were meant to get better at things with age, she was annoyed that her parents couldn't keep up with telemarketers, struggled with simple sentences, made her feel like she came from a family of dumb people. As she got older, though, that embarrassment morphed into resentment. Why did they choose to stay in Cabramatta, where everyone spoke Vietnamese, ensuring that they never had to get better at English? Why didn't they try a little harder?

"Oh, quit ya whinging," Minnie had said when they were both fifteen, after Ky had complained again about having to translate for her parents. "Learning a new language is way hard."

"We managed to learn English!"

"Girl, we were little kids."

"So?"

Minnie grimaced at Ky.

"First, you're being willfully ignorant—"

"*Excuse me?*"

"And second, they *obviously* get us to translate because they're afraid people will be mean to them."

"Um, no, it's because their English is still so bad after all these years and they don't understand anything the person on the line is saying."

"That's also true, maybe," said Minnie, who was also her parents' translator, but who had weaseled her way out of most of the work by simply throwing out anything that contained too many words. The only mail that survived Minnie's scourge were bills, because she didn't want the water or power to be cut off. "But they also have the worst FOB accents. They're probs worried the white people on the other end will be mean."

Ky hadn't considered that before. But after their conversation, she couldn't stop considering it. It made her feel bad for her parents. It made her feel worse for herself. Because, if Minnie was right, it meant that she had another thing to worry about. It meant it wasn't enough to simply understand or speak English; it meant there was a right and wrong way to sound, and that sounding wrong could be justification for someone to be mean to her. Overnight, she began answering phone calls with the thickest Aussie accent she could muster and, once at the *Herald Sun,* worked so hard at ridding herself of any trace of her southwestern Sydney upbringing that interviewees mistook her for British.

Still, despite understanding why her parents foisted translation onto her, she couldn't fathom why they didn't ask for a police report. Surely their son's murder was reason enough for them to crack open a dictionary.

"Why couldn't you do it?" she now said to her father, agitated. "The police were right there. You could have just asked them—"

"Would an explanation of why something was not done in the past make you feel better?" he said, defaulting to a line he often used on Ky's mother whenever she re-litigated his past decisions, from his failure to invest in the stock market before it popped in the mid-eighties, to why the family had settled in Australia instead of America—she'd heard that California's Little Saigon was bigger, better, and safer than Cabramatta. It was the closest Ky had seen him get to anger. "Because if it would change your life for the better and put happiness in your heart, pull up a chair and I will explain everything I have never done."

Ky stood silent, wanting to argue with her father, but not knowing what to say. She was already pushing the limits of respectfulness, and she didn't want to test her tantrums with him. Besides, she knew he was right—whatever sense of satisfaction she derived from getting him to admit his faults would be swallowed by the guilt of making another person feel rotten. It always caught up to her—the shame and disappointment in herself for making others feel the way she had so often been made to feel.

"What *did* the police tell you?"

Her father now rested his hands in his lap, his shoulders hunched. "I already told you everything."

"No, you didn't," Ky said, struggling to contain her frustration. "Denny gets bashed to death at Lucky 8, and the only thing the police tell you is that he got bashed to death at Lucky 8?"

"I told you about the camera and the Mr. Successful sash in his jacket pocket."

"That's not what I mean."

"Then what do you mean?"

Ky could now feel the heat in her ears.

"You're telling me stuff about what he was wearing and what was in his pocket and I want to know the *important* stuff, like what actually *happened* and whether there are any suspects and what the witnesses said and—"

"My memory is bad."

"This was just last week!"

"It was late at night."

Her father kept his head down, though Ky could see his face flush. She tried to make sense of what he was saying—what his memory had to do with the time of day; how anyone could forget the details of their son's death. Then it clicked, and she immediately felt sick.

"For Christ's sake," she said, suddenly dizzy as the blood drained from her head. "You were drunk."

Her father kept looking at the floor.

"You were drunk when the police came," Ky repeated, taking his silence as an admission of guilt. "Why the hell couldn't you—"

Ky's mother had told her in her years away that her father had cut back on his drinking; that these days he stuck to beer. Denny had said that he still cracked open the cognac from time to time, but only ever at home, and only ever late at night, when everyone had gone to bed. As far as drunks were concerned, Denny said he wasn't as bad as other people's parents. Still, her father's drinking had always bothered her, and any time she imagined him with so much as a beer in his hand, she felt a tightness in her chest. She felt even worse when she thought of him and Lucky 8. At every wedding the family attended, Ky's mother used to usher them out of Lucky 8 before her father had a chance to switch from beer to cognac. Once he crossed over to Hennessy, there was no turning back. Perhaps her mother thought that it was more dignified to harangue her husband into leaving early than to wait for him to fall over himself and throw up on someone. Ky always thought it did the opposite by drawing attention to their family. Just as everyone returned to their seats for course six or seven, the Tran family made their hurried, graceless exit.

"Why doesn't Dad just stop before he gets loopy?" Denny, who was seven at the time, had asked Ky as they held hands and descended the stairs of Lucky 8, the wedding singer's voice still echoing from the main banquet hall. Several steps in front of them, her mother was supporting most of her father's weight. His arm slung over her shoulders, they lumbered down the narrow staircase in fits and starts, her mother swearing under her breath while her father had a goofy smile stretched across his face, like he was imagining a holiday in Hawaii, oblivious to his children's embarrassment.

"Because he doesn't love us enough," Ky said.

"Don't say that to your brother!" her mother snapped, trying to turn her head to face her children, but her own husband's head was in the way.

Ky hadn't just been angry that they had to leave her second cousin's wedding early—although she did resent missing out on cake, the sweet and soupy red lentil dessert, and the plate of meticulously sliced oranges. She was angry that they had to leave everything early whenever her father and booze were in the same room. She was angry that all the muscles in her chest instinctively tightened whenever she saw a case of Crown Lager or VB next to the Coca-Cola and Fanta. She was angry that whenever her uncles and aunts welcomed her family to backyard barbecues, they always handed him a can dripping with condensation before telling no one in particular that it was just one drink, that it was a party, let the man have one drink, what harm could it do? She'd wanted so badly to yell in their faces, to ask them why they cared so much. What harm did it do to *them* if he *didn't* drink? Why weren't they satisfied until he had an opened beer in his hand? Why couldn't they just leave him alone?

"Your dad loves both of you plenty," Ky's mother had said as they struggled their way to the parking lot. "He's just a useless man."

Later that night, as her mother got her father into bed and Ky stood watch over Denny to make sure he brushed his teeth, he asked her who was right.

"About what?" she said.

"About Dad."

"I think he loves you plenty, because you're a boy and you're smart," Ky said. "Don't forget to brush the back of your teeth or they'll rot."

"But what about you?"

"I always brush the back of my teeth."

"No," Denny said, pausing his brushing. "Does Dad love you enough?"

Ky thought of the times she'd asked her father to drink less, to limit himself to just one beer. She thought of the breath-seizing anxiety she tried to communicate to him through her eyes, the hope that he could read the way she dug her own fingernails into her palms and crossed her arms at birthday parties, the way she kept an eye on him from a distance, those same eyes and nails begging for him to *please stop, please stop, please stop.* She thought of how she learned about liver cancer in Health, how she couldn't stop talking about it at dinner that night because she needed her father to know of all the ways his liver could die, because if his liver died, something else would happen, and she was too scared to say it, so she left it there, she left it at liver death, and she thought, she hoped, that maybe, if he loved her enough, he would take the hint.

"I don't know," Ky said. "But you don't have to worry. Mum and Dad love you. And I love you heaps."

Denny got on his tiptoes to spit. Saliva and toothpaste still dribbling out of his mouth: *"Aye grub yoo haaps, tah."*

Ky's father appeared to sink further into Denny's bed as she waited for a response, but she knew he wouldn't say more.

"Fine," she said through a constricted throat. "Is that all?"

Her father straightened his shirt collar and dusted his pants. His face was still pink, his eyes weary. He then switched to English, each word delivered in his musical Vietnamese accent: "Do your best."

Cabramatta Police Station sat across the street from a park where Ky's mother used to take her for the precarious swings and metal slides, before the drug dealers and junkies moved in, before the parched, prickly weed lawn was littered with used hypodermic needles, before teenagers loitered in broad daylight with heroin-stuffed balloons in their mouths.

Ky had been to the police station only once before. When she was nine, her primary school had done a unit on convicts and had organized an excursion to the station. She'd been nervous, clutching Minnie's hand as they stood in two straight lines, waiting to enter.

"Be on your best behavior," Ms. Price had warned. "Because if you're bad, the police will lock you up."

"I have a right to a lawyer," Minnie said, prompting Ms. Price to shush her.

The police station hadn't changed. The building still consisted of a light brown brick exterior, a white roof, and a flagpole that rose into the air, with the Aussie flag flapping in the breeze.

When Ky had first visited as a child in the eighties, the station was calm enough that it could host students. An officer had shown her class how handcuffs worked and displayed all the bits and bobs hanging off a policeman's chunky belt. When he drew the students' attention to his gun, which he never removed from its holster, the class gasped. It was the first time any of them had ever seen a real gun.

Now the station was chaos. The air-conditioning system struggled against the Australian summer. The air inside was thick and smelled like a person who'd spent too much time in the sun. Every officer glistened with sweat and appeared preoccupied. No one noticed Ky's entrance. In the cramped reception area, half a dozen tanned Asian boys in school uniform, each no older than fifteen, sat in a row of chairs against a wall, fanning themselves with whatever they could lay their hands on— brochures, school-books, caps—miffed expressions on their faces.

"Hey, Miss Police, can we go now?"

The white officer behind the counter didn't look up from her files. "No, you can go when your parents come get you."

One of the boys, who wore a sweat-stained uniform that Ky recognized as belonging to Canley Vale, a school just down the street from the station, groaned. "I already say they're not gonna come," he said. "Come on, miss, just let us go."

"So you can go back to selling drugs at Cabra Station?"

"I already say we weren't selling nothin'!"

After the officer ignored the boy's protest that he hadn't done anything wrong, that even the officer who arrested him hadn't been able to prove a thing, he pleaded again for her to let him go.

"You need to shut your mouth," she finally said.

Ky considered leaving, perhaps coming back when the person behind the front desk was in a better mood. But before she could turn to leave, a white man in jeans and a pit-stained T-shirt came in, guiding a teenage boy, maybe seventeen, dressed in the same Cabramatta High uniform Denny used to wear, by the neck. Each time a new person entered the police station, the air got heavier, the smell of body odor more pungent.

"This moron tried to sell to us," the man said to the woman behind the counter.

The woman shook her head, muttered something under her breath.

Ky's feet felt impossibly heavy. She hated how easily intimidated she was, how many mental exercises she had to run through before she could force herself to act. She now drew

36

on the words of Ian, the *Herald Sun*'s chief of staff, on her first day as an intern.

"Nothing a reporter does is actually that hard," he'd said, sitting on a chair turned backward, his arms on the backrest. "What sets us apart is that we're willing to do it."

As someone who didn't believe she was naturally gifted at anything—Ky hadn't been as gutsy or street-smart as Minnie, as academically brilliant as Denny—she liked the idea of willingness being important. Who cared if she wasn't the most talented person in the room? She was willing to stake out a convicted felon's house to get the story. Or go on any death knock she was assigned. Or follow the rules and trust in the process even when no one else was doing it. And so, according to Ian, it didn't matter if any part of her job made her feel sick or if she was constantly pumped with anxiety and dread. Nothing was too hard. Ky just had to be willing. Which was how she managed to force herself to approach the counter.

"Hi," she said to the officer, whose name tag read NELSON.

Officer Nelson looked up from her paperwork. She had the austere face of a PE teacher, her sun-bleached hair tied in a low bun, the edges of her lips naturally pulled downward.

"I'm really sorry to bother you," Ky said, "but I'd like to get a copy of a police report, please."

"What's the case number?"

"I . . . I don't know. I don't have it. It's concerning Denny Tran. He's my brother. He was killed a week ago, December 6."

The officer lowered her head, but her icy blue eyes remained on Ky. It was the look Ky's primary school teachers gave her and Minnie whenever they got into trouble for talking too much or laughing too loud. While the look simply made Minnie roll her eyes and get into even more trouble, it had always worked at silencing Ky.

"Why aren't you scared of getting into trouble?" Ky had asked Minnie when they were in year three after they'd both been scolded for being too chatty during class.

"I dunno," Minnie said as she picked through Ky's lunch box, shaking a paper box of raisins. "Why would I be scared?"

"Because getting in trouble is . . ." Ky said, stumbling over her own ideas, unable to articulate why she herself quivered at the thought of stepping out of line.

"The sad corner is the most boring punishment ever," Minnie said. "That's the worst thing they can do to us if we do something bad—make us go sit in the sad corner for fifteen minutes. It's dumb as crap."

"But—"

"Seriously, Ky. They can't do anything to us. Try it. Talk as much as you want, sing the words to the national anthem wrong, do a big fart during roll call. You'll just get the sad corner and Mrs. Waterson will give you the stink eye and that's it."

And *that* was it, Ky thought. It wasn't the punishment itself that Ky feared. It was the look. The look that said, *I expected more from you. I'm disappointed in you. You should be ashamed of yourself.* And it always worked on Ky, a reminder that there was a narrow path to success she could follow, and if she strayed by even a hairbreadth by speaking up, talking back, being loud, doing anything other than what people in power expected of her, then rejection was certain and her failure was her own fault. She didn't know how to explain this to Minnie because she could barely explain it to herself. But it always started with the look.

And now, looking into the eyes of the police officer, she felt small, scared—like she was about to fall off the path.

"Miss, we don't give out police reports for homicides."

"Why not?"

"Because that's the policy."

"But I'm family," Ky said, feeling flustered. "I'm his big sister—"

"It doesn't matter. We don't release any information on homicides—not even to family—unless it'll help with the investigation."

The officer adjusted her work shirt, which was stuck to her body.

"But how will you know if I can help if you won't even tell me what happened?" Ky asked. "For all you know, maybe—"

Ky swallowed, broke eye contact with the officer. She wondered if she was out of line. She pictured the narrow path, her mind's eye seeing the way it looped and wound itself in impossible bends, narrowing more and more the farther she traveled. It was hard to be good. It didn't get easier with time or experience. As she watched the officer tug at her uniform, Ky became aware of her own sweat marks, which were expanding from under her arms. She felt like she might pass out from how stuffy the police station had become.

Officer Nelson pursed her thin lips, which made the two pink lines around her mouth disappear from her face. After staring at Ky for a moment, she picked up her phone and wedged it between her shoulder and chin. "Let me find out which officer is on the case."

Twenty minutes passed, during which a middle-aged Vietnamese woman with a short, tight perm came to the police station to pick up her son. She announced her presence by yelling in Vietnamese, making a beeline for one of the boys in school uniform, and repeatedly smacking him in the back of his head with an open palm. "You stupid, stupid, good-for-nothing, useless, worthless, stupid son! You are so stupid you are killing your mother. You are killing your mother!"

The boy cowered in his seat as the others shuffled away from him, staring at their shoes, all too familiar with what their own mothers would do if they found them here.

"Stupid, stupid, killing your mother! You have killed your mother with your stupid! Getting arrested! What did we ever do to you? Why do you do this to us?"

"Oi!" Officer Nelson said as she slammed a hand against her desk. "This isn't an outdoor market. If you don't restrain yourself, I'll have you arrested."

But the Vietnamese woman wasn't listening or didn't understand, because she continued to smack her son and he continued to cower, tears in his eyes. Ky fought the urge to watch the unfolding scene like she was watching television. She had been doing her best to be invisible in the police station, standing next to a potted plant with her hands clasped together. But she worried that the Vietnamese woman would actually get arrested, so she took a few steps forward.

"Auntie," Ky said in Vietnamese. She awkwardly reached out

a hand to pat the woman's back but recoiled before she made contact. It felt too weird to try to comfort a stranger. "Auntie, the officer said she will arrest you if you don't stop."

The teenage boys looked at Ky, their faces spelling both relief and confusion that someone who spoke Vietnamese was intervening.

The woman kept slapping her son's head with open palms.

"Auntie!" Ky tried again. "You have to stop or they will put you both in jail!"

It was only then that the woman paused, panting, her face red and wet, her tattooed-on eyebrows angled like an angry cartoon character. "My stupid, good-for-nothing son!" she said to Ky, pointing at the boy, who reminded Ky of a younger Denny. "We gave him everything and this is how he repays us. He is killing his mother! I should feed him shit! That is all he deserves!"

The officer watched the scene play out, grimacing. Then she spoke slowly, pausing intermittently, in the way white people try to make themselves comprehensible to older Asians. "Is . . . this . . . your . . . son?"

"Yes. He my son."

"You . . . need . . . to fill out . . . this paperwork . . . before . . . you can go."

The Vietnamese woman's face went blank, like a confused child who had been called on to answer a question. She turned to her son, but he kept his head down, trying to hide the fact that he was crying. Ky recognized the look on the woman's face: her son was her translator, her bridge to Australia. At this moment, she needed him. At this moment, she was also ready to bury him alive.

"Auntie, I can translate for you," Ky said.

By the time Ky had helped the woman sign for her son's release, the police station door had been propped open in search of a breeze, an officer had complained that the air coming in was hotter than the air inside, and more women had come to claim their sons, grandsons, nephews, and brothers. Each of them wore the familiar helpless expression of incomprehension; each looked to their sullen, sweaty teenagers for help; each of those teenage boys looked to Ky. Sighing, Ky instructed these mothers, grandmothers, sisters, and aunts, who reminded her so much of the women in her own life, to fill out their addresses and sign their names. She helped a woman named Vuong, who understood no English, who fretted the whole time in Vietnamese about whether she'd lose her job at the fish market for leaving early to come get her grandson. She helped a woman named Mina, who showed up with a toddler in a pram and an infant strapped to her front. Mina spoke only Laotian, which Ky didn't understand, but she pantomimed under the weight of her baby what she needed Ky to know. And Ky helped a woman named Flora, whom Ky thought she recognized from somewhere, but she couldn't put her finger on it, who was as sweaty as Ky was, whose skin was ashen, who looked like she was going to throw up, who had come to claim her nephew, William. She told them which fields to leave blank, detailed what their boys had done wrong, explained that loitering, believe it or not, was an actual offense.

"Worse than in Vietnam," Vuong muttered in Vietnamese as she gave Officer Nelson the stink eye.

"What did she say?" the officer asked, looking between the woman and Ky.

42

"Tell her that I'm not scared of her pale-ass ghost face," Vuong continued in Vietnamese. "Tell her I've made a Viet Cong soldier cry."

"She's just upset with her grandson," Ky said.

"You the sister?"

The voice came from behind Ky. It belonged to a tall officer who emerged from one of the back rooms.

"Denny Tran's sister?" he added.

Ky nodded.

The officer introduced himself as Constable Ryan Edwards. "I'm swamped right now, so I can't get into it, but it's too early in the investigation to release anything, anyway."

"I'm just here for a police report," Ky said.

The constable gestured for Ky to come into one of the empty back rooms with him. "Sorry, just needed some privacy," he said, rubbing his brows. Ky noticed that he was sweating, the bags under his eyes deep and glistening. "Look, we can't release anything. This is all really sensitive, and the notes are disturbing. We don't want to upset the family any more than—"

"But I *am* the family," Ky said. And her brother was already dead. How much worse could it be?

"It's just due process, miss, and I'm still waiting for the homicide squad to get back to me before I can—"

"But," she said, feeling like she was treading water with stones in her pocket, "but isn't the . . . isn't all of that for the family's benefit? Like . . ." She cringed at the way she sounded, how every line she spoke drained her of what little power she had. She wondered how Minnie, even as a child, was able to sustain her razor-sharp edge, how she could be so fast without effort.

43

"What I'm trying to say is, sir, I can handle it. I'm his family. I can handle it. Really."

Constable Edwards sighed.

"Please," Ky continued. "My family is completely in the dark on all of this." One word after another, her inner voice coaxed. *Keep going, keep going.* "We cremated him, and we don't even know what happened to him, who he was with, who the witnesses were."

The constable's eyes narrowed in disbelief. "Are we talking about the same Denny Tran?"

"I—" Ky said. Her inner voice went quiet—it had not anticipated this. "I'm sorry?"

"You're saying that you're related to Denny Tran, the kid who was killed seven days ago?"

"Yeah," Ky said, suddenly able to hear her heart in her ears. "He was seventeen, straight-A student, had just finished high school—"

"At Lucky 8."

"Yeah."

Constable Edwards scratched the back of his neck. "Miss, I don't know what to tell you, but it seems like your family *wants* to be in the dark."

"Uh . . ." Ky's mouth went dry. "I'm . . . I'm not sure what you mean."

"Well," he said, now thumbing a freckle under his chin, "they declined an autopsy."

Ky swallowed, barely able to hear her own thoughts over how loud her heart was now beating. "Is that even allowed?" she managed to say, her legs feeling weak. "Why would they do that?"

The constable nodded. "If we didn't know what killed him, then no, the coroner would've pushed for an autopsy. But—" He trailed off, distracted by the noise of another Vietnamese woman—perhaps a mother, an aunt, a sister—entering the lobby of the police station and yelling at one of the boys. "It would've been useful," he continued, still eyeing the door that led to the lobby. "Kid gets bashed to death in Cabramatta, you might wanna know what was in him—"

"Wait, *what?*"

Constable Edwards looked at Ky like he'd just remembered that she was still in the room. "Look, I know no one wants to think their brother or son or whoever is using, but this town has a big problem, and he fits the profile—"

"*What* profile?" Ky said, pressing her nails into her palms in an attempt to contain a feeling rising inside her that she couldn't yet identify—she knew only that it was hot and red and threatened to overflow. "He came *first* in *everything.* He was the most hardworking, studious, nerdy—"

"Miss, please calm down."

"I *am* calm."

"Look, users and dealers around here are getting younger and younger. We've picked up twelve-year-olds with balloons in their mouths because the gangs know that little kids can only be charged as minors. Just look outside—those boys sitting out there are, what, in year seven? Year eight? All I'm saying is that your brother was a young guy, and maybe it could've told us a few things about him—"

"Are you sure they declined an autopsy?"

Constable Edwards crossed his arms. In the reflection of

his eyes, Ky could see herself wilting under the look he gave her—*I expected better of you, better of your family; your failure is your own fault*—and she tried to pull herself together. She noticed his face soften. He probably felt sorry for her.

"For what it's worth," he said, relaxing his shoulders, "we know *how* he died. Clear as day. Kid didn't stand a chance after taking a beating like that."

Ky winced.

"Autopsy might've helped explain the why—"

"Denny wasn't a junkie."

"Miss, I didn't say he was."

"I know my brother."

"Then maybe you can come in for a formal interview, answer some questions about him."

Ky clasped her hands together, nervously rubbing the skin around her thumb. This wasn't how things were meant to go. She'd expected the constable to hand over a detailed police report, show her the list of suspects, tell her that he had detectives on the case, that they would catch the killer, and whoever it was would be put away for good. She'd expected—in hindsight, unrealistically—that the entire local police force would be dedicated to righting the injustice that had been committed against her brother, that there would be some form of acknowledgment of how deeply disturbing it was that Denny, of all people, could be murdered. Instead, she'd never felt more invisible; her brother, alive only a week ago, had already been forgotten.

"Miss?" the constable said when Ky didn't respond.

"Yeah."

"You all right?"

Ky tried to bring her focus back into the stuffy room, which was now filled with the nauseating scent of BO and the constable's pungent Lynx body spray. She breathed through her mouth. "Uh-huh."

"You were close to your brother, right?"

Hearing her relationship to Denny spoken of in the past tense made her feel sick. It would probably be the hardest part of losing Denny—the constant tense corrections, and by extension, the constant reminders that what was once there and real was now little more than a memory.

"Close." At least she had *thought* they were. She didn't believe that Denny was a heroin user. He didn't have it in him. It was impossible. But hearing the constable's doubts suddenly introduced the smallest kernel of doubt into her own mind, and she hated that she'd even made room for it. She shook her head, as though trying to dislodge the idea, but it held firm. What if she wasn't as close to Denny as she'd thought? What if the constable found out she'd left for Melbourne years ago, hadn't answered Denny's last phone call because she'd been on deadline, had sat on his emails for weeks, had been the one to convince her parents to let him go out the night he died? What if things had happened—big things, things that would lead to a murder—while she was away?

"Close enough to tell us about his schedule, his social life, who he hung out with, what his friends were like, any secrets—"

"You keep talking about him like he did something bad—"

He sighed. "Miss, we're just not ruling anything out. Since there's no autopsy report, and no one will talk, we're just trying to understand who he was and—"

"What do you mean, no one will talk?" Ky said, feeling unsteady again. This wasn't the kind of information she'd expected to hear. "Wasn't this a big restaurant? Lucky 8 is huge. Has Eddie talked? Eddie is his best friend. They go everywhere together. Eddie would have been there, because they were coming from their year twelve formal. Did Eddie—"

Constable Edwards closed his eyes and pinched the bridge of his nose. "Miss, just answer the question. You were close to your brother, yes? If so, can you come in for an interview sometime this week? Maybe Thursday? It might help us."

Ky nodded, but her mind was snagged on what the constable had said. She could understand if no one knew who the killer was. But what did it mean that no one would talk? If someone could get in trouble for loitering, couldn't they get in trouble for not telling the police what they saw?

"I'm sorry, but I don't really get what you mean," Ky said.

"What confuses you?"

"You said no one will talk."

"Yes."

"What does that *mean*?"

Constable Edwards rubbed his brows again. "It means what it means. Look, it's surprising, but it's not. The reason . . . well, actually, one of the many reasons it's almost impossible to solve anything in Cabramatta is that no one knows anything. Everyone plays dumb or *is* dumb. I don't know which is worse. If you ask me, they're doing it to themselves."

If Minnie had been in the room, Ky knew she wouldn't let that one go. *Doing* what *to themselves?* she would have asked as she circled the constable. *Tell me, how exactly are the people you're sworn to protect at fault? And in what world is it appropriate or rational to conclude that they won't talk to you because they're dumb? Have you considered that maybe, oh, I don't know, you're fucking dumb?*

But Minnie wasn't here. Ky was on her own.

"Even Eddie Ho didn't talk?"

"Miss," he said, defeat creeping into his voice, "no one who was there will tell us what they saw. Including Mr. Ho."

"What if I try to talk to him?" Ky said, unsure of what she actually meant.

Ooooooh boy! Minnie said, her voice ringing in Ky's ears.

Quit it, Ky thought.

She's gettin' wiiiiild now!

Shut up.

Come on, I'm being supportive here. Git, git, giiiit it!

"I'm sorry?" Constable Edwards said, his voice pulling Ky back into the humid room.

"What if the people who won't talk to you . . . are willing to talk to me? I mean, it's worth a shot, right? If you give me a copy of the police report and whatever notes you took—people's names, where to find them—I can talk to them and—"

"Miss, I absolutely cannot share that kind of—"

"But what if I can do it?"

She had no idea if she could pull off what she was offering—the words tumbled out of her in desperation. She hated feeling out of control, and she couldn't bear to leave the station with more questions than answers. She needed something—*anything*—from the officer. And if her nascent career in journalism had taught her anything, it was that no matter what uniform, badge, or title someone wore, they were still just a person. No one *had* to follow the rules. It was, after all, how reporters broke some of their biggest stories—someone from the inside decided to leak information, to do what they wanted instead of what the system expected of them. Everyone had it in them to be sneaky.

Constable Edwards chewed on the inside of his mouth. He was baby faced, but his skin looked sun damaged. Ky learned to figure out how old white Aussies were not from the quality of their skin but from how filled in their faces were—whether the flesh around their chins sagged, the depth of the creases around their mouths when they smiled. The constable's sun-speckled cheeks looked like they'd still bounce back if poked, his jawline smooth and untouched by gravity.

When he didn't say anything, Ky kept going. "Denny was killed in Lucky 8, so most of the people who were there would have been Asian, right?"

Constable Edwards hard-blinked, a yes.

Work it! Minnie said.

"Probably Vietnamese?"

He blinked again.

"I'm Vietnamese. I know this community. I might have an in."

Ky didn't know if this was true. She could speak Vietnamese with the thick tongue of someone who had grown up in Australia, fumbling her way through conversations, substituting English for the Vietnamese words she didn't know. The only in she really had was that she wasn't white.

"I can't have some amateur playing detective, Miss Tran."

"I'm not playing anything. Your police force is one hundred percent white in a town where most people are not."

Owned!

Constable Edwards shifted his gaze to the floor.

"I'll just be talking to them, like a member of the community. Community members talk, right? People talk. And if they'll talk to me, isn't that better than no one talking?"

Constable Edwards's sweat stains now showed through his uniform as he rubbed the back of his neck.

"I swear it won't get back to you," Ky said, her voice gaining confidence, if only because she could see the fissure in his veneer. Also, she had to remind herself, she wasn't technically lying. People did talk. They wouldn't necessarily talk to her. But could it hurt to try? "If any of these people ask how I found them, I'll just say someone else who was there that night pointed me in their direction. Everyone knows everyone in this town."

Oh, is that right? Minnie said.

That part, Ky could admit, was a lie—Cabramatta had tens of thousands of residents, most of whom were quiet, private, and kept to themselves. But in Ky's defense, people gossiped, became friendly or at least familiar with one another. Shopkeepers recognized regulars, pharmacists knew who used hypodermic needles to shoot insulin and who used them for heroin, and *everyone* could recognize the wedding singer from the last wedding they attended.

"Off the record," she said, a magic string of words that nearly always worked on her interviewees, who saw it as an opportunity to vent with impunity. "I promise."

Constable Edwards held up his hand. "Wait here."

How does it feel? Minnie's imagined voice asked.

Leave me alone.

Aw, come on.

Go away.

Feels good to be bad, eh?

Who says anything about being bad? I'm just . . . being proactive.

Baby steps, baby.

This isn't, like, a gateway to me selling heroin or anything.

Uh-huh.

It's not!

I believe you.

No you don't. You're making fun of me.

Um, Ky, I'm a figment of your imagination. This is all you, man.

Whatever.

All I'm saying is I'm proud of you, even if you're, like, twenty years late to the party.

What party?

"Alrighty," Constable Edwards said, returning to the room with several photocopied sheets of paper and a yellow highlighter. "These . . ."—he put the stacked sheets in front of Ky—"are my notes from the night. It's what went into the report. You never got it from me. You never even saw it, okay?"

"Okay."

"And these . . ."—he flicked through the pages of ant scrawl, highlighting names that Ky could barely make out—"are the people who were there, with addresses, phone numbers."

He pushed the sheets toward Ky. "Don't say I didn't warn you—we don't normally share any of this stuff with family. It's really distressing material. Get rid of it when you're done. Shred it. Burn it. Especially those names and numbers. Whatever you do, don't let it get back to me, understand?"

Ky placed a hand on top of the paper pile. The photocopying job was crooked.

"Miss Tran?"

"Yes."

"Yes what? I need you to say it."

"Yes," Ky said again, pulling the sheets toward herself. "No one will know you gave this to me, I promise. I will get rid of it as soon as possible."

"Because if this gets back to me, it blows up the entire investigation. You'll never get answers, no arrests, no closure for anyone. Got it?"

"Got it."

"Come by late Thursday. I usually have time in the arvo, maybe fiveish. You can tell me what you know about your brother, the kinds of people he spent time with. If you get anyone to talk—not that you're playing detective, of course—you can let me know. Maybe we'll get somewhere."

Ky read and reread the officer's handwritten report more than a dozen times. Based on the number of used bowls and pairs of chopsticks that were still sitting on the banquet tables when police arrived, the constable concluded that in total, there were at least seventeen diners and restaurant workers at Lucky 8 when Denny was killed. Only ten stuck around until the police told them they could leave. Ky didn't recognize most of the names and addresses that the constable had written down in tight cursive that leaned so far to the right it looked like each word was at risk of tipping over.

> *Guang Woo (diner)*
> *Hong Woo (diner)*
> *Lucia Woo (diner)*
> *Flora Huynh (wedding singer)*
> *Jimmy Carter (dishwasher)*
> *Thu Ly (cook)*
> *Phat Luong (waiter)*

The names she did recognize:

> *Eddie Ho (diner)*
> *Kevin Truong (diner)*
> *Sharon Faulkner (diner)*

That afternoon, she called her boss, Ian.

"Hey, kiddo." Ian's familiar deep voice echoed through the receiver. Decades earlier, Ian had been a spritely newsroom heartthrob. In his fifties, he now looked slightly melted and had grown into an impatient curmudgeon who lived for asking interns what more they could do. What weren't they thinking of? Who hadn't they interviewed? How else could they verify information? Although he intimidated all the young reporters, Ky liked that he seemed to believe that they could be great—if only they were willing.

"Everything all right up there?"

"Yeah. Hey, Ian, I have a question for you."

"Shoot."

"Back when you were a police reporter, how long were the police reports in homicide cases?"

Ky could hear her own question rephrased for her as "How long is a piece of string?"

"Well, it depends."

Sitting cross-legged in her childhood bedroom, chunky receiver pressed to the side of her face, Ky explained how she'd gotten a report from an officer on Denny's case, and even though they were just handwritten notes as opposed to a formal report, it seemed laughably sparse and difficult to believe.

"It says that the restaurant's tables were covered in uneaten food, that there was evidence that at least a dozen people had been there for dinner—they even counted the bowls and chopsticks—but a lot of them were gone by the time police arrived."

Ky fought the urge to throw up as her eyes read the description of Denny: the thick pool of blood, his body still warm but lifeless, his disfigured face, his crushed neck, exposed bone, the CPR that failed, each chest compression causing blood to spray from his nose, his white formal shirt stained a deep red.

"This report is saying that a bunch of people, the perpetrators or something, did a runner, and the remaining witnesses said they didn't actually witness anything. Denny's friends were apparently in the bathroom at the exact same time and swear they didn't see a thing. His high school geography teacher, Ms. Faulkner, was there. I had no friggin' idea. She was at the funeral and never said anything about it. I don't even know if my parents know . . ." Ky paused, considered the possibility that the police told her father, but the information had disappeared in his drunken fog. "Anyway, Ms. Faulkner was there and made the Triple Zero call, but even she was somehow in the bathroom when he was killed." Now Ky felt a lump in her throat as she imagined someone beating Denny to death while no one helped; in a restaurant of seventeen people, no one helped. "The report says Lucky 8 only has two toilet stalls. The other diners said they were facing the wall and closed their eyes when they heard the commotion. The restaurant staff said they didn't see what happened, either. This can't be for real, right?"

There was a pause on the line. Ky hadn't told anyone at the *Herald Sun* how her brother had died. This was Ian's first time hearing it.

"Christ, Ky. This is bloody awful."

Ky pressed her fingernails into the squishy part of her stomach, leaving half-moon impressions in her skin. She tried to distract herself from the nausea, from the need to puke or scream.

"Tell me again what kind of document you got from this cop."

"He photocopied his handwritten notes for me. It looks like it's from a notebook or something."

"Hm, okay. So normally, in the event of a homicide, the police don't have to release anything, especially if the homicide is still under investigation, so good onya for managing to get something from this guy." He cleared his throat. "The length of any of these reports is gonna depend on how detailed the officer is, how much there is to write about. There's no set length. And honestly, us journos don't normally get to see it anyway."

"So what do we get to see?"

"Coroner's report, which you should be familiar with. If there's an inquest, and there might well be one for your brother, the timeline will depend on how complex the case is and how backed up they are. Normally the coroner will send the family a letter with an inquest date, and it can be anywhere from a few weeks to a few years away."

"Are you serious?"

"Unfortunately. These things move pretty slow."

"There's something else."

"Shoot."

"There wasn't an autopsy."

"What do you mean? Usually in homicide cases the coroner will order one—"

"My parents declined."

Ian went quiet. Ky would have thought the line had gone dead if it wasn't for his breathing, followed by a delayed "Huh."

"Well," he finally said, "families do have a right to do that, on religious or cultural grounds—"

"But you just said that in homicide cases the coroner will—"

"To determine the cause of death. If your brother had died of suspicious *and* mysterious circumstances, then I can see the coroner pushing for it."

"He *did* die of mysterious circumstances," Ky said, feeling pressure behind her eyes. "He was a *really* good kid. Like, I know people are always describing people as being a 'good kid,' even when they're just average, but Denny was exceptional. He came first in *everything*."

More silence, during which Ky thought she might break the skin of her belly if she pressed her fingernails any harder.

"I don't want to be cynical," Ian said, pausing as though searching for the right words, "and I've never been to Cabramatta . . . but I've read about it, seen the crime coverage, and . . . look, if *I* was the coroner, I'd have made an autopsy happen, no doubt about it. But maybe the coroner who saw your brother . . . maybe he or she . . ."

Ky held her breath. She could see the outline of what he would say next, and she prayed he wouldn't do it, even as the voice of Minnie repeated it over and over again.

Didn't care didn't care didn't care didn't care didn't care didn't care because no one cares no one cares no one cares no one cares no one cares no one cares.

". . . was just having a bad day," Ian said. "I've seen people make mistakes, even when the stakes are high. They're all human, you know? People do incompetent or just dumb things all the time, and that's just how it is."

Ky wasn't hearing Ian anymore. Minnie was now conducting a monologue in her ears, distracting her from whatever explanation Ian was giving about the overworked and overwhelmed system.

Isn't it funny? Isn't it just the funniest *that these dudes get to be so incompetent and dumb and make mistakes when it's literally life and death and they* never *get in trouble for it while you* agonize *over your stupid, narrow, pointless path like it matters? Isn't it* hilarious? *Doesn't it make you just want to* die *from frustration and humiliation and indignity and—*

"STOP," Ky said, surprising herself by speaking.

"Excuse me?" said Ian.

"I'm sorry," Ky said, embarrassed. "I was just . . ."

"It's fine. I get it. You're going through a lot."

"I . . . I have something else."

Ian was quiet again, waiting for Ky to go on.

"I have a list of witnesses."

"How so?"

"I got a list from the officer. Names, addresses, phone numbers. People who were there."

Quiet again.

"Wow," he finally said. "I mean, good onya for that."

"I should . . . I could track these people down, right?"

Another pause.

"Unless it would be inappropriate?" Ky continued, feeling a wave of nausea come over her, unsure of what she was meant to do. "But the officer said no one will talk, so it means they have the answers, which means—"

"Look, Ky," Ian said, letting out a long sigh, "this is a personal matter for you. This isn't work. This isn't a yarn for the paper—"

Ky could feel her chest begin to deflate at the thought of Ian shutting down an idea that could bring her closer to an answer.

"—but if it *was* a yarn for the paper," he said, speaking slowly, "then you know what I'd tell you to do."

Ky felt a jolt in her heart.

"You mean . . ."

"Yeah."

"I should call the people on the witness list," she said, stating it as a fact.

"What more could you do?"

59

"I could start from the outside and work my way in."

"Keep going."

"I could go see them in person."

"And?"

"Thank you, Ian," Ky said. Without saying goodbye, she hung up, the receiver clacking against the rotary phone. Her hands trembled at the thought of what she was about to do.

Chapter 3

So my name is Lulu Woo (yeah, it rhymes—so what?) and I'm ten years old and live with my parents in Cabramatta in an apartment upstairs from a savory donut shop that ventilates its grease fumes outward and upward and into our living room, so our apartment always smells like used cooking oil and no amount of shampooing can get it out of our hair. Let me tell you, Cabramatta is heaps dangerous and Mum tells me I have to run home from school, because if I walk too slow, then maybe a junkie will stab me in the neck with a needle full of heroin and get me hooked—because that's what junkies do; they're all zombies trying to turn more people into zombies—and Mum's like, "Listen to me, Lulu, don't walk, run." So every day after the three o'clock bell, I grab my Hello Kitty bag and push my fellow year threes out of the way, and my friends are like, "What the—?" but I'm already whooshing out the school gates, like, "Sorry! No time to explain!" and I run so fast that by the time I get home and jam the key into our dead bolt I can feel my heart in my eyeballs.

Anyway, until about a week ago, or maybe it was two—I don't know, it's hard to keep track of time—every day was basically the same, which was fine with me because I liked eating instant mi goreng and watching cartoons until the six o'clock news, which was also when my parents came home from work. After dinner I would spend, like, five minutes on homework because school was easy. Mum would look over my math and shake her head at the baby stuff they had us doing, and then she'd make me do math drills she'd photocopied from some library textbook meant for twelve-year-olds, and when I complained about being only ten and having to do extra work she'd say, "You want to be dumb like a white kid?" and if I talked back and was like, "Yeah! Dumb white kids rule!" she'd pinch the top of my ear and tell me I would never be white, so I may as well get used to being Vietnamese Chinese, and I thought it was pretty unfair for her to rig a conversation like that, but what's new?

One December day, when the weather had turned into summer, I was at home after school watching *Power Rangers* with the dress of my school uniform rolled all the way up to my armpits because I was so hot and our fan was so weak. The episode was about how the pink Power Ranger couldn't do gymnastics at school anymore and she was heaps sad about it, and it reminded me of the pink Power Rangers at my school, also known as white girls, also known as girls named Kimberly, who would get all cry-face about sports, and I rolled my eyes at the TV while I picked at the dead skin that crusted my lips, and I peeled off so much skin that I felt a sting and knew that I had gone too far, and when I looked down at my lap it was specked with all the dead skin that I'd picked.

On this day I heard a knock at the door and I literally jumped to my feet, dress still rolled up to my pits, because no one ever knocked on our door (exception: the Avon lady, but she gave up years ago when she realized that Mum was interested only in free samples). I crept to the door in my bare feet, hoping whoever was out there wouldn't hear the sound of the bottoms of my feet sticking to and pulling away from floor tiles, before realizing that they could probably hear the TV. I groaned on the inside and thought about turning the TV off, but that would be too obvious, so I just kept creeping toward the door and hoped that whoever knocked would think that we were one of those families that kept a radio playing all day to ward off burglars. As my heart pounded at the thought of someone wanting something from us, I recalled Mum's rules about people knocking on our door: if it was white men in neat white shirts and black ties, be very quiet and pretend you're not home because they'll try to kidnap you for a church; if it was someone dressed like a handyman, be very quiet and pretend you're not home because they will probably try to do rapes; and if it was the Avon lady, be very quiet and pretend you're not home, but check after she leaves to see if she has left free samples, and make sure to bring them inside so the super cheap Come-from-China neighbors can't steal them. I put my eyeball to the peephole and held my breath. There was an Asian woman outside, and I was heaps confused because Mum didn't have rules about Asians at our door, and the woman wasn't an old lady like most of the other Asians in our building, and she reminded me of the assistants who worked at the dentist's office, how they were kind of young but definitely adults and also probably not junkies because they dressed so tidy and looked alert and this lady even wore the kind of glasses that were so high-tech that they didn't need frames.

When I didn't answer, she knocked again, and I was panicking so hard because what if she had a legit reason for being here and I was doing something wrong by pretending no one was home? But also, what if she tricked me and did a kidnapping? She knocked again, which made me jump. I covered my mouth and tiptoed backward to our sofa, and as I gently lowered myself onto it, the plastic cover, which my parents hadn't removed since they won the sofa in a raffle seven years ago, squeaked under my weight. I kept both hands over my mouth and squeezed my eyes shut until I heard her footsteps travel down the hallway and disappear.

That night I had weird dreams. In one of them I was trapped in a dark box, and there were people outside the box screaming like crazy, and I wanted so bad to get out but I was also scared of what was waiting for me, so I tried to call for Mum but I couldn't because all of the skin on my lips had come off, and when I looked in the mirror (I had a tiny handheld mirror, and for some reason, even though it was pitch-dark I could see myself clearly) I had these big red clown lips and they were raw and gross and I wanted to open my mouth to scream for Mum, but I was also scared that it would hurt my mouth too much, so I just felt around in the dark, crying without moving my humongous no-skin lips. This went on forever and I was so angry and sad and frustrated that I thought I would die from it, and I don't even remember how the dream ended, only that it did. In another dream Nick Carter from the Backstreet Boys came to my house and asked me to be his girlfriend and I told him I was too young to date, but if he could wait for me, my parents said I could have a boyfriend once I finish high school if I score like a hundred in everything, and he was like, "Of course. For you, anything," and I flicked my hair, which, for the purposes of the dream, had grown from the mushroom cut Mum gave me to some Barbie-doll swooshy locks, and Nick Carter literally swooned. And in my last dream, I was a tiny cactus, but that dream lasted maybe three seconds and then I woke up.

When I went to the bathroom, I almost screamed because my real-life lips were huge and red, and I seriously thought all the skin was gone. But when I looked closer, the skin was still there—it was just dry and super flaky and had turned rusty red and everything was so tight that it hurt for me to open my mouth, and when I washed my face, the skin stung heaps, so I did the only thing I knew how to do when dealing with dry lips, I twisted my stick of grape-flavored Lip Smacker and filled in all the dark, sandpapery skin on my face, and then, because this is the rule with Lip Smacker, I licked it all back up so I could taste the grape flavor. When Mum saw me at breakfast, she was like, "Ai-ya! What you do to your lip?" and I shrugged, because how could this be my fault? And she was like, "You lick your lip again? Don't lick your lip!" And she lectured me on how saliva was bad for skin, and I would have argued with her, but I was trying to move my mouth as little as possible, so I ate my breakfast one Froot Loop at a time with chopsticks, and Dad was like, "I'm off to work—bye," and Mum was like, "Don't eat at that Cambodian place for lunch; you know you always get the runs," and I kind of wished one of them would take me to school, like before, when I was younger and it was their job to take care of me.

At school my friend Chao immediately noticed my lips and said, "Whoa, dude! What the heckin' frick!" and I told her I didn't know how it started but now I couldn't stop licking my lips, because the moment they felt dry, I had to swipe my wet tongue over them, because to not do that would make me feel like the skin would crack and my whole face would split apart. Chao told me that she once had big clown lips, too, and her mum was so freaked out she took her to the doctor, who said it was because of stress, and I was like, "What the frick do *you* have to be stressed about?" and Chao shrugged, and I thought that it probably had something to do with her alcoholic dad, who was way into alcohol because he had P-E-S-T or P-T-S-D or whatever, something about how the Viet Cong cut off his ear and then her mum tried to sew it back on, but it didn't work and fell off again. Chao said he loved alcohol so much he always got drunk at weddings, and one time it was so bad that he threw up on the bride, which was kind of funny except Chao never laughed when she told the story. So anyway, Chao said it was maybe stress, because the stress makes your lips dry, and then you lick them, and the saliva makes it worse, and I was gonna say, "Ugh, you sound like my mum," but then she said the solution was lip balm, so I went through half a tube of Lip Smacker before lunchtime, smearing it onto my huge clown lips and extending my tongue as far as it would go to lick lick lick up the grape flavor that was starting to make me feel nauseous.

After school that day I had to eat my mi goreng one noodle at a time because my lip skin was so dry and tight that the corners of my mouth cracked and wet stuff came out and it stung like heck-nuts whenever water or food touched it. I watched *Power*

Rangers and the Pink Ranger was still super depressed about school gymnastics and I was like, "God, she's such a crybaby," but at the same time I wanted to be her because she was prettier than the Yellow Ranger, who was Asian, and pink was my favorite color, and whenever we played *Power Rangers* at school the white girls would make Chao and me play the yellow one, and we thought it was heaps bull crap, but we liked that they wanted to play with us at all, so we took turns being the Yellow Ranger while they all got to be the Pink Ranger, and we asked why there could be four Pink Rangers but Chao and I couldn't be one of them, and Madison Stone said, "Because you're both yellow, duh," and I could see that Chao was about to cry, so I held her hand and was like, "They just mean we're bright! Like the sun! HA-HA! They think we're smart! Because we are!" and that totally saved the day.

So anyway I was watching TV and had my bowl of mi goreng resting on my exposed belly (hot day, dress was rolled up again) when someone knocked on the door and I freaked out so hard I tipped the bowl of noodles onto the sofa and I finally understood why my parents kept the plastic covering all these years. I tiptoe-ran to the door and eyeballed the peephole and it was the Asian woman again, the tidy young one from the day before with the high-tech no-frames glasses, and even though our peephole was grimy with donut oil, I could make out her neat ponytail, her ironed collared shirt, the kind of pants women wear when they work in an office, the kind with belt loops, and I could see that she was holding her hands together really tight, like she was digging her nails into her palms. For a moment I fantasized about office ladies because Mum always

67

said if I work hard and go to uni I can get a good office job, then I won't have to suffer like her and Dad, like how Dad works in a factory that makes metal sheets and Mum is a yum cha cart lady, and at night she shows me these gross purple spider veins on her legs and she makes me touch the bumpiest bits and says, "See? See how I suffer? You will not suffer. Not your generation, because you can speak good English," and I'm like, "Duh, tell me something I don't know," and she shakes her head and says no one likes an arrogant girl, but I'm thinking, No, seriously, tell me something I don't know, like, will her generation *ever* stop suffering?

The tidy lady knocked again, and this time I was freaking out so bad my face accidentally bumped into the door, which made her say, "Hello? Is anyone there?" and the first thing I noticed was that she had a full Aussie accent, like me, which was weird because anyone older than me was usually an FOB who spoke FOB English, like my parents and our neighbors and basically everyone in Cabramatta. And then I had the sudden urge to poop, which was super weird because I'm normally a pre-breakfast pooper, but my butt felt stiff, like a brick was lodged there, and I couldn't think straight, so I said, "*Yeah?*" and she said, "Is this where the Woo family lives?" and without even properly processing it, I said, "*Yeah?*" and she said, "Are your parents around?" and I said, "*Maybe?*" and she was silent for a while, and when I checked the peephole again she was jotting something down in a notebook.

"Do you know when they'll be home?" she asked.

How did she know for sure that my parents weren't at home? I hadn't told her. But what if I'd given too much away? What if she was a kidnapper after all? But I needed to poop so bad, so my thoughts weren't the smartest, so I said, *"Maybe later?"* and she said, "Okay . . ." and paused a little, then asked me what my name was, and because of poop I called out, *"Lulu!"*

"Lulu . . . as in, Lucia?"

"Yeah!"

"Okay, Lulu," the lady said, all calm-like. "Can I come back tomorrow? I'd like to speak with your parents. And with you."

She slid a piece of paper under the door, and before she could explain, I snatched it up and made a run for the bathroom and I thought I heard her say, "Hello? You still there?" but my butt was exploding into the toilet, and all I could do was feel embarrassed and relieved at the same time.

It turned out that maybe I shouldn't eat mi goreng every day and that the lady's name, which she'd written on the piece of paper along with her phone and pager number, was Ky Tran. I could barely pay attention to cartoons the rest of the afternoon, so I decided to take a shower, but my lips were still dry and cracked, so I washed my body but didn't let any water near my mouth, and every time a droplet accidentally splashed onto my face I winced and wondered what I did to deserve this kind of suffering. I emerged from the shower smelling like fake green apples, but my mouth was still a giant brownish-red crust that now included food specks and the dried-up Lip Smacker that my tongue couldn't reach and I looked like a rejected clown, but I didn't know what else to do, so I put on more Lip Smacker.

That night I wanted to tell my parents about the lady named Ky, but Dad was busy with the runs because he ate at the

Cambodian place again, and Mum was too busy yelling about how she should never have married him, that it was the biggest regret of her life, that if only she'd chosen an uglier man she would be treated better, and then she said, without even looking at me:

"Listen, Lulu, don't ever marry a handsome man. He will never listen to you. You will have no power over him. And one day he will be old! He will be old and ugly anyway! Like your dad! But who he is on the inside will not change! He will still have his head stuck up his butthole, so far up that it pops out of his neck and is a normal head again! And people will say that they don't understand why you are complaining because your husband's head looks like it's in the right place, but only you will know that it is not in the right place at all! Only you will know that it went into his butthole first! Marry an ugly man, okay? Your auntie Sum-Sum married so ugly. A man so fat. Nose so big. Eyes tiny, like little dessert beans. You know dessert beans? Very small. The smallest bean. My god. So ugly. But he treats her so good! She has all the power! She says walk, he walks. She says sit, he sits. She says give me all your income and I will manage our finances and you will not buy anything until you ask me for permission first, he does not argue with her! Such a good man. But he's only good because he is ugly. You see what I mean, Lulu?"

Mum said these kinds of things all the time and it made me feel heavy, not in the nice sleepy way like when you go to the dentist and they put that lead apron on you before they X-ray your mouth, but in the way that made it hard to take a deep breath. I spent a lot of time feeling heavy, like when I watched the news and that Pauline Hanson lady said that Asians were swamping Australia, which wasn't true because how could I swamp anything if I didn't even know what swamping was? Or when I asked Dad why he called my grandparents auntie and uncle and he said it was because they were superstitious and believed that if kids got too attached to their parents, terrible things might happen, so growing up he was never allowed to call his parents mum and dad, and when I said, "But didn't bad things happen anyway?"—like the Vietnam War and the communists stealing his things and him becoming a refugee and yada yada—he said, "Can you imagine how much worse it could have been?" And of course I couldn't, so I felt heavy instead. Or the time when I was at school, which is basically every day, and some Britney or Kimberly would say, "Ha-ha, gross, you're eating grass!" when I was eating a pork floss sandwich, or "Friggin' yuck, your lunch smells gross!" when I was eating mi goreng, and the worst was when it came from another Asian kid, another Vietnamese Chinese girl with nicely braided hair, who would say, "My dad says only poor people eat soy sauce sandwiches," and I'd want to say, "We're not poor! We just didn't have time to buy ham!" but for some reason I couldn't summon the power to save the day for myself. Chao would say, "Don't listen to her. She's just a snob because her dad's a doctor," but I couldn't help it, and I learned that in the pyramid of people there were the Kimberlys at the top, and then there were the girls who had just come from Yugoslavia and sucked at English but looked pretty so no one made fun of them, and then there were the Samoan girls who won at all sports, and then there were the Asian girls whose dads were doctors, and maybe if you kept going down down down you'd find the Asian girl who eats soy sauce sandwiches. I didn't say any of this to Chao, because I was too heavy to find the right words.

So no one looked at me that night because Dad was on the toilet forever and Mum was busy reading about OC classes, which she was totally obsessed with because she said if I got into an OC class I would only be around smart kids, and if I was only around smart kids then I wouldn't become a junkie or gangster or violent murderer, and she started listing off all the math and general ability skills I had to practice in order to ace the OC test, and I went to bed early because I couldn't stand that no one was paying any real attention to me. I closed my eyes and imagined what it would be like to work in an office, to wear pants with belt loops, to have someone say, "Good morning, Lulu. You want some coffee?" as I came to work each day, and to respond with "God, I'd love a coffee. I sure cannot start the day without one!" and the more I thought about it, the sleepier I got, and that was basically how I fell asleep every night, by imagining myself drinking coffee.

That night I had weird dreams again. I was in a dark box and could hear people outside going, "NO NO NO!" or "STOP STOP STOP!" and then a million bowls and plates smashed, and then I woke up and was wet all over: my face was wet, and my mouth was wet, and my thighs were wet, and I was like, "What the heck! Why are my—"

I pulled the damp sheets off my bed and put them in the laundry basket with the rest of my clothes. When I walked into the bathroom to wash, I almost screamed for real because

I caught my reflection and my lips were bleeding, the skin had cracked, and if I stretched my mouth even a little bit I could see the pinkish red wetness. Standing all nudie in the bathroom with a cracked clown face and a damp bed and no idea how to fix anything, I wanted to cry so bad, and I did, I did one of those totally silent cries where your face is the ugliest it will ever be, but I made no noise at all, and my whole head hurt so much from loneliness that I forgot how much my lips burned and stung, and after I washed myself and put on clean pajammies I crawled back into bed, sheetless, and I curled up like a prawn, my body perfectly avoiding—or wrapping around—the wet spot, until everything turned dark again.

The next day at school we had a fire drill. Mr. Hidson sat with us on the soccer field, wearing the big straw hat that he got from Mexico. All the popular girls sat around him, telling jokes that weren't funny; it was like the Britneys and Kimberlys were friends with him and it made me want to be friends with him, too, because maybe if I was friends with the teacher then no one would make fun of my sandwiches, and maybe I would have protection, like how the Cabramatta gangs say they will protect the yum cha restaurant where Mum works if the owner agrees to pay them money every month, except I wouldn't pay Mr. Hidson anything because we'd be pals for real. I scooted toward them without letting my butt leave the ground, and when they laughed at something Britney said I also went *HA-HA-HA* to fit in. I figured Mr. Hidson might like to talk about politics because he was a grown-up, and maybe we could gossip together about how Pauline Hanson was a mad racialist, and he would see how smart and in the know I was, and even though I didn't really know anything about Pauline Hanson, I did know that she wanted to get rid of Asians because every time her powder-white face and bright orange hair appeared on the TV Dad would say, "I hate her! I hate her to death!" and then Mum would say, "She hates Asians! I read it in the *Sing Tao Daily*! She thinks we are bad people!" and Dad, who seriously never said anything most of the time, would get all veiny in the head and say, "Hate, hate, hate!"

So I said to Mr. Hidson, "Sir, do you hate Pauline Hanson?" and his shiny pale face that looked like a raw chicken breast tilted to the side all confused.

"Why do you ask, Lucia?"

"Because," I said, frantically licking my lips again because I'd stopped for like ten seconds and it had gotten unbearable, "because she hates Asians, so I hate her."

Mr. Hidson looked at the other girls, who had each made their eyebrows lopsided, and then he looked back at me, and his eyes definitely moved to my brown crusted clown lips, and he said, "It's not good to hate anyone, Lucia Woo," and something about that dropped a heavy curtain in front of my face, and I felt soiled from rejection, and Britney Nichols said, *"Anyway . . ."* and I knuckle-dragged myself back to where I sat before.

The cartoons that afternoon kept getting interrupted by breaking news alerts about a body being found in the Georges River and how it was probably drug and gang related and Cabramatta this and Cabramatta that and they brought out Pauline Hanson again, who said something about whatever and I groaned so

74

ALL THAT'S LEFT UNSAID

loud I slid off the plastic of our couch and kind of just stayed there with my knees on the floor and my face on the squeaky cushion, wondering when they would cut back to *Rugrats,* when a knock came at the door. It wasn't that I'd forgotten that the lady named Ky was coming back, I had just been hoping she wouldn't, that maybe she was unreliable, like how my parents promised to get me a Barbie or a Cabbage Patch Kid and then never did, and I didn't hold it against them because people can be like that.

She was dressed like an office lady again with a collared shirt that she had tucked into belt loop pants, and she called through the door, "Lulu? Are your parents around?" and I felt like I knew her at least a little bit because she had come around three times now and she sounded exactly like me (like, not an FOB) and I had her name and phone number, and what kind of kidnapper would be dumb enough to give someone their phone number? So I said, with my eyeball to the peephole, "No . . ." and she looked at the floor, which I tried to never do because the carpet in our hallway was so old and dirty that my skin felt itchy whenever I thought about it, and she dug her fingernails into her palms again, and then she said, "May I come in? I just want to ask you a few questions," and I said, "What for?" and she said, "It's about my brother," and I had no idea what she was talking about, but now I wanted to know, so I opened the door but kept the chain latched, and there she was, her rimless glasses looking even more classy and fashionable and high-tech up close, her eyes wide at the sight of my lips, then a friendly smile, and in a soft voice she said, "Hi! How's it going? May I come in?" and I eyed her up and down, and her hands were empty and had little half-moon marks on them from where she'd been digging her nails, and I said, "Okay, but you have to take your shoes off," and she nodded like, *Of course,* and I liked her even more.

She asked me if she could sit down and I pointed at one of our fold-out dining chairs, and then she asked me if my parents were at work and I nodded, and she asked me if I was home alone most days after school, and I nodded then, too, and I thought of how much trouble I would be in if Mum found out that I'd let a stranger into the house, but maybe I didn't even have to tell Mum, maybe this could just be for me.

She pointed at the TV and said something about how she liked *Rugrats,* too, and I thought she was maybe a bit too old for it because it was literally a cartoon about babies, and then she said she liked my school uniform, which, whatever. "How old are you, Lulu?" she asked, and I said ten, and she swallowed real hard and looked at her lap, and I had no idea what was going on or if she was maybe sizing me up to kidnap me and sell me on the black market, and just as I started thinking about the possibility of being tricked by an office lady she said, "I have a brother named Denny. Well, *had* a brother, I guess . . ." Here her eyes kinda drifted out of focus and she looked heaps sad. "He was at Lucky 8 a little over a week ago. Do you remember going to Lucky 8 with your parents, Lulu?"

Mum and Dad had promised to take me out for king crab if I came first in school. They made me that promise when I was in year two, and when I came first in everything four terms in a row, they didn't take me out for king crab because they said we were busy, even though they meant that *they* were busy, because

I was free as all heck. So this year, after I came first three terms in a row, and after I complained about how I was so hungry for king crab that I was too tired to do homework, too tired to study, too tired to come first and get into an OC class, Mum looked worried, and she gave Dad the same worried look, and he was like, "Fine, okay," so they took me to Lucky 8, which does king crab, and you can even choose the crab you want from the fish tank and they'll fish it out for you, and I remember Mum saying to the waiter, "Pick one with lots of meat! Don't try to trick us with a watery crab! I am watching you!" and—

"Lulu?"

"Yeah," I said, my mind snapping back to our greasy dining room. "We went for king crab."

"Lulu," Ky said, looking me in the eye in a way that made my skin tighten around my body, that made me want to look away, "my brother Denny was killed that night. At Lucky 8."

She paused, maybe to let it sink in, but nothing was sinking anywhere, and now my heart was going nuts, and I swore I was more heart than human because I could feel it beating everywhere.

"The police say they've interviewed you and your parents, but you all said you didn't see anything . . ." She stopped again, pushed her hair behind her ears, looked down at her lap, then looked back up at me. "Look, Lulu, I'm not with the police. I'm just Denny's sister. The police are still investigating the murder, but . . . I just need to know what happened. This is just for me. You won't get in trouble if you tell me what you saw. I promise."

I felt embarrassed all of a sudden that I had invited someone into our donut grease house, that maybe I should have mopped the floor, even though it never did anything anyway because the more we cleaned, the more the savory donut shop pumped oily air through our window, and I didn't want the office lady to think we were gross or anything, but here I was covered in grease with lips that looked like the surface of Mars.

"Lulu?" she said again, and I snapped back again. "Can you tell me what you remember from that night? When you went out for king crab with your parents?"

I remembered the first thing that came out was a soup, my favorite, canh chua, and it had a whole fish head in it, and this was before my lips went bad, so I was able to slurp like four bowls before my parents told me to slow down or I'd get a stomachache. And then the fried rice came out, and Mum complained to us about how they skimped on the seafood, how this couldn't possibly be seafood fried rice if it only had three prawns, that we were getting ripped off, that we should never have come to Lucky 8, and Dad ate in silence because he was good at ignoring Mum, and I was like, "Uuuuuugh!" because why did she always have to complain, and then a man with a super wet apron and a limp came out with a big, big plate that smelled like so many flavors my tongue tingled and my mouth filled with saliva, and on the plate was a glossy, steamy, bright orange king crab cooked in garlic sauce, and for a moment Mum actually stopped complaining and we all looked at it with hearts in eyes, like in the cartoons, and we felt so good, so successful, like our all our dads were doctors, and then a bowl smashed, and another bowl smashed, and we looked over at a table near our own that was big and round with lots of people wearing black sitting around it, and a guy with long hair, who was probably a naughty person because Mum said that any man with long hair is bad—anyway, this naughty long-haired man was towering over a skinny boy. The skinny boy didn't look like he belonged with the big round table because his hair was all neat and short, and I didn't know why a neat person like him would want to go near naughty people, but maybe he was sick of being so tidy and wanted to be bad, or maybe he was asking them how much he would have to pay them to get protection like Mum's yum cha restaurant, or maybe he was giving them advice and telling them they didn't have to be naughty and they could change their ways, and if they just cut their hair and did good in school and didn't cause trouble, then they could be heaps successful one day. Well, back to the real story—this tidy boy's eyes were huge and scared-looking, and the long-haired man grabbed him and pushed him so hard that I felt my insides shake, and before the boy hit the floor I saw darkness, and my head was in Mum's lap, and she was squeezing it so tight, like I was wearing a helmet, and my eyes were squeezed shut, and everything was dark except for the screaming, and the plates, and the screaming and screaming.

"I don't know," I said, because I suddenly felt so heavy it was like someone had put dumbbells on my throat, and when she asked me what I saw, whether I saw her brother, and she said he was a skinny kid, with a center hair part, who wore glasses just like hers, who looked a lot younger than he was, whether I saw what happened to him, and how it happened, and how it all started, I could only think of the shiny crab on our table and how it glistened and even made Mum smile, and all I could say was "I didn't see anything," because it was true, everything had gone dark, and Mum was hunched over holding my head, and Dad was hunched over holding Mum, and we were a tight ball of Hugging Woos while people around us screamed, and once the screaming stopped, Mum wouldn't let go of my head, so everything stayed dark for me, and we never even got to touch the king crab—I remember that now, we never even got to touch the king crab.

"Lulu," Ky said, her eyes red—she looked like Chao whenever Chao was about to cry—and she said, "please don't lie to me," and I got all huffy and said, "For serious! I'm not lying!" and something in her forehead twitched, and her voice went wobbly, and she said, "Why won't you help me?" And on the inside I was like, "*What?*" but I had dumbbell throat, so nothing came out, and then she was like, "I'm not the police, okay? I'm not *them*. I'm like you. I'm just like you. Why can't you just tell me what you saw? What's so goddamn hard about that?" Then she swallowed the words that were meant to come next, slouched, and closed her eyes, her forehead still quivering. For a moment she looked like she had fallen into a twitchy sleep, but then I thought maybe she was praying, like my parents when we were hugging in the restaurant, how Mum was rocking back and forth while squeezing me and repeating over and over, "求观音保佑我的家人," and I would have been like "What are you even saying?" except I was too busy having my head squeezed.

Ky opened her eyes after seriously forever, leaned forward, closer to me, and apologized. "I'm sorry you had to see that," she said, and I said it was okay even though I felt heaps uncomfortable because I didn't like seeing Asian girls get sad, and it was even worse if the Asian girl was an adult, but then she said,

"No, it's not okay. You never should have . . . you're only a kid. And what you saw was . . . I can't imagine what it must be like, to have seen that, you know?" And I wanted to say, "For real, I didn't see anything," but I had serious crazy heart, so I said nothing, and she was like, "I'm really, really sorry, Lulu. You shouldn't have gone through that. It wasn't fair to you. It wasn't fair to anyone. I'm sorry."

She went quiet, so I stared at my toes and made them flex, and I noticed that my longest toe looked like E.T.'s finger. Then she asked me where my parents worked, so I told her because I was scared she would cry, and she jotted it down in her tiny notebook, and she studied it, and then she sniffed twice, flaring her nostrils each time, and then she thanked me for my time and said sorry for bothering me, and I said, "No worries, mate," like a true blue Aussie. Then she got up from our fold-out dining chair, stood still, looked at my big crusty lips, and said, "You should use Vaseline." And as she walked out the door, I was like, "What?" and she said, "For your lips. I used to have that problem, too. Just smother the whole area with Vaseline," and she raised her hand to her face, and that was the clearest thing I'd remember about her—this office lady, whose brother I didn't see die, who saw me and said sorry to me—walking out of our apartment and down the hall, face still turned toward me, motioning her hand all over her face like she, too, had big, cracked clown lips.

Chapter 4

Before Ky could even focus her vision, her eyes still bleary with sleep, her mother had woken her and left the room. The clock by her bed read eight in the morning. She rolled onto her stomach, buried her face into her pillow, and remembered Lulu Woo's apartment from the day before—the greasy floor, the air thick with cooking exhaust, how much the furniture and complete disregard for aesthetics reminded Ky of her own family's home.

"I think, when I move out, I'm going to decorate my house in a Western style," Denny said during one of their last phone conversations. Ky had called from Melbourne to wish her brother good luck in his upcoming HSC exams—the final hurdle between him and his university of choice.

"You mean like Wild West?"

"No, no, like white people."

"You ever been in a white person's house?" Ky asked, genuinely curious.

"I watch *Better Homes and Gardens*," Denny said. "Mum watches it, too, but I think she does it to feel superior to white people."

"Huh."

"She reckons they're super impractical and waste money on decorative junk they don't need."

"Like?"

"Like, on last night's episode, they knotted some white rope, framed it, and called it nautical art. Mum hated it."

"I bet she did."

"But," Denny continued, "they got this really nice rug with an anchor on it. Mum also hated that because she was like, 'Why would you cover your floor with a carpet?' And I told her it was to make a room look nice, and she said it just made the floor harder to clean."

"She's not wrong."

"She spends every episode shaking her head and saying how dumb the ideas are, but she still hate-watches it every week," Denny said. "Anyway, when I move out, I'm gonna get a rug, and take the plastic covering off the sofa and remote control, and buy real shelves for my closet, and—"

"What, you *don't* like having shelves made from empty baby formula tins?" Ky said, picturing the Nestlé S-26 canisters that their mother had saved from when Denny was an infant and stacked to form platform shelves.

"Don't tell Mum, but I think baby formula shelves look bad."

"Yes, they do."

"And they're not even that practical. It's not even really a shelf."

"But they're free," Ky said.

"When I move out, I think I don't want to be cheap."

"You sound like a terrible Asian right now, Denny."

"Maybe, when I move out and have a real job and money, I can buy Mum and Dad a real closet?"

"Mum'll just yell at you for wasting money when she has a perfectly free solution."

"Man."

Ky laughed, felt the tingling warmth that bloomed within her whenever she talked to someone for whom she didn't need to fill in the blanks—someone who understood that the act of complaining about her parents was not an invitation to trouble-shoot her problems, because there was no solving the problem of refugee parents; someone who could commiserate without casting judgment; someone who accepted the contradiction of the things that annoyed her most about her family being the same things that signaled to her that they cared.

She used to be able to talk to Minnie and Denny about it. With Minnie gone, it was just Denny. Now that Denny was gone, too, Ky felt so alone lying in her childhood bed that she had to force herself to get up and get moving, if only to momentarily take her mind off her feelings.

She dragged her feet down the hallway, stopping at the door to Denny's room, where she could see her father's socked feet on Denny's bed. Her parents had been a ghostly presence in their home. In the mornings she could hear their movements through the walls, could see cups of tea still warm on the kitchen counter, could feel steam lingering in the bathroom. She couldn't tell who was avoiding whom. It occurred to her that she reminded them of Denny, that her presence emphasized their loss. It occurred to her that they were upset with her—having the nerve to move away for four years, to rarely call; being checked out and fretting about work any time she visited; returning only after it was too late. It occurred to her that they had something to hide—the fact that the autopsy had been declined had sat heavy in her chest since she'd talked to the constable, and she'd wanted to corner her parents, to demand an explanation for why they had so many questions about Denny when he was alive and why they'd lost all interest now that he was dead. Seeing her father, once again fully dressed for work, spooning a pillow atop the mattress, she saw her opportunity.

"Dad?"

Her father sat up in one swift motion, as though Ky's voice was an alarm clock he'd anticipated. "I'm going to work today," he said, smoothing down his hair without looking at her.

"Okay," Ky said. "I didn't ask, but—"

"Oh," he said, hands resting in his lap, "your mother wants you to go to the temple with her. She's already outside."

"Okay."

"Did you . . . did you go to the police station?"

"Yeah," Ky said.

Her father turned his body to face her, but his eyes were somewhere else—focusing on the dresser, the doorknob, the air above her head. For as long as she could remember, he had been distant in a way that exceeded even the limits of immigrant father aloofness. With the exception of Minnie's dad, who was negligent at best and more likely belonged in jail, Ky's own father was the most uninterested person she knew. He seemed to care about only two things: *Paris by Night* and finding a phở restaurant that came close to making the phở he ate as a child.

"The best phở I've ever had was made by a man in our village who came from Hanoi," he once told Ky and Denny when they were eleven and six. It was one of the few occasions that he shared a story, and both children, realizing that something rare was happening, dropped their LEGO bricks and paid attention.

"Aren't Hanoi people communists?" Ky said. By that age, she had heard enough about Vietnam from her mother to know which side they were on.

"Not everyone from Hanoi was a communist," her father said. "Besides, we don't hate their people—we hate their system."

Ky scrunched her nose as though he had just lied to her face.

"When I was five, I asked the cook what his secret was, and he told me that he made the phở in a soldier's helmet," her father said, leaning forward and tapping his head. "All the salt from the human sweat makes the broth extra flavorful."

"No way," Ky had said in English, even though, back in those days, her father had been strict about the members of the household speaking only Vietnamese. He reasoned that they'd already lost their native home; they weren't about to lose their native tongue.

"It's true!"

"Wow," said Denny.

"Nope nope nope!" Ky said, covering her ears.

In his quest for soldier helmet phở, every year her father would cycle through the Vietnamese restaurants in Cabramatta and choose the one that most closely resembled the flavors of his childhood. His pick became the family's local. Whenever a restaurant changed cooks or tweaked its recipe and the phở no longer tasted right, he moved them on to the next best restaurant. He expressed no strong opinions about anything else.

"Did they give you anything?" he now asked Ky, still sitting on Denny's bed.

With one hand, he rubbed the protruding, robust veins on the back of his skinny hands. He looked old, tired, and Ky couldn't imagine that he was ever the young man she'd seen in her family's black-and-white photos, the ones that showed him smiling with his eyes, laughing with his whole body, his lanky arms draped over her mother's shoulders, both parents looking in love and unburdened. The question of the autopsy burned in her throat, but she couldn't get it out. He looked frail, barely there, and she worried that if she brought it up now, the confrontation would make him crumble to dust.

"Not really," Ky said, focusing on her father's wrinkled neck so that she didn't have to look him in the eyes.

"Oh."

"They just told me what they probably already told you."

"I see."

He scratched the backs of his hands, and Ky thought she registered skepticism on his face. Minnie had often told Ky that her parents were probably more perceptive and resilient than she gave them credit for—they did, after all, survive a war—but Ky wasn't convinced. There were moments, like right now, where she felt that she knew what was best for them, and that as their bridge to Australia, she had a responsibility to protect them from the country's own horrors. She couldn't tell him what she knew until she knew it all. She couldn't drop Constable Edwards's incomplete notes that raised more questions than answers into her father's lap.

"What did they tell you?" he asked.

"Just that they're still investigating," Ky said, unable to conceal the wobble in her voice that often gave away the fact that she was lying. She hoped that her father didn't know her well enough to spot the tell.

After standing in the doorway for what felt like an eternity, Ky told her father that she was going to the temple.

"Okay," he said as she turned to leave, his fragile frame slumping.

By the time Ky had showered and dressed herself in gray slacks and a white button-down—an office outfit that doubled as mourning attire—her mother was waiting for her in the car, fingers impatiently drumming on the steering wheel while her mouth was set in a frown.

"There are creases in your shirt!" her mother said when Ky climbed into the passenger's seat.

"It's fine," Ky responded in English.

"Is this how you live in Melbourne? You forget everything I've taught you? You just live like an unclean person? People must look at you and think, 'Wow, that girl is so—'"

"Mum!" Ky shouted, her adult veneer all but dissolved. "Can you just not?"

Her mother backed the car out of the driveway, shaking her head. In the back seat sat a box of waxy nectarines and stacks of joss paper offerings for Denny. Ky spotted the yellow prayer sheets that from a distance resembled coffee table doilies, and the wads of afterlife money that she, Minnie, and Denny used to play with.

"Whoa, check out these *hell* bank notes!" Minnie had said when they were both eleven. It had been Tomb Sweeping Day, which, as her mother had explained, was a day for people to remember their ancestors. The Tran family had bought joss paper clothing, servants, prayer sheets, and money to burn for Ky's grandparents.

Minnie had opened a packet of joss paper money, which could have passed for American singles were it not for the Chinese print, the old Asian man's face in the center of the bill, or the words, written in English, HELL BANK NOTE.

"We probably shouldn't play with that," Ky said.

Minnie fanned herself with the ink-smelling wad of paper, ignoring Ky's protests.

"Okay, so we're in the Gold Rush, and I own all the land, and if you want to pan for gold on my territory, you have to pay me a fee," Minnie said, divvying the joss paper money among herself, Ky, and a six-year-old Denny. "Ky, you're a hardworking bloke from the outback, and Denny, you're the first Chinese man from China to come to Australia, and . . ."—Minnie smacked her own stack of money against the palm of her hand—"even though white people like Ky hate you, you work really hard and are way more successful than them, and maybe that's why they hate you, because you're so smart and successful, but also because you're a Chinese, so—"

"This is too complicated," Ky said.

In school, where they were learning about the 1851 Australian Gold Rush, their teachers had devised games in which the students played prospectors exchanging pounds and shillings for a chance to mine gold. There was no real backstory, no real role-playing. The school's game was essentially a lottery. The students lapped it up.

Denny began folding each note individually and putting them in his pastel bum bag, while Ky and Minnie bickered over whether it was better to play Minnie's game (Minnie: "I'm just making mine *realistic,* okay?") or to replicate what they'd been playing in school (Ky: "We already know the rules for it." Minnie: "*What* rules?").

The three of them didn't get in trouble with Ky's mother until, days later, while doing laundry, she emptied Denny's bum bag to find dozens of neatly folded hell bank notes.

"*Who do this?*" she'd yelled in English before reaching for her feather duster, hand clutching the soft feathery part, waving the hard plastic handle in the air. "Bad luck!" she continued as she stomped into the living room, where Ky and Denny were playing Connect 4, the older sibling surprised by how well her brother kept up.

Her mother shook a fistful of the joss paper money between their faces, knocking over their game.

"Mum!" Ky yelled. "What the heck!"

"Who do this? Huh?"

Both Denny's and Ky's eyes widened when they realized what was in their mother's hand.

"Did you take this from Tomb Sweeping Day?" her mother asked, switching back to her native Vietnamese. "Who did this?"

Denny's mouth quivered. His face, which Ky saw in its chubby entirety, was pleading. Denny's greatest fear, after the prospect of a durian falling on his head, was getting in trouble with anyone. This was one of the things they had in common: a fear of authority, a fear of falling off the path, and the shared belief, absorbed from school, from strangers, from TV, from the sun-warmed air they breathed, that it would pay off—that being good paid off. The difference was that Denny was also afraid of their mother and Ky was not. Ky couldn't help it—in the presence of the woman who yelled at her the most, Ky devolved into a brat. Watching her mother continue to wave the feather duster in the air, half a dozen possibilities ran through Ky's mind, from throwing Denny under the bus, which she knew she couldn't do, to pinning it on Minnie, because it was Minnie's idea, after all, to feigning cluelessness, to some rationale about it actually being good luck, that she'd read somewhere that—

Her mother began smacking the duster handle against their linoleum floor, which meant that if someone didn't fess up soon, the next thwack would be against their hands and butts.

"Ma—" Denny began.

"I'm sorry, Mum," Ky said in English, cutting her brother off, surprised to find her own mouth now quivering, even though she couldn't explain why. "It was me."

Denny's mouth hung open. He made the same face he always made whenever his sister fell on a sword for him—a mixture of guilt and gratitude, the inability to hide the truth.

Their mother looked at both of them, rolled her eyes to the ceiling, and sighed.

"You stupid, *stupid* children," she said. "You . . ."—she pointed her feather duster at Ky—"hand, out."

Ky kept her hand close to her body, unfurled her fingers, palm upward. She squeezed her eyes shut, preemptively wincing in anticipation of the sharp smack of the duster.

Her mother grabbed Ky's hand, squeezing it until her own hand began to sweat. After a silence that went for so long that Ky allowed herself to open one eye to see what was going on, her mother gently tapped the handle of the feather duster against Ky's palm, tickling it instead.

"It is very, very, very bad luck to play with this," she said, releasing her daughter's hand. "This is not for the living! This is only for the dead! Do not invite this bad luck into our house!"

When her mother then stormed away, Ky rubbed her hands together as she calculated how much bad luck the joss paper money, which spent three days stewing in Denny's bum bag, could possibly have brought into their lives.

"Next time we go to the temple, you better ask Buddha to take back the bad luck," she said to Denny, who nodded like a child relishing a second chance. "Because I swear to god," she said, leaving her sentence hanging, "I swear to god."

Back in the car with her mother, they now drove in silence to the Mingyue Lay Buddhist Temple in neighboring Bonnyrigg, where Denny's cremains were interred. Ky had always liked the novelty of the temple: her family went only a few times a year; she got to see people burn joss paper offerings of clothing, houses, origami boats, gold, and servants; and each visit was a pleasant reminder that her family's take on the afterlife—that you could chill out in luxury until it was time for you to reincarnate—seemed a lot more forgiving than her rudimentary understanding of Christianity's concepts of heaven and hell. Her mother had explained that the Buddhas weren't something to be feared; rather, they were wish granters. She taught Ky and Denny to hold a lit joss stick between their palms, kneel before the Buddhas, and make a wish. She always dictated the wish, though—that they should ask to do well in school, that they should ask to be obedient to their parents.

"What do I ask for now?" Ky said a year earlier on one of the rare occasions she attended Tomb Sweeping Day. It was the first time she'd been back at the temple since moving to Melbourne.

"What you mean?"

"I've finished school . . . what now?"

Her mother had looked at her with a puckered mouth but didn't offer an answer.

"What do *you* wish for?" Ky asked.

"For you and your brother to do well in school and to listen to me."

"Don't you think it's time for an update?"

"Your brother is still in school."

"But what about when he graduates?"

"Long time away."

"He finishes school next year!"

"But then he have university."

"And then?"

"What?"

"Never mind."

So novel was her family's brand of Buddhism that Minnie, who'd accompanied them to Tomb Sweeping Day several years in a row, drew a connection between Ky's mother's superstitions and the plot of *Monkey,* which they'd been watching after school.

"For serious, dude," Minnie said when they were fourteen and pulling into the temple parking lot, "I think she got it from TV."

"Or maybe," Ky said, "the TV is based on true facts?"

Minnie gave Ky a pitying look.

As the car now turned into the parking lot, Ky considered the Sisyphean task ahead of her, didn't know whether she'd be able to push on if every person she talked to was going to make her feel as brick-in-the-stomach sick as Lulu Woo did. She felt like she was doing death knocks in reverse. A disproportionate part of her job as a rookie reporter was tracking down people who had recently lost loved ones in car accidents, killings, or natural disasters to get a quote for an article. These death knocks drained Ky with such intensity that she couldn't even cry at the end of the night, even though it was all she wanted to do. She hated being the person who interrupted, sometimes hounded families in mourning. She hated being the person who visited them in their grief while having the luxury of leaving. It so often felt wrong, gross, completely unnecessary. But a journalist had to be willing, and she was doing what her managers expected of her. She wondered whether in tracking down the supposed "witnesses" to Denny's death, she was subjecting them to her grief. In inflicting this much discomfort on herself, in forcing herself to find out what happened to her brother in the most excruciating way possible, was she trying to obtain absolution? She didn't know who exactly could absolve her. But she saw no other way of emerging from the guilt that had been suffocating her since she learned that her brother was gone.

Arriving at the temple, Ky and her mother passed the main

hall that housed the enormous gold-leaf buddhas and headed straight for the columbarium. Ky, Denny, and Minnie were never allowed into this part of the temple when they were younger because Ky's mother worried that they would offend the dead. The family had seen *Mr. Vampire,* a Hong Kong comedy about ghost hunters, which warned that if someone offended a dead person while standing near their grave, a ghost would follow them home. Ky's mother had taken the warning to heart and made the girls and Denny wait outside every Tomb Sweeping Day.

Following her mother into the narrow room toward Denny's cubby, Ky now understood why her parents hadn't wanted any children in there. Surrounded by unsmiling portraits, Ky felt a cold draft brush against her neck and back. She found herself weighed down not only by the sadness of her brother's death but by the sheer concentration of the deaths around her, each face crammed into a hole in the wall. She tried not to look at the portraits but couldn't help it. In her mind, she heard Minnie providing a running commentary that would have gotten all the ghosts to follow them:

Holy crap, that's a photo of a baby! A baby died, Ky! That's so sad. And look at this lady—she was so young. And pretty. What a waste. And look at this dude! He looks so miserable! Why don't Asians smile in their photos? Like, come on, you just have to say cheese. Bro, this one defs had Down's syndrome, I think. Look at his eyes!

Ky's mother pointed to the top shelf, where two urns were nestled in a shared cubby. Ky recognized the framed photos leaning against the urns—her grandparents.

"We saved up for so long to buy this cubby space so that

your grandma and grandpa could rest side by side," her mother said, pointing at the black-and-white portraits that Ky had seen every day while growing up, the same portraits that sat in her family's ancestral altar. Four cubbies below them, at eye level, was Denny's. His year twelve school photo—dressed in his Cabramatta High uniform, the tie done all the way up, his hair neatly parted down the middle, his glasses thick and shiny, his face glowing, a big smile in place—leaned against a ceramic urn. On either side of his photo were tiny vases that each held a plastic flower.

"We were very lucky," her mother said, "to get a spot for your brother here, close to your grandparents, at this height."

Not lucky enough, said the voice in Ky's head. Her imagining of Minnie's commentary hadn't stopped. *Also, in what world is it lucky to be stuck in this cramped, dank room with all these other sad-ass dead people? It smells like stale incense in here. And have you noticed who he has to stare at all day? Angry grandma. Look! The woman directly across from his cubby! She looks like Chairman Mao's wife. The mean one. Get him outta here, man!*

Ky's mother, who hugged the joss paper she'd brought from the car, lifted the offerings up to Denny's photo, as though he could see her, as though she needed him to know that she had brought him something nice. With her other hand, she stroked the picture frame and ran a finger down the smiling boy's cheek.

The hell bank notes and doily-looking prayer sheets blackened and curled in the trash-can fire outside the columbarium. Ky dropped sheets of joss paper painted silver and gold into the can, mesmerized by the way the flames gobbled them up. It was another dry December day. The air was so warm, she couldn't tell how much of the heat was coming from the fire and how much had simply been there all along. She tried to picture her brother in the afterlife, accumulating so many precious metals with no idea what to do with them. Did the afterlife have a commodities market? Did he need a broker? Would he have to barter? She paused when she got to the joss paper servants—origami dolls that, when burned, were meant to appear at Denny's service, wherever he was.

"You know," Ky said, putting the dolls back on the ground, "I don't think Denny would appreciate servants."

"What?" her mother said in English, fanning the thick smoke out of her face. "What it mean?"

"Denny wouldn't like servants," Ky said, switching to Vietnamese to save herself from having to translate herself.

"Why not? Who wouldn't want a servant?"

"He'd feel weird about it."

"Why would he feel weird?"

"Because," Ky said, thinking of how she always tidied her hotel room at checkout because she didn't want housekeeping to judge her harshly, "he wouldn't want to be anyone's boss."

Her mother grimaced—at the smoke that was blowing against her body, at Ky.

"Don't be dumb," she finally said, stepping out of the smoke's way. "Everyone likes to have servants. This way you don't need to cook, don't need to clean. You think your brother knows how to do laundry? You think your brother can cook? You want him to eat instant mi goreng every day in the afterlife? Because that's all he can make. Is that what you want for him?" She picked up the origami servants and waved them in Ky's face. "We're doing him a favor."

Had Ky known that her mother took the offerings so literally, she would have brought the latest Kmart and Target catalogues with her. She imagined her dead brother in the afterlife, lying atop a bed of cash, servants feeding him pizza pockets. She imagined everything they burned from the catalogue appearing with a *poof!* in his room: a Nintendo, tube socks, a CD player with a compilation of all the hits of 1996, a jumbo box of Roses chocolates, T-shirts that change color when they get wet, every flavor of Lip Smacker. She would have made stick-figure drawings in her notebook and burned those for him, too: the DeLorean from *Back to the Future,* the phone booth from *Bill & Ted's Excellent Adventure,* the genie lamp from *Aladdin*—anything that could help her brother travel back in time.

"Mum," Ky said.

"What?" her mother said, not looking up, prodding at the charcoaled paper with a temple-issued poker stick.

"Do you ever think about Minnie?"

Her mother looked up, studied Ky's face through the residual smoke. "Why?"

"No reason," Ky said, returning her eyes to the glow of the dying fire.

Don't lie, Minnie's voice continued in Ky's head. Ky hated how little control she had over her own thoughts. *Tell her! Tell her how you can't stop thinking about me. Tell her how I'm the best friend you ever had and you feel super bad for what you did—as you should—and the guilt eats away at you every time you're in Cabramatta, and, in fact, you are now more guilty than you are person. If doctors put a piece of you under the microscope, they'd be like, Hey, this girl is composed of mostly guilt! Guilt and, I dunno, dumpling meat—*

"She turned naughty," Ky's mother said, waving smoke out of her face.

"I know," Ky said.

"A long time ago."

"I know."

"Such a waste."

"I know."

"We tried to save her."

This, Ky didn't know.

"Your dad and I . . ." she said, shaking her head.

Ky waited for her to continue. When her mother's mouth rested in a scowl, Ky prodded her. "What did you and Dad do?"

"We tried to be good people, you know?" her mother said, still focused on poking at the embers in the trash can.

"Yeah?"

"We have nothing in common with that family. Everyone thinks that because we were all refugees and we all came from the same country that we should be friends. But I would never have been friends with them in Vietnam, and I don't want to be friends with them now. They weren't like us. Do you know what I mean?"

Ky nodded. She'd heard this before, the complaints her mother had about Minnie's family. Ky's mother was repulsed by the Le family's poverty, their wastefulness, their lack of investment in the future. Her mother liked to talk about how there were two types of refugees—the kind who knew how to help themselves and the kind who didn't, and how Minnie's family gave all the other refugees a bad name.

"We are poor, too," her mother said. "But we never go hungry. You know what I mean?" She continued prodding at the trash can, which threw tiny embers into the air. "You can be poor and full, or poor and hungry. And that family, they are not like us."

When Ky said nothing, her mother continued: "But when I saw Minnie playing with you at school, when you were both little, she was so skinny and so dirty. It made me sad. And then, when I learned about her parents, I was so angry! Her dad had a union job, did you know that? He made more than your dad, with benefits! They paid him even when he didn't work! Do you know what I get when I don't work? Nothing! I've worked at that fabric shop for fifteen years, and if I miss one day, that's it, she docks my pay. I'm not working today because I'm mourning my dead son, and she's not going to pay me. Fifteen years!"

Ky had heard the story before. Every time her mother talked about the fabric shop, it was the same list of injustices—no paid time off, no sick leave, no overtime. But instead of running off at the mouth as she usually did—cutting her mother off, telling her that this was a choice she'd made by not learning English, that she should just get another job—Ky felt something shift inside her, like room was being made for her mother. It was small, just a sliver—maybe inspired by the temple, maybe inspired by Denny—but it was more patience and understanding than she'd ever had before for the woman who raised her. She thought she finally understood, for the first time, that it wasn't a choice—it couldn't possibly have been a choice. It was a trap, and her mother was stuck. For fifteen years, she'd been stuck.

"And do you know what Minnie's dad did with all his money and sick leave?" her mother continued. "He gambled it! I don't know if he still does, but back then he took everything to the RSL club and fed it to the slot machines. And his wife, instead of leaving him or killing him in his sleep, which is what I would have done, did nothing! She let him throw all their money away! And when he lost all his money, he would take her money from her sewing job and gamble that! Do you see what I mean? How they are not like us?"

Ky now tried to interrupt because she knew that if she didn't, she'd get Minnie's life story, which she already knew. But her mother was on a tear.

"It broke my heart. So your father and I offered to babysit Minnie after school, by which I mean I offered, since, honestly, when has your father ever done anything? Minnie's parents were never around, and we thought, this way, at least we could feed her and make sure she did her homework and give her proper baths, and untangle her hair. And her mother had the nerve to get defensive! She kept reminding me that she was Minnie's mother, told me that it wasn't my place to try to steal her daughter from her. She was crazy! I didn't want another daughter. You and your brother were enough. I'm not some child kidnapper, collecting other people's children for fun. You think I liked having to feed another person? But that Minnie, you loved her so much. You were obsessed with her. So I assured her mother I was just going to watch her for a few hours each day after school, and she said fine, but she wanted her daughter home by dinnertime. Which was stupid, because neither of them were ever home for dinner, and there was never any food for Minnie. I'd walk her home with a lunch box of rice, tell her to lock the door and not answer to strangers. I tried to keep her at our house for dinner once, and when her mother found out, she went crazy again, accused me of trying to steal her daughter. I just hoped, so badly, that if we did enough, she would turn out well. She was such a smart girl."

Ky had never heard her mother speak of Minnie like this. While she'd always suspected that there was some charity involved—Minnie didn't like talking about her home life, but she often dropped hints of what went on—she'd convinced herself over the years that her mother took in Minnie after school only so that Ky and Denny would have company. She didn't think that her mother saw what she saw, understood the things she understood, felt the sympathy and compassion and enormous love she had felt for Minnie. Ky didn't allow her mother to have feelings, because to grant her these would mean acknowledging that she was a person who had desires and dreams beyond what Ky saw. It was easier to imagine her as a caricature, as an immigrant Cabramatta parent, whose only desire was for her children to become doctors and lawyers (or ideally both), whose only means of expressing love to them was through cooking their meals, washing their clothes, and criticizing them into being better people. And despite wanting more from her mother, despite wanting the expression of love that came with warmth and acceptance, despite wanting her mother to actually know who she was, Ky had convinced herself that it was beyond her mother's capabilities, that people from the old country simply didn't do things that way. They'd give their life for you, but good luck getting them to see you.

"Minnie's parents are useless," her mother continued, the lower half of her face twisted, like she'd tasted something bad. "I don't know how they could let her go like that. If you or your brother turned naughty, I would have locked you in your room," she said, waving the hot poker in Ky's direction. "I would have put metal bars on the windows. I would have tied you up and never let you go outside again. I would have—"

"Okay, I get it, Mum."

"I just . . ." Her mother's voice wobbled. "It hurts me here . . ."—she beat at her chest—"to . . . to . . ."

"It's not like she was your daughter," Ky said. She knew the comment came across as catty, mean even, but something about her mother's emotional response to Minnie made her feel jealous. In all her years of knowing her mother, she had never seen this kind of tenderness directed at her.

"Doesn't need to be daughter!" her mother said in English, the frustration breaking her voice. She switched back to Vietnamese. "We cared for her nearly every day, from when she was in year one to year ten, from when she was tall like this . . ."—her mother tapped her hip with her free hand—"to when she became a woman. You think about that. How do you think it makes me feel to lose her like that?"

I guess your mum totally liked me more than she liked you, dude, Ky heard Minnie gloat. Ky didn't even know if that was a thing twenty-two-year-old Minnie would say, but she let the imagined remnants of her former friend rile her up anyway.

"Maybe don't be such a dick to your mum," Minnie had

said when they were in high school, after witnessing the way Ky talked back to her mother.

"Mind your own business, Minnie."

"Nope," her friend said while peeling the rice paper off a piece of White Rabbit candy and putting it onto her own tongue.

"Don't eat that paper, it'll give you cancer," Ky said.

"Don't be a dick to your mum, her heart's good."

"Why are you taking her side?"

"Because, objectively, you, my friend, are being a brat."

Ky didn't even remember the particular tantrum that had sparked that conversation, nor did she remember how it ended. Two things lived with clarity in her memory: One was the way she felt being called out by Minnie—the shame from someone seeing right into her, through to her ugliest parts. How it bear-hugged her, made her feel known; how much it made her squirm.

"Well, maybe if she wasn't such a dick to *me*—" Ky began, doubling down on being wrong because it was all she felt she could do.

"For fuck's sake, Ky!" Minnie finally said, straightening up like she did whenever she had something serious to say. "Do you know how friggin' lucky you are to have a mum like that?"

"You always take her side—"

"There are children starving in Africa!"

The comment was so unexpected that Ky couldn't control the laugh that escaped from her. "What on earth does that have to do with—"

Ky stopped herself from finishing her sentence when she saw the change that had come over her friend: the subtle pinch between Minnie's eyebrows; the way her lips pursed; the way light reflected from her eyeballs, suggesting the surface had gotten wetter.

That was the second thing she remembered clearly about that conversation—the way she'd managed to hurt her friend. The way she did it then. The way she'd manage to do it again and again and again.

Ky fumed on the drive home. She kept her arms folded in front of her body, angry at her mother for getting angry at her; angry at herself for feeling angry at her mother when she meant to be angry about Denny's being gone. Reverting to her teenage self, she sighed every time her mother slowed down for yellow traffic lights or waited too long at stop signs.

"Do you want to drive?" her mother finally said in Vietnamese. "Or are you just going to keep groaning like a dying animal?"

Ky turned her head to face the passenger side window, dug her teeth into her lower lip.

"Because if you're going to keep making noises, you can get out and walk," her mother said, eyes on the road. "You have no idea how lucky you are to have someone drive you around. No idea. You and your generation, you grow up so lucky and all you do is complain. Do you know what my generation would give to be as lucky as you? To grow up here and have everything—"

Ky felt a familiar heat rise in her body. It was as if she were fifteen again, her mother easily getting under her skin, igniting a frustration from which there was no relief. As a kid, she didn't have the words to describe that feeling; she knew only that it was glowing and hot and impossible to touch without burning herself. Now that she was twenty-two, the words were there in her head, jumbled. The feeling was still too hot to approach but was slowly beginning to make sense. If she would just give herself the time and space to think about it, to examine the thing she'd spent her whole life avoiding, she would realize that what she wanted to say to her mother was that *she* was the one who had no idea—no idea how badly Ky and people like Ky needed a break. No idea how speaking perfect English and having an office job and being born in Australia didn't mean what any of them thought it would mean. No idea how hard it was to walk the narrow path where everyone expected her to be quiet and smart and hardworking and good—a narrow path not even laid out by her or people like her. No idea how it felt to suffer the slow death of a thousand cuts: from the things people said, from the way people looked at her. The looks she got when she knocked on doors, walked into a room, boarded a flight; the way they saw her skin before they saw her, wanted her to shut up and be grateful, expected her to take a joke when she *was* the joke. The way she was expected to feel lucky, so lucky, like her life was abundant and full, when all she felt was depleted and diminished. It made her feel crazy to be called lucky, and her mother had no idea.

"We do everything for you," her mother continued.

"Then why didn't you get an autopsy for Denny?" Ky said, her voice raised, the inside of her lip bleeding from how hard she had bitten herself.

Her mother slammed on the brake at another yellow light. There were no cars around them. "You do not yell at your mother."

"I'm not yelling!" Ky said, still yelling. "You say you do everything for us, but you're not even doing anything for Denny right now—"

"I am giving him what he needs in the afterlife!"

"What about justice? What about finding out what happened to him?"

"We already know what happened to him."

"What is *wrong* with you?"

"Do not talk to your mother like that," her mother said again, her hands gripping the steering wheel.

"But don't you want to find out who did it? Or why they did it?"

"What good would it do?"

"Are you fucking serious—"

Her mother now clapped her hands in front of Ky's face, the smacking sound so loud Ky thought she'd been slapped. "I said *do not* talk to your mother like that! Show some respect!"

"I can't believe this. An autopsy would let us know if there was something in his system, or if he did something—"

"My son did not do drugs."

"But how can you be sure? You don't even know us!"

"What makes you think *you* know your brother? You don't live here anymore. How many times have you seen him since you moved to Melbourne? Do you think you can just come back and accuse my son of taking drugs?"

Ky pressed her fingernails into her palms. "I didn't say that," she said, a wave of guilt washing over her. "I just meant—"

"And so what? What would it change? I don't know who killed my son or why," her mother said. Her face was red, her eyes were deep pools. "Having the police cut him up won't bring him back."

"The coroner would do the autopsy—"

"I don't care. I don't want anyone to cut my son up. It won't bring him back. Nothing will bring him back. I can only make sure he has a good afterlife."

Ky kept her nails in her palms, trying to focus on the sting of physical pain so that she didn't have to confront everything she felt inside.

They continued the drive in silence, her mother cooling off enough to resume her slow and steady driving while Ky counted houses to distract herself.

"Giời ơi!" her mother said after she'd pulled the car into their driveway. "We forgot the fruit!"

The box of nectarines was still in the back seat. It should have been brought into the temple to be blessed by the Buddhas, to be offered to Denny, then brought home for eating. Ky's mother smacked her forehead several times with an open palm.

"Chill out, Mum," Ky said, reaching for the box from the front seat. "You can just take them tomorrow."

"No, no, no," her mother said. "They'll go soft by tomorrow. In this heat. No good."

Ky balanced the box on her knees and gently squeezed one of the nectarines. They had already started to soften from car heat.

"You bring to school," her mother said in English.

"What?"

"You bring to school."

"What school? I gradua—"

"For Denny's teachers. They come to funeral, we thank them."

Her mother gave the box a quick shove so that they sat further up in Ky's lap, like the matter was settled. "You go today, before fruit go bad. Give to Mr. Dick-sun and Miss Fuckna and Miss Buck."

"Dickson," Ky corrected. "Faulkner. God, Mum—"

"What-ever," her mother said, slamming the car's door as she climbed out, leaving Ky to cradle the box of fruit on her own.

Chapter 5

When the first Indo-Chinese refugees arrived in Australia, Sharon Faulkner was a high schooler in Sydney's Inner West who had seen Asian people only in photos, on the news, and in World War II textbooks that showed propaganda posters of the Japanese as bucktoothed rats.

When the first Indo-Chinese refugees left the Commonwealth migrant hostels in Villawood, Fairy Meadow, East Hills, Mayfield, and Dundas—equipped with a handful of English phrases ("Hello, how are you?" "Very good, thank you." "What it mean?"), a distaste for porridge, and the newly acquired knowledge that they couldn't digest cow's milk—Sharon Faulkner was on her way to Newcastle, farther north, to study education, with a cohort that was completely middle-class Anglo-Saxon Protestant.

And when the first Indo-Chinese refugees settled in Cabramatta, opened the first phở restaurants, established the first Vietnamese grocery stores that sold packets of dehydrated rice noodles, bottles of pungent fish sauce, and tubs of nose-prickling spices, Sharon Faulkner accepted a job straight out of university at a high school in Hay, some 725 kilometers from Sydney, town population: 1,300.

Hay was a comfortable place for Sharon Faulkner to teach. In a place like Hay, teachers were on a first-name basis with parents, and the kids themselves weren't too different from her: they all burned easily in the sun, watched cricket on Boxing Day, and used the term *mate* in a passive-aggressive manner to signal that they'd run out of patience ("Sit down and shut up, mate").

But Sharon was a city girl at heart. She wasn't made for Hay's scorching summers or the vast ring of nothing that surrounded the town and stretched for hundreds of kilometers in all directions. The first time she saw a tumbleweed, she ran out of her cottage in pajamas and a pair of flip-flops to follow it, giddy to see where it would go (a neighbor's driveway)—she'd never thought they were actually real. By the second, third, fourth, and fifth time they rolled by her house, by her classroom window, or alongside her 1981 Toyota Corolla hatchback as she drove down Hay's quiet roads, they reminded her only of how far she was from the tree-lined suburbs she so dearly missed, with the milk bars run by Greeks and Italians, the diversity of colorful neighborhoods where heads of rich brown hair dotted a sea of blonds, with olive-skinned blokes who said *youse* when they really meant to say *you*.

Sharon spent three years in Hay. She took the first transfer available, to a metropolitan school, in a suburb with a name that she thought sounded Italian.

When the first Indo-Chinese refugees—motherless and fatherless—found one another in southwest Sydney, banded together, created their chosen family—them against the world; when they enrolled in high school without understanding a word the teachers said; when the parents who came with babies and toddlers raised them as best as they could, put them in secondhand school uniforms, ordered them to work hard, to be good, to claw back the success and stability that had been torn from them; when a sixteen-year-old black-haired boy smoked a white powder off a piece of aluminum foil, then passed it to his friend, who passed it to his friend, who passed it to his friend; when the police and politicians decided that a certain ethnic enclave didn't have the DNA to be Australian, and the prime minister of the country said Vietnamese sob stories didn't wring his withers, and the friction of fear and hate coalesced in an Italian-sounding suburb of four square kilometers, Sharon Faulkner, freshly transferred from Hay, hair bleached golden by the sun, arrived in Cabramatta.

A week after Denny Tran's death, Sharon found herself outside the office of Cabramatta High School's counselor. For years she'd sent troubled students there and, over the same period, lost faith in it when instead of coming back calmer and better behaved, her students stopped coming to school altogether. Her colleagues, noticing her recent despondency in the staff room and the way she now ignored her students as they ran wild in the hallways, urged her to talk to someone. When it seemed like Sharon might zombie lurch her way through to the end of the school year, Barbara Stone, the fifty-something head teacher of social sciences, snatched Sharon's car keys from her desk and threatened to not give them back until she marched herself over to the counselor's office for a chat.

"The counselor is for kids," Sharon protested, her voice flat and lifeless.

"If she can handle our kids, then she can handle you," Barbara said, dropping the keys into her handbag. "Look, Shaz, you've been traumatized. I wasn't even there and *I* feel traumatized. Denny Tran was a good kid, and I'm no psychologist, but I know that you need to talk to someone." She put her handbag in her desk drawer, made a point of slamming it shut. "You can get your keys back once Lena Lao writes a note proving that you've talked to her."

The door to the counselor's office was ajar, but no one appeared to be inside. Sharon knocked before pushing it open, revealing a messy and lived-in room. A cheap pinewood desk was littered with lolly wrappers and empty takeaway coffee cups. Atop the desk was a computer in sleep mode; a Windows 95 logo drifted back and forth against a darkened screen. Three cardigans hung haphazardly off the back of the office chair, and a tattered brown sofa took up the bulk of the green carpeted floor space. The place was a sty compared to the previous guidance counselor's sterile setup of one desk, two plastic chairs, and a framed poster commemorating ABBA's 1977 Sydney tour. Sharon noticed that the ABBA poster was now gone, replaced with student art, holiday cards, and photos of the new counselor with friends and family. In one framed picture, Sharon recognized a younger Lena Lao in the Fairfield High School uniform—fresh-faced, hair unevenly streaked pink, on her hands and knees, forming the foundation of a human pyramid. Sharon rarely felt old—she was only in her mid-thirties, her newly grayed hairs still passing for ultra-blond while her body clung to the memory of eighteen years of track running. But she couldn't help but feel strange when people young enough to have once been her students ascended the ranks and became her colleagues. She'd just gotten used to being the youngest teacher in the room. Every time she encountered someone younger, it was like a spring in her chair released itself and she was cartoonishly thrown into the air.

"Ms. Faulkner!"

Lena Lao, petite and deeply tanned from months of playground duty, rushed into the room, clutching a stack of paper and an opened box of Band-Aids. To Sharon's surprise, up close, she looked as youthful as she did in her high school photo, except her long hair was now cropped into a tidy bob, the pink streaks long gone.

"I've been expecting you," she said. "Ms. Stone told me you might come by. Sorry I'm a bit all over the place right now, just had to break up a fight near the canteen, and—" She cleared room on her desk for the papers, found a spot in one of her overflowing drawers for the Band-Aids, and used a foot to kick the door closed. "And, well . . ." She sighed, looked at Sharon, who was standing in the middle of the room. Lena dropped herself into her office chair, knocking one of the cardigans to the ground. She picked it up, bunched it behind her. "Please, sit."

Sharon settled onto the sofa and immediately sank further than she'd anticipated.

"How are you?" Lena asked, looking at Sharon in a way that made her feel like she couldn't hide. It was a stark contrast to the previous counselor, Mrs. Humphreys, who couldn't seem to make eye contact with anyone. So aloof was Mary Humphreys that she'd become a joke even among teachers: If you wanted to lose a student, just send them to the school counselor. Mrs. Humphreys routinely dismissed students early from sessions, failed to keep track of who had visited, and confused the Asian students for one another. To everyone's relief, she retired at the start of the year. The school went two terms without a counselor. Lena Lao, only a few years out of university, started in term three.

"I'm fine," Sharon said.

"I heard that you might not be. You witnessed something really horrific, Sharon."

"I didn't witness anything," Sharon said, steadying her hands.

"But you did. Maybe not while it was happening, but afterward—"

"Please, stop," Sharon said, now gripping her fingers to stop them from shaking. "This feels like an interrogation, and I didn't come here for that."

"Okay, okay," Lena said, leaning back in her office chair. "It wasn't my intention. I'm sorry. What I'm trying to get at is: you were there. And that couldn't have been easy. Especially when the student is someone you know."

Sharon took a deep breath. She didn't want to cry, not at work, not in front of the counselor. "Look," she said, "I really don't need to be here."

"Then why did you come?" Lena asked, still looking at Sharon in a way that was so soft, so sympathetic, that she felt excruciatingly exposed.

"Because Barbara Stone took my car keys and said she wouldn't give them back unless I spoke with you."

"I see."

"It's nothing personal," Sharon said, realizing that she was coming across as rude and dismissive, but unable to help the fact that she was struggling to hold herself together. She hadn't been sleeping. She'd been snapping at her mother whenever she called. She was having daytime nightmares when she was awake—she didn't even know that was possible.

"Hey, no offense taken. Barbara Stone is a force to be reckoned with."

"So," Sharon said, tonguing the back of her teeth to anchor herself to reality, to remind herself to be polite and respectful, "I just need a note from you to prove that we've spoken, and then she'll give me my keys back."

"No problem," Lena said. "I'll write you a note once we've spoken."

Sharon's brows furrowed, unsure if she'd heard right. She wondered if Barbara had already spoken with Lena, if this had all been prearranged. The counselor's face was still soft, kind.

"So, tell me about Denny."

"You can't be serious."

"We both have fifth period off, Sharon. Let's talk."

"I can't believe this," Sharon said, eyeing the door, considering a dash for it. But she knew that her refusal to cooperate would signal to her colleagues that something really was wrong with her. It would be an invitation for them to worry, to be nosy. And in any case, Sharon *did* need to talk to someone about what had happened. She couldn't go into detail. And she knew she couldn't tell the whole truth—she'd nixed that possibility when she lied to the police. But that didn't mean she couldn't talk around it.

Lena now inched her chair closer toward Sharon, stopping before their knees touched.

"Fine," Sharon said. "Did you know Denny Tran?"

"I only knew of him," Lena said. "Students like him don't normally get sent to my office. At my last school I did some mediation between a few ultracompetitive, overachieving girls who were about to kill each other—not literally, of course—but that kind of thing didn't seem to apply to Denny Tran."

"No, he was very sweet to everyone," Sharon said, picturing Denny, with his thick glasses and center part. In her mind's eye, she saw the photo of him that his family had framed on their ancestral altar. Then she saw Ky, passing her a plate of noodles at the wake. Sharon knew it was a bad idea to attend the funeral. She could barely hold herself together, and she constantly worried that the Tran family would ask her questions that she couldn't answer or see through her lies. But she felt like she had no choice. Being at the funeral and wake was her way of being there for Denny, even if it was far too late. Every day since the funeral, details of the Tran family home dominated Sharon's thoughts: the photo of Denny, the narrowness of the townhouse, the year of the rat calendar, and the presence of Ky. "His sister was like that, though," Sharon said.

"Like what?"

"One of those ultracompetitive girls you mentioned. She was a very hard worker—but she seemed to derive no enjoyment from it."

"You taught her?"

"Yeah," Sharon said, picturing the year ten class of 1990, the begrudging faces of fifteen- and sixteen-year-olds who had no interest in geography but were mandated to take it. "When she was in year ten."

"That's a tough year," Lena said, appearing to lose herself in thought for a moment. "Not as tough as year twelve, but it's usually the time when students realize that there are stakes in all of this and that their friends are actually their competition."

"I didn't feel that way when I was in year ten," Sharon said, remembering that her own experiences with school were perfectly pleasant, with tight-knit friendships and a levity that she often longed for as an adult.

"Hmm," Lena said. "It can be different in these parts. I don't want to generalize, but I'm going to. When you're in the minority, the world makes you feel like there isn't enough room at the table for you. If you're lucky, maybe there's room for one. So you gotta fight it out, unfortunately. Speaking from experience."

Sharon nodded, although she wasn't sure that she bought it. She'd always prided herself on being more empathetic than her colleagues and had chalked up student competitiveness to parental pressure.

"And there is a lot of pressure from parents," Lena added, as though reading Sharon's mind. "But I think at some point, you realize the nature of the game."

Sharon thought she detected bitterness in Lena's voice, but the young counselor looked serene. Sharon didn't know how to read her. "That's cynical," Sharon said.

Lena shrugged. "It's how these kids feel. Better to recognize it than to dismiss it."

"But it's not true," Sharon said. She'd seen her own students work hard and be rewarded, earning spots in law schools and medical schools, winning full scholarships to university. Several of her own students had renewed her faith in the idea of the

ALL THAT'S LEFT UNSAID

Aussie fair go—children of refugees who, through sheer hard work and the right attitude, could go on to do whatever they wanted.

"The point is," Lena said, "that it's not easy for a lot of students, even the smart and studious ones. I'm not surprised his sister had a hard time."

"I keep thinking about her, actually," Sharon said.

"Why is that?"

"I was at his funeral over the weekend, and she was there. It was unsettling."

"Of course," Lena said, nodding. "Did you meet the rest of his family?"

"Sort of. Not really. His sister was the only one who spoke."

"I see."

"I don't know. I keep thinking of the year that I taught her."

"What about it?"

Sharon thought for a moment. In her head she drew lines from 1990 to 1996, from Ky to Denny, from her classroom to Lucky 8.

"I don't know," she said. "I guess . . . I keep thinking how everything is connected, somehow?"

"Hmm."

"It sounds crazy."

"Say more."

"Well, I keep thinking that maybe the writing was on the wall, way back then. But I also know it's crazy, and I have no proof, and I'm not even trying to prove that there's a connection. It's just where my head's at."

"When did you teach her?"

"In 1990."

"And was there a lot of overlap between your experience with her and Denny?"

"What do you mean?"

"Well," Lena said, leaning further back into her office chair, "I wonder what keeps bringing you back to her when it's her brother who died."

"I . . ." Sharon paused, flustered. She could feel a rash that appeared whenever she was nervous climb her chest. "I can't explain. I'm just stuck on it, the year I taught her. I can't stop thinking about it. It's probably because I just saw her. Maybe that's just how my head is processing things. I don't know."

"What do you remember from that year?" Lena asked, her lips pursed in thought.

"Jeez," Sharon said, letting out a long sigh. "It was so long ago. Nothing? Everything? I don't know."

The names were not the hardest part of Sharon's first year at Cabramatta High. She still butchered them—all the teachers did—but she quickly learned that Nguyen sounded more like "Newen" than "Noogooyen," that Ngoc was basically "Knock," and Phuc was more "Fook" than the other phonetic option. She even got used to the roomful of Asian faces that greeted her each morning at roll call, the sleepy Vietnamese, Chinese, Cambodian, and Lao students who tried to squeeze in a catnap before first period.

"You're like Anna!" her mother said whenever Sharon called to complain that each new week hadn't improved on the previous.

"Who?"

"From *The King and I*!"

"Strewth, Mum," Sharon said, remembering a scene from the movie where the King of Siam's fifteen young children greeted the English governess by kissing her white-gloved hands. "It's not like that."

"Isn't it, though? You're doing such a generous thing, sweetheart. I hope they appreciate it."

Like so many people outside of southwest Sydney who had heard about Cabramatta only from the news, her mother had initially been fearful about Sharon's move. But Sharon never encountered the criminal gangs that dominated headlines. She never got mugged, threatened, or targeted by dealers. Some people were just lucky like that. And her mother eventually came around on her new job when she landed on an analogy that made perfect sense to her: that her daughter had essentially entered a war zone to save the children. Sharon rolled her eyes, hoping her mother could sense it through the phone's curly cord. She told her mother that the hardest part about teaching at Cabramatta High had nothing to do with the crime rate—it was that the students didn't seem to like her. They weren't exactly hostile. But they weren't friendly, either.

"Nonsense," her mother said. "How can anyone not like you? You are the most charming, radiant, delightful young woman in all of New South Wales, and—"

"Tell that to a bunch of fifteen-year-olds."

"It's probably because they don't know you. And you don't know them!"

Her mother wasn't wrong. Sharon had spent the first week

of term memorizing names, going as far as writing the phonetic pronunciations in the margins so that she'd remember that the *h* in Thao was silent, Minh preferred to go by Minnie, and Ky was pronounced "key." She'd learned to match her students' names to their physical traits, too, so she wouldn't get them confused if they changed seats. Victor spiked his hair so aggressively with gel that his head resembled an echidna. Hue was the only chubby Asian kid in class and was always angling for a joke. Jason had straight black hair cropped to his ears, but inexplicably grew a rat's tail that brushed against the center of his back. Minnie, although painfully thin, had the roundest face of any student and unusually dark eyes that bore right through her. And to Minnie's left or right was always Ky, the devoted puppy dog of a best friend, the yin to Minnie's yang, highly strung, acne-chinned, a girl who wore every emotion on her face. Sharon similarly learned to identify the handful of non-Asian students. Spiro was the boy whose hairline Sharon could tell would soon recede. Maura wore green eye shadow to school every day. Mikey was an actual giant.

But what did Sharon really know about any of her students?

"You should tell them about yourself!" her mother said, as though landing on a jackpot of an idea. "Open up to them and they'll open up to you. It's a good cultural exchange. They can tell you all about where they're from, and they'll be smitten with you once they know your story, love."

What story? Sharon thought. She was born here, and so were her parents, and so were their parents, and so were their parents. Still, she didn't have a better idea, short of bringing in cookies and cakes as bribery, but she didn't want to seem desperate or reward standoffish behavior. So the following week she began each of her geography lessons with an icebreaker that every student—herself included—would answer. When she announced the activity, half of her year ten class signaled their lack of interest by twirling pens, graffitiing pencil cases, and yawning. The other half looked skeptical. Minnie and Ky grimaced. Sharon understood that her students probably thought she was treating them like babies, that this was the kind of thing kids in primary school did. She powered on.

"Today's question is: Where are you from? Who wants to go first?"

The roomful of students diverted their eyes—the universal gesture for "Don't pick me." Only Minnie and Ky continued to look; Minnie's thick brows raised into rooflike arches, Ky's furrowed in thought.

"Ky, how about you?"

The girl's face immediately transformed into one of horror and embarrassment. Her classmates giggled.

"Well," she said, her voice barely emerging from the back of her throat, "I was born in Vietnam."

"Speak up!" yelled Cora, one of the Greek Australian girls, from the back of the classroom that Sharon recognized by her tight curls, which were always pulled against their will into a full ponytail. Her friends stifled laughs.

"I was born in Vietnam," Ky repeated, louder.

"Việt Nam!" Hue called out, leaning into his Vietnamese accent, and now the Asian students were giggling, too.

"All right, settle down." Sharon looked back at Ky, whose skin flushed. "Go on."

"I don't remember anything about it, but . . ." Ky continued, "my family spent a few years in a refugee camp in Malaysia. I barely remember that, either. That's it."

Sharon nodded. "How about you, Hue? You seem to have a lot to say."

The class collectively went *Ooooh* as Hue shook his head, suddenly embarrassed.

"Việt Nam," the boy said.

"Same as Ky!"

"I dunno exactly where she from, miss," Hue said. Like many of her students, he spoke English with a singsongy rhythm that Sharon quickly came to associate with native Vietnamese and Cambodian speakers. She didn't mind the way it sounded, but wondered whether these students would ever sound Aussie, or if their speech would forever brand them as outsiders. Some students, like Minnie and Ky, didn't have much of an accent, but they still had tells: Ky had a tendency to end her sentences with *either* or *but*. Those could probably be corrected. Sharon wasn't so sure about the thicker accents.

"Vietnam," Sharon said. "Ky said she was from Vietnam."

Hue continued to shake his head as the boys around him snickered. "Miss, Vietnam is very big country. Who know where she from?"

"I'm from South Vietnam," Ky said.

Hue drawled, as if telling off a child: "Jay-sus, girl, you know how big is South Vee-et-naaaaaam?"

Now the whole class was united in laughter.

"Okay!" Sharon said, unequipped for heckling so early in the school year.

"How about Minnie? Where are you from?"

The girl with dark eyes looked directly at Sharon. She felt cold in her spine.

"Where are *you* from, miss?"

"Me?" Sharon had planned to go last. She had a whole story prepared about how her family had been here for more than a hundred years, descended from the English, but that her nanna's dad was half Italian and had blue eyes—could you believe? But Minnie's question, so soon into the icebreaker, caught her off guard. "Oh, I'm from here."

Minnie smirked. "Me too."

"No you're not," said Cora.

"Sure you are," said Minnie.

"What?"

"Exactly."

"Oi!" said Sharon. "Cora, don't speak 'til it's your turn. Minnie—you were born here?"

The girl rolled her eyes again. "Does it matter?"

As an undergraduate, Sharon had sat through a seminar devoted to breaking up student fights, conducting mediation, and helping both sides see eye to eye. There had been a separate day devoted to dealing with students who were rude, who talked back, who took out their rage on the teacher. Whatever was now happening in Sharon's classroom was neither of those things. Still, the tiny hairs on her body poised themselves to stand.

"Well, no. I guess it doesn't matter," Sharon said. "But the question was—"

"We're all Aussie here, miss. Even Hue."

The chubby boy perked up at the mention of his name,

seemingly unsure of whether the dark-eyed girl was dishing out support or a diss.

"I wasn't suggesting—"

"This is where I'm from, miss," she said, opening the palms of her hands like this was all she had to offer before clasping them into fists.

As reluctant as Sharon was to admit, she hadn't hated the forty minutes she'd spent with Lena Lao that first session. The young counselor had agreed to write her a note but had asked her to come back again during her next free period—nothing formal, they could treat it as colleagues having a chat. Sharon had said maybe, but once at her desk, she compared her teaching schedule against the counselor's.

"How'd it go?" Barbara said, looming over Sharon with both hands on her hips, a set of car keys dangling from a hooked index finger.

"Fine," Sharon said, covering the counselor's schedule with her own. Over the years, she'd learned to tolerate Barbara, understood that the head teacher simply treated everyone—even the principal—like they were one of her year seven students. Still, Sharon wished she would buzz off.

"She any good?" Barbara asked.

"She's nice."

"Nice doesn't always mean good," Barbara said. "In fact, nice is rarely ever good."

"Right," Sharon said. "I suppose she was nice *and* good."

Barbara's eyes were expectant, and Sharon knew she was waiting to hear more. But Sharon had no interest in talking, and certainly not with Barbara Stone. She pulled her mouth into a tight smile and pushed the signed slip from Lena across the table.

"Very well, then," Barbara said, her mouth suddenly small and disappointed. She placed Sharon's keys on the desk, gave them a tap.

On the walk to her car, Sharon replayed her conversation with the counselor to make sure that she hadn't given away more than she'd intended. Lena Lao was a good listener and came across as genuinely curious rather than nosy. Not long into their first chat, Sharon had found herself seeking the counselor's approval, if only to have her efforts validated.

"It's good that you learned to pronounce everyone's names correctly," Lena had said during their first session. "It can be really demoralizing for a student to have their name constantly mispronounced, or worse, to be confused for another student. A lot of the time people brush it off as a harmless mistake or not a big deal, but to the student, it becomes apparent that they're not being seen or thought of as an individual. I don't want to keep saying that I'm speaking from experience, but—speaking from experience—it makes a student feel like the people around them see their race before they see anything else."

"I would never," Sharon said, quietly pleased with herself for keeping up the practice of writing students' defining physical traits in the margins of her roster, even when her colleagues made fun of her for it.

"So it sounds like it was a challenging year for you," Lena said.

Sharon nodded. She felt herself transported back to 1990,

to the year she taught sixteen-year-old Ky and Minnie, to the unchanged social sciences staff room.

"What are they even learning in ESL?" Barbara had said back then, complaining for the third time that day that students were graduating from ESL classes too soon and that, instead of just being a social sciences teacher, she now had to double as an English teacher for every student passing through her history and geography classes.

"They are learning that they don't know what it mean," said Greg Kosta, another social sciences teacher, cackling at his own joke.

"Good grief. What it mean. What *does* it mean, Greg? What *do* they mean? What is the *meaning* of anything?"

"Think of how the English teachers must feel. Trying to teach *Macbeth* to these kids. Oof."

Sharon took her packed lunch—a tuna, pickle, and lettuce sandwich—to the conference table where Barbara and Greg sat with the papers they were grading and their coffee mugs.

"Oiya, Shazza," Greg said, consolidating his homework spread to make room for Sharon. "Do your kids know what it mean?"

Sharon shrugged. Some of her students' poor grasp of English grammar had bothered her during her first few weeks on the job—she'd groaned at the thought of how much heavy lifting she'd have to do. Sometimes she still worried about her students' integration into Australian society. Would people be mean to them because they both looked *and* sounded different? Would they ultimately feel unwelcome? But after a few weeks, she saw less of her students' accents and poor grammar and more of their personalities, and when she heard, "What it mean?" she thought of the chubby jokester in her class, his sassiness toward his peers, his warmth and respect toward her, always ending his sentences with "miss."

Barbara Stone huffed, theatrically licked her middle finger, and used it to flip the pages of a student worksheet.

"Have any of you taught Minh Le?" Sharon asked.

Both Barbara and Greg paused, the former putting down her worksheets, the latter swallowing his coffee.

"Trouble," said Barbara. "Trouble trouble."

"Yeah?"

"The attitude of that girl." Barbara shook her head, returning to her grading. "Bloody ungrateful."

"She seems very smart, though. She's scoring full marks on all my quizzes."

"But?"

"But, yeah, attitude. I can't put my finger on it."

"I taught her last year," Greg said. "Her and that Ky girl. Inseparable. Top marks in everything. Ky's definitely the rule follower, which, hey, doesn't cause me any problems."

"She's a good example," Barbara added. "Head down, work hard—she's got the right idea."

"The other students call her a snob because if she comes first, she tries to make sure that everyone knows about it. But I think she's just insecure. Classic teenager needing to prove something. As for Minnie, I have no idea what she's trying to prove."

"Some kids are just trouble," Barbara said, not raising her eyes from her work. "She was all right in year seven. Everyone's all right in year seven. But puberty creates some real monsters."

Sharon pictured younger versions of Minnie and Ky at the start of high school—their hair in pigtails, their hand-me-down school bags cartoonishly oversize, both girls holding hands on the walk to school. She couldn't help but wonder how two people who seemed so different from each other could be best friends. She wanted to be a fly on the wall when Minnie and Ky were alone, perhaps nestled in the shirt pocket of their school uniforms, her fly ears a mini microphone picking up every word in the baffling conversations the two girls must have.

"It's not gonna last," said Greg.

"What's not gonna last?" Sharon asked. She began separating the crust from her sandwich.

"That friendship."

Sharon balled a piece of bread between her thumb and fingers, not realizing that her colleagues were watching her play with her food. She did it whenever she thought of something she wanted to say but knew she shouldn't. She wanted to ask Greg how he—or any teacher, really—could be so confident in their assessment of a student. What did they know that she didn't? And what did he think he was, anyway? A psychologist? Instead, she said, "Oh?"

"There's always a blowup in year nine or ten when one girl rebels and the other doesn't. Just watch."

"Puberty!" Barbara said again, too loud this time. "Bloody monsters."

During that first session with Lena, Sharon didn't divulge this memory, but instead spoke about her frustration with the school for not doing more to understand students. "I feel like people just write them off," she said, picturing Barbara Stone licking her middle finger over and over again as she graded papers. "And I think my first few years were especially hard as I adjusted to that culture."

"Hmm," Lena said, resting her chin in her hand. "How did people write students off?"

"Well," Sharon said, careful with her words, "I don't think any students are ever just bad. I think there are a lot of factors at play, like what's going on at home, and I think a lot of people here just didn't care, or at least didn't think it was their job to care."

"Did you feel like it was your job?"

"Yes, absolutely. But I'm also not a social worker. I did my best. Well, I think I did. Maybe I did too much."

"What do you mean?"

Sharon felt a sudden rush of heat to her face. "I don't know," she lied, even though she knew there was truth to her words. The thing itself was hidden deep in the layers of her brain. But the tip of it had started to show. *Maybe I did too much.*

Three days later, during a free sixth period, Sharon was outside Lena's office again.

"Sharon!" Lena said, her face lighting up. Then, like she'd just remembered that she was speaking with an adult, she adjusted herself, relaxing back into her office chair. "I'm glad you came back."

"I saw you had a free period," Sharon said. "Just needed to get out of the staff room and figured I'd swing by, you know, for—"

"I welcome any and all distractions from staff rooms."

Lena offered Sharon a Chupa Chup lollipop from her top

drawer, which was filled with an array of sweets. "I recommend the cola one," she said. "The Cherry Ripes have fully melted, the Wonka Nerds might be expired, and kids love the Starbursts, so I save those in case I need them in an emergency."

Having never been to counseling of any kind, Sharon had assumed that Lena would want to ask her about her mother, her childhood, her dreams. Instead, the counselor seemed perfectly content to have Sharon talk about whatever she wanted, and unlike the shrinks she'd seen on TV who silently listened, judged, and wrote notes, Lena wasn't afraid to pipe in with her own opinions, from her take on the school's cross-country carnival ("We let them be sedentary 364 days of the year, and on the 365th day we expect them to run a 5K without puking?"), to disciplinary measures ("I've never understood getting in trouble for talking too much"), to school party food ("Fairy bread is gross").

"Your students seem to like you," Lena said, swinging one leg over the other and resting her elbows on her knees.

Sharon, not expecting the sudden pivot in the conversation, blushed. "Oh, well, they didn't, back in the day," she said.

"No need to be modest. I hear things. And here's the thing, no kid likes geography. They all think learning to read atmospheric pressure is beneath them."

"Oh," Sharon said, her bubble popping.

"But that's what I find remarkable. Geography is unsexy, but they like you. What's your secret? Cocaine? You giving these kids coke?"

"Ha!"

"That was obviously a joke. Public school teachers can't afford coke. Now, heroin would be a different story."

"I can't say I know how much any of it costs," Sharon said, feeling increasingly relaxed around Lena. Being in her company was a stark contrast to the stuffy social sciences staff room, where fellow teachers raised brows in response to jokes that were borderline risqué.

"For the record, I have never bought or used heroin," Lena said, raising both hands as though to plead innocence. "But I do know that it's cheap, and there's definitely an Asian discount."

"I don't know what to say."

"Yeah, same. Anyway. The secret to your success, let's hear it."

"Well," Sharon said, considering the key thing she did differently from her colleagues, "since coming to Cabra High, I've started every class with an icebreaker."

"Like, at the start of the year? Or the start of term?"

"No, every class."

"Wow."

"I end up recycling a lot of the questions, and they all get reused with each new cohort."

"Still, that's a lot of questions."

"It pays off, usually. We all get to know one another better."

"Give me an example."

Sharon recounted how in her first year of using the icebreakers—asking questions about dream vacations, favorite movies, short-term goals—her once-standoffish year ten class warmed to her. She left out the part about Minnie, who was the source of the class's hostility, and Ky, who never embraced the activity because Minnie was in the way. As bright as Minnie was, she had a way of poisoning the well with her presence; everyone was quieter, more self-conscious when she was in the room. Fortunately for Sharon, Minnie's attendance began slipping not long into the first term, and without the girl's eyes boring into her, Sharon felt like she was able to establish a rapport with her students, who started entering her classroom with a "Sup, miss?" and volunteering answers to questions about their favorite food—"Macca's," "Macca's," "Bún bò Huế" (Sharon: "What's that?" Hue: "You for serious, miss?"), "KFC," "Macca's"—and their worst fears—"heights," "cancer," "Thai pirates," "the smell of durian" (Sharon: "What's durian?" Hue: "Oh my gawd, miss"), "my mum," "Jason's mum" (Everyone: "Ha-ha-ha!").

"Did Denny's sister warm to you?" Lena asked.

"Who, Ky?"

"Yeah. You said she was in your class that year? Your first year teaching at Cabra, right? A year ten class?"

"Oh, yes. Sort of. But not really."

"Why was that?"

Minnie, Sharon thought, but didn't want to say the name. She felt herself getting close to something buried deep within her, something she wanted to stay buried.

"I think she thought she was above it," Sharon said, before a gnawing feeling told her that she was being unfair to Ky, that Ky's story became wildly skewed when Minnie was removed from the equation. In Sharon's memory, there was no Ky without Minnie. There was no Minnie without Ky. This proved to be true even now—she'd seen Ky only days earlier at Denny's funeral; she saw Minnie a week before that at Denny's death. She tried to suppress the most recent image of Minnie, the gaunt girl at Lucky 8, but it kept fighting back. Maybe, she thought, if she talked around that, found a way to talk about Minnie without talking about Minnie, it would alleviate some of the pressure.

"Actually, she had this friend, who was a handful," Sharon said, speaking dangerously close to what was on her mind. "I don't want to say her name, for privacy reasons, I guess. She was very resistant."

"This friend," Lena said, pushing her hair behind her ears, "what did she do?"

"Rolled her eyes a lot," Sharon said. "Sloppy attendance."

"Say more."

"Confrontational."

Sharon had had students get in her face—tantrums, swearing, an empty juice box thrown at her. And as shaken up as those incidents made her feel, there was always a sense of resolution, an eventual apology, an understanding that things were said and done in the heat of the moment. But Sharon had never gotten over her confrontation with Minnie. Sharon had called the girl aside on one of the rare occasions when she made an appearance. She remembered seeing Ky waiting outside in the hall, worry etched on her young face.

"Hey," Sharon had said to Minnie, being as gentle as possible, "is everything okay?"

Seated behind her scratched-up wooden desk, Sharon looked up at the girl who stood slouched before her, the whites of her eyes pink. Sharon had always thought that Minnie was intimidatingly pretty—she suspected it was one of the reasons so many of her peers left her alone and instead went to town making fun of Ky. But in the space of three school terms, she looked like she'd aged years. Her once-glossy, curtain-straight hair now looked stringy and greasy. Her pale skin took on a grayish hue.

"Everything's fine," Minnie said.

"We need to talk about your absences, Minnie."

"I'm doing good, aren't I?" Minnie shifted her weight from foot to foot, growing agitated. "I'm doing better than most of these dumb shits, aren't I?"

"Hey!" Sharon snapped. "Don't insult your peers."

Minnie was right, though—she was still doing better than most people in the class. But if there was one thing that got on Sharon's nerves, it was an arrogant student. She'd take a hardworking straggler over a cocky whiz kid any day.

"This isn't just about doing well on tests, Minnie. Any monkey can do well on a test. You actually need to be in class consistently. You don't want to repeat year ten, do you?"

"Monkey?" Minnie's pupils were pinpricks. Sharon imagined a laser shooting from those eyes, slicing through her insides.

"It's a figure of speech, Minnie."

"I'm sure it is," she said, rolling her eyes in a way that made Sharon want to slap them straight and still.

"If you don't start attending every class for the rest of the term, I will not let you pass year ten. You will be repeating."

The girl seemed incensed at the idea, and for a moment Sharon thought she could read what was going on in Minnie's head: the humiliation and injustice of the cohort's highest academic achiever being left behind, all because she didn't want to sit in a classroom where everything was too easy, anyway. If anything, Minnie should have skipped a grade.

"That's bullshit, man. That's fuckin' bullshit."

"Watch your language, Minh Le." Sharon found herself raising her voice for the first time. "You do *not* talk to me that way."

"Maybe you should stop talking to us like we're a bunch of dumb cunts, then. You're not on safari, okay? You're not saving the monkeys. And I don't have to like you, you patronizing *bitch*."

Sharon felt like the girl had kicked her in the teeth. It took her a moment to understand what Minnie meant. Sharon had never thought of herself as condescending. She'd tried so hard with these kids, made every effort to get to know them, to make them feel like she understood what they had been through. Then her own mother's words snaked their way out of the crevices of her brain: *You're doing such a generous thing, sweetheart. I hope they appreciate it.*

Sharon sat stunned as Minnie walked out of the classroom. She heard from the hallway the footsteps of Ky chasing down her friend, her tiny voice asking, "What happened?" followed by a distant "Oh, fuck off."

Back in the office with Lena, Sharon felt the hairs on her arms stand at the memory, and she fumbled her way through a loose recounting of the incident.

"So then what did you do?" Lena asked.

But before Sharon could respond, the bell for the end of school started ringing, and Sharon picked herself up and power walked to the parking lot.

As she approached her car, Sharon remembered why she usually waited a good twenty minutes until after school was over before trying to leave the grounds. There were students everywhere—groups of girls taking their time walking to the front gates, boys pushing one another out of the way, and serial truants standing in the parking lot, oblivious to the teachers trying to leave. She got into her Corolla, but immediately got back out after she felt the start of a panic attack brought on by the fear of being trapped in a furnace-hot car. She stood next to her Corolla, attempted to tap its roof, but it was so hot she instead took to standing with her hands by her sides. She watched as a small Daihatsu fought against the traffic of students into the parking lot, starting and stopping like a first-time driver. It took Sharon a moment to recognize the person behind the wheel: Ky Tran.

"Watch it, woman!" A boy in year seven slammed his hands onto the hood of the Daihatsu.

Sharon kept watching as Ky called out an apology to the kid, who gave her a prolonged glare while shaking his head. Even from a distance, she could see Ky's mounting frustration as she sat in her car with her right blinker on, trying to turn into an empty parking spot—every time she inched forward, more students would appear in front of her car, forcing her to brake. It made Sharon think of the traffic advice that her own students had given her earlier in the school year.

"You just have to close your eyes and go, miss," said Eddie Ho, who always sat next to Denny.

"That seems a bit dangerous, doesn't it?"

"He's talking about Vietnam," Denny had said.

"Yeah, you can't do that here, miss. You'll cause an accident. Duh. But in Vietnam, if you wait for a break in traffic, it'll never come."

"So is everyone just closing their eyes and going at the same time?"

"Basically."

"That doesn't sound right."

"Miss, don't listen to Eddie. He hasn't even been to Vietnam, and he doesn't know how to drive," Denny said.

"But my dad has!" Eddie said. "Trust me, miss, if you're ever in Vietnam and you need to cross the road, just go. It's the only way."

Sharon let out an unexpected laugh at the memory. She tried to swallow it when she saw that Ky had successfully parked and was now approaching her with what looked like a ten-kilo box of nectarines.

"Hi, miss," Ky said, stopping at Sharon's car.

"Hi," Sharon said, straightening herself. "Nice job navigating this—" She gestured at the parking lot, which still had dozens of stragglers.

"I hate driving."

Even though Sharon couldn't recall any of her former students dropping in after they'd graduated, she suspected that Ky was here to see her. She cleared her throat, tried to think of something to say.

"Oh, these are for you," Ky said, hoisting the box toward Sharon. "Mum wanted to thank you for coming to Denny's funeral."

Sharon took the box with both hands. Her mouth tingled and salivated at the smell of the ripened fruit.

"This really isn't necessary," she said. "But thank you. I'll . . . I guess I'll share these with the staff room."

She gave Ky a weak smile, hoping the girl would turn and leave.

"I know you're about to go home," Ky said, still standing next to Sharon's car, "but can I talk to you for a sec?"

No, no, no, Sharon thought. She'd already been sweating from the heat, but she now felt her body ramp it up. Sharon considered whether she'd manage to hold on to the lie she'd told, or whether a conversation with Ky Tran would force her to spill the beans. Her lie had been a careless, panicked decision, anyway. If she'd been in the right frame of mind, if she hadn't just seen her favorite student's body bloodied and pulpy, she probably wouldn't have told it. But what was done was done, she'd kept reminding herself. Changing her story wouldn't bring Denny back to life. She had to keep lying.

"Well, I was just about to—" Sharon said, reaching a hand to open the door of her car.

"Please?" Ky said.

Sharon wanted to say no, but she couldn't do something so cruel. She was a teacher; she'd lied only to protect a student; she wasn't in the business of hurting people, certainly not if she could help it.

"Yeah," she said, hearing her heart in her ears. "The staff room might still be busy." She looked up at the clear sky, where the unforgiving sun was already making the skin on her cheeks tingle with a pink sunburn. "But my classroom is free."

"That works," Ky said.

They walked in silence back into the school, toward the very classroom where Sharon had taught Denny, Ky, and Minnie. She felt foolish carrying a box of nectarines with her.

The classroom was sparse, the desks disorderly, the chairs untucked. Sharon had in the past week stopped reminding her students to push in their chairs when they left the classroom, and because she had stopped caring, her year eight and year nine classes had stopped caring, too. She instinctively dropped the box of fruit onto her desk, switched on the classroom fan, and took a seat at the front of the room. Ky stood frozen at the entrance. Sharon grabbed a chair, gestured for her to sit.

"Weird," Ky said.

"What is?"

"Being back."

"Mm."

"I used to sit there," Ky said, pointing to a desk by the window.

"Denny sat over here," Sharon said, pointing to the other side of the room.

"Do you remember all your students?"

"Oh," Sharon said, taken aback by the question. "Um . . ."

"I'm just curious," Ky said. "I'm not, like, judging you or anything."

"Right," Sharon said. "Yes. I remember some students better than others, but I don't think I've ever forgotten a student."

"That's cool."

Sharon stared at Ky, who was avoiding eye contact. Both women were fidgeting—Ky with her nails and the palms of her hands; Sharon with her fingers, tapping her thumb against her pinkie over and over again. Sharon was struck by how much Ky and Denny looked alike. They had the same expressive forehead that gave every feeling away, the same ink-black brows. When Sharon had been in the Tran family home days earlier for Denny's wake, she'd studied the photos in the ancestral altar, noticed that Ky and Denny's grandparents also had broad foreheads. She imagined a family that spoke using only the movements of their foreheads—how much they could say through fine lines and folds.

"I want to ask you what happened that night," Ky finally said, sitting without looking up.

Sharon took a deep breath. She was glad that a student who she once worried about being too meek, too easily pushed around, and too susceptible to following others had found a way out. The Ky she had taught six years earlier would never have raised a hand in class to ask a question, let alone pose such a skin-crawling conversation starter. But she also wished that Ky would apply her newfound gutsiness to something else, to someone else.

"And I also want to know why you didn't mention it at the funeral," Ky said.

Sharon could feel the sweat trickling down her back. The ceiling fans were useless against a Sydney summer.

"You didn't ask," Sharon said, telling the truth. She didn't know if she would have told the Tran family everything, but had they asked, a part of her would have given in.

"So you thought it was okay to just not tell us?"

"Hold on," Sharon said, taken aback. "Your parents should have known I was there."

"How?"

"Because the police interviewed me that night. And I'm pretty sure they would have told your parents. Right?"

Sharon noticed Ky clench her jaw.

"They didn't say," Ky said, releasing her jaw just enough for the words to escape.

"Oh."

"What happened that night?"

"Honestly, Ky, I don't know," Sharon said, which was not untrue. The evening of Denny's murder, she'd been having a celebratory dinner with her former students—Eddie Ho, Kevin Truong, and yes, Denny. She'd gone to the bathroom. When she returned, Denny was dead. She couldn't explain what had happened to the boy. She didn't know who had done it. She couldn't begin to fathom why someone would do what they did to him.

"But you were there," Ky said, her jaw still stiff, as though she was doing everything she could to stop herself from losing her composure. "Why were you even there?"

"They invited me," Sharon said. It had been the night of the graduating class's formal. The boys were in suits that they'd clearly borrowed from their fathers—ill-fitting jackets and too-long pants—and the girls were in the same style of strapless satin gowns that reappeared every year around graduation time. When the formal wrapped at eight-thirty, the students dispersed to after-parties. Denny, Eddie, and Kevin had decided to stay in Cabramatta and get a second dinner instead. "Every high school formal since, well, basically the dawn of time has served overcooked chicken schnitty and chips," Sharon said. "So your brother and his friends had planned to go to Lucky 8 afterward."

"But why would they invite you?" Ky asked.

Sharon tried to not be offended, but she couldn't help but

remember the grudge she still held against Ky and Minnie for not embracing her like her other students had. "Believe it or not, Ky, some of my students actually like me."

"That's not what I—" Ky began, but Sharon could tell by the chastised look on her face that it was exactly what she'd meant. Sharon immediately felt bad. She was a teacher talking to a grieving sister—she had to be better than this.

"But who knows," Sharon said, backtracking, hoping to soften the tone of the conversation, "maybe they felt bad for me because I'd never eaten a whole fish before. They seemed really bothered that I'd never tried fish eyes."

When Ky just stared at her own hands, Sharon kept talking, hoping she could fill enough air to satisfy the young woman so she would leave and not ask any more questions. "Plus, not a lot of year twelve students here take geography, so it was a tighter-knit class," she said. "They were all good kids. They'd just graduated. I didn't see the harm in joining them."

"Were you really in the bathroom?"

"Yes."

"Was everyone else?"

No, Sharon thought. She'd gone to the unisex bathroom at the same time as a former student, Kevin, each in their own stall. Her stall had run out of toilet paper, so she'd had to unwrap a new roll sitting on top of the cistern. She'd taken her time, sitting and smiling and peeing and feeling like this was a turning point in her career, like she finally knew what it meant to succeed as a teacher, like this was her reward—these were the students who were going to remember her, who were going to come back to visit her long after they'd graduated and gotten jobs and started families. And when she came out of the bathroom, an entire table of diners had disappeared, the restaurant was silent, and a body that she recognized only by its oversize suit was mangled on the floor. The room had spun, she'd heard a shriek that somehow came from her own mouth, and the next few minutes were a black hole during which she had no recollection of calling Triple Zero, getting blood all over herself attempting CPR, and throwing up everything she'd eaten that night on the carpet—the fried rice, the jumbo shrimp, the fish eyes, the overcooked chicken schnitty from the graduation formal. And when Eddie Ho begged her to tell the police that he had been in the bathroom with her and Kevin, even though he clearly hadn't, and she saw in his face a deep and paralyzing fear that she didn't understand, she'd said yes. And when he'd begged her to promise, to promise with her life, she'd promised. And it wasn't until later, much later, after she'd lied to the police, after she'd re-created the evening in her head and analyzed it from every conceivable angle, that she realized the mistake she had made.

"Kevin was in the bathroom. And so was Eddie," Sharon said.

"Ms. Faulkner," Ky said, "Lucky 8 only has two toilet stalls."

"We all went at the same time," Sharon said, repeating to Ky what she'd told the police. "I was in my own stall, so one of them must have waited."

"Who was waiting?"

"I don't know," Sharon said, barely able to hear herself think over the sound of blood rushing to her head. "I don't remember."

"You didn't hear anything from the bathroom?"

"No," Sharon said, feeling good that she at least didn't have to lie about it. The Lucky 8 toilet stalls shared a wall with the kitchen, which vibrated from the running of exhaust fans. "It sounded like a generator in there."

A look of defeat spread across Ky's face. As she exhaled, it seemed like her body deflated. "You're one of the last people who saw him alive," she said, pausing as though to process what this meant. "How was he?"

Sharon pictured the boys in their baggy suits, their ear-to-ear grins, the way they took on an air of authority when they instructed Sharon to use a chopstick to poke out a fish's eyeball and suck on the goo. She recalled how Denny couldn't stop laughing when she accidentally swallowed the whole eye because she couldn't gracefully get the shell-like bits out of her mouth.

"He was happy," Sharon said. "Excited, optimistic. Didn't stop smiling the whole night."

Sharon felt pressure behind her eyes. She had been so proud of her students that night—proud of what they'd overcome, proud of the meaningful breakthroughs she'd had with them, how she'd convinced Eddie to stop leaving assignments to the last minute, how she'd supported Kevin in his decision to apply to universities outside of the state, and how she'd helped Denny understand plagiarism so that he wouldn't do it again. They were good students who listened to her, who saw that she had something valuable to offer, and the thought of them made her feel warm inside. She'd told them that they could finally call her Sharon because they were no longer high schoolers, no longer her students, but they kept defaulting to calling her *miss*.

"It's too weird," Denny had said over their Lucky 8 dinner. "It's like whenever someone at the doctor's office calls me Mr. Tran. I just think they're talking to my dad."

"All I'm saying is you're all basically adults now," she'd said. "You can call me Sharon."

"What about Shazza?" Eddie said.

"I do, unfortunately, respond to that."

Ky lifted her head and Sharon saw that she was fighting back tears, too.

"And how was he before that?" Ky asked. "As a student."

"Well, you've seen the awards your parents framed," Sharon said.

"Yeah."

"He was basically the dream student—did his work on time, scored full marks, never complained, and really took on feedback. After I caught him plagiarizing at the start of the year—"

"Hold on, what?"

"It wasn't a big deal. I mean, plagiarizing *is* a big deal, but once I explained to him why it was a problem, he took it to heart and really made an effort to—"

"You're saying that Denny didn't *understand* plagiarism?" Ky said, her forehead bunched and lined.

"Even the smartest kids need help," Sharon said. "He probably just thought there wasn't anything wrong with borrowing from a sample paper. But really, what's remarkable was how well he took the feedback and how genuine he was—"

Sharon paused. Ky put her head in her hands, her fingers massaging her scalp.

"Is . . . is everything all right?" Sharon asked.

"How many times did he do it?"

"What do you mean?"

"How many times did he plagiarize?"

Sharon scratched the back of her ear in thought. "I would assume just the once. I only caught it because I happened to have read the old HSC student sample papers a few weeks earlier and thought his work looked familiar. But really, Ky, I wouldn't overthink it. It was probably an honest mistake."

Ky kept her head in her hands. She looked pained.

"Did you see anything else?" she said, finally raising her head, strands of hair poking out of her ponytail. "Before you went to the bathroom, did you notice who else was there?"

Sharon hated that she was about to lie again. She hated even more that she wasn't even protecting a scared student with this lie—she was protecting herself. "No," she said. "I was just focused on our dinner. I didn't notice anyone else who was there."

Ky closed her eyes and remained still for so long that Sharon fought the urge to clear her throat, to remind Ky that what she was doing was excruciating for both of them.

"Is there really nothing else you can tell me?"

"No, I'm sorry," Sharon said, wishing Ky could know how much she meant it.

"Yeah," Ky said, her eyes returning to her hands. "I guess that's it, then. Thanks for talking to me."

"Of course," Sharon said. "That's it. I'm sorry."

But of course that wasn't it. And as Sharon drove home, hands gripping the steering wheel so hard her fingers felt numb, she thought of everything she hadn't told anyone, like how even though she didn't get a good look at all the diners who sat several tables away from her and Denny—the diners who disappeared after she came out of the bathroom—she did get a good look at one of them. She almost didn't recognize the woman, whose eyeliner was so thick and smudged that it looked like a shadow had been cast over her eyes, whose skin was sallow and elbows were bony, and who was chain-smoking cigarettes in defiance of the NO SMOKING sign at her table.

Minnie.

Sharon hadn't seen the girl in years. Minnie had never officially dropped out of school, but her absences during the year ten exams meant she'd failed by default. The girl never reenrolled, never petitioned for a place in year eleven, and as far as Sharon was aware, never stepped foot in Cabramatta High again.

Sharon couldn't say with any certainty that Minnie had anything to do with Denny's death. She herself hadn't seen anything. Eddie had started repeating to no one in particular that he hadn't seen anything, either, that he'd been in the bathroom. Sharon's own memory of the night was filled with splotchy gaps; she was unable to recall what was real and what she had imagined. She couldn't bring herself to believe that Minnie—so thin and clearly unwell—had anything to do with it. Because if she did, then Sharon also had something to do with it. Sharon had set the wheels in motion.

As she pulled into her driveway, a memory she'd long ago buried began bubbling to the surface, popping and sputtering against her attempts to suppress it. It was the final parent-teacher night of the year. She'd been looking forward to it, hoping to meet Minnie's parents, to get to the bottom of what was going on in the girl's life, to make sure she showed up to the upcoming year ten exams so she wouldn't be forced to repeat the grade.

Ky's entire family came that night. Her father wore a suit so large it looked like he had shrunk in the wash. Her mother had put on a full face of makeup, including blue eye shadow. An eleven-year-old Denny was there, still in his Cabramatta Public School uniform. She remembered speaking with the Tran family, telling Ky's parents that she was a fantastic student, and if there was one thing she should do more of, it was relax, have fun, and find a balance between study and play. When the Tran family looked at her with blank expressions, Sharon looked to Ky to translate. Ky hesitated. She spoke to her parents in Vietnamese, and their faces read confusion. Mrs. Tran then said something to her daughter that sounded like a reprimand, to which Ky said in English, "I'm not lying!" Sharon then tapped Mrs. Tran on the forearm to get her attention, pointed at Ky, and gave her a thumbs-up. The Tran family looked at Sharon like she was a sad clown, then moved on to meet with Ky's other teachers.

Sharon remembered waiting for Minnie's family. She remembered feeling hopeful that they would show up. She remembered Greg and Barbara telling her that Minnie's parents—along with half the parents of all Cabramatta High students—had never once attended any kind of school meeting.

"We've sent letters," Barbara said at the end of the night. "At least half a dozen."

"In English?"

"What else?"

"You know that English is not the first language for most of our students' parents, right?" Sharon had said, feeling like she was at the end of her rope with her colleagues, her students, the entire goddamn school.

"Well, English *is* the first language of this *country*," Barbara said before turning away in a huff.

Sharon remembered that the next day, she went to the front office with a letter for the Le family. She asked the school's interpreter to translate the letter into Vietnamese. She then told the receptionist to mail it in a plain envelope—she'd heard of students intercepting mail that displayed the school's insignia so that their parents would never get to it. When the front office assured Sharon that the letter, in Vietnamese, had been sent, following her instructions, Sharon checked in every day to see if the family had responded. She never heard back from them. She never saw Minnie again.

At home she tried to call her mother. When no one picked up, Sharon called Lena Lao. "I'm sorry to bother you so late."

"I'm usually here 'til five anyway," Lena said, her voice distant and tinny in Sharon's ear. "What's up?"

"I have a question," Sharon said. She knew she was skirting dangerously close to saying too much, but after seeing Ky that afternoon, she could think of nothing else, and she needed an answer. "It's just something unrelated to anything, something that's been bugging me."

"Shoot."

"When I first got here, to Cabramatta, I had a student who was brilliant. Intimidating. Street-smart and book-smart with an attitude you wouldn't believe. But she stopped coming to class, so I sent home letters. First in English, then in Vietnamese—"

"Was this Ky's friend?"

"No," Sharon lied, even though she saw a crystal-clear image of Minnie and Ky in her mind. "Totally different student."

"Okay."

"Anyway, when I sent the letter, I made sure it was sent in a plain envelope, so the student wouldn't toss it out, so the parents would get it."

Lena was quiet on the other end of the line.

Sharon went on. "Before that, she still sporadically came to class. After I sent that letter, I never saw her again. She never officially dropped out, but she didn't turn up to any classes after that, either. I've . . ."—Sharon now pinched the fleshy part of her palm, rubbing it between her fingers as she continued to sweat—"I've thought a lot about whether I did the right thing. I've continued to send letters home when students have chronic absenteeism, and I've followed the school policies, and I haven't done it in plain envelopes since. But I just wonder, sometimes . . ."

Sharon let out a long sigh, not wanting to say any more until she heard some verbal confirmation from Lena that she was still there.

"It's good that you cared enough to try something different," Lena finally said. "But it's also good that you're now following proper procedure."

Sharon nodded, even though she knew Lena couldn't see her. "I just wonder if that letter . . . if it did more harm than good."

"Hmm," Lena said, taking her time to respond. "It's possible that you didn't see this student again because she transferred to another school. It's not uncommon. A lot of parents who have gotten desperate will borrow money to send their kids to a private school. I knew a girl whose parents shipped her off to live with an uncle in Bathurst so she could get a strict Catholic education. It didn't work. She was back in Cabramatta a year later, playing in the streets."

"Playing?"

"It's what they call it here. Street life. When you hit the streets, you're 'coming out to play.' We have kids at this school who came out to play when they were ten."

Sharon had heard of kids being described as "naughty"—the Cabramatta euphemism for wagging school, causing trouble, or even just smoking cigarettes. But coming out to play was a new one for her.

"Are they all on drugs?" she asked.

"Nah," Lena said. "They're all at risk of it, no doubt. But it doesn't start with drugs. It never does."

"Oh, okay. That's good."

"It's also possible that your student's parents beat the shit out of her after they got your letter."

At that, Sharon flinched.

"I know that's crude, but when you mix poverty and PTSD with zero community support, it can happen," Lena said, her tone matter-of-fact. "Or her disappearance from the school system could be completely unrelated to your letter. If her attendance was already bad, she may have already gotten deep into something else. Or she may have felt ashamed, like it was too late for her to come back. Or . . . who knows. It could be any number of things."

"But," Sharon said, "if she was really bright, she could feasibly have enrolled somewhere else and just not told anyone, right?"

There was another long pause, during which Sharon tried to picture how Lena would look at her if they were in the same room. Whatever warmth the counselor usually exuded did not come across the phone line.

Sharon continued: "I just feel like . . . I think what has been bugging me is when a student drops out, I feel like I've let them down, somehow."

"It's good to hear that you care," Lena said. "But you shouldn't blame yourself for—"

"But I can't help it. I do—"

"No, let me finish. It's *never* just one person," Lena said, her voice coming out of Sharon's receiver crisp and cold. "By the time one of our students is ready to drop out, the whole world has let them down."

Sharon felt the wind knocked out of her.

"We can only do the best that we can," Lena said, "but the problem is bigger than us."

"Okay," Sharon managed to sputter. She felt like if she stayed on the line with Lena any longer, she would finally say too much, and she wouldn't be able to take it back. "Thank you. And sorry again, for bothering you."

"No bother at all," Lena said, her voice softening over the line. "Good luck."

Sharon sat on her sofa hugging her knees for the rest of the afternoon. Her mind cycled through memories, thrusting her back into classrooms of years earlier, to the first time she taught Denny in year seven, to the bright green pandan cake he and Eddie had brought to class in year eleven to celebrate her birthday, to the day that a class full of year nine students wouldn't let her move on with her lesson until she could pronounce phở correctly.

As the sun began to set, she found herself remembering the year she taught Ky and Minnie. It was the first week of school and Sharon hadn't yet learned their names. Standing in the playground on lunch supervision duty, she spotted both girls sitting together, away from everyone else. Minnie sucked on a juice box while Ky tore a sandwich in two, giving her friend half. Sharon noticed that they were sharing an apple and a Le Snak out of Ky's lunch box, too. She scanned the rest of the playground, making sure nothing was amiss, and whenever she returned to the two girls, she couldn't help but smile. The wind blew. She sneezed. When she looked back up, she caught Ky's attention, who, after holding eye contact for a beat, appeared embarrassed, self-conscious, her eyes shooting from Sharon to the ground. When she turned to Minnie, the skinny girl's face was expressionless, a challenge to Sharon. Sharon had tried to smile, but she felt chilled to her spine. Minnie kept staring, her sunken eyes dark and focused like she was seeing through to Sharon's soul. Sharon looked away first. She felt vulnerable and exposed. With her body turned, she suspected that Minnie was still staring, but she couldn't bring herself to look.

Chapter 6

Ky crawled back into bed after her encounter with Sharon Faulkner. The day had drained her. In the hours between going to the temple with her mother and seeing Sharon, she'd had a quick and uncomfortable confrontation with Lulu Woo's mother, Hong Woo, outside the dim sum shop where she worked. Hong had demanded to know how Ky had found her, and when Ky refused to say, Hong accused her of harassment, ordered her to leave the Woo family alone, threateningly shook a pair of extra-long chopsticks at Ky. Then there was Hong's husband, Guang Woo, who had initially been more subdued. When Ky found him in the break room of the Comalco aluminum factory, he wasn't happy to see her, either. But instead of confronting Ky, he had simply repeated that he hadn't seen anything, that his family had faced a wall when it happened, that their ears had been covered and their eyes closed—just as he had told the police. After Ky followed Guang from the break room to the edge of the factory floor, pleading with him to tell her the truth, he pleaded back, asking her to believe him, because he *was* telling the truth, and when she wouldn't, he literally ran from her, hands covering his ears. Meanwhile, Denny's classmate Kevin Truong, who was supposedly in the restaurant bathroom at the time of Denny's murder, was conveniently in Perth, having accepted an early offer from the University of Western Australia. And the day wasn't even over yet—the constable wanted to interview her at the police station at five.

Lying in bed, Ky clutched her stomach, feeling queasy about what she'd learned about her brother. She couldn't believe that Denny had plagiarized his schoolwork. He'd always been so academically gifted, so hardworking, everything that everyone wanted him to be. It wasn't in his nature to cheat. At the same time, Ky didn't buy for a second Sharon Faulkner's rationale that he simply didn't know what plagiarism was, didn't know that he was doing something wrong. Of course he knew—as hard-core rule followers, both Ky and Denny had to know what it meant to be bad in order to make sure that they were good. They understood cheating, they understood stealing, they understood risk-taking, and most important, they understood that people like them couldn't afford to do any of it. So what the hell was Denny thinking?

Ky curled further into herself, sick with guilt. Had her brother changed while she'd been away? Did he change *because* she was away? And what if she was wrong? What if Sharon was right and Denny just had a momentary lapse in judgment, and it was unfair of her to suddenly question his character? She gave herself emotional whiplash as she swung between extremes, with both ends suggesting the same thing: either she didn't know her brother or she didn't know her brother. She hated feeling out of control, like she didn't understand people, like she couldn't predict what they would do, like they were drifting away from her. The last person who had made her feel that way was Minnie. Ky remembered how angry she used to get at Minnie for sabotaging their chances at being likable, at being teachers' pets, at being invited to call their teachers by their first names. There was no reason for her *not* to be well liked—she was a straight-A student, she never caused trouble, she was *good*. If only Minnie would mellow out and get on the same page and stop challenging every teacher that crossed her path.

"Why are you always antagonizing them?" Ky had asked when they were fourteen. It was the first time that Ky felt Minnie's attitude could become a liability; the first time that the friend who had for so long been her savior threatened to derail her from the path they both needed to be on.

"I do nothing of the sort," Minnie had said, feigning a posh British accent as she colored in countries on a map using expired nail polish.

"Yes, you do. It's like you're always looking for a fight."

"They have it coming. You ever notice that New Caledonia looks like a perfect turd?"

"What? Ew."

"Look at it." Minnie raised the map, which they'd gotten for free from the newspaper's education supplement. "It's like a poo you do after you have Weet-Bix."

"As if you know what my poos look like."

"It's a compliment—a Weet-Bix poo is a great poo."

"You're gross."

"How smart do you reckon you have to be to become a PE teacher?" Minnie said, returning to the map.

"I dunno," said Ky. "Not very?"

"Mm, yeah. I didn't think so."

"Why?"

"If we met all our teachers when they were fourteen . . ."

Minnie kept coloring the map, piping up every now and again with a comment about how, geographically, Australia made more sense as an Asian country than as a European country, and how Hawaii had no business being part of the United States. Minnie was a mystery to Ky. She hadn't minded so much when they were children. They were different from each other, with Minnie never having a packed lunch for school, always having unbrushed and unbraided hair. Unlike Ky, who got welts from mosquito bites, Minnie's welts were dark and scabby and man-made. But they liked each other, and every difference could be bridged. Ky shared her lunch, helped put Minnie's hair in lopsided pigtails, convinced her to wear her hair down whenever the bruises on her neck were too obvious. They were able to sit in silence with each other without feeling awkward. They could laugh at each other's farts. When they became teenagers, though, this no longer seemed to be enough. Ky needed affirmation that they were on the same team; she needed Minnie to wholeheartedly endorse the decisions she was making by making the exact same decisions. She needed Minnie to join her, arm in arm, so that together they could be successful and well liked, and whenever a teacher or a police officer or a lady at the shops or a woman with a name tag or a man in a business suit looked at them, it would be the kind of look that came with a smile, the kind of look that said, *Look at you!*, the kind of look that made Ky feel proud of herself, because these strangers were proud of her, because she was good, she was so good, she was good good

good even when it was hard. But Minnie kept refusing to do it. And her refusal felt like rejection, like judgment, like an attempt at destabilizing everything Ky had worked for.

"Where do you think the people who skip class go when they're skipping class?" Minnie asked Ky one day in year eight as they were packing their bags after the final school bell.

"I dunno."

"What could they be doing that's so interesting?"

"Who cares?" Ky had snapped. In addition to feeling like Minnie was rejecting success, at fourteen Ky started to feel insecure about the fact that she and Minnie weren't curious about the same things anymore. Minnie grew increasingly preoccupied with what other people were doing, what motivated them, what rules they followed, and how those could be broken. She'd started showing interest in boys, and not just any boys—she wouldn't stop talking about the boys who hung out near the school gates, the ones who wore all black, the ones who had clearly dropped out or failed. She told Ky about a boy named Thien, who was older than them, who drove a white car, who kept cigarettes behind his ears, whom she'd never actually had a conversation with but couldn't stop thinking about. Whenever Minnie brought him up, Ky would be baffled by why someone as smart as Minnie was wasting her energy on some naughty guy who probably didn't even get into university. Compared to Minnie, Ky had no interest in boys, and certainly not the ones who hung out by the school gates. She didn't care how tall or good-looking they were—to her, they were a blur of irrelevance. Ky was more interested in herself and how she could outperform her peers, how she could leave Cabramatta, how she could be special. The fact that Minnie didn't seem to want the same things made Ky feel agitated and alone.

Minnie slung her bag over her shoulders and began the slow march toward the school gates. "But haven't you ever thought about how they spend their time while we're here learning baby shit?" she said.

"Math and English are kind of hard."

"That's beside the *point*," Minnie said, exaggeratedly throwing her head back like the conversation was the biggest slog in the world. "What are they *doing* that's so much better than what we're doing? And why do they get to hang out with Thien?"

"What do you mean, why do they *get* to? It's not like he's the queen or whatever."

"You know what I mean."

"No, I don't. I don't get why you care so much about him. He doesn't even know your name."

A wounded look flashed across Minnie's face.

"Besides," Ky added, enjoying the effect her words were having on her friend, "I wouldn't hang out with him even if you paid me."

"Whatever."

"I'm serious," Ky said. "They're naughty kids. They're wasting their lives."

"How do you know that?"

"Because that's just the facts. If someone doesn't go to school, it's because they've turned naughty. And if they've turned naughty, it means they're going to do drugs and join a gang and never get a real job, and one day we'll be rich and powerful and they'll still be naughty."

"You seem to know a lot for someone who knows so little."

Ky came to a halt and gawked at her friend. "What's *that* supposed to mean?"

Minnie stopped a few steps ahead of Ky and cocked her head as though the answer was obvious. When Ky remained still, her eyes saying, *Well?* Minnie raised and dropped both hands.

"I'm just saying, aren't you curious at all about what other people are doing?"

"Sure I am," Ky lied out of defensiveness.

"Like who?"

"I dunno! You're putting me on the spot!"

Minnie sighed.

"I sure don't care about what *Thien* is doing," Ky said, crossing her arms over her body. "I'm sick of hearing about him, anyway. Can we talk about something else?"

Back in her bedroom, adult Ky made a mental list of all the things that interested her, all the ways she was curious. She was a journalist, after all, a professional curious person—able and willing to be curious about anything she was assigned. Outside of her job, she was also curious about: the love triangle between Prince Charles, Princess Diana, and Camilla Parker Bowles; conjoined twins; Ouija boards; hair extensions; whether Tasmanian tigers could be cloned back into existence; Christmas; Dolly the sheep; car phones; how much musicians made on *Paris by Night;* Jupiter's moons; Freudian slips; and American serial killers, who always seemed to be the worst ones.

It was an exercise she often did to make herself feel better, to remind herself she was interesting and curious enough to be worthy of friendship, even though sometimes she struggled to convince even herself. Because the truth was, she'd never recovered from losing Minnie. When Minnie stopped attending classes, stopped coming over after school, rejected Ky's path wholesale, plunged cruel words into Ky like a knife and twisted it, Ky had felt broken. She'd fantasized about fist-fighting Minnie, about using violence to fill the void. In her final two years of high school, which she finished without her friend, she felt a hollowness expand in her chest as she walked home each day. She got used to the heavy mask she wore as she made new friends, withheld her true feelings, her deepest, pettiest thoughts, through fear that they'd reject her, walk away like Minnie did. Not interesting enough. Not curious enough. Not smart enough. Not good enough. It all started with Minnie.

Ky went through Constable Edwards's photocopied notes one more time, marking off Sharon, Kevin Truong, and the Woo family. She checked her bedroom clock—it was a quarter to five. Tired of the suffocating sensation that swallowed her whenever she sat around feeling sorry for herself, she stuffed the constable's notes back in her bag, slung it over her shoulder, and made her way to the police station for her interview.

Cabramatta Police Station was once again in chaos. A different group of high schoolers in uniform sat in the waiting area; officers escorted a belligerent white man whose jeans were down to his knees to a holding cell; and mothers with crying infants on their hips tried to navigate the language barrier between them and the frustrated on-duty police. Ky waited half an hour before being shuffled to a sterile room to then await Constable Edwards, who himself kept ducking in and out, distracted by incoming phone calls, at one point handing Ky a blank sheet of paper and asking her to write down her witness statement before remembering that she wasn't a witness and telling her to just hold on to it "for later."

When she was sure that the constable had forgotten about her, Ky couldn't help but think of the care she'd put into talking to grieving relatives whenever she was sent on death knocks.

"You need to make the families feel like they're the most important people to you," Ian had said when Ky was still an intern. "Because they are. I don't care what's going on in your own life or if you have a kid at home—in that moment, when you are sitting across from those families, *they* are the most important people to you."

Ky had taken the lesson to heart. She'd never been the most socially graceful person, but on a death knock, she pulled out everything she had ever learned about making others feel comfortable—the eye contact, the body language, not talking over her interviewees, being okay with silence and waiting for others to fill it, the contortions in her forehead that she hoped communicated how deeply sorry she was.

"Couldn't pay me enough to do that," Penny Trautman had said to Ky on the last day of their internship, right after Ky had recounted a death knock in which she got to the parents of a woman killed in a car accident before the police did.

"I didn't know the police hadn't told them yet," Ky said, still pale from the experience. "I heard about the accident on the police scanner, so I just went straight to the parents."

"And you know what's crazy?" Penny said, leaning in as though sharing a dirty secret. "In Ian's eyes, you did the right thing by getting there first. That's fucked up."

Ky wanted to defend Ian and death knocks. But she was still too shaken by the experience—the way the woman's mother seemed to experience a fast-forwarded version of the stages of grief as the squad car pulled up to the curb.

"Corporate law's where it's at," Penny had said, nudging Ky.

Ky had nodded but knew there was no world in which she would leave journalism—not until she felt like she'd succeeded, not until she felt like she'd done what no one else could do. She told people that she couldn't help what she was drawn to, couldn't help that her calling was so unaligned with her personality. She had repeated it so many times she actually believed what she said was true—that it wasn't, like so many other things, a result of Minnie.

Many years earlier, when she and Minnie were in year nine, the school had organized a careers seminar, complete with a personality questionnaire that every student filled out ahead of time. The day of the seminar, a white woman who looked like she cohosted *Play School* stood before Ky's cohort in the gymnasium, asking students if they knew what they wanted to be when they grew up.

"Doctor!"

"Lawyer!"

"Doctor!"

"Doctor!"

"Butcher!"

"Ha-ha-ha!"

"Jesus," Minnie had said under her breath. "How many friggin' doctors does Cabra need?"

"I don't want to be a doctor," Ky whispered back.

"I know you don't."

"Do *you*?"

Minnie looked at Ky out the side of her eye. "Why would I wanna be around sick people all day?"

"True. What about lawyer? You're good at arguing."

The corners of Minnie's lips curled upward. "I don't wanna wear a stupid wig."

"What wig?"

"Haven't you seen on TV? The court lawyers wear those—"

"Alrighty!" said the *Play School* woman, her voice now amplified over the gymnasium's delayed speaker system. "It's wonderful that some of you already know what you want to do. I'm here today to talk to you about options. Maybe there's a job you'll be good at that you haven't even thought of! Maybe, instead of going to university, you might want to get a technical education. Australia needs all kinds of workers, from doctors and lawyers, to plumbers, electricians, construction workers, nurses—"

Their packets contained the results of the questionnaire, highlighting strengths and interests so basic—math, science, English, sports—that both Ky and Minnie squinted in disbelief.

"What is this dumb-ass—" Minnie began before the *Play School* lady's voice echoed across the gymnasium again.

"On the back, you'll see recommendations for careers that might suit your strengths and interests. Now we're going to get into groups, and—"

Ky looked at the list of careers that floated inside bubbles on the page. According to the sheet, she was best suited to be a K–12 teacher—subject specialty to be determined. In a smaller bubble were the words *quality control engineer.* And below that, in an even smaller bubble, *paralegal.* She felt indignant. These were not the glamorous careers commensurate with what she believed she was capable of. She knew she wasn't the smartest person in the world, but she'd always been a diligent worker, someone destined to be more impressive than a schoolteacher, because that's what she'd been taught—that if you grew up in Australia and had all the opportunities your parents didn't, you'd never have to settle, never feel like you could have done better, never feel like you were living anything but the best life a person could live. Besides, no one she knew had ever talked up teaching or paralegaling or quality control engineering like it was an exciting or brag-worthy job; no one ever said, "Wow!" or "That's *so* cool!" when they heard that someone was a schoolteacher; no one who was actually good at anything ever vocalized dreams of doing legal work without actually being a full-on lawyer; no one understood what a quality control engineer even did, and honestly, what was the point of doing something if you couldn't brag about it? The questionnaire results stung in a way she couldn't have anticipated.

"This is so friggin' random," she said, showing her results to Minnie.

Minnie was engrossed in her own packet. For the first time in months, she seemed to be taking something seriously, or at least giving it her undivided attention.

"What did you get?" Ky asked, looking over her friend's shoulder.

In the smallest bubble was *actuary.* In the larger bubble, *lawyer.* And in enormous font, hovering above the smaller two bubbles, was *JOURNALIST.*

"Huh," Minnie said.

Inside, Ky felt something akin to a fire igniting in her chest and swallowing her breath.

Later that afternoon when they were eating plates of bánh cuốn that Ky's mother had prepared, Ky couldn't stop picking at the mental scab that had formed over her scratched-up ego. "I don't even like kids!" Ky said.

"You like me," Denny said, looking at Minnie for affirmation that he'd said something funny. Minnie gave him a wink.

"But that's different." Ky shifted in her seat, feeling frustrated, like her clothes were suddenly too tight and no one understood what she was saying. "I *have* to like you. You're my brother."

"They're just recommendations," Minnie said through slurps. "It's not like it's a crystal ball or anything."

"Still, it's messed up. And . . ."—Ky felt her skin tingle at the thought of what she was about to say—"why would they make nonsense recommendations? Like, why would you be a journalist? Asians don't get to be on TV."

Ky noticed Minnie freeze. Her friend raised both her brows before returning to her plate of food.

"What about Lee Lin Chin?" Denny asked.

"Lee Lin Chin doesn't count," Ky said. "No one watches SBS, and when have you ever seen an Asian on the real channels?"

"Well," Minnie said, tapping her chopsticks against her plate, "in our small groups, the lady said journalists can work in print and radio, too. I could write for newspapers and magazines."

"But do you even want to?"

Minnie shrugged. "Why not? Seems pretty cool. The lady said journalists hold truth to power and expose corruption and unfairness. She also said journalists get to travel and see the world, and every time they publish an article their name gets to be on it, so I could write an article and millions of people might see it, and—"

"And what the frig is an actuary, anyway?" Ky said, cutting Minnie off. "It's like some FOB trying to say *actually*. Is that what it is? Is it a job for FOBs? Oh, *actuary,* this job is only for FOBs, so if you're not super fresh off the boat, we can't hire you, madam."

Ky felt herself overheating. She saw from the corner of her eye that Denny was looking back and forth between her and Minnie; he'd always been sensitive to people's moods and could tell when something was off, but he was too young to understand the root of the problem.

Minnie looked back at Denny to reassure him that whatever he'd sensed was right, that he wasn't crazy to think that his sister was being a jerk. Then she gave Ky a familiar pitying look. "Well, *actually,* the lady said an actuary is like a super accountant. They're good at identifying risks, or something."

"As if you're good at that!"

Minnie picked at bits of fried onion and scallions on her bánh cuốn. "Sure I am."

"No, you're not, you do risky things all the time."

"Exactly. I'm good at identifying risks. Doesn't mean I have to avoid them, right, Denny?"

A sheet of rice noodle hung from Denny's mouth. He gave Minnie a half shrug, like he wasn't sure of the correct answer.

"This is so dumb!" Ky said, dropping her own chopsticks on the plate, sending specks of fish sauce onto her school uniform.

"Then don't take it so seriously," Minnie said, reaching her own chopsticks toward Ky's plate to pick at the remaining scallions. "I wouldn't be caught dead being an actuary—sounds boring as heck. Their recs are probably wrong anyway."

"I'm *not* taking it too seriously."

"Yes, you are."

"No, I'm not!"

"Okay, you're not."

"Thank you," Ky said, raising her hands palms up, as though praising the lord.

"Except that you are," Minnie said, smiling with teeth, her eyes icy and flat.

How do you sum up a life? How do you capture who a person was, what they meant to you, and who they could have been? When Constable Edwards finally sat across from Ky with a notepad in hand, Ky didn't know where to start. She listed off Denny's schooling achievements—things she knew about his grades, his awards, the extracurricular activities he did during recess and lunch. She talked about his friends—how he was closest to Eddie Ho; how, for as long as she could remember, their primary recreational activity was playing board games and watching cartoons; how it didn't take a genius to see that they were both sweet and innocent and dorky. She spoke in generalities and clichés—good kid, good brother, wouldn't hurt a fly.

As she watched the constable sporadically scrawl onto his notepad, distracted by the noise outside the room, nodding without looking up at Ky, she wished he'd at least pretend to care, pretend that she was, if not the *most* important person in the world, at least someone who wasn't completely invisible to him. Because if he would only look at her, acknowledge that she was someone who was still hurting, she would have shared more, gotten specific. She would have told him how most people thought that Denny was a quiet person who didn't have a lot to say, but the truth was he had so many opinions—he just didn't share them with everyone. She would have told him that Denny was one of the most sensitive and perceptive people she knew—he could always tell when something was wrong even though he rarely knew the right thing to say or do. And she would have told him that despite Denny's awkwardness, despite his routinely letting the wrong words out of his mouth, at times he blew Ky away with how well he understood her.

"I guess I'm just worried I'll never change," Ky had told him on one of her last visits home, after another of her explosive mother-daughter tantrums. "When I'm away from Cabra, I feel like I've shed my old skin. But whenever I come back here . . ."—Ky gestured to their surroundings; they'd walked downtown to buy chicken chips from Red Lea—"it's like I didn't shed anything at all. It's like I've just flipped a switch, you know? And my old self was there all along."

"Dormant," Denny said, stroking his hairless chin.

"Yeah! It just . . . I dunno. It scares me that our old selves follow us everywhere, and they're lying dormant, and all it takes is a flip of a switch and we're pieces of shit again, you know?"

"If you can be self-reflective like that, then I think you've changed," Denny said.

"I guess."

"Everyone changes, whether they like it or not."

Ky had looked at Denny then, wondered whether behind his boyish face was a wrinkled old man.

"You've been pretty consistent," Ky said.

Denny stared at the ground as they walked.

"Do you think you've changed?" Ky asked after a beat.

Denny shrugged.

"Probably. Yeah," he finally said.

"How?"

"I dunno."

"Instead of becoming a doctor, you now want to become a lawyer?" Ky said with a smirk, nudging her brother in the ribs.

A pained expression crossed his face. At the time, Ky thought that perhaps he was agonizing over what university to choose, what degree to pursue. Unlike most of his peers, he'd be spoiled for choice.

"I get it," Ky had said in an attempt to make her brother feel better. "I got lucky—I knew exactly what I wanted to do and what I wanted to major in, but not everyone knows that right away."

"Yeah . . ." Denny said, looking everywhere but at his sister.

"You wanna talk things out?"

Denny seemed to perk up in response.

"I *think* UNSW has the best medical school, but if you're gonna do law, then I don't think it matters which of the big three schools you go to," Ky said. "I can ask around for you, if you'd like?"

He shrugged again, losing interest.

"Do you know if he was taking anything?" Constable Edwards said, dragging Ky back to the present. "To help with the pressure or the stress?"

"What do you mean?"

"Kids these days take all kinds of things, and you never know what ends up being the gateway drug. Was he using stimulants to help him finish assignments? Stuff to help him pull all-nighters? Or marijuana to help him unwind from all the pressure—"

"*What* pressure? What are you talking about?"

Constable Edwards finally looked up from his notepad at Ky, both brows raised. "Well, based on what you've described, it sounds like Denny was under a lot of pressure. Coming first in almost every subject four years in a row? Quiet, hardworking, future doctor? Seems too good to be true."

"It *is* true."

"Look, Miss Tran," the constable said, resting both hands on the table between them, "I'm not trying to give your brother a bad name, it just . . ."—he gave a one-shoulder shrug—"it adds up."

"He wasn't a junkie," Ky said, although the more time she spent in the constable's presence, the less confident she felt about Denny. "He wouldn't even know *where* to buy drugs, let alone—"

"Miss Tran, your brother lived in Cabramatta."

"And so *what?*" Ky said, feeling defensive. She knew the constable was right to a point—there was a reason Cabramatta was known as the heroin capital of Australia. But she resented that an outsider—a freckle-faced blondie with a thick drawl that suggested he wasn't from southwest Sydney—was painting her home in the same unflattering wash that made everyone who lived there two-dimensional, hopeless, the same. Because it wasn't like drug dealers were going door to door like the Avon lady. It wasn't like Ky was tripping over mounds of heroin on her walk to Woolies or Red Lea. And it wasn't like everyone's lives revolved around drugs and gangs and crime. There was more to Cabramatta than that. Every time the constable opened his mouth, Ky saw how her brother, her family, everyone around her was squished flatter and flatter.

"Okay then," Constable Edwards said, snapping shut his notebook, "I think we've got what we need."

"That's it?" Ky said. She looked at her watch—they'd been talking for no more than fifteen minutes.

The constable was already on his feet. "Unless you've got anything else to share."

He stood at the door and gave Ky a moment to respond. When she said nothing, her hands wringing in her lap, he left the room, leaving her alone to dig her fingernails deeper into her palms.

Ky couldn't shake the guilt. She kept replaying in her head conversations with Denny, reexamining them from new angles. Had he been so down the last time she was home because he had changed for the worse? Had Ky been too oblivious to notice, too stubborn to listen? Had she done to Denny the very thing that she hated when other people did to her—flattened him, chosen to see only what she wanted to see? As much as she couldn't stand how the constable had written Denny off, she couldn't stop wondering whether there was truth to it. Ky *had* put Denny under a lot of pressure. What she expected of him *was* unrealistic and unfair. She pictured her brother walking by Cabramatta's train station and asking a teenage dealer—maybe someone from his own school, in his own grade—if they could sell him something to help him take the edge off. She saw him getting in too deep, perhaps stealing money from his parents, promising dealers that he would pay them back, that next time he would come back with double. She saw her own absence from his life, the cascading effect it could have had.

Back at the townhouse, she could tell her parents were home by the sound of her mother in the kitchen and the dreary music coming from her parents' bedroom. The previous few nights her father had given the *Paris by Night* tapes a rest. But the melancholy music was now back, somehow sounding sadder than before.

"If I get the depression and kill you, it will be because of this music!" Ky's mother used to threaten whenever her father replayed songs about the devastation of war and the fall of Saigon. "You're making everyone sad with your miserable music! Cut it out!"

"But didn't you listen to *Paris by Night* when you lived in Vietnam?" Denny once asked after their mother had taken to smacking the top of the television with her feather duster to make her point.

"Giời ơi, my son is so stupid!" Ky's mother had said, taking the handle of the duster to her own head. "*Paris by Night* is made by people who *left* Vietnam. *After* the war. Look . . ."—she waved the duster at the television screen, obstructing everyone's view—"you think they're filming in Vietnam? That's Orange County! That's America! They make this depressing junk for people who miss Vietnam."

"Don't you miss Vietnam?" Ky asked in English. "It's all you ever talk about. Back in Vietnam this, back in Vietnam that, back in—"

"The past is the past!" her mother responded in English. "I go forward. Your dad go backward. This sad music make me crazy. I kill him!"

At this, Ky's father turned up the volume.

Hearing the ghostly shuffling of feet in the townhouse, enveloped by the smell of freshly burnt joss sticks, and unable to confront her parents, Ky backed out of their home and stood in the driveway, losing track of time. She had never felt so tired. Even on her busiest days as a reporter, she rarely talked to as many people as she had that day. But despite the exhaustion, she also felt wired. She pulled the constable's original notes from her bag and studied the names again—most of them were Lucky 8 employees. Ky didn't want to talk to any more people. But she thought of how they might hold answers—how they might tell her whether Denny was in fact killed because of a drug deal gone wrong, whether he *looked* like he was on something that night, whether it really was all Ky's fault.

She took a deep breath, turned around, and got back into the little white car.

Chapter 7

Onstage, dressed in a glittery green áo dài, hair in a beehive, face painted with rosy blush and a winged cat eye, a Valium dissolved in her stomach, Flora Huynh crooned for a bride and groom—the first wedding held at Lucky 8 since the incident nearly two weeks ago. The bride looked like a cupcake. The groom wore a rented tuxedo. He struggled to hold his new wife against his body, the skirt of her dress so puffy and full that when he finally managed to pull her in by the waist, her feet left the ground. Flora sang Elvis Presley's "Love Me Tender," and her audience of drunken wedding goers cheered and applauded when, midway through, she switched to a Vietnamese rendition of the song. As friends and family joined the couple on the dance floor, faces flushed and bodies swaying, Flora's mind traveled. She'd always preferred to be anywhere but the present, and when she sang, her voice went into autopilot while her consciousness traveled back in time, deep into the past, to when she was a child, the earliest Lunar New Year she remembered, the new clothes to which she awoke, the clacky new shoes. Her mother, a pretty woman who always wore lipstick and rouge, took Flora to a relative's salon, where her silky locks were spun into a beehive. Mother and daughter, both in matching new áo dài and hair-spray-hard updos, walked through the festive streets of Saigon, hips swinging from side to side.

Her mind momentarily returned to the present when a song came to an end, and making eye contact with the sleepy live band behind her, she launched into another song, the Righteous Brothers' version of "Unchained Melody," the first few lines in English before switching to Vietnamese. She looked at the dance floor, which had been scrubbed clean by Lucky 8's dishwasher, Jimmy Carter, and she found her hand over her stomach, pinching and grabbing and pressing against the body-hugging áo dài.

She closed her eyes and traveled again, saw the skin of her brother Bao's once-youthful face—the emergence of pink rashes, grease slicks, dry patches when he turned thirteen. When they were children in Vietnam, Flora and Bao's mother routinely smacked Bao's hand from his face when he picked at his acne, warning him that he would leave scars—deep craters that would make his cheeks look like the surface of a dirty rice bowl. She offered to treat his bad skin with a sewing needle and a candle. She had shown Flora how to do it—the passing of the needle through a candle flame to sterilize it, then the piercing of the skin through the pimple's core.

"You need to release the poison from your body," Flora's mother used to say when her own needle-punctured wound glistened with yellow pus and blood.

Bao never allowed their mother near him with a needle, preferring instead to grow out his bangs to cover his spotty forehead, concealing his chin with his hands. But the more he touched his face, the more inflamed it became, until one day

Flora couldn't remember what her brother had looked like before his skin declared war on him.

Flora remembered how the eruption of every bulbous pimple on his face meant the loss of a kindness he'd once reserved for her. As his face grew spottier and his moods sourer, he stopped letting Flora, who was six years younger than him, sit on the handlebars when he rode his bicycle; stopped doing the voices and sound effects when Flora played with her dolls; stopped singing along whenever the Beatles came on the radio. When he turned fourteen, he lost all interest in amusing Flora. Instead of doing voices for her dolls, he asked her how she could still play when there was a war going on, when the communists were so close, when the entire family's gruesome death was imminent. When he was fifteen, he'd become a stranger in their house—a person who spent more hours asleep than awake, who obsessively listened to the radio for the daily death count, even when those deaths were happening in faraway places. This was well before anyone in her family had heard of ideas like mood disorders and chemical imbalances, well before anyone understood the insidious trauma inflicted by war. This was when people still thought that a person's problems could be blessed away by the Buddha.

Then when Bao was sixteen, a peasant woman as old as their mother arrived on their doorstep with a swaddled new baby, still sticky with afterbirth. Even though the woman's clothing was worn through and her hands looked calloused and her skin impossibly dry, she was unintimidated by Flora's family—not by her father's brand-new business shirt, nor by her mother's perfectly painted lips, nor by the new dolls Flora clutched in her hands. The woman's back was straight like a stick and her chin looked like it was being pulled into the air by string. She shoved the fresh baby in Flora's mother's arms, told the Huynhs that the baby was Bao's, that it was their problem now. Flora's father had refused to accept the child, had yelled at the woman, and had told her that though Bao was a useless son, he was not in the business of fathering illegitimate children. When Bao remained silent, all but confirming that that was exactly what he had done, her mother sat down, baby in arm, eyes unfocused.

The woman said she didn't care whether the Huynhs wanted the child—it was theirs now. Her face creased and her teeth black, she wanted the Huynhs to know that they had ruined her family's name, that Bao had seduced her innocent teenage daughter, that the humiliation of the unwanted pregnancy meant that they now had to move farther south to rural Vietnam where they could get a fresh start.

"Don't blame us for your daughter being a slut!" Flora's father yelled after the woman had said her piece.

"Your son is a scoundrel!" the woman yelled back.

"We don't want this stupid baby! If you're already going to leave town, take it with you! We don't want it!"

"Your son destroyed my daughter's life!"

"Your daughter is lucky to have been fucked by a Huynh!"

"Go to hell!"

"No, *you* go to hell, you hag!"

"A curse on all of you! Bad luck for a million years! Fuck you and fuck your mothers!"

Which marked the arrival of Thien. The baby cried constantly, and on the rare occasions when he stopped, his face was twisted in discomfort, his soiled cloth diaper reeking unlike anything Flora had ever smelled. Unwilling to hire a wet nurse because Flora's father was too embarrassed for anyone to find out that Bao had gotten a peasant girl pregnant, the family paid a premium for cow's milk powder. That Thien continued crying even after being fed something that cost so much only further enraged Flora's father, who took it out on Bao, demanding to know why he created such a defective child. It wasn't until years later, after the family arrived in Australia, that they learned that Thien was allergic to cow's milk.

Whenever Thien cried, Flora's father suggested that the child be thrown into a river. Even after the matter was settled by Flora's mother, who said she would care for the baby, he carried on about all the ways they could rid themselves of the stain on the family's name. In his crueler moments, he implied that both Bao and Thien were the stain, and that both should go—drowned, immolated, buried alive.

"Stop it, Long," Flora's mother said, her voice weak, like she was unable to muster the air from her lungs to speak. "He's our grandson."

"I would rather fuck a communist than have him for a grandson!"

Flora, who had been trained to respect her parents above all else, flinched whenever she heard her father speak of Bao or Thien. She could never bring herself to leave the room—too afraid that it could be read as rude or disrespectful—so she bit down on the insides of her cheeks to maintain her composure, even as his words rattled her, even as she desperately wanted to defend her big brother, whose kindnesses she still remembered and clung to.

Back at Lucky 8, the wedding party was still slow dancing to Flora's singing, but her mind jumped to the day before. She wasn't scheduled to sing; she'd come to work just to see if she could do it. When she saw that waxy dance floor again, her skin crawled, her breath went shallow, and she was certain that her pulse had given up on a steady rhythm.

"You know, Miss Flora, no one expects you to come back to work so soon," Jimmy Carter said in Vietnamese when he brought her a cup of tea. Older than Flora by five years, he had a slight hunch to his back, a limp he'd gotten after an encounter at sea with pirates, and leathery hands. But his face was gentle, open, and easy to read. "No one expects any of us to come back to work so soon."

"Then why are you back?"

"Because keeping busy is the best way to forget."

"Well, same goes for me," Flora said.

"You're shaking."

"No, I'm . . ." Flora started to say, but there was a tremor in her hand and her mouth was dry. She started seeing stars. She sat down at one of Lucky 8's large round dining tables, each covered with a white tablecloth and decorated with napkins folded into swans.

"Miss Flora," Jimmy said, "Big Boss Tang will understand if you need to take more time off. He can get another wedding singer for tomorrow—"

"No, I'm fine," Flora said, making a mental note to get

a prescription for something that would calm her. "I can work tomorrow. I'll be fine."

As she now sang, she caught glimpses of Jimmy emerging from the kitchen, his apron drenched in dirty dishwater. He scanned the restaurant, checking out the stage, and his face relaxed when he saw Flora, a look of relief that she was there. Or maybe that was what she wanted it to be. The live band began playing the opening bars of Frank Sinatra's rendition of "Fly Me to the Moon," and Flora left her body again, this time traveling to months earlier, in the dialysis wing of Liverpool Hospital, where her liver-spotted and increasingly senile father sat as a machine cleaned his blood. "Do you know what they would call you back in Vietnam?" he said from his chair, loud enough so that the other Vietnamese patients could hear. "There are no words for what they would call you in Vietnam! A woman! Thirty-five! So old! No husband! They would not call you anything! It is too embarrassing! No words, none at all!"

Her father was right on only one of those counts, though. Flora was thirty-four. And she did have a suitor—one of the rare men she encountered who, instead of creating problems for her, helped her forget. A man who asked her how her day was and actually cared about what she had to say. A man who wanted to know about her ambitions and goals and encouraged her to pursue them. A man she worked with, who brought her tea, who stood in his dirty dishwashing apron to watch her sing. But she had recently learned that Jimmy was from North Vietnam, which according to her father meant that at best he was a communist sympathizer, at worst a communist—either way, a no-go. Flora hadn't pushed back.

Her father had tried to help her situation. Photos had been exchanged; introductions made. Vietnamese men in their forties and fifties agreed to meet with Flora, curious as to why a fair-skinned and by all accounts not ugly woman had gone single for so long.

"They all say you're not bad," her father back-channeled to her when she helped him sand the calluses from his diabetic feet. "They think you are okay-looking, and they like that you are not fat, but . . ."—here his prune-like face, prematurely wrinkled from decades of relentless stress (twelve months in one of Vietnam's New Economic Zones, two years in a Malaysian refugee camp, the death of his wife just before they were granted resettlement, his deranged son, his unwanted grandchild, his unmarried daughter), twisted into an expression that almost looked sympathetic—"they worry that you are not a good girl, because of your work. People think a wedding singer is indecent."

She had considered a career change. But because she lacked a high school certificate and spoke broken English, any work she was qualified to do paid too little. And, besides, Flora liked how she felt when she sang onstage. She liked to sing. She liked the way her mind was free to wander, how she could escape the present and hide in the folds of memory that she liked best. She liked it so much that she even sang on days when Lucky 8 didn't have a wedding to host. The restaurant's owner paid her a reduced rate to perform to the weeknight dinner crowd with the support of a taped backing track instead of a live band.

Flora's father never gave up on the hope that she would marry, so on days when he didn't berate her for being single, he passed on leads. "This one is different!" he said from the dialysis chair one day in spring. "This one will be a very, very good match for you. It is Porky's nephew."

Porky, whose real name Flora didn't know, was a fellow patient at Liverpool Hospital who, like her father, came in for dialysis twice a week. Porky got his nickname because of his physical features. "Back in Vietnam," he liked to say, "only the very, very rich get to look like this." Flora's eyes were always drawn to Porky's fingers, which looked like sausages.

"Right," Flora said, pulling up a chair next to her father as the dialysis machine whirred.

"This is different!" her father insisted, grabbing her forearm with his needle-free hand. "Porky, you tell her!"

Porky, who was asleep in his own dialysis chair, startled awake.

"Hi, Uncle Porky," Flora said, her eyes tracing his arms to his pudgy bundle of hands, which rested on his protruding belly.

"What? Someone call me? Hello, pretty girl."

"Porky!" Flora's father said, his free hand waving Porky toward him, even though neither could leave their chairs. "Your nephew! Tell her about your nephew!"

Flora retrieved an orange from her handbag and began to peel it.

"Oh yes, my nephew. Very good boy. He's a student, I think. I have a photo. Can you get my wallet?"

Porky pointed to a frayed leather wallet that sat on the wooden table beside him.

"My hands are sticky," Flora said.

"Then take my word for it, he's a handsome boy. Very, very good. You will like him a lot. He will make a good husband."

"And he doesn't look like Porky!" Flora's father said. "He is a skinny man!"

Porky shrugged.

"And what else, Porky? Tell her!"

"Of course. I have told my nephew all about you. I know your search for a husband has not been easy—"

Flora shifted in her chair, glad that the only other patients were the Chinese-speaking regulars, who didn't understand Vietnamese, and an old Greek woman.

"I didn't want to get anyone's hopes up, you know? So I told him everything. I told him that you are thirty-six—"

"She's thirty-five," Flora's dad corrected.

"I'm thirty-four."

"Well, that will be a nice surprise for him. Anyway, I told him that you are thirty-six, not fat, have very fair skin, you take good care of your father, you can cook, and you sing at weddings. But I assured him that you are a very good girl."

On a date with Porky's nephew, Flora learned that although he was skinny and from some angles he could be considered handsome, he didn't have teeth. Besides a few molars that stood like islands on his gums, his mouth was a dark hole when he smiled, his lips slapping against each other when he spoke. She also learned that the reason he didn't mind her line of work was because he was in Australia on a visa and needed spousal sponsorship to become a permanent resident. It didn't matter what Flora did for a living or who she was as a person or what she wanted out of life. Flora was an Australian citizen, which meant Flora was his ticket to staying in the country.

She said she would think about it. She didn't want to disappoint her father, but the thought of having to make more compromises after everything she'd already given up for her family left her wondering whether this was it. Was she doomed to be this unlucky in life? Was there no hope for a brighter day?

She took so long to think about it that Porky's nephew married someone else. Her father berated her for letting the opportunity slip from her fingers. Secretly, though, Flora had never been more relieved. Maybe there was hope.

Back onstage, her hands clammy against the microphone, she sang, the wedding party swaying on the dance floor. Her mind now leapt from her memory of the man with no teeth to a lazy day in Saigon when Bao stopped her from crushing a cricket. "They're friendly!" Bao, ten at the time, said as he threw his body between Flora and the bug, almost flattening it by accident. "Look—" He showed her that she could tickle its antennae to make it jump and explained that crickets were different from cockroaches. Cockroaches were dirty and drawn to filthy homes. Crickets were friendly neighbors who would only move into clean houses.

She sang, and now she was watching Thien take his first steps. She wasn't much older than him; she was a child herself. But she remembered the way his soft, tiny hands reached for her like she was so much bigger, older, wiser. She remembered the unbridled joy that spread across Thien's face, the way he giggled and squealed as he grabbed onto Flora's fingers and hung off them as if they were a trapeze.

She sang, and now they were in Australia, Bao in jail for the first time, Thien, only twelve, stealing the money from her wallet. She'd caught him red-handed, and he'd lied about it. She pressed him, at which point he'd put the twenty-dollar bill down his pants, rubbed it against his crotch, and asked her if she wanted it now.

She sang, and a full year of savings that she'd hidden in a cookie tin under her bed was gone. Her gold ring, left to her by her mother, kept safe in a pouch inside a box, in that same tin, was gone. Her checkbook, which she needed to pay rent, to pay bills, was gone. She checked the room Thien shared with his younger brother, William. Thien was gone.

She sang, and Thien, who towered over her after a summer growth spurt, shoved her into a wall when she confronted him about the white Honda with the tall rear spoiler parked outside their townhouse, demanding to know where he'd gotten it, how he'd afforded it, whether it was stolen. She remembered the way his eyes went dark, like a light had been switched off, like no one was home, a young man possessed. He could have killed her; she couldn't explain how she knew this with such confidence, but she did. Had she not made a dash for the bathroom and locked herself in, she knew that he could have killed her, that he wouldn't have stopped until it was too late.

She sang, and there they were, the Huynhs, in a tent in a Malaysian refugee camp, her mother shriveled skin and bone. There had been cancer in her lungs, her ovaries, up and down her spine. Flora remembered that final gasp, her mother's futile attempt at air, the violence that erupted the moment Flora's father realized his wife was gone: the way he had kicked Bao over and over again; the way Bao never fought back, never even shielded himself; the blood in Bao's urine for days after the beating. She remembered the way Thien, barely ten at the time, had watched—the way Thien had watched Flora watch; the way they had locked eyes, hearts bruised by the ways the world had let them down, by the ways they'd let each other down.

She sang, and she saw the black hole in the man's mouth, the marriage proposal that chilled her insides.

She sang, and remembered the conversations with Jimmy Carter, the cups of tea they shared, the way he encouraged her to go to TAFE with him so they could improve their English and earn certifications that would allow her to teach music and him to do plumbing work. The way he looked at her when he said that it was hard if you did it alone, but everything was easier when you had someone to share it with.

She sang, and she had to make herself swerve from the waxy dance floor, the boy's body, gurgling, dodging memories, finding a different fold in which to hide.

She sang, and it was just a string of men, date after date with skeptical, uninterested men who scowled when they thought she wasn't looking. And there was the man with no teeth again, his face morphing into the face of the man with teeth, Jimmy, whose skin was dry and thick, who walked with a limp, whose appearance was so ordinary that she found it comforting, who liked her—no, who *loved* her—and whom she had to walk away from because her family would never allow it.

She sang, and had that been Thien? Thien, with friends, hair as long as his father's, head to toe in a black suit, arm over a skinny young woman's shoulders? He was a grown man. The last time she'd seen him, he'd broken into her house again, but this time to *leave* money, a thick wad of hundreds for William. She'd caught only the back of him as she chased him out, worried that he might do something to her younger nephew, worried that he was now recruiting new gang members from their childhood bedrooms. If the man in Lucky 8 was Thien, his face had sunken deeper than she'd ever remembered, his eyes glazed and unfocused, his hollow cheeks emphasizing the height of his cheekbones. Was it him? Did she remember right? She had been singing then, just as she was singing now, a backing track playing, her bottom on a stool, watching as Thien and his friends arrived, noisy, demanding, watching as they ordered, watching as he kept trying to hang his arm off the skinny woman's shoulders, the way the woman kept pushing him away, spitting words at him she couldn't make out, her arms crossed, her back turned. Flora watched Thien until he watched her back, and then, a change in his eyes. Was it recognition? Had he seen her? Did he know she worked at Lucky 8? She kept singing, as she was singing now, her eyes on her nephew as the curtain of hair fell over his face, like it fell over William's face, like it fell over Bao's face, and she wondered why she couldn't break from her instinct to protect those who hadn't spared her a shred of kindness in recent or even distant memory.

And before Flora could travel any further back in time, the band began winding down in preparation for wedding speeches, and people returned to their seats, and at the back of the banquet hall, right by the flower arch, she spotted a young woman, the same young woman from days earlier, with the rimless eyeglasses at the police station.

Flora stopped singing. The audience clapped. Inside her ears she could hear only the pounding of her battered heart.

Three days earlier, Flora had been at the police station, hands shaking, stomach churning, her hair matted from how much she'd been sweating.

"My nephew," she said, pointing at a thirteen-year-old boy who sat against a wall with a group of teenagers. "William never do anything bad. William a good boy. What he do?"

She'd already been sweating all day, but the heat inside the police station was oppressive, the smell of people's bodies making her feel sick. Her hand grabbed at the soft part of her belly to keep herself from throwing up.

The unsmiling female officer behind the counter stared at the plum-colored skin under Flora's eyes and said a word that Flora didn't recognize.

"Lottery?" Flora asked, looking back at her nephew to translate. He kept his head down, his long hair covering the angry acne on his forehead and cheeks.

"Loi-ter-ing," the officer said. Flora felt a familiar frustration, like the world was playing a joke on her; if this officer could expend energy breaking down the syllables of a word, why couldn't she just tell Flora what it meant?

"Auntie," a young woman in rimless eyeglasses, whom Flora hadn't even noticed, said in Vietnamese. "Loitering means—"

"So he isn't in trouble for selling drugs?" Flora asked, her native tongue affording her the dignity of being able to say what she meant.

The young woman, who Flora assumed was the police

station's interpreter, looked confused. "I don't know," she said. She looked at the form that Flora had to sign before she could take William home. "It just says he was loitering."

Flora squeezed her eyes shut; she could feel the pits of her shirt getting wet, she could see the waxy dance floor of Lucky 8. She remembered the strange and far-too-loud burp—more of a belch—that escaped her mouth when the restaurant's patrons fell silent and the only remaining sound was the music coming from the speaker system and the labored, gurgled breathing of the boy.

When she opened her eyes, the young woman was staring at her. Flora stared back and couldn't tell if the woman's eyes were blurry because of the thickness of her glasses or because Flora's own eyes struggled to focus. She wanted to take the woman's glasses off. She wanted to take the woman by the face and pull her close to let her see what Flora was going through. She wanted to explain to the woman that she wasn't actually that old, certainly not old enough for a stranger to call her auntie, and if she looked old it was because of the weight of what she carried, and could this young woman with her whiskey-glass-thick eyeglasses see that? Could she see what Flora bore on her shoulders every waking hour of every exhausting day? Instead, she mouth-breathed shallow breaths as she signed for William's release. She checked the boxes she understood. She let the interpreter help with the rest.

Outside the police station, Flora rested her hands on her knees and dropped her head between her legs.

"Auntie," William said in English, prodding at her shoulder with a finger. "You okay?"

Flora's eyes were closed. She saw the waxy dance floor. She heard the gurgled breathing. She raised her hand to indicate to William that she just needed a moment.

When they started walking, Flora told her nephew to not say a word about the police station to his grandfather. "He have liver problem and blood sugar problem. If you tell him, he have heart attack. Okay?"

William nodded, keeping his eyes on his scuffed black shoes.

Maybe it wasn't a lie to say that William was a good boy. As far as Flora knew, he didn't use or sell drugs, wasn't in a gang, hadn't committed murder. But he came from a line of men who struggled to do the right thing; men for whom violence and unrestrained anger were as natural as air. She worried that her nephew might end up like his father, Bao, or worse, his older brother, Thien. A block from their unit, Flora stopped to face her nephew, her eyes welling with tears. "You selling drug?" she asked.

William finally raised his head, his face flashing anger and offense. His skin, once baby smooth and evenly colored like a pear, had in the past six months flared up red and bumpy, just like Bao's.

Standing on the street in Cabramatta facing William, Flora saw Bao and Thien in the shape of William's eyes, in his sharp cheekbones, in the crisp definition of his upper lip.

"Why does everyone think I'm selling drugs?" he said, his own voice shaky. "Is that what you want me to do?"

"Then why you lottery?" Flora said.

"*Loi-ter-ing!*"

"What-ever!"

"Do you want me to turn out like Thien?"

Flora felt her heart in her throat. Did William know what his brother had done? Beyond the drugs. Beyond the gangs. Flora hadn't told anyone what she'd seen. Even when the police interrogated her at Lucky 8 the night the high school boy was killed, she'd lied, had said she was in the dressing room, had said she hadn't seen a thing, even though now, when she closed her eyes, it was all she could see: the waxy dance floor, the boy's body, the sound of breath forcing its way through blood, the jangly music coming through the Lucky 8 speaker system.

"Because it's like that's what you want," William continued. "It's like you won't be happy until I say I'm selling drugs."

"I am not happy if you selling drug—"

"Then why do you keep asking? I already said I'm not!"

"Then why you lottery—"

"We were just hanging out, okay? Where else can we go? There's nothing for us to do around here and we can't even be anywhere, so my friends and I were just hanging around Cabra Station and the cops picked us up. Fucking anh hai, you know how they are!"

Flora shuddered. She'd heard those same words before from both Bao and Thien. Any time they were fired from a job, arrested by police, it was never their fault, it was always the police, fucking anh hai, you know how they are.

"And is it anh hai's fault you went to jail?" Flora had asked Bao years earlier, after his second stint in a minimum security prison. "Is it anh hai's fault you got caught breaking into people's cars?"

"The car doors were unlocked," Bao had said. "I didn't break into shit. They should have charged me with something lesser, but fucking anh hai, you know how they are."

"Why the hell were you going through people's cars anyway?!"

"Because heroin costs money!"

"And is that anh hai's fault, too?"

During that conversation with Bao, he'd been sleeping on her sofa; his skin was sallow, with hair so greasy that it looked like it had been painted onto his scalp. As Flora spoke, he'd rubbed his temples so vigorously that she thought he might break skin.

"Stop that," she'd said, smacking her brother's hand from his face like their mother used to. She resented that he was older than her and should have known better but didn't. She resented that whatever affliction took hold of him when he became a teenager had all but consumed him, leaving him a shell of who he once was. She resented that she no longer felt like his little sister.

"It's worse now," Bao had said.

"I know."

"You don't even know what I'm talking about."

"Then tell me."

"You wouldn't understand."

"William asks about you," Flora had said, hoping to snap her brother out of his self-pity, to remind him that no matter how bad he felt, he still had responsibilities for which he had to show up, like how she had shown up for every member of their family even when she hadn't wanted to, even when it had pained her to, even when it came at the expense of the life she had wanted for herself. In addition to having Thien with the peasant girl in Vietnam, Bao had fathered William with a woman named Sophea soon after the family arrived in Australia. Sophea, who had introduced Bao to heroin, had no interest in being a parent and disappeared from their lives within months of giving birth. This left Flora to care for William.

"I'm tired, Bao," she'd said when he let his hair fall in front of his face, the curtain separating him from the world.

"I'm sorry."

He began rocking back and forth on the sofa.

"You're out of jail now. You're free. You can get a job. You can be a father to William. It's not too late."

Bao had kept rocking. A few weeks later, he was back in jail on drug and assault charges.

A musty smell that made Flora grimace hung in the air of their public housing unit when she and William arrived home. Her father, skinny and sinewy, had sunken into the sofa, sleeping with his mouth ajar. His upper dentures, detached from his gums, appeared to float in the center of his mouth.

"Is Grandpa dead?" William said.

"Dad!" Flora said in Vietnamese, the only language he understood.

Her father coughed himself awake, forcing his dentures further out so they dangled over his lips. He used his fingers to push them back into his mouth.

"My boy!" he said, waving for William to come sit with him.

The teenager reluctantly dropped himself onto the sofa. Her father slapped William on the knee and asked him how he was, whether he was off to university, whether he'd saved a down payment for a home.

"I'm in year eight," William responded in English.

"Vietnamese," Flora said as she made her way to the kitchen.

She listened as William struggled through a conversation with her father. His Vietnamese was stilted, like he had to think about every word as he lay one in front of the other, sometimes in the wrong order, with the wrong inflection. Flora had given up on correcting him after her efforts were met with groans and *whatevers*.

"It's important to learn proper Vietnamese!" she'd stressed after the first time he'd pushed back.

"But why?" William responded in English when he was nine years old. "We're Aussie. We speak English."

Flora, steadfast in Vietnamese: "Maybe *you're* Australian, but *I'm* not."

The young boy had looked at her, puzzled. "You live in Australia, auntie. You're Australian. Like me."

Flora couldn't find the words—in any language—to explain why, despite having been an Australian citizen for years and firmly rooting her life in Cabramatta, she didn't think of herself as Australian. The nebulous outline of it, which she could sometimes make out, usually when she did something mindless with her hands like washing dishes or sanding calluses, was this: Wouldn't being Australian mean that she belonged in Australia? And wasn't belonging meant to feel better than this?

"You can't forget your roots!" she'd said to a pint-size William. "Whatever."

Within a year, his Vietnamese had gotten so bad that she'd had to use English if she wanted him to respond in full sentences.

William remained slumped on the sofa with her father, who flicked between channels, stopping on *The Price Is Right*. Flora swung a duffel bag over her shoulder and pointed at her young nephew to get his attention. In her head, in perfect Vietnamese, she told him that dinner was in the fridge and warned him to stay home tonight, to not have any friends over, because she was tired, so tired, and she needed a break. She carried so much guilt from lying for her family, and she didn't want to lie anymore. The human spirit could take only so much before it crumbled.

In English, she said: "I put rice in fridge. You don't go anywhere, okay?"

By the time Flora got offstage and the live band had put on a *Paris by Night* CD to signal that the party was over, the young woman was waiting outside Flora's dressing room. Although Flora recognized her—she was in the same button-down and gray slacks she wore days earlier, and Flora now noticed that her rimless glasses added unnecessary years to her face—the woman didn't seem to recognize Flora through her thick mask of makeup.

"Are you with the police?" Flora asked in Vietnamese, her pulse quickening. The doctor had said the effects of the Valium would last for up to six hours. It had been only four.

"Oh, no, not at all," the woman said. She introduced herself as Ky Tran.

"But I saw you on Monday. You were at the police station."

Ky looked at Flora, confused.

"Lot-ter-ry," Flora said in English.

Recognition lit up Ky's face. "Oh. Ohhh! No wonder I thought you looked familiar. I didn't recognize you without your—" Ky moved her hands over her hair and face, gesturing at Flora's beehive hair and made-up face. Flora pursed her lips—she got that a lot from people, the unsolicited comments on how she looked, the questions about whether she was feeling unwell because the color was gone from her face. Jimmy Carter was the only person who told her that he could spot her a mile away with or without her makeup. "Your beauty shines through everything," he'd tell her, and she'd smack his arm and tell him to stop being cheesy, but he'd insist that it was true.

Flora nodded, not sure what to say.

"Auntie, I don't work for the police. I was there on Monday to get information, and I ended up helping—"

Flora noticed that Ky spoke with the thick tongue of someone whose Vietnamese was rusty. She wasn't as bad as William, but Flora could tell that every word was siphoning off the young woman's brainpower.

"What do you want from me?" Flora said, moving past Ky into the cramped dressing room that also stored the restaurant's overflow of bottles of soy sauce and sesame oil.

"I just spoke with the other people at the restaurant," Ky said, following Flora into the room. She looked around, her arms tightly pressed against her sides as though she was afraid of knocking things over. "The cook and the dishwasher. They both said they didn't see anything because they were in the kitchen."

"I'm not sure I follow."

"You see, my brother—" Ky said, pausing as though she'd forgotten her place in her sentence.

"Miss Flora," said Jimmy, who'd appeared at the door of Flora's dressing room with a tray of tea and two cups. He looked surprised to see another person with her.

"Thank you," Flora said.

Jimmy lingered in the doorway, watching Ky. "Miss Flora," he said in Vietnamese, "is everything okay here? I told this woman not to bother you. I already told her no one here saw anything—"

"I'm not here to cause any trouble," Ky said, her face dropping in a way that read like fear to Flora—fear that their conversation would end before it even began, fear that she would lose Flora. "It's just that the boy who was killed here—he was my brother."

Flora's stomach lurched. She grabbed at the softness of her belly again.

"I don't work for the police. I'm just trying to find out what happened, what you saw."

"We didn't see anything," Jimmy said, louder this time. "I already told you, Thu is the cook, and he never leaves the kitchen during his shift. I wash dishes, so I'm stuck at the sink."

"But you couldn't account for the waiter—"

"I already told you, he's a useless slob who spends most of his shifts on smoke breaks out back." He looked to Flora for affirmation. "That's why our service is so slow, no one's ever working."

Flora gave a barely perceptible nod in support. She was looking at herself in the mirror, at the way her makeup was drying into the creases of her skin.

"And Miss Flora," Jimmy continued, "she was back here—"

"It's fine," Flora finally said. She had spent the past two weeks pushing memories of that evening as deep as they would go; she hadn't even begun to process what she had seen, or what it meant, or how ridiculously she had acted to protect her nephew. She knew that the young woman in her dressing room threatened to unravel her, but she felt herself move toward telling the truth even though the voice in her head tried to pull her back. "This young lady and I are just going to talk for a little bit."

Ky lit up. "I only have a few questions. I promise not to take up too much of your time."

Jimmy focused on Ky, his eyes narrowing. He looked back at Flora, who nodded again. "Okay then," he said before handing Flora the tray and turning to leave, his eyes on both women as he took slow steps away from the dressing room, his pace emphasizing his limp.

Flora gestured for Ky to take a seat. They sat on fold-out chairs as Flora took inventory of everything Ky wore—anything to distract herself from where she suspected the conversation would go. Ky carried a practical satchel-like handbag that didn't strike Flora as expensive. Her hair was in a sensible low ponytail. Her chin bore faint acne scars, reminding Flora of Bao's acne scars, which were much worse, leaving deep craters on his face that shattered his self-confidence.

"I can't be a father," Bao had said to Flora the last time he was a free man, the last time he was clean, the last time Flora had urged him to take responsibility for William. "Look at me," Bao had said, pointing to his face. "You think anyone wants a dad who looks like this?"

"Your son doesn't care what you look like!" Flora had said. "He just needs a parent! He needs someone who isn't me!"

"It's like roulette in my head."

"What?"

"I stay up at night and I can't sleep because my brain plays roulette. It always lands on memories where I let someone down, and I relive it, over and over again. The memories swallow me, then spit me back out. Then the roulette wheel spins again, and I never know what sad, shameful feeling I'll have to drown in. It never stops."

"Bao, you need to see a doctor."

"I have a doctor."

"Your dealer is *not* your doctor!"

"I can't be a father. I'm sorry."

"Bao, I need my life back."

"I'm sorry."

"I've taken care of your children since I was ten."

"I'm sorry."

"It's not fair, Bao."

"I'm sorry."

"I don't even know what I want anymore," she said, one of the few occasions when she'd allowed herself to cry. She had been so desperate for relief, so in need of being heard that she wanted to scream. Instead, she'd sobbed and pleaded for her big brother to help her by helping himself because she didn't know what else to do. "I feel like I can never breathe, like any time I win a little bit, I find out it was all a joke, like a big joke was played on me, like I'm stuck. Why does everyone else get a second chance in Australia but me? Why won't you help me?"

"I'm sorry."

"Stop saying you're sorry! If you were really sorry, you'd step up and take care of your sons and take care of our father and give me a shred of a chance to live the way I want to!"

"I'm sorry."

"You're not sorry at all!"

"I wish I'd never been born."

"Don't say that."

"I'm sorry."

Three weeks later, Bao was in jail, picked up in a drug sweep.

"Auntie," Ky said, reeling Flora's consciousness back into the tiny dressing room, "my brother Denny was killed here at Lucky 8. I know you've said that you didn't—"

"I didn't see anything," Flora said so unconvincingly that she even surprised herself. How could she lie when she saw it clear as day? The boy being knocked down before he even had a chance to defend himself; the way the body didn't recover quickly like it did in the movies; the waxy dance floor; the backing track that kept playing even when she stopped singing; the way he bled, darkening the floor; the way she belched, the sound catching in her handheld microphone and echoing through the banquet hall.

Ky went quiet and looked Flora in the eyes. "Auntie," Ky said again.

Flora blinked and realized that she was crying. She made a mental note to not look in the mirror again, afraid of her own reflection.

"The worst part of it," Ky said, pausing between sentences the way William did whenever he came up against the limits of his Vietnamese, "the worst part of it is I think I let him down. And the fact that I don't know for sure whether I let him down *proves* that I let him down."

Flora looked up. Her eyes fell on Ky's acne scars again. She kept seeing her own brother. "I'm not sure I understand," Flora said.

"My brother was a really good person," Ky said. "I don't

know where he got it from. Not me. I'm petty and jealous and weird. I hated him when he was a baby because he didn't even cry a lot. He was perfect. I was *so* jealous. But then I realized that there was no point in being jealous, because everything that was good about him made him a better brother. I'm sorry that my Vietnamese is bad and I can't explain exactly what I mean, but . . . the good things about him were good for me, if that makes sense."

Flora felt the full weight of her own sadness. She was envious of Ky. She wished her own brother had been half as good.

"But what if he wasn't good in the end?" Ky said, her face distorting to keep herself from sobbing. "I thought I knew him, but what if I didn't? What if I'd been gone for so long that he changed and I just didn't care enough to pay attention? What if . . . what if I could have done something?"

"Do you think your brother was in a gang?" Flora asked. She pictured the skinny boy with the center part, his shirt tie done all the way up, his face full of color. He looked nothing like Thien. He looked nothing like the people who followed Thien. Their worlds had no business colliding.

"I don't know," Ky said, using her knuckles to wipe her eyes. "And I hate that I'm even saying that. A week ago I would've said no way, Denny is perfect and would never do anything like that. But now I really don't know. What sort of big sister doesn't know?"

Flora felt her stomach gurgle. She thought of how she'd always known too much: what Bao had done, what Thien had done, what her father had done—the violence they'd committed against one another, the pain they'd inflicted on strangers. She'd turned a blind eye again and again, lied for them when she had to, bailed them out even when they were better off behind bars, took care of them even though she knew they would never do the same for her—all in the name of family.

"My family doesn't know what happened to him," Ky continued. "The police don't know what happened to him. No one in my house can sleep. I keep finding my dad in Denny's bed, and my mum doesn't go to work because she goes to the temple every day, and I feel like it's my fault, like I let him down—"

Flora instinctively grabbed at the softness of her belly. She wondered what it was like to come from a good family—one where the siblings cared for each other, where no one was an island. She wondered how her mission to do right by her own family had resulted in her doing so wrong by another. She wondered whether any of her actions—the sacrifices, the compromises, the high price she'd paid again and again—had been worth it.

"—and . . . I just need to know. I just need to know what happened to him. Even if it was his fault—if he did something to get himself killed—I need to know. I don't need him to be perfect anymore. I just . . . I don't know what else to say. The police are stuck, and I know that someone saw something. I just need to know what happened."

Flora pulled the tray of tea toward herself and filled both cups. She handed one to Ky, trying her best to steady her hands, which suddenly felt weak and numb.

"I had a brother, too," Flora said.

Ky blew on her cup of tea. Flora saw Bao in her mind's eye, how sick he looked when she last visited him at Silverwater, the way he had described the shakes, the sweats, the nausea, the diarrhea. He was still her brother. But she'd lost him a lifetime ago.

"I'm sorry," Ky said. "You must miss him."

"Every day," Flora said.

"How long ago?"

Flora closed her eyes, tried to remember that final year when some light emanated from Bao's eyes. He'd been fifteen, Flora was nine. Although Bao had passed the point of wanting to entertain Flora and often slept entire days away, he still had enough warmth for her that he'd allowed her to tag along with him to Cholon one time to buy candied fruit on a stick. As they sat side by side on a stoop sucking the caramel off the apple-like hawthorns, the wind blew and sent their hair—equally long and silky—into their faces. Flora tucked a piece of hair behind her ear, jerking Bao's head toward hers. And when Bao went to pull what he thought was his own hair out of his caramel candy, Flora felt a tug against her own scalp. The wind blew again, entangling their locks, and even though Flora wanted to scream from the sand that was being blown into her face, she laughed and couldn't stop, and next to her she could feel Bao's body shake with the giggles as the wind whipped at their faces, bringing their heads closer together in a nest of sticky, candied hair.

"Before the war ended," Flora said.

"What happened?"

"I wish I knew."

"So you know how I feel, then."

Flora sipped her tea. What she would give to know what had happened to Bao. But also, she thought as she studied Ky's hopeful expression, what would it change?

"It's not the same," she said.

"You know what I miss the most about Denny?" Ky said, cutting Flora off before she could justify her opacity. "I miss the things that haven't even happened yet. I miss all the times in the future where I won't be able to tell him about the things I'm doing."

"What would knowing change?"

"What's stopping you from telling me the truth?" Ky said. Flora noticed that she didn't sound desperate anymore. She sounded angry.

At the center of her mind, images of her family—once crystal clear and firmly planted—shivered. She saw Bao's youthful, spotty face dissipate; Thien as a baby faded; her father, wrinkled and weak, an unrecognizable blur.

"Nothing," she said, putting down her cup. "There is nothing stopping me."

She told Ky that a large group of people had dined at Lucky 8 the night Denny was killed. She told Ky that her nephew Thien had been there, was part of that group, that she knew he was also part of a gang, that maybe it was the 5T gang, but she didn't know for sure, because every gang seemed to be a 5T copycat. She told Ky that Denny had approached the table, which surprised her, because he was dressed like a sensible boy—even from the stage she could see that he was different from Thien and his friends. She told Ky that Denny's movements were unusual, that she had no idea what to make of them. She saw him leave his own table and approach Thien's, only to turn back and sit down, then get up again, where he proceeded to hover near

Thien, and just as Thien was getting into a heated argument with a heavily tattooed, skinny woman—a skinny woman who Flora assumed was another one of his addict girlfriends, the same addict girlfriends Bao was drawn to, who dragged him back into his addiction every time he got clean—Denny snapped a photo and said something. Flora couldn't make out what was said. Moments later, he was on the ground, his body lifeless. She told Ky she didn't know why someone would want to hurt her brother, that it was inexplicable, that it was just bad luck.

She didn't tell Ky that Thien was the one who did it. She didn't tell Ky that she sat and watched, unable to move, unable to help. She didn't tell Ky that she feared for life—maybe hers, maybe someone else's—when she saw the way the light in Thien's eyes flickered off, the separation of body and soul, the demons of Bao and the demons of Flora's father coalescing in an unwanted child who never stood a chance. She didn't tell Ky that she always knew Thien would hurt someone—that it was born from his genes, but also from the ways he'd been treated, rejected, unwanted—and that her lies, her bail, her excuses enabled him. She didn't tell Ky that even now, knowing that her nephew was dangerous, she couldn't bring herself to say the words: He did it. He did it. The young boy who had reached for her fingers, he did it. Her flesh and blood, he did it. She didn't tell Ky that she wanted to throw up right now, because her body was revolting against her, because her own body was ashamed of her for still protecting a killer, even though she'd now uttered his name, even though the police would now easily find him because of her, even though—

"Who exactly did it?" Ky asked, her face red.

"I don't know," Flora lied out of habit.

"Auntie—"

"I don't know," Flora said, seeing the waxy dance floor, seeing the violence, feeling sick, spinning.

Ky adjusted herself on the stool. "Then did your nephew tell you why it happened? What did Denny say to him? Can you describe what the girl looked like or any of her tattoos? If your nephew was part of that group, then wouldn't he—"

"I don't talk to him anymore," Flora said, which was true. She wouldn't know where to find Thien. Ever since he first ran away, he had always been the one to find her, usually by coming home, usually by breaking in.

"Then what about the girl?"

"I don't know," Flora said.

"Auntie—"

"She was just a skinny girl with tattoos. I didn't get a good look at her."

"Did you see anything else? Was it . . ." Ky hesitated, the words coming out slowly. "Did my brother die fast? Was it at least a quick death?"

Flora rested her face in her hands. She didn't care that her makeup was becoming further smudged. The boy's death wasn't slow, but it had been drawn out enough that he must have feared it, must have seen its approach, must have struggled against it. Flora saw his bloodied neck, the blow that ended his life, and her stomach flipped on itself. Before she could do anything else, she felt a lurch in her belly and threw up chunks of her lunch and the evening's tea onto the dressing room table.

Ky sat stunned, mouth open. Flora began to retch from the smell of her own vomit.

"I'm so sorry," she said, wiping her mouth with the back of her hand.

"No, I'm sorry," said Ky, getting up to rub Flora's back. "I can help clean up—"

"No," Flora said, resting her head between her knees, her face wet and nose blocked. "Please, just go away. I've told you everything."

"But, auntie—"

"Just go away. Please. I have nothing left."

Flora squeezed her eyes shut so tight that white blotches came into view. But even before she saw it, she could feel it coming again: the waxy dance floor, the boy with the tidy center part, Thien looking like Bao looking like her father. And then she saw herself, the curtain that fell in front of her own face, the separation between her and the world. Thien looking like Bao looking like her father looking like her. She didn't know how much longer she kept her head down, but when she finally opened her eyes, Ky Tran was gone, the lights in the banquet hall were off, and Jimmy was standing in the doorway, a steaming cup of tea nestled in his calloused hands. Flora was overwhelmed by his presence, surprised by the relief. She couldn't bear to be alone anymore.

Chapter 8

Ky left a message with the police station immediately after her meeting with Flora Huynh. She called again the following morning. "Did Constable Edwards get my message from last night?"

"He doesn't get in until the arvo," said the officer on the line.

"Can you make sure he gets the message?"

Ky heard through the receiver a rustling of paper.

"What's the message again?"

Ky spelled out Thien's name and told the officer that she believed Thien was connected to Denny's murder, and if he wasn't directly involved, he at least would be able to identify the person who did it.

"Hang on, so it's Thee-en?" the officer said.

"No, the *h* is silent."

"So it's T-i-e-n—"

"No no, it's still spelled with an *h,* you just don't pronounce it."

"Okay. And the surname is what again? H-o-o—?"

"I think I know him," Ky said after spelling out Thien's name.

"Yeah?" the officer on the line said.

"I think so," Ky said. Thien was a common Vietnamese first name. Huynh was an even more common Vietnamese surname. But how many Thien Huynhs in Cabramatta were in a gang? Ky pictured the Thien Huynh who drove the white Honda, the Thien Huynh who was a high school dropout, the Thien Huynh whom Minnie had chosen over Ky. She felt a pang of resentment, as fresh as if it had happened yesterday, at the memory of her best friend running off with Thien.

"He'll just friggin' dump you in a month and hook up with another slag," Ky had said when she learned that Minnie had been sneaking off to see Thien after school.

"What do you mean, *another* slag?"

"You know what I mean."

"What, so you think I'm not good enough? You think I'm only good for being used?" Minnie said. It was one of the few times Ky had seen Minnie on the brink of crying.

"No! That's not what I mean. God, I'm just saying that he's *trouble* and he's probably a player and I bet he has, like, five girlfriends and he doesn't actually care about anyone."

"You don't even *know* him."

"I know enough."

"No, you don't. You've never even spoken to him. You don't know *anything*."

Ky didn't know for sure that the two Thiens were the same. Still, she spoke through the receiver. "I think he's in a gang," Ky said.

The officer on the other end of the line made an inaudible noise. Ky thought she heard "No shit."

"Okay, is that all?" he finally said with clear enunciation.

Ky thought about how she was right—how, all these years later, she had been vindicated. If it was the same Thien, he'd ditched Minnie for some tattooed chick. He'd probably ditched her years earlier. She was right. Minnie should have stuck with her instead.

"Hello? You still there?" the officer said.

"Oh, yeah," Ky said. "That's all."

When Ky hung up, whatever petty thoughts she had about Minnie were overtaken by the central question of what had happened to Denny.

You're getting close, said the imagined voice of Minnie, her presence filling Ky's childhood bedroom.

Doesn't feel like it, Ky thought.

I'm not talking about the case.

Then what *are* you talking about?

Come on, don't be dense.

Stop insulting me.

You're insulting yourself.

Shut up.

Think about it, girl.

How about *you* think about it and help me understand what the hell was up with Denny?

Ky, I only know what you know.

Then why do you keep talking to me?

That's a good question for yourself.

What did Flora even mean when she said Denny's movements were *unusual*?

One woman's unusual is another woman's regular.

Not helpful.

My point is—
What?
You're figuring things out.
Uh-huh. Like what?
Like, what if your silly, narrow, keep-quiet-and-be-polite path . . .
Not this again—
. . . leads nowhere?

Ky clapped her hands against her ears to cut Minnie off. She made her way to Denny's bedroom. In the five days since the funeral, she'd only allowed herself to stand outside her brother's room, to watch as her father lay still in his bed. Part of her was afraid of disturbing what was left of her brother; part of her was afraid of what she might find. But in those few days, things had changed. Her need for closure now outweighed her fear of the truth. And whatever it was—whatever she might find—it had to be better than being suspended in limbo, not knowing, riddled with guilt, guilt about feeling guilty, questioning who her brother really was.

As she stepped across the threshold, she entered a time capsule. Her parents dusted, vacuumed, and mopped around Denny's knickknacks. On his desk: neat stacks of folders labeled by school subject; the complete set of Looney Toons KFC mugs, each serving as pencil and pen holders; a framed photo of Denny with a half dozen friends, all tidily dressed in school uniform, throwing a *W* sign with their fingers—a symbol that Ky and Minnie had also thrown in high school. The *W*, as far as they were aware, stood for Westside, as in southwest Sydney, as in near enough to Cabramatta.

"It can also stand for West Coast," Denny had said to Ky over dinner on one of her last trips to Sydney. "Like, how Tupac is West Coast and Biggie is East Coast."

"You sure about that?" Ky asked, unconvinced that her brother knew of the intricacies and politics of American hip-hop. His favorite singer was Mariah Carey.

"That's what Eddie told me."

"And how does Eddie know?"

"He just knows stuff," Denny said.

Sitting at her brother's desk, Ky now thumbed through the folders. His handwriting looked like the models used for teaching little kids how to write the alphabet.

She spent the morning going through folder after folder, reading the extensive notes he took in classes, the stick-figure doodles he drew in the margins. She went through a folder that contained the prospectuses of every university he had applied to—including two that were in Melbourne. Another folder held clippings from the local paper, including a puff piece on Denny's year eight debating team winning the district championship. There he was, plastic trophy in hand, wearing an oversize blazer jacket that he had borrowed from the school. Denny was always the fourth speaker, which meant he never actually spoke.

"I'm not charismatic," he'd told Ky when she'd asked why he let others do the talking.

"Oh, come on."

"I'm serious. Even Mr. Dickson said so."

"What a dick thing to say."

"He was nice about it, but it's true. I'm not the kind of person that people listen to," he'd said matter-of-factly.

At least a dozen local articles over the years featured Denny, most of them filler stories about awards won, murals painted, school raffle nights. She stopped at one clipping that had yellowed over time. The headline was about student art on display at Cabramatta's public library. The photo showed four children in school uniform, pointing at a wall of lush green landscapes and still life paintings of fruit bowls. Caption: "Year seven students from Cabramatta High School admire their paintings. *L-R:* Minh Le, Ky Tran, Holly Nguyen, Sid Dokic."

Ky remembered how Holly Nguyen's and Sid Dokic's mothers had shown up for the photo call. Ky hadn't been able to convince her own mother to come.

"Is it an award?" said her mother, who by then was full time at the Cabramatta fabric shop and relied on Ky and Minnie to perform after-school pickup for Denny.

"No, but they chose our art for the library," Ky had said. "And the *Fairfield City Champion* is going to be there to take our picture."

"If they're taking your picture, then why do I have to?" her mother said. "We'll save the newspaper when it comes out."

"But Holly's mum is going!"

"Well," her mother said, putting down a plate that she was washing and turning off the faucet, "Holly's mum doesn't have a job because Holly's mum doesn't need a job. Holly's dad went to *university.* Holly's dad is a *doctor.* You want a doctor dad and a mum who doesn't work? You can go join Holly's family, go be their daughter."

Ky resented how her mother made her feel bad about wanting what everyone else seemed to have. It wouldn't even cost her mother any money to go to the library and see her paintings.

It was the *library*—everything was *free*. And when her mother tried to explain that *time* was money, that not going to work was money, Ky stormed out of the kitchen to her bedroom, where Minnie was reading a Kmart catalogue.

"I swear to god," Ky said, dropping herself onto her bed.

"So it's a no?"

"She won't come because it's not an award."

Minnie continued reading the catalogue, making tears along the edges so that they'd dangle as she turned the pages. "My parents won't come, either."

"But that's because you didn't even ask them," Ky said. "I swear, if our parents were white, we'd be, like, the perfect children. Have you ever noticed that? The white parents come to everything, and they're *so proud* of their children, even when they're all kind of dumb?"

Minnie yawned, dropped the catalogue, and leaned forward to touch her toes. "I reckon," she said, body folded in half, face in lap, "they just have a lower bar to clear."

"It's not fair."

"I know."

"But we'll have the last laugh," Ky said.

Minnie sat back up, rested on her elbow. "How?"

"We'll get the best scores and go to uni and become super rich and powerful, and then they'll have to work for us, and—"

"What if we just go take over Vietnam?" Minnie said, reclining with her eyes closed.

"What?"

"It's a Third World country. We could totally take it over."

"Minnie, be serious."

"About what?"

"About—" Ky said, suddenly unable to pinpoint what exactly she wanted Minnie to take seriously. "I dunno."

"I don't want white people to work for me," Minnie said.

"Why not?"

"Because then I'd have to *pay* them. Screw that. Let me be rich and powerful and left alone."

"But don't you want to boss your enemies around?" Ky said.

Minnie sighed, sitting up again. She raised both hands as though to shrug, then let them drop.

Back in Denny's folder of clippings, Ky learned that her brother collected articles with any mention of Cabramatta. A clipping from September 1994 in the *Sydney Morning Herald* covered the assassination of John Newman, Cabramatta's representative to the state legislative assembly. His killing in the driveway of his Cabramatta home became Australia's first-ever political assassination. Ky recalled the mixed feeling of excitement and dismay when she heard the news: the thrill that came with the thought of people finally paying attention to her home; the dread that came from the fact that, of all things to finally get people to pay attention, it had to be this.

"You know, they think the gangs did it," Denny had told Ky over the phone the day after news broke with Newman's death.

"Does that scare you?" Ky asked. "I hear the gangs love recruiting fifteen-year-olds."

"Not this fifteen-year-old," Denny had said. "Plus, I don't think they would target our family."

"Why not?"

"I read in the paper that they target homes with money.

They bring machetes and they tie people up and they demand to know where the safety-deposit box is, and then they threaten the families, take their photo albums so that they can identify all the relatives, and tell them if they go to the police they'll come back and kill the children."

"Jesus, Denny."

"I know, but we don't have money, we don't even have a safety-deposit box, and Mum says that only certain kinds of people attract gangs, and we're too timid and poor to be on their radar."

"But aren't you worried," Ky said, phone wedged between her shoulder and ear, "that you might get caught in the cross fire?"

"Huh," Denny said, like it had never occurred to him that violence could be indiscriminate, that a bullet didn't always land where it was intended.

"What if a gang gets the wrong address? What if they think they're going to some rich person's house and end up at our house instead? Ever think of that?"

"But that won't happen," Denny said.

"And why not?"

"Because energy follows thought."

"What?"

"That's what our PE teacher said—energy follows thought. If you think you're going to get hit in the face with a ball, you'll get hit in the face with a ball. So just don't think that you'll get hit in the face with a ball."

Ky laughed. "And how's that working for you?"

"Not great."

"That's too bad."

The last sleeve in the folder housed an article on the best Vietnamese food in Sydney. Two restaurants in Bankstown ranked first. A Cabramatta restaurant came in third. Ky scoffed. Denny seemed to agree—in the margins of the article, he'd written *Booooo!* As she held the sleeve between her thumb and forefinger, it felt oddly thick, like there were additional sheets of paper sandwiched between articles. Ky reached in to pull them out.

One of the booklets was a year twelve math exam where Denny had scored full marks—his teacher had circled the grade and included a doodle of a smiley face. The other booklet was the same exam, photocopied, date stamped a year earlier, also scoring full marks, but belonging to a different student. Ky blinked, holding both sets of exam papers side by side. As she turned each page in tandem, she noticed that the questions and responses were the same. It wasn't unusual for teachers to recycle exams from year to year, and she'd heard of students tracking down old student exams to cheat. But she'd never done it herself, nor had she known anyone who had done it.

Ky's throat went dry and her palms broke out in a sweat. Plagiarizing. Approaching gangs. Unusual behavior. *Cheating.* Who had her brother become while she was away?

She looked back down at the papers, then at the photo of Denny with his friends. Next to Denny was Eddie Ho. Ky touched the photo—she'd put off talking to Eddie, had hoped she wouldn't have to. The closer she was to someone, the harder it was to confront them. How else could she explain how she had said more to, revealed more to, expected more of strangers than she had her own family? Eddie had grown up with Ky and

Denny, had been like a younger brother. The thought of talking to him, of confronting him or forcing answers out of him, made Ky want to escape her skin. But now she had to either see him or resign herself to a dead end. She had to do it. For Denny, for herself—she had to do it.

During the day, when local businesses bustled, when the streets were filled with shoppers, when schoolkids and retirees gathered on the long red benches in Freedom Plaza to soak up the warmth of the sun and women in plastic visors pushed carts full of groceries through the center of town, it was easy to ignore the open-air heroin market, the addicts who loitered and swayed outside pharmacies, the white police who stopped and searched people outside the train station.

Ky never worried about being stopped and searched herself. Years earlier her mother had said that neither she nor Denny looked mean enough to rouse police suspicion. Ky had initially taken this to mean that she looked friendly. But her mother had continued: "You look like the kind of people who get pushed around. You look like people who are soft and never fight. You look like people who are easily tricked—someone will scam you for all your money and you'll be too simple to notice. You look like people who wouldn't survive on your own in a refugee camp. You look like—" But just because she wasn't worried about an unfair arrest didn't mean she didn't worry about everything else—getting mugged, stepping on a used syringe, and since Denny's death, a run-in with gangs. She remembered a time when Cabramatta didn't scare her. Back when she and Minnie were still friends, neither of them thought twice about using the pink-walled public restrooms near Dutton Lane because, unlike today, people weren't routinely overdosing in the stalls. Back then, the greatest threats in their lives were quicksand, which seemed like the worst natural phenomenon in the world, and boa constrictors, which they'd sung about in school ("Whaddaya know, it nibbled my toe, / Oh, gee, it's up to my knee").

Across from the train tracks, on a road where single-family homes stood in overgrown grass, Ky recognized the terra-cotta-colored brick house where she had picked up and dropped off Denny on countless occasions when he was still a kid. The one-story home had a black roof, with white stone lions the size of Chihuahuas sitting on the edges of a tiny porch. Ky rapped on the metal frame of a fly screen door, producing a tinny noise that barely registered as a knock. When no one answered, she stretched out an arm and knocked on one of the house's front-facing windows. The blinds were drawn, but she saw a flicker—a finger push down on a blind, the flash of an eye, before a retreat. She knocked again.

"Eddie, I saw you," she called to no response.

It was a game she was familiar with, one that she, Denny, and Minnie had played whenever the Avon lady came to their house.

"Pretend you're not home," her mother had instructed them. "That woman is trying to steal our money."

"It's not exactly stealing if she's giving you something in exchange for your money," Minnie had said, not in the interest of defending the Avon lady, but simply because by age twelve she couldn't help herself, calling out things that didn't sound right.

"You know how much they charge for lipstick?"

"You don't have to buy it, auntie."

"And I don't! Because if I give them money, then the thieves win!"

From then on, when the Avon lady came knocking, the girls would peek through the blinds to see who was there, then immediately duck, hands covering mouths, afraid that the redheaded woman outside their door would hear them breathe.

"Eddie Ho!" Ky now shouted, hand rapping the fly screen. "I saw you! If you don't let me in, I'm going to tell the police what I know!"

Less than a beat had passed before the wooden door swung open, a gangly teenager with a side part standing behind the fly screen, dressed in oversize track shorts and a Homer Simpson T-shirt.

"*Ssshhhhh!* Stop shouting!"

Eddie was a head taller than Ky, with a panic in his eyes that made her feel bad for him.

"Let me in and I'll hush," Ky said, taking on a sudden authority. To her surprise, she felt like she was bossing Denny around—the feeling came on so suddenly, with such intensity, that she lost steadiness and had to rest a hand against the doorframe for support.

Eddie stood with his hand on the doorknob, shaking. There was something about the clothes Asian boys wore at home that made them seem younger than they were. Like Denny, Eddie was on the cusp of eighteen. In baggy clothes, he was just a kid. He unbolted three separate locks before the fly screen exhaled open.

The Ho family home was mostly unchanged from what Ky

remembered. The floor was still covered in a pale blue tile that kept the house cool in the summer and freezing in the winter. The leather sofa, bought more than a decade ago, remained covered in the manufacturer's protective plastic. And the ancestral altar looked as sad now as it did back then; Mr. and Mrs. Ho spent so much time at their bakery that they often forgot to replace the fruit offerings. Oranges routinely shriveled on their plates. Bananas were left long enough to turn brown and, eventually, black. And now there were persimmons showing the first signs of rot—a brown bruise that likely reached deep into the heart of the fruit.

"Your parents not home?"

"No, they're at the bakery," Eddie said, closing the door behind him, triple-locking it, and peeking out the window again.

She noticed all the things about the house that had changed. The television was bigger. The Super Nintendo in the TV cabinet had been replaced by a brand-new Nintendo 64—Denny had told Ky about it in an email she never responded to, about how it wasn't available in Australia yet, but Eddie's cousin in America had shipped one to him.

"So," Ky said, dropping her backpack onto the plastic-covered sofa.

Eddie played with his knuckles.

"You gonna tell me what happened?" Ky said.

Eddie looked at her, his expression pained. "Do you want some water? Or tea? I can make you tea. We have the little teacups." Eddie was speaking fast, his thumb still rubbing his hands. "Like the ones from yum cha. Let me make you tea."

Ky followed Eddie to the kitchen as he moved with his head down, his hands clumsy, sweat glistening on the back of his neck.

"Eddie—"

"I didn't see anything, okay?" He lit the stove burner with a matchstick, shook the stick more times than he needed to to put out the flame. "I told the police everything. I didn't see anything, I was in the toilets, I was—"

"I don't believe you."

The boy's eyes were now pools. Ky felt a dull pain in her stomach—the feeling of seeing a younger sibling get hurt, the desire to make things better for them.

"I've seen the report, Eddie. You, Kevin, and Ms. Faulkner told the police that you were all in the toilets. At the same time. And when you came out, Denny was dead? Come on, man."

As Eddie's hands shook, Ky fought the urge to switch into big sister mode, to tell him that everything would be okay, that she would take care of things, shoulder the burden of whatever ate away at him. But she had to remind herself that just because this boy reminded her of Denny, was Denny's best friend, was the last person with Denny before he was killed, it didn't make him her brother. She didn't owe him anything; he owed *her*. She felt it in her chest, standing in the Ho family kitchen, that Eddie had the answers. She knew that unlike Sharon Faulkner and the Woos, who probably didn't see with their own eyes what had happened, Eddie had seen everything. It was in *his* eyes. It was in his nervous white knuckles. It was in the way he was quietly sucking snot back up his nose as he put the teakettle on the stovetop.

"Also, you didn't come to the funeral."

"My parents wouldn't let me," Eddie said, still facing the stove.

"He was your best friend."

"You don't get it."

"Then help me get it."

Eddie remained quiet and still.

"Look," Ky said, taking a step forward, causing Eddie to back further into the kitchen counter, "I've been in touch with the police. If you don't start telling me the truth . . . I'll tell them you're lying to them."

"But I didn't do it!"

That much was obvious to Ky. She knew there was no way he was responsible for Denny's death. He was an awkward kid whose mother still dressed him, who spent weekends playing video games, who made Mariah Carey and Tupac cassette tapes for Denny—the latter to ensure that Denny had a "balanced diet" when it came to music. But he knew something about the night at Lucky 8—at the very least, he had to have known what was going on with Denny—and if scaring him was the only way to make him speak, Ky was willing to do it.

"I'm not saying you did, Eddie. But . . ."—Ky's fingernails were deep in her palms again—"I know about the cheating, Eddie. I saw the math test. And I know about the plagiarism. And how he was . . . *unusual* the night he died. I just . . . I just need to know *why*. Was he doing drugs or something? Had he joined a gang? I can handle it, Eddie. If he was off the rails and fucking up his life, I can handle it. I just need to—"

Eddie's mouth formed grotesque shapes as he tried to stop his lips from quivering. "He . . . he was under a lot of pressure," Eddie said, wiping his nose with the back of his hand.

Ky held her breath. Maybe she couldn't handle it.

"But he wasn't *bad*," Eddie said.

"Like how the naughty people and junkies in town aren't bad, right?" Ky said, her tone sarcastic and mean. "Those screw-ups are just *misunderstood*, right?"

"What? No, that's not it—"

"Then what is it, Eddie?" Ky said. Her anger was rising—at Denny for veering off the path, at herself for not stopping him sooner.

"He didn't do any of that! He didn't do drugs. Ever."

"How can you be sure?"

"Because we have eyes! You think we haven't seen what heroin has done to people who went to school with us? You think we could look at how sick and messed up they are and still think it's a good idea to try drugs? We're not idiots."

"But what about other stuff?"

"*What* other stuff?"

"Like, I don't know, weed or pills or—"

"God, no. He never messed with any of that."

"But he messed with cheating and plagiarism, and who knows what else—"

"Yeah, fine, that was dumb," Eddie said, sounding annoyed. "But it's totally different, okay? He only cheated and plagiarized once. And he didn't even have to. He was doing fine. He did better than me even without cheating. But he kept saying he needed to get a hundred in everything or else—"

"Or else *what*?"

"I don't know! Or else he wouldn't be perfect? Or else your parents would be disappointed? Or else people would think he was dumb?"

"That's ridiculous."

"No, it's unfair," Eddie said, struggling to hold himself together. His voice wobbled as he spoke. "He felt bad. He was so embarrassed when Ms. Faulkner caught him. But he only did it once, and only because he felt like he was cornered, like he couldn't afford to *not* come first. That's why he wouldn't wear the Most Likely to Succeed sash he won at the formal. He felt like he hadn't earned it, so he put it in his pocket."

"I don't believe you," Ky said. It seemed like everyone she'd talked to in the past week had lied to her, withheld information from her, thought nothing of her. She wanted to slap Eddie for doing the same, for thinking he could hide anything. "Tell me the truth. What shit was Denny getting into? People don't get bashed to death for no reason. What was he doing that was so—"

"Just because we're not perfect doesn't mean we're bad!" Eddie said, hot tears streaming down his face.

The words landed against Ky like a blow to the chest. She envisioned the narrow path she'd been on her whole life. The narrow path that perhaps led nowhere. The narrow path that she didn't create, but perhaps she'd helped maintain by never questioning its existence, by never wondering who it served: pushing her brother, pushing Minnie, pushing herself onto it even when there was no proof that it was correct. You were perfect or you were bad. You couldn't afford to be bad. You couldn't afford to be anything else. It was impossible. It was her fault.

"It's not fair," Eddie said again.

Ky tried to swallow, but her body just wanted to cry. She blinked tears out of her eyes. "Yeah," was all she managed to say.

After a moment, during which they both wiped their faces and took deep breaths, Ky asked: "If he wasn't doing drugs and he wasn't trying to join a gang that night, then . . . what happened?"

"I don't know," Eddie said, unable to look at Ky. "I was in the bathroom—"

"Come on, man!" She found herself reaching upward to grab Eddie by the shoulders. "None of this explains why someone killed him. Why won't you help me?"

"I already . . ."—now he was gasping for air, his own grief putting him in a choke hold—"told you . . . I was . . ."

A deep cry escaped his mouth, his face already a wet mess. Ky saw herself standing in her own kitchen in Melbourne, a teakettle full of vinegar bubbling away, a wail she couldn't control. She let go of Eddie's shoulders and he almost fell; her firm grip had been supporting him.

Ky closed her eyes and massaged her temples, focusing on the line of gray that floated up and down behind her eyelids. She thought of the times when Eddie was at her house, when Minnie and Ky came home to hear her mother yelling at someone on the phone. How the four of them—Denny, Eddie, Ky, and Minnie—would lock eyes, and how the boys could tell them, through facial expressions alone, whether her mother was yelling because she was angry and everyone should stay out of her way, or if she was yelling because Cabramatta women sometimes did that for no good reason.

"Okay," Ky said, "let's try no words."

Eddie wiped his eyes again. His face had turned puffy.

"Were you, Kevin, and Ms. Faulkner actually in the toilets when Denny was killed?"

Eddie chewed his bottom lip and stared at the ground, his thumb still over his knuckles. He raised his head to nod, but Ky stopped him.

"Hold on. Let me be more specific. Was the teacher in the toilets?"

Eddie looked up and nodded without hesitation.

"Okay. Was Kevin in the toilets?"

He continued to nod.

"Were you?"

His eyes returned to the floor, where the kitchen's yellowed linoleum was pockmarked with air bubbles.

"You were at the table with Denny," Ky said.

Eddie's head seemed to want to shake and nod at the same time. She noticed his fist relax, the color returning to his fingers.

"But you lied to the police and told them you were in the toilets . . ."—Ky kept her eyes on Eddie, hoping he would look up—"so that you wouldn't have to be a witness. Because you were scared. And your parents—"

Eddie's parents had an even greater distrust of the police than most families Ky knew. Eddie's father had been conscripted into the South Vietnamese army because of the police. They'd stopped him in the streets of Saigon, ignored his protests that he wasn't old enough to enlist, shredded his identification documents that proved that he was underage, and dragged him to a hospital, where a doctor took one look at his mouth, noticed wisdom teeth, and declared him to be over eighteen. Eddie had told Denny that it was a miracle his father had survived the service. Ho men weren't made for war. Ho men weren't fighters. Ho men were skinny and savvy but lacked coordination. But this particular Ho man—Eddie's father—was blessed with good luck, which the Ho family didn't take for granted. Which was why Eddie's parents had a dentist on John Street remove Eddie's wisdom teeth the moment they showed up on an X-ray, well before they even had a chance to poke through his gums. And it was also why they looked at the police with disdain. To them the white cops of Cabramatta were no different from the cops that dragged Eddie's father from the streets of Vietnam into the ranks of the poorly trained, underprepared military.

Eddie continued wiping at his face with his bare hands. Whatever height he had gained over the years he lost in that moment, hunched over, sobbing.

"Which means," Ky said, "Ms. Faulkner lied for you."

Eddie sniffed, sucking snot back up his nose.

"Eddie, is that it? Is it because of your parents?"

"I didn't see anything," Eddie said, his eyes squeezed shut, his head shaking.

"Is it because of what happened to your dad in Vietnam?"

"What? What are you talking about—"

"Because what happened in Vietnam isn't relevant here," she said, feeling a twinge in her heart; she wasn't sure if she meant what she was saying, but she knew she had to say something, and this was the best she could do. "This is about catching the guy who killed Denny, and if you saw something, if you know who did it, you have to—"

"No, it's not about Vietnam or whatever. And I didn't see anything."

"Who are you trying to protect?!"

"I don't want to hurt my parents!"

Ky stood stunned, unsure of how telling the truth amounted to hurting anyone. "What are *you* talking about?" she said.

Eddie took gasps between words, his body shaking. It was hard for Ky to watch, but she kept her eyes on him, ready to catch him as soon as he looked up.

"If I *did* see something, which I didn't, it would break my parents," Eddie said, the collar of his T-shirt now damp from crying. "They'd feel like . . ."—now he was panting, trying to talk through his tears—"like they failed me. They'd feel like . . . like . . . it was their fault . . . that they couldn't . . . they couldn't . . . protect me . . . from . . . from . . . seeing it."

Ky continued staring at Eddie, the muscles in her face aching from trying to hold back the urge to cry. To anyone else, Eddie's reason would have been baffling. But Ky understood. She hated how well she now understood. After all, hadn't she kept every hurt she'd ever experienced from her own parents? Hadn't she hidden the bullying, the name-calling, the cruel acts of strangers, the times she'd been told to go back to where she came from, the ching-chongs, the pulled-back eyelids, the blondies with the Cabbage Patch Kids, the way she was forced to play the monster, the way she was asked why she couldn't just take a joke, the times she was told that Asian women were ugly, kinky, docile, crazy, nerdy, unworthy, the way she was dismissed by men, the way she was dismissed by white men, their comments about what Asian women were and weren't, what Asian women could or couldn't be, the way she smiled with her tongue pressed against her teeth even as an ache beat in tandem with her heart—hadn't she hidden all of that? And hadn't she lived her own ambitious, exciting, anxious, uncompromising life while knowing that she could never, ever, ever, *ever* tell her parents about what she had been through? Because knowing would break their hearts. Because she had to help them believe that their sacrifices had paid off. Because she had to help them believe that moving to a country where they didn't speak the language and weren't seen as individuals had been worth it. Because she had to convince them that they'd done right by their children, that no one had failed, that no one had been let down, that they were one of the lucky ones who'd followed the path and found success. It made perfect sense. You lied to protect. You lied because of love.

The teakettle whistled. Eddie was too distraught to switch off the flame. Ky reached over to turn the knob.

"Is that it?" she said. "Is that really a good enough reason to let Denny down like this?"

Eddie rubbed his white knuckles again, unable to look up at Ky. "I already did."

"You already did what?"

Eddie was now blotting his nose with the sleeve of his oversize T-shirt. "Let him down."

Ky wasn't sure what he meant. She waited for him to say more. He continued sniffing, his shoulders hunched, his breath uneven.

"If I told the police that I saw something, which I didn't, I'd also have to tell them that . . . that . . ."

"What?"

"That I didn't do anything. If I was there. If I had seen it. I just . . . froze. I couldn't move. I just watched him get killed and I didn't do anything to stop it. I didn't try to help. I just couldn't. I was paralyzed or something, like it wasn't real. If I saw something, then that was what would have happened. But . . ."

"But . . . ?"

"But I didn't see anything," Eddie said, his voice breaking again. "Because I wasn't there."

Ky kept looking at Eddie, but her vision had blurred. Among everything her family refused to acknowledge, refused to talk about, this detail was possibly the most painful—no one had helped. Even if they could explain Denny's encounter with a deranged gang member as bad luck, there was no explaining why a roomful of ordinary people—people who looked like Denny, people who could have been related to Denny, people who were friends with Denny—did nothing. It haunted Ky, hurt her in ways that made it hard to be awake. Ky understood why Eddie had to lie—to her, to the police, to himself. Because to admit the truth would be to admit that he was a coward, that as his best friend was being beaten to death, all he'd managed to do was sit and watch. He was lying to save his parents. He was lying to save himself.

She felt herself deflate. As she turned to leave the kitchen, her pager buzzed. It was from the police station.

"Can I use your phone?" she asked, gripping the little plastic device in her hand. "This might be important."

Eddie nodded and gestured toward the living room, where his family kept a cordless telephone. He stayed in the kitchen while Ky made her call.

"Miss Tran?" said a voice through the receiver. It was Constable Edwards.

"Yes. Hi," Ky said, clearing her throat to hide that she'd been crying. "Did you get my messages? I called last night, and this morning, and left them with the other officer. This Thien guy, he was there. He would have seen who did it, and I bet he can identify—"

"Miss Tran—"

"There was, like, some big group, maybe they were a gang, and one of them killed Denny, and Thien Huynh was there with that group, and he might—"

"Miss—"

"—know something about what happened to—"

"—it was him."

"What?"

Constable Edwards went quiet, during which Ky could picture him in his uniform, the sweat under his eyes, the way he dragged out his sighs as a precursor to sharing bad news. And here it came, the sound of air pushing out of the constable's mouth.

"Have you talked to Flora Huynh, Miss Tran?"

"I—" Ky said, her words getting caught in her throat, seized by a familiar fear—the fear of getting into trouble with authority, even though Constable Edwards was the one who had told her where to find Flora in the first place. "Yes," she said.

"And what did she tell you?"

"What I already told you," Ky said, feeling her own breath grow shallow, because for once, Minnie wasn't there; there was no imagined friend, and Ky felt on her own, small and scared and meek. "In the messages, I said that there was a guy named Thien—"

"Did she tell you what Thien did?"

And now Ky strained to hear Constable Edwards over the racket of her raucous heart, and she tried to slow her breathing, but it was like her nostrils were blocked and she couldn't get enough air.

"Only that he was there," Ky said. "That he saw something."

"Are you sure?"

"Yes," Ky said, irritated, because if she was in trouble for something, she wished the constable would just say so. His line of questioning reminded her of the way her grade school teachers reprimanded students with a string of accusatory questions that always led to a self-indictment.

"Miss Tran, we got a call early this morning, at about two, for an overdose. Thien Huynh broke into Flora Huynh's home and shot up in her younger nephew's bedroom. She called Triple Zero when she found him, and when we showed up, she told us what had happened."

"Wait," Ky said, the room suddenly spinning. Her hand felt sweaty against the receiver. "*What* happened?"

Constable Edwards cleared his throat. "Flora Huynh admitted that she'd lied to us. She told us that her nephew, Thien Huynh, killed Denny."

And now Ky's sweat felt cold, her stomach like she'd just gotten off a roller coaster.

"Miss Tran?"

"Yeah," Ky said. "I'm still here."

"Thien Huynh is known to us. This wasn't his first offense. We had some officers go to his apartment earlier today, and we found shoes that match the prints left at Lucky 8, covered in dried blood. We've sent them off to the lab, just to cross all our

Ts, but, and I wouldn't normally say anything so definitive, but in this case, I think we have our guy."

Ky's heart was now beating with such intensity she thought she might have a heart attack. "Is there going to be a trial?" she asked.

Again, a pause. "Miss Tran . . . we don't put dead people on trial."

Ky couldn't think of what to say. She tried to swallow again, but her mouth and throat were so dry she made herself cough.

"When Flora Huynh got home, she found Thien unconscious. He'd already gone cold. We have reason to believe it was an accidental overdose."

"And you said he broke into her house?" Ky said, a croak in her voice.

"Correct."

"Why would he do that?"

Ky pictured Constable Edwards shrugging.

"Your guess is as good as mine. Apparently he's done it before, previously to steal from her, but in recent years she said he left money or snacks, and on this occasion, he was sleeping on the floor next to her younger nephew's bed. The younger nephew didn't think anything of it. He had no idea his brother had overdosed until Flora came home."

Ky tried to imagine how Flora must have felt after speaking with her and finding her nephew's cold body.

"Is Flora going to get in trouble?" Ky asked.

The constable sighed. "It's not my place to say."

"But . . ."

"But . . . Miss Tran, look: Did she do the wrong thing

by lying to law enforcement? Yes. Do we have bigger fish to fry? Absolutely. You ever heard of a home invasion? That's a Cabramatta specialty. We didn't even have a term for that before these Asian gangs got here, and there were two of those last night. We're just glad this particular case is now closed."

"So that's it?" she said, not wanting to believe that this could be it, that justice could feel this bad, that a resolution could be so unsatisfying, that she could get this far and still feel like the biggest questions had been left unanswered.

"Miss Tran, homicide cases often don't get solved. And even when we know gangs like 5T are involved, eyewitnesses almost never come forward to help us pin anything on them. You got lucky here."

"But do we know why he did it? I mean, Denny didn't even *do* anything. Why did this Thien guy—"

"These gangs don't seem to care about anything, and they're not scared of our laws," Constable Edwards said.

Ky squinted, wondered why those particular words sounded so familiar. Then she remembered: Years earlier, just before her falling-out with Minnie, she saw John Newman on television, his forehead deeply lined and his eyes blue as ever, telling a reporter that the only thing that Cabramatta's Asian gangs feared was deportation back to the jungles of Vietnam, "because that's where, frankly, they belong."

"Can you believe this guy represents us?" Minnie had said, scowling at the screen. "Like, maybe say they belong in jail or something. But fuck you if you think that criminals 'belong' in Vietnam."

"But our parents got out of there," said Denny, who had been sitting on the floor with a comic book, only half paying attention. "So it's probably not wrong to say that Vietnam is a bad place?"

"*No,*" Minnie said, pointing a finger at Denny to make sure he was listening. "Our parents fled authoritarian shit. Don't confuse a regime with a country and its people."

"Chill out," Ky had said. "Who made you Miss Vietnam?"

"Can't you see why shit like this is a problem?" Minnie said, her back now perfectly erect, like she was ready to leap onto the television. "This guy reps Cabra and he fucking thinks we're trash—"

"Whoa whoa whoa, he thinks the *gangs* are trash."

"There's no difference! We're all the same to him!"

"Umm, it doesn't take a genius to tell the difference between, say, Denny and some gangster dude," Ky said.

Denny beamed.

"You're missing the fucking point," Minnie said, allowing herself to sink back into the couch.

"Stop swearing."

"Seriously. If all the bad people *belong* in Vietnam, does that mean only *good* people belong here, in Australia?"

"I dunno."

"*Think* about it, Ky!"

"You're overthinking it," Ky said. "We don't have anything to worry about because we're good."

"Ugh! You're not listening!"

Over the phone, Constable Edwards continued speaking, trying to explain the violence as an Asian gang problem, and going on to say that ultimately they might never know why Denny was targeted, and for that, he was sorry.

"Okay," Ky said through her teeth.

"That will be it for now, then," Constable Edwards said. "If there are any developments, I'll let you know."

He hung up first. Ky sat with the phone in her lap, staring at Eddie's Nintendo. She supposed that she would walk home and break the news to her parents. She supposed that she would book a flight back to Melbourne, return to work, because there wasn't anything left for her to do in Cabramatta. But first she bent over, rested her head on her knees, and allowed herself to cry in a way she hadn't since she'd gotten those first calls from her father informing her of Denny's death. She cried so hard her whole body shook, her wails trailing into silence before she gasped for breath and unleashed another. She didn't care that Eddie had poked his head from the kitchen and was watching her. She didn't care that her grief, which was meant to be private, hidden, kept from view, was now pouring uncontrollably from her, because how could this be it? How could she do everything right *and* try something new and still end up here? She cried, she finally, *finally* cried, for her brother. She cried for her family. She cried hard and loud for herself, to be heard.

Ky lost track of how much time she spent folded over on the couch in tears. At some point, when her body was finally quiet, she felt a nudge against her shoulder. It was Eddie.

"Are you okay?"

Ky sat up. The knees of her pants were soaked from her tears. "No," she said, "I am obviously not okay."

A long silence passed. Then Ky, thinking of what Constable Edwards had told her, asked Eddie what he knew about gangs.

"You mean, like, Tupac and Biggie?" Eddie asked. "Bloods and Crips? I know a bit about those."

"More like 5T."

"I'm not in a gang, if that's what you're asking."

"No," Ky said. "No one would mistake you for being in a gang." Her eyes moved to his Homer Simpson T-shirt before returning to his face. "I just want to know what 5T stands for."

"Oh," Eddie said, putting his hands in the pockets of his shorts. "That's easy. It's five Viet words that all start with *T*."

"And what are the words?"

"I don't know Viet—my family speaks Teochew."

"Right," Ky said.

"But I do know that it translates to 'love, money, prison, punishment, suicide.'"

"I see."

"Yeah."

Ky placed the cordless phone back on its recharging dock and stood to leave. As she picked up her bag, she fought another wave of uncontrollable grief that threatened to wash over her. "Fucking *why?*" she said, closing her eyes and letting her head fall back—a final plea to the universe for answers.

Before she opened her eyes, she felt Eddie's hand on her shoulder. He immediately withdrew it when she turned to face him.

"It was because of your friend," he said, sucking on his bottom lip.

"Excuse me?"

Eddie's fingers began rubbing his white knuckles. "Your friend. The one who used to always go to your house. She was there that night. It happened because of her."

"You mean Minnie?"

"Yeah."

"Hold on. *What* happened because of her? What did she do?"

Eddie was crying again, but this time he was quiet, steady. "I . . . she was there that night. I saw her. But then I went to the bathroom. So I didn't see anything else—"

"Jesus Christ, Eddie, what the hell are you talking about?"

His face went red. Ky could tell that Eddie was both fighting to hold things back and regretting that he'd said anything at all.

"Eddie," Ky said, trying to be gentle, "you can't just say something like that and expect me to let it go—"

"Forget I said anything."

"Goddammit, Eddie!"

"I went to the bathroom and I didn't see anything after that. Just . . ."—now a vein throbbed in his neck—"you should talk to your friend. I went to the bathroom. I didn't see anything. I'm sorry."

Ky stared at Eddie, hoping the longer she kept him uncomfortable, the more likely he would be to divulge what he saw. But Eddie just stood and cried, sucking up snot as his eyes were glued to the ground. Ky was exhausted. But she now knew what she had to do next.

"All right, Eddie," she said, unlocking each of the bolts to let herself out. "I'm sorry, too."

Chapter 9

Hanh Tran hadn't been able to fall asleep in his own bed since Denny's death. His mind refused to switch off. When he closed his eyes, he submerged in memories of missed opportunities: the times he could have played with Denny but didn't; the times he could have feigned excitement when Denny bought him gifts from the primary school's Father's Day Gift Fair (handkerchiefs, cuff links, fuzzy coat hangers, a tea cozy) but didn't; the times he could have simply talked to his son, told or asked him anything at all, instead of silently sipping a beer until his chest felt sufficiently warm and the edges of his world sufficiently blurry and the idea of sleep particularly alluring. And even though he still had one living child, the loss of his younger only amplified his sense of regret—what if he had wasted her time, too?

Yen climbed into bed. Judging by the tense energy that her body radiated hours into the night, he suspected that she hadn't been sleeping, either. But they didn't talk about it. Instead, when his eyes throbbed with so much exhaustion that he couldn't bear to be awake any longer, he would get up, tiptoe to Denny's childhood bedroom, and lie upon the single mattress that his wife kept perfectly made—a last-ditch effort to feel closer to a son who was no longer around. Curled up with his knees to his chest, he allowed himself to bury his face into the sheets until a different kind of exhaustion washed over him, pushing him deep, deep down into sleep.

On this night, though, as they lay side by side, eyes to the ceiling, his wife broke the silence. "What do we do?" she whispered, her blanket pulled up to her chin, her hands gripping each other as she rested them atop her belly. "Why is our daughter like this?"

Yen had gone with Ky to the temple earlier in the week, and as was the case any time mother and daughter spent more than a few hours together, Ky had lost her temper, had talked back, had behaved like a disgruntled child who was always spoiling for a fight. They hadn't spoken since. Hanh knew that Yen wasn't blameless—she, too, had a knack for escalating arguments and a firm belief that she was always right. Hanh never got involved—he didn't see the point in fighting, didn't believe he could win, didn't think anyone ever wanted their mind changed. It didn't make it any easier to hear the two of them going at it; his skin crawled whenever he heard Ky grumble and grunt or Yen raise her voice so loud that it triggered an itch deep in his ear.

Hanh wanted to blame Australia. He wanted to tell Yen that, in Vietnam, a child could never speak to their parents the way Ky had without repercussions. He'd heard of sons and daughters being outright disowned for refusing to study what their parents wanted them to study or marrying a person their parents thought was a poor fit. But here, what difference did it make? Ky didn't even live with them, could easily avoid them for the rest of her life if she wanted. Besides, had he and Yen ever owned their children? Or had they given them up when they gave up their first home? Hanh wanted to tell his wife that Australia made it easy for Ky to be the way she was. And it also made it hard for him to be the father he thought he was meant to be.

"Are you coming to the end-of-year assembly?" Ky had asked him when she was eight years old. "We're gonna dance the Nutbush onstage, and me and Minnie are in the front row."

Hanh had seen the two girls practicing in the living room, taking turns singing the Tina Turner song as they vigorously line danced until sweat beaded on their temples and their hair became matted and damp.

"We get to wear costumes," said Minnie, who at that point was spending every afternoon with the Tran family. "We get to dress like disco people."

Hanh had shaken his head. "I'm busy."

"Doing *what*?" Minnie said.

"Yeah," Ky parroted. "Doing *what*?"

Hanh had imagined the comforts of an evening to himself. With his wife, daughter, and toddler out of the house, he would be able to eat his dinner in peace, drink his beers alone, and listen to Khanh Ly's music on cassette tapes while missing the life he had in Saigon. He knew it was morose and unproductive. His wife liked to tell him to forget the past, to stop listening to Khanh Ly's tinny voice as she sang about heroic soldiers and brave dead sons. But the more she told him to move on, to move forward, and the more white-faced strangers yelled for him to speak English, and the greater the pressure to shut up and disappear, the more he felt like he was in a bizarre dream where the world had collectively agreed to erase his past. So whenever he was by himself, Hanh fought back with memory. Because life had been good in Vietnam. The very end, when the new government took control and bank accounts froze and private businesses were forced to shutter, had been rough. Their lives had been ruled by uncertainty and fear, and the straw that broke them was when Yen returned from collecting rice rations for the month and found that the bag had been weighed down by gravel. With a crying baby Ky in their lap, the couple picked out individual rice grains from the bag, salvaging what little was edible. Yen had been so angry that she threw a piece of gravel in her mouth and attempted to chew. She immediately chipped a molar, bloodied her gums, and cried. "What kind of life are we living?" she said, sobbing.

Before all of that, though, life had been good. That was what Hanh tried to remember as often as he could. He hadn't been born a refugee. He was more than that. Before they'd lost their home, before they had Ky, Hanh and Yen had gone dancing every weekend. He remembered when he took his new wife to see *Ben-Hur;* neither of them could follow what was being said in English, and both could barely keep up with the French subtitles. But the movie was so big, so colorful. He had gotten a Beatles haircut. She styled her hair into a bouffant at record speed. At the disco, he moved his feet so fast, the other dancers formed a ring around him and cheered. Yen could limbo lower than anyone else. And when they were both flushed from booze, and they allowed their faces to touch, the warmth from each other's cheeks made them feel like they were too big for their bodies, because they were—they sometimes felt like they were bigger than Saigon, bigger than Vietnam, bigger than the war. They were so big that, together, they could create life. That was worth remembering.

"Well?" eight-year-old Ky said, arms crossed. "Can you come? Mum will probably need help with the camera."

Hanh had shaken his head again.

"Ugh!" Ky said as both girls left the room, backs hunched, heads tipped backward. "You never *do* anything!"

Hanh remembered being baffled by the girls. Wasn't it enough that he gave Ky a home and Minnie a respite from her own family life? As a child, he had been sent to Can Tho to live with relatives because his parents' Saigon apartment was too small to accommodate him and his six siblings. He was raised by his grandmother until he was five. When his parents came into enough money to buy up the remaining floors in their Saigon apartment building, Hanh finally joined them. It had been confusing—painful, even—to leave the only home and caretakers he had ever known to live with people whose greatest act of love had been to send him away. But so what? Hanh now thought. The pain had dampened with time, the bruise in his heart an ache that he grew accustomed to, and life had carried on. Didn't Ky know how lucky she was?

Yen continued fidgeting with her hands in bed. "She rarely comes home to begin with, and when she does, she acts like this," she said. "And you know what she said to me? She told me it was wrong to refuse an autopsy for Denny. Can you believe that? She wanted us to let some stranger cut up our son. And for what? To check that he's really dead?"

Hanh bit his tongue. Had he been in the right state of mind the night that Denny died, he wouldn't have listened to his wife, wouldn't have declined the autopsy. Because even though he knew that Yen was right—that no amount of information would bring Denny back—he wanted to know how, wanted to know why, and maybe if he got those answers, he'd understand something about his son.

"She probably just wants the details," Hanh said in his daughter's defense. Thinking more about his own desire for answers than Ky's, he continued: "Maybe she thinks there's something important to understand."

"What could be more important than the fact that he is gone? That is the only detail that matters. He's gone. And nothing we do will change that."

"But—"

"We should have never allowed her to go to Melbourne for university. It changed her, it—"

"Yen—"

"—it made her forget where she comes from, it—"

"Yen, the two of you always fought, even when she lived here."

"It's worse now! She's like a bull. All horns."

"A bull needs another bull in order to lock horns."

He felt his wife open her mouth to refute, but nothing came out. Instead, she pulled her sheet over her head.

"Yen," he said, letting his hand rest against hers under the sheets. "She lost Denny, too."

He heard his wife sniffle. He rolled to his side to face her. She'd always been such an expressive woman, and her face seemed designed to say more than most—her eyebrows were thick and dark and could arch in surprise, furrow in thought, or form straight lines when she was angry. Her eyes were enormous, with crow's-feet that amplified the power of her smiles and made unbearable the sight of her crying. And she was loud—at times uncomfortably so, her expressions of joy or fury ringing off every surface so the neighbors could hear. He studied the white sheet, the bumps and grooves created by his wife's nose, chin, and cheeks.

"When we came here, to give them a better life, did you know what it would mean?" he said, his mind barely a step ahead of the words tumbling out of his mouth.

"What are you talking about?" Yen said through the sheet.

"Because I didn't. I thought that a better life was the life we used to have. I thought that Ky would be able to grow up like we did, but in Australia. I . . ." He paused, shifting his shoulder. It was something Hanh had thought about over the years, which had only recently crystallized in his head—that a "better life" could be something alien to him; that it might be something that he couldn't even imagine. Did Yen know that a better life meant that their children's Vietnamese would be terrible? Did she know that it would mean that Ky and Denny would know nothing about either of them, would reduce their stories to refugee clichés, would look at them like they didn't know the first thing about life? A wave of grief passed through him. He felt his throat tighten, pressure behind his eyes. "I didn't know that I would fail like this."

Hanh could barely see through the tears that blurred his vision, but he could feel his wife lowering the bedsheet from her face and the shifting of her body as she rolled to her side to face him.

"Like most men, you are lazy, inconsiderate, and useless," Yen said. Hanh could feel the breath of her freshly brushed mouth against his skin. "As a husband, you annoy me to death with your lack of interest in everything, and you are not the man I fell in love with. You haven't been for a long time."

Hanh's heart felt like a punching bag, each of Yen's words making his body tremble. These were all things Yen had said before, but usually during one-sided arguments, when her voice traveled through the walls of their townhouse and she declared to whatever Buddhist deity she had developed an interest in that her husband was a waste of her time, that her skills and talents were wasted on a man like him, and could a Buddha please make him disappear. Harsh words yelled in moments of passion didn't faze Hanh. But the gentleness of his wife's current delivery punched through muscle and skin.

Yen reached for his face, took his exposed earlobe between her thumb and forefinger. "But . . ." she said, massaging his lobe, "you have not failed as a father."

Hanh began to cry. He covered his mouth with both hands to muffle himself.

"Our children know that we would die for them," Yen continued. Hanh noticed that she referred to Denny as though he were still alive. It made him splutter through his palms. "They are not idiots," she continued. "They might do dumb things, inexplicable things, but they are not idiots. They know our love."

Hanh used one of his tear-dampened hands to cup his wife's

hand, pressing her palm against his ear and cheek. He hadn't felt her hands in so long. They had become rough, calloused, and thicker than he'd remembered. For the first time in a week, he curled up on his side of the bed, let his wife keep her hand on his face, and let sleep swallow him whole.

The next morning, though, Hanh still made his way to Denny's bed. Until his son's death, he had never taken an interest in the boy's room, couldn't tell if the furniture had been moved, the sheets had been changed, or a new poster had gone up. But since the day he learned that Denny was gone, the room had taken on the weight of a temple, and Hanh had come in search for answers. Maybe, while lying on the tidy single bed, Denny's ghost would speak to him. Maybe, surrounded by the objects his son had touched, he would absorb the information he'd once so readily ignored and arrive at an understanding of who his son was. But Denny's ghost never spoke, and the boy's bedroom paraphernalia only confused Hanh. Why was he so obsessed with a Black American man who could throw a ball through a hoop? What was the point of the knickknacks he collected on his desk? What was with the smiley faces he drew on his schoolwork?

The great emptiness followed Hanh to work, where he helped people deposit checks, open bank accounts, and send wires. It followed him on his lunch break, where he slurped a bowl of phở without enjoyment and walked the compact commercial district of Cabramatta to pass the time. And it expanded when he walked to Lucky 8, down the road from the bank, which had reopened just days after the murder. He found himself drawn to it—because there had to be answers inside—but also afraid, because what if he couldn't handle it? This was how Hanh passed the days following Denny's death—in a blur of exhaustion, basketball posters, cashed checks, and wire transfers, with his daughter standing in the doorway to Denny's room, a judgmental look on her face, his daughter offering no answers for how she was spending her days, his daughter missing dinner and returning home just as his eyelids felt heavy enough for sleep, his daughter storming into the bank that morning—although who knew what day it was?—asking if he knew where she could find Minnie, that it was important, that she needed to find Minnie *right now,* and when Hanh said he would look into it when he got home, his daughter raised her voice, because this couldn't wait—she couldn't explain and she couldn't say more, but this absolutely couldn't wait—and so Hanh raised his own voice, the first time he'd done so in years, demanding that Ky show some respect and leave the premises before she made any more of a scene.

Why is our daughter like this? Hanh heard his wife's voice as he walked Cabramatta during his lunch break, wondering himself whether this was it, whether the family was finally unraveling—his son was dead, his daughter was unhinged, his wife was all prayer, and Hanh had been emptied of purpose and joy. His boss had told him to take an extended lunch; his colleagues tried to stay out of his way—whether they were afraid of an outburst or scared of his family's bad luck rubbing off if they got too close, Hanh didn't know. So he ate his lunch and he went for a walk, taking himself to Lucky 8, where he once again stood on the other side of the street, imagining a banquet hall of answers that he was simply too weak to take. When he saw a thin man about his age in a stained apron come out of the restaurant, a cigarette pack in hand, Hanh followed him, hoping that if he just got close enough to someone who had been inside, answers might emerge. The thin man, who Hanh noticed had a slightly hunched back and a barely noticeable limp, went through an alleyway, and by the time Hanh himself emerged, the man was seated on a milk crate outside Lucky 8's back entrance, lit cigarette hanging from his mouth, eyes staring into the multistory garage of Dutton Lane.

"Back entrance is closed," the man said to Hanh in Vietnamese after he'd stood long enough that he looked like he was lost.

"Oh," Hanh said. He hadn't expected the man to notice him.

"Someone broke a bottle of fish sauce on the carpet. I had to cover the back stairs in carpet shampoo."

When Hanh continued to not move—he'd never been so close to answers, and the prospect of finding out what had happened to his son both paralyzed him with fear and gave him a reason not to turn and leave—the thin man asked if everything was all right.

"Do you work here?" Hanh asked.

The man nodded, his cigarette ash dropping into the gutter.

"May I sit down?" Hanh said, pointing to one of the spare milk crates. "I'm feeling a bit dizzy."

The man studied him through a cloud of smoke. He shrugged, which Hanh took to be a yes. The man offered him a cigarette.

"Got any beer?" Hanh joked. When the man didn't laugh, Hanh introduced himself, giving his name and the fact that he worked at the Commonwealth Bank.

"Jimmy Carter," the man said, extending his hand to shake Hanh's. "I'm not interested in a bank loan, if that's what this is about."

"Oh, no," Hanh said, "I'm just a bank teller."

When Hanh didn't elaborate, Jimmy Carter offered him the packet of cigarettes again, as if to say that if Hanh wasn't going to talk, the least he could do was smoke. Again, Hanh declined.

"Did you choose the name Jimmy Carter?" Hanh asked.

Jimmy Carter nodded.

"On Bidong," he said.

"My family went through Bidong Island, too!" Hanh said with more enthusiasm than he felt. It wasn't much of a surprise or even coincidence that Jimmy Carter had been processed on Bidong—most of the Vietnamese in Cabramatta had stayed at the same refugee camp.

"Oh yeah?" Jimmy Carter said. "What year?"

"Seventy-eight."

"You must've had money to get out that early."

Hanh wanted to tell Jimmy that yes, he *had* money, past tense. Fleeing Vietnam early ensured that anyone who had money arrived at their new home flat broke.

"The immigration officials told me my name was too hard to pronounce," Jimmy said. "They suggested that I change it."

"What was it?"

"Cung Đặng."

Hanh frowned. "That doesn't sound hard at all."

"I was desperate. I'd been in Bidong for a very, very long time. I was willing to do anything for resettlement," Jimmy said.

"So you chose Jimmy Carter?"

"Well," Jimmy said, chuckling in the rote kind of way that suggested he knew he was meant to laugh while telling the story, even though he didn't find it funny, "I told them I wanted the same name as the president, because why not? If I was going to get an English name, I might as well go big, be the leader of Australia. I didn't know that Australia has a *prime minister,* not a president. But because I had said president, the immigration officials told me it was Jimmy Carter."

Jimmy pinched the end of his cigarette and began lighting a second. "Now, if I had said prime minister, I would be Malcolm Fraser," Jimmy continued. "But because I'm an idiot, I'm now named after a short guy who's all top-row teeth when he smiles. He might even be shorter than me."

"Jimmy Carter was a good president," Hanh said, even though his criteria for measurement was narrow. In Hanh's eyes, a country's leader was good if they accepted refugees after the Vietnam War.

"I guess it doesn't matter," Jimmy said.

But a name *did* matter, Hanh wanted to say. Like Jimmy, he, too, had been offered the chance to change his name when he was resettled in Australia. They extended the invitation to Ky because they thought her name was difficult to pronounce ("Kai?") and could affect her ability to assimilate. Hanh had rejected the offers. He was proud to be Vietnamese, proud to keep the name that his parents had given him, proud that his name alone was an act of defiance against those who wanted to erase the memory of Vietnam. He'd relented into giving Denny an English name only because Ky had asked to name her baby brother.

"Have you worked here for long?" Hanh asked, inhaling Jimmy's plume of cigarette smoke and coughing.

Jimmy looked at Hanh out of the corner of his eye. "You sure you're not trying to sell me a bank loan?"

"No, no, I'm just a bank teller—"

"And you're just sitting here because you're dizzy?"

"Yeah," Hanh said, feeling exposed. "Just—"

"Diabetes?"

"Sorry?"

"My fiancée's father is a diabetic and gets dizzy all the time."

"Oh, no. It's not that. I don't think I have diabetes. It must just be the sun."

They both looked up to the sky; it was another cloudless day, the sun feeding a dry heat that made Hanh feel like he was sitting in a toaster oven.

"When are you getting married?" Hanh asked.

"No idea. I only just proposed last night."

"Wow. Congratulations."

"Thanks," Jimmy said, scratching behind his ear. "It wasn't the romantic proposal I wanted to do—I would have gotten a ring, flowers, taken her somewhere nice, but it was spur of the moment. It felt right, and I didn't want to miss my chance."

Hanh didn't understand what Jimmy meant about missing his chance, so he just nodded.

"It's a bit scary," Jimmy said to Hanh's silence. "Being someone's husband, taking care of them. I'm ready, of course, don't get me wrong, I am glad to be so lucky, but I've never done this before, you know? I've been on my own for so long. I'll need to get a new bedspread. I can't have her sleeping on my worn-through sheets. And a vase for flowers. There are so many different things you have to do to make a house ready. It's exciting but scary. I've dreamed about marrying her and opening a business with her and starting a family with her, but it was always just a dream. And now it's becoming real."

"My son was killed here."

Hanh could feel his own heart beating in his neck. He couldn't explain why he'd chosen that moment to bring up Denny, only that he couldn't contain it anymore. Jimmy froze; the only movement between the two men was the smoke wafting from Jimmy's cigarette.

"His name is—was—Denny Tran. He was seventeen," Hanh said. "You work here. Did you see what happened to him?"

Jimmy's body stiffened, the dreamy expression that emerged when he talked about his fiancée instantly wiped from his face. Hanh realized he'd probably given the man emotional whiplash. After a long pause, Jimmy said, "I wash dishes in the kitchen. I don't see anything, ever. I can't help you."

"But . . ." Hanh said, feeling small and pathetic, "what about the other people who work here? Did they see anything? Maybe you heard them say something?"

"Listen," Jimmy said, shifting his body to face Hanh, "Thu Ly never leaves the kitchen—he cooks all night and doesn't take breaks, so he didn't see anything. Phat Luong is a piece of shit of a waiter who is always sneaking smoke breaks when he's meant to be working, so he didn't see anything. *I* have to wait his tables for him half the time."

"But if you're waiting tables for him, then you must have seen—"

"I was back in the kitchen by then," Jimmy said, turning away from Hanh and looking into the parking garage, one leg crossed over the other. "I serve a table, I go back into the kitchen, I wash dishes, I stay in the kitchen."

"What about Lucky 8's wedding singer?"

"What *about* her?"

"I don't know, I just thought—"

"I'm going to tell you the same thing I told your daughter—I didn't see—"

"My daughter?"

"—or hear anything. I wash dishes in the kitchen, and that job doesn't come with a view—"

"What do you mean, you told my daughter?"

"That young woman who said she was Denny's sister—she was here last night. She asked for everyone who worked here the night it happened."

"My daughter was here last night?"

"Well, the woman said she was Denny Tran's sister, so, yes? She had a long chat with Miss Flora. She couldn't find Phat Luong because he's a flake who starts late, leaves early, and spends more time smoking out here than serving in there." He cocked his head toward the restaurant stairs. "But Mr. Ly and I—we were both in the kitchen the night it happened. We didn't see anything. We can't help."

"But what about afterward? When you came out of the kitchen? Did you see anything?"

"A boy on the ground, a screaming white woman, and a family that had turned their chairs to face the wall. Same thing I told the police. I didn't see what happened or who did it. I'm sorry."

Hanh's eyes had fogged up again, his hands still gripping the edge of the milk crate.

"I tell you what, though: you have a gutsy daughter. I don't know if I'd be able to do what she did—"

"What did she ask?"

Jimmy Carter scratched his ear. "Same as you. She wanted to know what I saw, what happened, how people looked. You know, details."

Hanh's fingers began to hurt from how hard he was holding on to the crate.

"But, you know, even if I did see something—even if any of us saw anything—what would it change? You can't turn back the clock."

"And you told my daughter that?"

"Yeah. What happened was tragic. I'm sorry for your loss. But doing what she was doing, going around to each person, digging—what does it change?"

"And did she listen to you?"

Jimmy shook his head. "Your daughter was on a mission."

Before he had time to process what he'd just heard, Hanh was back on his feet and walking away.

"You okay?" Jimmy called.

"I have to go," Hanh called back. He felt the pieces click

together in his mind. He should have given his daughter more credit. He should have known that she wouldn't retreat like him and his wife. He wanted to kick himself for not seeing sooner what she'd been up to. He power walked, legs and arms swinging, as he passed the turnoff for the bank and kept going in the direction of home.

Chapter 10

Ky overturned her childhood bedroom that afternoon, going through old Hello Kitty–bound journals in the hope of finding an address for Minnie. She checked her mother's phone book in the kitchen, but nothing was organized alphabetically, everything was in Vietnamese, and her mother liked to use nicknames that didn't correspond with any names that Ky knew. She felt embarrassed—how had she been so close to Minnie for so many years and not even know where she lived?

Ky thought her mother had returned home when she heard the front door click open, but it turned out to be her father, still in his work shirt and pants, without his briefcase.

"Where's Mum?" Ky asked in English. "The car's in the driveway, but she's not—"

"She took the bus to Wollongong," her father responded in Vietnamese, removing his shoes and making his way to the kitchen.

"What's in Wollongong?"

"The big Buddhist temple," he said. "She thinks the bigger

the Buddha, the better the chances of your brother reincarnating into something good."

"Dad . . ."—Ky handed the phone book to her father—"how do I find Minnie in here?"

He took it in his hands, flicked through its creased pages. "Why are you looking for her?"

Ky had been waiting to tell her parents what she knew—waiting for the moment when she knew the full story, waiting until she understood why it had to be Denny. She had hoped that if she was the one to figure it out, she could also be the one to share it in the gentlest way possible, to give her parents closure, to spare them from any more pain. She now felt close to knowing, but no closer to understanding.

"Because Minnie might know why it happened," she said, still unable to look her father in the eye.

That would be the last piece of the puzzle, Ky decided. Whatever Minnie held would help her complete the story. And then she could tell her parents.

"Are you going to tell me more?" her father said, still holding the phone book.

"I just need to talk to her first," Ky said, feeling impatient.

Her father took a breath as if to speak. Ky expected him to demand that she spill what she knew; that he wasn't going to help her until she explained what she'd been doing since she'd been home. Instead, he sighed, opened the phone book, and began ruffling through the pages.

"Your mother is insane. What is the logic of this phone book? I don't even know where to find . . ." He trailed off, running his finger down each page while squinting at her mother's cursive Vietnamese. Finally, his finger came to a halt. He mouthed something to himself before passing the phone book to Ky.

"She has her listed as 'Second Daughter,'" her father said, shaking his head. "I don't know if they still live there. Maybe they've moved, or maybe Minnie has moved, like you."

Ky tried to take the phone book, but her father kept holding on, his finger on a McBurney Road address.

"Dad," Ky said, giving the phone book a tug.

"Just because your mother doesn't want to know," her father said, "doesn't mean she doesn't care."

Ky looked at him, confused. "What do you mean?"

"Details. You want details. Your mother doesn't."

Ky took a deep breath. But before she could speak, her father continued. "It's a different way of thinking. She doesn't care about the why; she only cares about what is or what isn't—that's just how she is."

"And what about you?"

Time seemed to slow as they each held a different end of the phone book, neither of them willing to let go. When her father finally released his grip, the pages flopped and hung off the spine.

"I want you to tell me what you know once you find her."

Ky met his eyes—she noticed for the first time how much he'd aged since she left Sydney, the way gravity tugged at his skin, his posture the result of a man who carried a burden even in his sleep. She wanted to go back in time, to childhood, when she could still hug him without self-consciousness. She nodded.

"You promise?"

"Yeah," she said. "I promise."

"You are a brave girl," he said, "brave enough for you and me." Then he turned and left the kitchen, leaving Ky to grab her mother's car keys, start up the family's Daihatsu, and fight the urge to completely come apart.

Chapter 11

The first time Minnie laid eyes on Thien Huynh, she was nine and he was twelve and she thought he was the most mesmerizingly pretty person she had ever seen. His face was sharp, his skin the color of a freshly baked loaf of bread, and his cheekbones so delicate and defined that she imagined someone in art class building his head by painting on thin sheets of clay.

"Of course Minnie remembers Thien!" her mother said, giving Minnie a slap on the back so hard that she almost fell off her stool. They were at a birthday party for a family friend, where Minnie took note of the men chain-smoking in the backyard while doing shots of Hennessy and the women nervously eyeing their husbands—the same nervous look her mother had whenever her own father drank. Minnie looked across the room at the sullen-looking Thien, who sipped Fanta from a plastic party cup.

Her mother, who managed to look poor even when she wore her best clothes, was talking to a young woman who was holding a sleeping baby, the infant's droopy cheeks resting on her shoulder.

"We were all in Fairy Meadow together," the young woman said. "You called me Big Sister Flora. Do you remember?"

Minnie brought her shoulders to her ears before dropping them. "Do you remember *me?*" she asked in return.

The woman looked surprised, then smiled. "I guess there were a lot of people at Fairy Meadow, weren't there?"

Minnie remembered only fragments of her time at the Fairy Meadow migrant hostel: that she was already toilet trained on arrival; that, in those days, her parents exclusively wore donated clothes—the floral shirts and flare-legged pants that made them look like hippies, like their feet were poking out of trumpets; that there were curved wooden huts that rose from the grassy ground where she took English lessons with other children; that the teachers—all white—spoke slowly, and far too loudly, as though Minnie were dumb and deaf.

Among the things she didn't remember: teaching herself to sound like the teachers by copying the shapes of their mouths when they spoke; the revolving door of people who took her to the cafeteria several times a day because her parents were always working; the piles of donated children's books that her young mind used to make connections between letters, which formed words, which turned into sentences, which she understood without being able to explain how; wetting the bed once, which led to her father twisting her arm until something snapped. Sometimes she thought she remembered how her skin itched under the plaster, how much it stank when the cast came off, but she didn't know if these were her own memories or simply things she'd heard from her mother.

The birthday party had ended like so many others, with a couple arguing, a man vomiting, and a child being spanked in front of everyone for talking back. Minnie spotted Thien slipping packets of Marlboro Golds lying around into his trouser pockets. When he noticed her staring, he held a finger to his lips and gave her a wink. Minnie smiled, hypnotized by the way he drifted across the room, going unnoticed by the grown-ups, stealing a sip of one person's beer here, pocketing someone else's lighter there, then finally fishing a set of car keys out of his aunt Flora's handbag before disappearing from the party.

"Are there any boys you like?" she asked Ky the next day at school as they shared a Vegemite and cheese sandwich.

Ky thought for a moment. "Steven Kowalski," she said, before blushing at her own admission. "But it's not like I wanna be his girlfriend or anything!"

Minnie grimaced. "Even with his weird fang tooth?"

"I dunno!" Ky said, crossing her arms. "He's good at soccer, and he's kind of nice sometimes, and he didn't yawn when I did show-and-tell last year. But it's not like I wanna marry him or anything!"

"Is it weird to like a guy who's older?" Minnie asked.

"You mean, like, someone in year four?"

"Or maybe year six."

"Ew! That's too old," Ky said. "That's *high school*. No way, José. You don't have a boyfriend, do you? Oh my god, do you have a boyfriend? I can't believe you didn't tell me. That is so wrong! I thought I was your—"

"Chill out, Ky, I'm just doing a hypnothoughtical."

"A what?"

"It's when you think of a what-if situation."

"Oh."

The second time Minnie saw Thien was five years later. The

school year was winding down, Christmas beetles had begun clustering around the drinking fountains, and a restlessness was in the air. It felt to Minnie like half the school was wagging class.

"What could they be doing?" she said as she slung her backpack over a shoulder after the last bell, the same question she found herself asking in the lead-up to every school holiday.

"Who cares?" said Ky, whose own bag made her look tiny, who hunched under the weight of all the textbooks she insisted on bringing to school, even though they were rarely used in class. "They're gonna fail and we're gonna come first."

"Yeah, I know, you always say that, but what could they be *doing* that's so much better than what *we're* doing?"

Ky's mouth went tiny in thought. "Don't they just hang out on the red chairs, or something?"

"For *six hours* a day?"

"Why do you care? They're just wasting their lives."

"Doing *what*!?"

When they reached the school gates, they raised their eyes to the group of students standing on the sidewalk, cigarettes tucked behind their ears, shirts hanging out and trouser ends dragging beneath their shoes. Ky looked away, tutting under her breath.

It was easy to spot a truant. They made the effort of putting on their school uniform, but they always did a sloppy job of it—top buttons undone, pants unbelted, and most baffling to Minnie, neckties loosened and dangling so low down their chests that she didn't know why they bothered. Every now and again, Minnie and Ky would spot a student who had abandoned the pretense of coming to school altogether and dressed head to toe in black. Those people intrigued Minnie the most. Where did they go during the school day? And more important, why did they come back?

"Stop staring," Ky whispered.

But Minnie didn't feel like listening to Ky. She wanted to get closer, to understand what they were doing, to find out what she was missing, to—

"Hey!" one of the girls dressed in black said, locking eyes with Minnie. She looked about sixteen, wore thick black eyeliner, a spaghetti-strap top, and flared pants. "What you looking at?"

Ky and Minnie stopped in their tracks—Minnie could feel her friend's body tense beside her, while she herself was overcome with giddiness. Without thinking, she called back, "You!"

The group of about half a dozen truants, all older than Minnie and Ky, looked at one another. Minnie saw one of them mouth to the others, *For real?*

"Why you looking at me?" the black-clad girl called back, amused.

Minnie shrugged. "Looks like you're having fun," she said.

"You think this . . ."—the girl pointed at the ground where she was standing—"looks fun?"

"If it's not fun, why do it?" Minnie said.

She felt Ky's hand on her arm—it was time to go. But Minnie wasn't done. As long as the truants were willing to talk to her, she wanted to talk to them.

The girl in black smirked. "Who you think you are, chị hai?"

Minnie had only ever been called chị hai by Ky's mother, who used the term any time she or Ky didn't listen to her, like when they refused to wear turtlenecks under their school uniforms in winter ("You think you're immune from catching colds, chị hai? You think you're so tough that you can beat winter?!"), or when they resisted carrying parasols on their walks home from school ("You think you can beat the sun, chị hai? You'll both tan like refugees!"). In Mrs. Tran's mouth, chị hai was patronizing—a reminder to both of them of how little real power they had. But coming from a fellow teenager, chị hai seemed to take on its true meaning. It was electrifying for Minnie to think, even for a moment, that someone might actually respect her enough to call her chị hai and mean it.

"I—" she said. Though usually never at a loss for words, Minnie found herself so preoccupied with the thrill of the interaction that she lost her train of thought.

And that was when Thien appeared, pulling up to the curb in a white Honda—the kind that was low to the ground, with a rear spoiler so high that Minnie could have squeezed her head through it. When he stepped out of the car, she recognized him right away. He was taller and looked like he should be in year twelve—his Adam's apple was noticeably pronounced, and his jawline had grown solid and more defined. But the sharp cheekbones, the smooth appearance of his skin, the sullen face—none of that had changed. He was still the prettiest boy Minnie had ever seen.

"Oi," he called out, arms resting on the roof of the car, "who's coming?"

Everyone in the group raised a hand. When Thien cocked his head, they piled into his car, some of them sitting on one another's laps.

Ky started walking again, but it was now Minnie's turn to grab her by the arm.

"Hey!" Minnie called to Thien, her words finally returning to her. "I know you!"

Several heads poked out of the Honda's windows. Thien focused on Minnie, then looked behind himself, before returning his eyes to her round face. "Oh, yeah?"

"Yeah. We were at the same birthday party for some old guy, years ago. Your auntie talked to me."

Minnie watched as Thien shifted his weight from one foot to another, his tongue running over his teeth. The people in the car craned their necks to watch them.

"Oh, yeah, I remember you," he said, mouth pulled into a smirk—it was clear he had no recollection of her. "You were a baby, right? A big crybaby?"

The group in the car laughed. Minnie looked at Ky, who kept her eyes on the ground between her feet. "I was nine, and I never cry."

"Oh, is that right?" Thien said.

"Yeah, that's right."

"Careful, Thien," the girl in black said from the back seat. "Chị hai over there will fuck you up."

Laughter echoed from the Honda again. "Is she right? You gonna fuck me up? You a chị hai?"

"No, why would I—"

"Then what you want from me?"

A half dozen things raced through Minnie's mind: she wanted to know what he and his friends did all day if they weren't in school; she wanted to know why they came back to Cabramatta High even when they didn't have to; she wanted to know if she could come along, just to see for herself; she wanted to know if he'd be her friend, because even though she knew nothing about him, she wanted him to keep talking to her, because this sidewalk exchange inexplicably filled her insides with expanding bubbles and made her ecstatic.

"Nothing," she lied, worried about coming on too strong.

"You sure?"

"Yeah," Minnie lied again. "Just wanted to say hi."

Thien nodded and smiled. "All right, then. Hi, chị hai."

"My name is Minnie."

"Okay, hi, chị hai Minnie. I'm Thien."

Later that day, on their walk home from school, Ky gave Minnie the silent treatment.

"Why aren't you guys talking?" Denny said.

"Your sister's being moody."

"No, I'm not!" Ky said, arms folded across her body as she walked.

Minnie and Denny made eyes at each other. Hers read: *You see?* His: *Oh, yeah.*

"She's pissed that I talked to new people."

"No, I'm not!"

Minnie looked at Denny again—they both raised their brows.

The three of them instinctively held hands at every crosswalk and picked up the pace when they crossed the footbridge over the train station. At Ky's house, they made sunny-side up eggs on toast with soy sauce. Ky slammed cupboards and drawers and kept breaking the yolks because she was rough with the eggs.

"You need to be gentler with them," Minnie said, standing by the stove. "Here, I'll do it—"

"I don't need your help," Ky said, flipping one of the eggs, even though none of them liked it that way.

Minnie sighed. When she was younger, she'd loved spending every afternoon with Ky: the Tran family always had a full fridge, Ky and Denny were always down for whatever game Minnie devised, and they could watch TV together after finishing their homework. But the lack of time apart had started to wear on her. Sometimes she felt like she was suffocating under Ky's expectations, like her friend was trying to keep her perfectly preserved and contained in a vessel in which she no longer fit. And maybe she was grating on her friend, too. Minnie had noticed that since the start of year eight, without room to breathe, they both had grown short with each other, with every frustration, snippy comment, and disagreement between them never having a chance to be defused by time and space. Minnie knew that Ky was her best friend, her *only* friend. At the same time, she was sick of Ky. Sometimes she fantasized about throwing a mug at her friend's face.

"I think I'm gonna go home," she said, moving away from the stove toward her school bag.

Ky looked taken aback. Denny, who had been waiting for the toast to pop, also whipped his head around. "But Mum's not home yet," he said.

"I'm gonna walk home by myself."

"But," Denny said, looking to Ky for help, "it's not safe to walk by yourself."

"I'm old enough," Minnie said, making her way to the front door.

"But what if you get kidnapped?" Panic crept into Denny's

voice. "Just wait for Mum to come home and then she can take you—"

"For Christ's sake, Minnie, stop being an idiot," Ky said, dropping the spatula into the frying pan.

"Excuse me?"

"It's not safe to walk home by yourself. What if something happens to you?"

"I'd rather take the risk than deal with your bullshit," Minnie said, reaching for the doorknob.

"You were talking to naughty kids! How am I supposed to react?"

"You don't even know what naughty kids do when they're not in school!"

"So?"

"So you don't know anything about them," Minnie said, trying to not raise her voice, even though her frustration with Ky threatened to bubble over. "You don't know that they're bad people. You're just judging them because they don't wear their school uniform properly."

"And they don't go to school!"

"Whatever, I'm leaving."

Minnie stood with her hand on the knob, pausing for effect, and when no one said anything, she began to slowly turn it, letting it squeak like nails on a chalkboard.

"Fine! I'm sorry!" Ky said, stomping from the kitchen to the front door. "Happy now?"

"Sorry for what?"

"Sorry for being . . ." Ky crossed her arms again, a child reluctantly admitting wrongdoing. "I dunno!"

"A controlling bitch?"

"Is that what you think I am?"

"I dunno, Ky. Denny, would you say your sister was being a controlling bitch?"

Denny's mouth opened and froze in the shape of an O. He raised both hands in surrender.

"Okay, fine, sorry I was being a bitch. Now you happy?"

"I'd be happier if you weren't a bitch to begin with," Minnie said—surprising herself with her own meanness; with her inability to control how she felt. "But I'll accept your apology."

On the inside, she fought the urge to tell Ky that she wasn't satisfied at all. That beneath what little control she had left of herself were barbed-wire words and an anger she didn't fully understand, waiting to break free.

The third time Minnie crossed paths with Thien was weeks after their encounter on the sidewalk, on the last day of school. Ky's family had started their vacation early—a trip to Warner Bros. Movie World on the Gold Coast that they'd spent all year saving for—leaving Minnie to walk home from school by herself. Mrs. Tran had offered to take Minnie on the trip, but her mother had shot down the idea. When Minnie confronted her about it, asking why she couldn't go when the Trans were willing to cover the cost, her mother had slapped her twice without explanation. It was a familiar response. Whenever Minnie asked to have dinner with the Trans or sleep over at their house, her mother would slap her across the face. Minnie used to think that her mother hated her. Over time, she suspected that whenever anyone offered to care for Minnie, it triggered in her mother a shame so unbearable that her only way of finding relief was by shifting the blame to Minnie and accusing her of being ungrateful.

"Listen," Ky's mother said to Minnie the day before they left for the trip, "as soon as the last school bell rings, I want you to run home. Don't walk at your usual pace. Don't make stops. Don't talk to anyone. Run straight home."

Minnie had agreed, even though she had no intention of following through. Cabramatta didn't scare her. Junkies were slow, she didn't have anything for anyone to steal, and her family was too broke for her to be a ransom kidnapping target.

Mrs. Tran sent her home with eight hefty bánh tét, each weighting at least a kilo, to tide her over for the ten days that the Tran family was away. She showed Minnie how to unwrap the football-size sticky rice cake from its banana leaves, slice off a hockey puck portion, and microwave it without drying it out.

"You'll never go hungry with bánh tét," Mrs. Tran said. "Sticky rice is dense, like this." She formed a fist. "It's like eating rocks. Your stomach will spend forever digesting it."

"Great," Minnie said, not afraid to be sarcastic around Mrs. Tran because, unlike her own mother, who hit her whenever she did anything that resembled talking back, Mrs. Tran found her funny. "I love eating rocks."

The last week of school without Ky left Minnie bored out of her mind. The teachers had nothing left to teach, so they put on VHS tapes of *Mary Poppins, The NeverEnding Story,* and *The Wizard of Oz*—the same three movies they'd put on during the last week of school the year before, and the year before that, and the year before that. When the last bell rang, Minnie didn't run.

Instead, she walked at a leisurely pace, brain fuzzy and somewhere in Kansas, her peers pushing past her to begin their summer break.

As she drifted toward the school gates, she saw the same group of truants from weeks earlier, half of them in school uniform, the rest in black.

"Hey, chị hai," one of the girls said when Minnie approached. "Where's your nerdy friend?"

Minnie felt an electrifying zap. She looked around to make sure the older girl wasn't speaking to someone else.

"On holidays," Minnie said, her voice croaky. She hadn't spoken all day, realized she hadn't said a word since the Tran family left for holidays at the start of the week. She snapped herself out of her VHS coma, her eyes rapidly searching the group for Thien. He wasn't there.

"Where she go?" the girl said.

"Movie World."

"Wah, so lucky. And she don't take you with her?"

The group laughed. Minnie suddenly became aware of how hot her ears felt.

"I didn't want to go," she lied. "Queensland is lame anyway."

An older boy who was playing with a lighter nodded in agreement. "Yeah, man, Queensland is full of racists."

"*Australia* is full of racists," the girl said.

"Can't go anywhere," the boy said.

"So, what are you gonna do, chị hai?"

Minnie shrugged. No one ever asked her about her plans, so she never felt like she needed to make them; every holiday spent alone was the same, a weekslong window that passed in a hunger-panged blur. But the girl's question suddenly made the holidays daunting—a void into which she would disappear unless she had plans. She was usually never at a loss for words, but the question stumped her. What *was* she going to do?

"He's here," the girl said.

The low-to-the-ground white Honda pulled up to the curb. Behind the wheel, she saw the cheekbones that seemed to refract light and a handsome, tall-nosed profile. He rolled down the passenger side window.

"Yo, get in!"

The three girls and the boy who said Queensland was full of racists did as they were told. Minnie wanted to follow them. Instead, she awkwardly stood, one foot twisting back and forth on the spot.

"What you doing there, chị hai?" Thien asked, calling from the driver's seat. "You wanna come with us or something?"

"Thien, she's just a kid," Minnie heard one of the girls say from inside the car.

Imagining the next two weeks as a black hole that threatened to swallow her—no TV, no plans, no friends—Minnie panicked at the thought of Thien's extending her a lifeline, only for the girl inside the car to retract it before she could grab onto it.

"I'm not just a kid!" Minnie called back.

The girl in the back seat stuck her head out the window. Minnie noticed that she wore long, jangly earrings that were made of thin chains, and when she looked at Minnie, her lips pressed together so that her mouth resembled a bow.

"Can I come?" Minnie said, figuring she had nothing to lose.

The girl in black pouted, making her already full lips look like she was kissing the air. "You serious, girl?" she said.

"Yeah."

"How old are you?"

"Fourteen."

The girl turned back to her friends and waited for Thien to say something.

"You got nowhere else to be?" the girl asked, turning back around, her earrings shimmying to the Honda's vibrations.

"Everywhere's racist," Minnie said.

The girl smiled. The door to the back of the car clicked open.

"Come on, chị hai," Thien said. "Get in."

Squished into the back seat with three other girls, one of whom let Minnie have her seat belt, she finally learned the names of the people who for so long had been a mystery to her.

"I'm Sarina," said the girl who had earlier called Minnie a kid. Sarina had uneven splotches on her neck. When Minnie and Ky first learned about hickeys in year seven, they'd both decided that they looked tacky and painful. Still, the girls were curious about how hickeys were created, so they each sucked on their own wrists until the blood vessels burst and left behind faint bruises that faded the next day. Minnie, wanting to push things further, insisted on latching the long mouth of a vacuum cleaner to her skin. She left perfectly round welts on her thighs and stomach. She made a wine-colored moon on Ky's left butt cheek. "Wow," Ky had said. "That sucked." They'd vowed then and there that if a boy ever tried to give them a hickey, they'd karate chop him in the nuts.

Minnie now counted five hickeys on just one side of Sarina's neck, inconsistent enough in shape not to have come from a vacuum cleaner.

In the car, she learned that Sarina was seventeen and still technically a student at Cabramatta High but had missed so many classes that she'd likely have to repeat year eleven if she ever stepped foot back in the school.

"And this is Chanlina," Sarina said, nudging the girl next to her. "But we call her Miss Soy Sauce."

"Whatever," Chanlina said. Everyone in the car laughed. Minnie was wide-eyed, amused, her fingers tingling with excitement. Her eyes tried to take in every detail about the girls: how they all wore their hair long and silky straight with face-framing layers, how Chanlina had four piercings on one earlobe alone, how the bottoms of Sarina's black flared pant legs were frayed and dirty from rubbing against the ground, how their postures were all so relaxed—unlike the tense, uptight way Ky carried herself. It was like they were made of spaghetti.

"What? We mean it nice," Sarina said. "She's Miss Soy Sauce because she's so black."

"Shut up." Chanlina crossed her arms. "Cambodians have naturally dark skin, okay? It's totally normal and even beautiful."

"And that's Alani," Sarina said, looking to the last girl in the back of the car. Alani couldn't have been much older than Minnie, but she was covered in flaky scales and her skin looked so dry it creased, making her look much older. Alani acknowledged Minnie with a nod and went back to staring out the window as the car sped through a school zone into the heart of Cabramatta.

"I'm Phil," said the boy up in the passenger's seat.

"He tells people that, but his real name is Phat Phuc," said Sarina, who made Minnie unexpectedly snort-laugh.

Minnie's eyes kept drifting back to Thien. She liked the way he drove with just one finger on the steering wheel. She liked the way the light hit the tops of his cheekbones. She liked how whenever the car erupted in laughter, his lips only ever curled upward the slightest bit.

"Yeah, okay, shut up, Sarina," Phil said.

"I'm just filling her in, mate."

"Chị hai, ignore Sarina, she full of shit sometimes."

Minnie felt the familiar rush of warmth from being called chị hai by the older kids, but she wanted to make sure they knew her real name, too.

"You can just call me Minnie if you want."

"Like the mouse," Phil said.

Before Minnie could respond, the car swerved into a parking spot on a street dense with noodle restaurants, Vietnamese bakeries, and a dumpling house that Minnie had only ever heard of but never stepped foot inside.

"Yum cha or bún bò Huế?" Thien asked as he removed the keys from the ignition, twirling the key ring on his index finger.

"Yum cha!" everyone collectively shouted.

"Chị hai Minnie," Thien said, twisting his body to look at the girl, "you ready to eat like a king?"

The next ten days were the best of Minnie 's young life. With the Tran family in Queensland and her parents present only in the shoving she heard at night through her thin bedroom walls, her new friends picked her up every day to eat at restaurants she'd only ever fantasized about: the cramped establishments that served phở and bún bò Huế, the yum cha restaurants that kept refilling her teacup without her having to ask, the dessert stands that made strawberry shakes from fresh berries blitzed with sugar syrup and ice cubes. She wished Ky could have been there to try all the foods the two of them had only ever salivated over, and to also see how wrong she was to be scared of truants. They were harmless. They were better than harmless. She thought Ky would be able to appreciate that they were funny and smart, like how Chanlina had a calculator for a brain and could add up the cost of any meal before the bill even came, or how Phil could perfectly mimic any server immediately after they spoke, or how Alani was good at never making a judgy face, or how Sarina, who was definitely the smartest, could explain why colonialism was super messed up and schools were teaching it wrong. Thien remained a mystery—he rarely spoke, liked to stare, and although Minnie couldn't explain why, whenever she said something that made the corners of his lips curl upward ever so slightly, she felt like a hot water bottle had been pressed against her chest.

After they ate and Thien paid—his wallet was always fat with fifties—they would sit on the red benches in Cabramatta's Freedom Plaza, snack on hot chips from the Red Lea Chicken shop, and feel the sun on their skin while Chanlina hid in the sliver of shade.

"So what do your parents do?" Alani asked.

Minnie, drawing smiley faces into the condensation of her plastic juice cup, had to think for a moment. She rarely spoke of her parents. With Ky, the girls had an understanding, their own shorthand, developed from seeing each other nearly every day since year one. Ky could tell from a look, a throat clearing, a fidget, what might have happened in the Le household the night before. It was both comforting and frustrating for Minnie to be understood in this way. She liked that she didn't have to talk about home. But sometimes she wished that Ky would ask. She wondered whether Ky knew that not talking about it didn't make it go away.

"Mum sews clothes for people," Minnie said.

"She do it at home?" Alani said.

"No," Minnie said. "Someone else's garage."

"That's good. You don't want it in your house," said Alani, who picked at a scab that had formed in the dry crook of her elbow. "Both my parents sew in our house and it's terrible."

"Yeah?"

"It's just fabric fluff everywhere. You can't breathe. Nothing can breathe. That's why I'm like this." She rubbed her parched, inflamed skin that looked angrier today than usual. "Doctor said I'm allergic. The fluff makes my eczema worse."

Minnie felt bad for Alani, whose skin stretched taut when she smiled or frowned.

"Would they ever move their sewing machines somewhere else?" Minnie asked. "Or change jobs?"

"Ha!"

"Why don't your parents change jobs so they can be home to take care of you?" Thien said, lighting a cigarette that smelled like her dad's Marlboro Reds. Minnie felt a jolt of embarrassment, like she'd been caught saying something stupid.

"Because . . ." she started, hoping that by simply speaking, her mind would pluck out the words to spell the truth.

"Because how do they even do that?" Sarina interrupted.

She tilted her chin toward Thien, indicating that she wanted a cigarette. He put one directly between her lips and lit it for her like Minnie had seen people do in the movies. Never had Minnie wanted so badly to smoke. "Most people who leave Vietnam are just normal, you know?" Sarina said. Minnie loved listening to her, how weird her accent was, how it was equal parts thick Aussie drawl and FOB. "They are not superheroes. They don't have superpowers. You don't just go from being a normal person to a refugee to a successful person just like that."

"What about all these shop bosses?" Phil said, squatting atop the red benches with a straw sticking from his mouth like a toothpick. "They FOB as fuck and they rich."

"They're exceptions," Sarina said.

"They got lucky," said Alani.

"If you survive being a refugee, you got lucky," Sarina said. "You make it out alive, you don't get raped, you don't drown, you don't get blown up, you come here, you got lucky."

"Well, I don't feel lucky," Alani said, scratching at her raw elbows again.

"You get lucky, then you get bad lucky," Sarina said, smiling at Minnie, who beamed. "Look, everything sucks, but if you're pissed off at your parents 'cause they work a shitty job, you're pissed off at the wrong people."

"But *you're* pissed off at your parents," Thien said, his head in a cloud of smoke as he looked off into the distance, coolly disinterested. "You hate them."

"Yeah, well, it's not because of their jobs," Sarina said, looking at the space between her knees.

"Yes it is," Thien said, his eyes still far away. "You never had someone at home to look after you."

"I don't want to talk about this," Sarina said, letting her head hang. Thien began rubbing her back with his hand, stopping at her neck and stroking the wisps of stray hairs with a finger. Minnie wanted that.

"What about your dad?" Alani asked, turning the conversation back to Minnie.

Minnie's brain cycled through at least a dozen possible responses to the question. Her father was: A gambler. A chain-smoker. A heavy drinker. An anticommunist. A veteran. A former prisoner of war who escaped a reeducation camp and then escaped Vietnam with his young family. A toe amputee. A person who had broken her arm. A person who choked her mother. A person who sometimes had lots of money and sometimes had zero money. A possible womanizer, although she didn't have proof. An owner of a busted-up red Camry that wouldn't start if the weather was too hot or too cold. An absent father whom she hadn't seen in weeks. She could word vomit all the English she knew. But she didn't want to scare away her new friends.

"He works in a factory," she said.

"Doing what?"

"Comalco."

"Dang," Alani said. "That's a stable job."

"Yeah," Minnie said, feeling let down by her parents again.

Before she could ask everyone else about their own parents, Thien told them it was time to go. He offered to drop everyone off at their respective homes before he took off for work. He never elaborated on what he did.

"Come on, Thien, I don't want to go back to my shithole," said Alani.

"Either I drive or you walk."

"Can't we come with?" Minnie asked.

"Fark no, girlie," he said, shaking his head like one of those Chihuahua bobbleheads Minnie had seen in people's cars. "Now come on, all of you. Home."

The next day, when Ky's family returned from vacation, Minnie found herself sitting at home, waiting for Thien, Sarina, Phil, Chanlina, and Alani to pick her up in the white Honda as they had done every day for nearly two weeks. She told herself that the Trans would need time to unpack, that Ky probably didn't need to see her so soon, and maybe she could ask Thien if Ky could join them next time, because despite the anxiety that radiated off her friend like a UFO glow, Ky was cool. Maybe not Sarina-cool, but in her own way cool—she was always there. She had always been there. From the first day of kindergarten when they both sported bowl cuts, and they both were lonely without having the words to describe that sad, empty feeling inside their chests, and a miniature Ky stood next to an even shorter Minnie while they washed their hands in the girls' restrooms and asked, "Are you my friend?" and Minnie, who had so many English words in her head that she never got to use at home, said, "Yes."

But her new friends were a no-show that day. Minnie tried not to worry—Thien had said that his work was unpredictable, and since her dad tripped over the telephone wire a week earlier when he was drunk and accidentally tore it out of the wall, there was no way for them to call her. Still, she got her hopes sky-high every morning, excited for the extravagant meals they ate, the ease with which they moved through the world, the tacit understanding between them that there was something very wrong in each of their homes and, when they were together, none of it really mattered.

When her new friends were still nowhere to be seen two days later and she felt faint from eating nothing but the crusted remnants of a bánh tét and a frozen bag of pandan-flavored mantou buns that had been in the fridge for so long they'd become part of the appliance, she finally walked to Ky's house.

"Where the heck you been?" Ky said when she answered the door, one hand on her hip. Her tan had deepened from the Queensland sun. "We've been calling your phone but no one answered."

"Whoa," Minnie said, surprised by her friend's darkened complexion. "Miss Soy Sauce."

It took a moment for Ky to register what Minnie meant. Her shoulders slumped in defeat. "Man, I know. I wore sunscreen and a hat and everything." Ky presented her browned arms to Minnie. "Mum says I look like a refugee."

Minnie gave her friend a sympathetic pat on the shoulder.

"Wait, how did you get here?"

"I walked," Minnie said.

Ky's mouth hung open.

"Don't," Minnie said, one hand raised. "I don't wanna hear it."

Ky crossed her arms.

"You gonna let me in or what?" Minnie said.

Ky moved out of the doorway.

"Anyway," Ky said, "I got you a Tweety Bird key ring from Movie World. And you missed two days of *Young Talent Time*. I recorded it for you."

The comforting familiarity of Ky wrapped around Minnie like a fuzzy blanket.

"We can watch the episodes I recorded, and then we can watch the ones my auntie recorded for me while we were on holidays, but before that, we can look at photos from Movie World, Dad developed like a hundred of them, and at some point we have to do the homework Mum left for us because she said we can't just watch TV all day—don't worry, it's just algebra for babies—and there's phở for lunch if you're hungry."

Minnie was always hungry. They reheated the soup Mrs. Tran left on the stove and rinsed a bag of bean sprouts from the fridge. When lunch was ready, she inhaled the phở—soup and all—so quickly that her belly bulged against her hand-me-down T-shirt that inexplicably read: SYDNEY PLACE SO GOOD TO GO ON HOLIDAYS.

She fought the need to yawn as Ky provided commentary on a stack of photos showing the Tran family with Bugs Bunny, the Tran family with a giant Tweety Bird, the Tran family when they'd journeyed farther south along the Australian coast to visit the Big Banana, one of Australia's many "big" things that served as tourist attractions. The banana was hollowed through the middle and could fit at least a dozen people. Minnie didn't get it.

"It's just screens with stuff for you to look at," Ky said. "It's near where they grow bananas or something. It was cool but also boring."

When Ky started narrating their encounter with the Looney Tunes characters in Movie World, Minnie turned the Tweety Bird key ring in her hand a few times, secretly disappointed that Ky didn't realize that she'd lost interest in Tweety a year ago. And when they got through their second episode of *Young Talent Time* and Ky sang along to the song's closing theme of "All My Loving," Minnie suddenly felt much, much older than her friend, like Ky had been frozen in time while Minnie had experienced life in warp speed. Maybe Ky didn't want to know about Thien and Sarina. Maybe she wasn't ready. Minnie pictured Ky freaking out, telling Mrs. Tran, who would tell her parents, who would ruin everything. Or maybe, even if she told Ky about her new friends, it wouldn't count for anything, because where were Thien and Sarina and Alani and Phil and Chanlina now, anyway? She kept her mouth shut as Ky continued flipping through photos and wondered: Was it worse to feel alone because you'd been abandoned, or to be in the presence of a friend and still feel alone?

Was there a world where Minnie did things differently? A world where, six months after last seeing Thien and friends, she spotted his white Honda in the street and ignored it? A world where, after seeing his gorgeous face again, she fought the hot water bottle warmth that spread across her chest and refused to speak with him? A world where, after hearing that he'd just spent six months in prison on drug charges and Sarina had been sent by her family to a strict Catholic school on the South Coast and the others had fallen off the radar entirely, she chose to stay away instead of allowing Thien back in and closer than ever? A world where, upon violently vomiting after smoking her first heroin-laced joint, she decided that it wasn't for her, and she would instead get her highs from doing well in school and going to university and becoming the fearless journalist that the career quiz said she could be? Was there a world where Minnie chose Ky over Thien?

Maybe. But it was beyond Minnie's imagination. She'd tried to picture it, tried to place herself next to Ky at their high school graduation, Denny carrying their bouquets of flowers for them, opening their university admissions letters at the same time, celebrating with the Tran family at Lucky 8. But the images were always distorted, incomplete, left hanging, because the undeniable truth was that it felt too good to be with Thien, and it felt too good to be chosen by someone so beautiful, and it felt too good to be wanted—desperately, possessively, unreasonably—and it felt too good to smoke and have her anger and disappointment dissolve, and even when she later realized that Thien was a disappointment, that what she mistook for mysteriousness was actually hollowness, and what she mistook for love was dependency, and what she mistook for empower-ment was a trap, she didn't know where to go. She'd waited too long, wasted too much time, and Ky was gone.

The barbed-wire words, exchanged between friends in the final months of year ten:

"You're jealous."

"Why would I be jealous of the naughty, no-future, waste-of-life losers you're hanging out with?"

"Because you don't have anyone else."

"*Pfft.*"

"You're lonely and alone because you're a judgmental control freak who's fucking miserable to be around."

"At least I'm not some piece of trash who hangs out with junkies."

"So that's what I am to you? See what I mean? You're a fucking snob and you don't even have a right to be."

"Oh, yeah, and why's that?"

"Because who the fuck are you?"

"Who the fuck are *you*?"

"Someone who tried."

"As if you tried. You ran off to join those naughty kids the moment you could. You're just always looking for something better, always ready to ditch the people who helped you, always finding ways to waste your stupid life. You're so ungrateful and—"

"Excuse me?"

"I said you're fucking ungrateful! If it wasn't for me, you'd be starved to death and the police would have put you in foster homes and—"

"Oh, go fuck yourself, you didn't do shit."

"Your dad's an alco and your mum's useless."

"Umm, earth to Ky, *your* dad's an alco—"

"Well, at least he doesn't hit us!"

"Real fucking high bar to clear, father of the year, bravo—"

"And we took care of you!"

"Oh, thank you *so* much for personally raising me, Ky, thank you *so* much for keeping me alive, I don't know what I would have done without you."

"Stop being sarcastic, it's ungrateful."

"Oh, thank you *soooo* much. Is this the part where you tell me how much I owe you? Where you tell me you own me and that I better be *grateful* for the opportunity to put up with your bullshit?"

"Why are you wasting your life like this? Why do you have to be so stubborn and—"

"Because why should I have to do whatever you choose to do? Why should I play some stupid game where we're meant to lose anyway?"

"What the hell are you talking about?"

"For Christ's sake, Ky, the game's rigged! It doesn't matter how smart you are or how hard you work or how many lamingtons you shove in your mouth, they'll never see you as one of them. Never ever ever ever. I bet you a million bucks—"

"I'm not gambling with you."

"Well, I'm not playing their stupid game."

"There's no point talking to you."

"I'm glad we agree."

"Where are you going?"

"I always knew you were a stuck-up cunt. Thanks for confirming it."

"Oh, fuck you."

"Bye!"

"Fuck you!"

"Bye!"

"I hate you!"

"Bye-bye-bye!"

★

Coming back had been a panicked decision. After Thien had dragged her by the hair from Lucky 8 into his car and their dinner party had dispersed at high speed down Cabramatta's residential roads, Minnie knew that this was it—in hurting Denny, Thien had crossed a line Minnie didn't even know she had. It was over between them, for good, and she had to go somewhere Thien wouldn't look. They'd fought in the frantic car ride from Lucky 8 to the filthy apartment they shared, Minnie out of control, punching and kicking and scratching and trying to explain who Denny was while Thien restrained her from behind the wheel, pulling over once and threatening to kill her if she didn't calm down. She had threatened to kill him in return. At the apartment, they'd both gotten dangerously high, Thien slurring apologies while Minnie felt so far from herself that she couldn't even form words. In the morning, the image of Denny's limp body seared into her eyes, she got up while Thien was still unconscious and ran.

Despite being gone for so long, she noticed that the public housing unit in which she'd grown up was mostly unchanged. The air was heavy with the familiar stale scent of mothballs; the furniture was covered in the same yellowed and mottled upholstery that her father had countless times thrown up on; and her childhood bedroom, which consisted of a single mattress on the floor and plastic storage bins, was exactly as it had been when she last lived with her parents. She'd been relieved to see that her father was gone, but it unnerved her how much the apartment felt like a time capsule, every corner reminding her of the early blind optimism that had swallowed her when she first met Thien.

It also reminded her of the ways her best friend had hurt her and the ways she had hurt her best friend. It reminded her of Denny, whom she'd seen grow from a nappy-wearing toddler to gangly teenager. She searched her mind for clearer memories, for better memories—ones that could push out what she'd seen at Lucky 8—but she managed only distorted flashes. She saw Denny playing Connect 4 with Ky. She saw the three of them walking home from school. She saw the letter, written in Vietnamese, sent from her high school. She saw the way the room spun after her father hit her so hard she collapsed. She saw Thien's white Honda, whisking her away from danger. A day passed. Then another. And another. She saw flashes, she got high, she hid under her sheets. Her mother never bothered her.

After a week at home, Minnie still flinched when she brushed her wet hair, her scalp tender from where Thien had grabbed a fistful and forced her out of Lucky 8. The burst blood vessels in her left eyeball were barely visible and the bruise across her eye had lightened to a sickly yellow. She didn't bother to apply concealer. No one would see her. Besides, seeing in her own reflection what Thien had done to her when she'd tried to stop him—the way he'd thrown her against the table when she tried to get between him and Denny—was an important reminder that under no circumstances was she to go back to him. She imagined how he would come for her, which he did every time she ran away—after the first time he'd hit her, just like her father had; after she'd heard about home invasions gone wrong and knew he was responsible; after his unprompted outbursts, like a demonic possession, that made his eyes go blank, that he couldn't control; after the times he'd tried to domesticate her, even as he sold her on their lives being acts of rebellion. It didn't matter if she'd been violent in return. It didn't matter if she'd hurt him with words. It didn't matter if she felt like trash that no one could possibly want—a fool who had made an irrevocable mistake, so far gone she might as well be dead—he always came for her. And every time she'd gone back to him because he was there, because he had come for her when no one else had, because he would never abandon her, because he made her feel wanted, *so* wanted, like she belonged, she finally belonged, if not in this country, then at least with him. But this time had to be it. There wasn't a world where she could forget the look on Denny's face when Thien towered over him, the yelp she heard when Thien pulled him to his feet by his shirt collar.

Back in her childhood bedroom, she put on clothes that her mother had left untouched from when she was in high school. Everything still fit and stank of stale cigarette smoke—her first-ever pair of black flared microfiber pants that a girl named Ngoc had given her; a Sydney tourism T-shirt that made her feel like she was a kid again. When Thien came for her, she would tell him that things between them were well and truly over, and if he didn't leave her alone, she wouldn't hesitate to call the police. When Thien came for her, she would float the possibility of detox, and it wasn't so much that she wanted him to detox with her, but if he didn't want to die young, maybe it was something he would take seriously. When Thien came for her, she'd lay out a plan that didn't involve him in her life, although what that plan was, she still didn't know.

And when eventually a knock did sound on the apartment

door, she froze, realizing that she wasn't ready at all for Thien to come for her.

"Mum?" she called.

But she was home alone. The knock came again, urgent and loud.

Minnie tiptoed across the carpet to the door. The peephole had been painted over with nail polish. Minnie pressed her ear against the peeling paint of the wooden door. The knock came again, this time vibrating through her skull.

"Go away!" she said, imagining Thien on the other side. Next he would beg and plead and apologize and give her a dozen reasons why she should go with him. She used to buy it. She used to ache at the thought of his childhood, the abuse he received, the sense of abandonment, his damage so much worse than hers. She used to fill with warmth at the sight of him, at how in certain moments he was able to overcome his own pain to put her first, to stroke her hair as she talked about her parents, about her friend, about how loneliness felt like hunger, how deeply familiar she had been with both, how tired she was, how much she hated that she still wanted to belong—even in a country that showed no love for her, she still so badly wanted to belong—at how he had held her and kissed her and told her she would never be alone again. She used to buy it. Not anymore.

The knocking kept coming.

"I'll call the police!"

Silence. She thought that must have done it. In all their years together, she had never pulled the police card.

Then another knock.

"What the hell?" Minnie said, unlatching the door and

swinging it open. It took her eyes a moment to register that she wasn't looking at Thien.

She looked the same as Minnie had remembered, but she was lamb dressed as mutton, her outfit oppressive in its properness, her rimless glasses, tidy low ponytail, and ironed slacks adding years to her petite frame, proclaiming to the world that she was here to fit in.

"Hi," said Ky, her voice caught in her throat, her face surprised, like she didn't expect knocking to yield to a door opening.

Minnie stood frozen. Her lips parted and stayed that way.

Ky's face softened. "Can I come in?"

Chapter 12

It felt like a balloon had expanded in her belly and was threatening to pop. It felt like spiders crawling up the back of her neck. It felt like she was looking at a ghost, except the ghost was a living person—although, barely, it seemed. Minnie didn't look healthy. Her color was off—if she had been paint, it was like someone had mixed in a spoonful of gray—and there was a hard-to-pin cloudiness to her eyes. She stepped back from the doorway to make room for Ky.

"Why don't we ever go to her house?" Denny once asked a few years after Minnie began staying with them after school.

"Because Mum says there are no adults there to look after us."

"But what if she has a Nintendo?"

"She defs doesn't have a Nintendo."

"But what if she *does* and we don't know because we've never been to her house?"

Ky had been sure that if Minnie owned a Nintendo, she would have said something about it. Still, she wanted to be sure, so the next day at school, she asked.

"Why would I have a Nintendo?" Minnie said, baffled.

"I dunno, just checking."

"Weirdo."

"Hey, why do you come to our house, but we never go to your house?"

Minnie had pulled back her long untied hair, moving it out of her sweaty face. The bruises on her neck had faded, but Ky knew it was just a matter of time before they reappeared. That was the cycle with Minnie—as soon as her skin returned to a uniform beige hue, the bruised splotches were just around the corner. Ky once asked, "Why the neck?" Minnie, wordless, gently placed her own hand around the back of Ky's neck. She squeezed until Ky's skin pinched. Ky allowed herself to imagine an adult's hand in place of Minnie's, how the grip of a grown man could easily snap their necks in half. She'd shuddered, wanted to blanket her friend in balls of cotton, roll her back to the Tran family home, adopt her and make her an official forever sister.

"Your house has better food," Minnie had said.

"Oh."

"Plus, my house is boring. The TV doesn't even work."

But even if Minnie's house had had a working TV and even if there had been adults to supervise, Ky now understood why her own mother would have been reluctant to let her visit. From the outside, the windows to the McBurney Road flats appeared darkened, the exterior brick stained. Entire units looked like they had bad breath. Inside was no better—the air was stale, the paint was peeling off the walls, and Minnie's home was so sparsely furnished—a wobbly card table, two fold-out chairs, a disgusting couch, and a TV stand without a TV—she couldn't imagine them spending time here as children or teenagers.

Ky followed Minnie into a bedroom where the bedsheet curtains were drawn, casting a suffocating orange glow across the already darkened room and worsening the stuffiness. She stood awkwardly, wondering why they had come into a room with no chairs.

"Oh," Minnie said, picking up a black handbag, "I didn't mean for you to follow me in here—"

"Oh, right," Ky said, backing out of the room. "Sorry, I just—"

"No, it's—"

"I'll wait out—"

"I just came in to get cigs," Minnie said, waving her handbag at Ky. "We can talk out there." She tilted her head toward the tiny dining room they'd passed.

Ky made her way back to the card table and sat on one of the fold-out chairs. As Minnie emerged from the bedroom with an ultrathin cigarette between her lips, the smoke already creating tendrils that trailed her, she wondered again why some people were able to move through life so easily while she was constantly gripped by anxiety, so afraid of a misstep. Sitting across from Minnie, she found herself holding her breath. Minnie must have noticed, because she looked at Ky, looked at her cigarette, and looked back at Ky.

"Relax," Minnie said. "It's not like it'll kill you."

"Are you kidding?" Ky said, the public service announcements of her youth rushing through her head: *Smoking Kills; Never Swim Alone; Slip, Slop, Slap.*

"Hm," Minnie said, studying the cigarette like it was her first time smoking one. "I guess I am."

They faced each other for a while without speaking, Ky opening her mouth several times but unable to form words. Maybe that's why people smoked, she thought, watching Minnie balance the cigarette between her fingers, sucking in and blowing out smoke in lieu of talking.

For so long Ky had fantasized about confronting Minnie. In her pettier moments, she imagined a fight where she finally came prepared—nothing like the fight they'd had in year ten, when the best she could do was swear and call Minnie names—a fight where Ky would eloquently lay out her list of grievances and relitigate all the ways that Minnie had wronged her, all the ways Minnie had been wrong. In her more mature moments, she imagined an apology in which she explained herself, analyzed her own shortcomings and anxieties and insecurities and acknowledged that they were no excuse for how she'd behaved, for how possessive and mean she became. The biggest fantasy, though—the one that occupied more of her daydreams than the thoughts of apology or spite—was the one where they'd remained friends all along. The fantasy in which they'd finished high school together, gone to university together, shared a stage at graduation, kept in touch through internships and first jobs and first apartments and family drama and everything in between.

Ky had made Minnie out to be so big, so essential in her daydreams. It was jarring to see the Minnie in front of her—skinnier than Ky remembered, her arms covered in tattoos that had already started to fade, giving her body an even more weathered appearance. Ky felt her stomach drop at the sight of the ink, which took the form of an enormous tiger crawling up one of her arms, hundreds of flower petals blooming across the other, and the black outline of flames filling the space between. Ky considered Flora's description of the woman who was with Thien: A skinny girl. A heavily tattooed skinny girl.

Minnie was there. It had been Minnie's Thien.

"So," Ky finally said.

"So."

"I thought I would know what to say when I got here."

"Okay."

"But now I don't know."

When Minnie didn't respond, Ky shifted in her seat, unable to get comfortable. She'd never been speechless around Minnie. As a kid, she couldn't shut up around Minnie. But the air between them had changed, and Ky didn't know what to do, how she was meant to be, what remained between them.

"This is really weird," Ky finally said after another long pause during which they stared at each other, Ky's skin tingling at both the familiarity and the newfound foreignness of her former best friend.

Minnie shrugged. Another long pause.

Then: "You look well," Ky said.

Minnie raised a brow. "You for real?"

"I don't know," Ky said, feeling exposed. "I was just, I don't know. Making conversation. It's what people say."

"Oh, Ky." Minnie crossed her arms. "This *is* weird."

She thought she saw a flicker of a smile on Minnie's face,

a blink-and-you'll-miss-it warmth. Ky's insides were in chaos—she wanted to bask in that warmth, to draw it out even more, to reacquaint herself with what was lost. But she also wanted to draw out the truth about Denny—a truth that she knew would make her want to kill Minnie.

"I have something to ask you," Ky said.

Minnie took a deep breath, as though bracing herself. On closer inspection, she looked exhausted—the skin under her eyes was dark and puffy, the side of her face splotchy and yellow, her back slouched like she was too lethargic or too defeated to sit up straight. Ky didn't want to ask what she was about to ask. She would have gladly talked about anything else—what Minnie had been doing with herself all these years, whether she'd always lived here or if she'd recently come back, whatever happened to her parents, whatever happened to all her new friends, when she'd started smoking, why her skin looked so sallow, whether it had all been worth it.

Minnie returned Ky's gaze, but her expression remained neutral. It was one of the things that had made Minnie who she was—her ability to look without flinching, without giving anything away.

"You were there that night, at Lucky 8," Ky said. She paused and hoped Minnie would volunteer information without her having to say more. But Minnie remained still. "What happened?"

Minnie shifted her eyes to the cigarette ash that was collecting on the card table. Ky could tell by the movement of her chin that she was chewing her tongue.

"And don't lie to me," Ky said, her voice almost breaking at the thought of all the people who were at Lucky 8 who could have helped Denny but didn't; all the people who could have told the police the truth sooner but didn't.

When Minnie continued to say nothing, the heel of her foot restless and jittery, Ky surprised herself by reaching across the card table to take the cigarette from her hand and snuff it out in the ash pile. Minnie looked up, her eyes intense, her brows furrowed.

"I didn't come here to sit in silence," Ky said.

"I don't know if I can help you."

A familiar frustration arose within Ky—the same frustration she felt when witness after witness told her they hadn't seen anything when they clearly had—but with Minnie, it felt worse. Didn't they at least owe each other the truth?

"I know we haven't talked in a long time," Ky said, "but . . ."

But what? Ky could hear her own voice echo deep in her ears. Did she still know Minnie? Did Minnie know her? She made fists with her hands, angry with herself for struggling to say what needed to be said.

"You're not going to get in trouble if you tell me," Ky finally said, trying to keep her cool. She pressed her fingernails into the palms of her hands. "You can tell me, Minnie. The police have already caught the guy—"

"What?"

For the first time since she opened the door for Ky, a spark of surprise lit up Minnie's face.

"What do you mean, what?"

"You said they caught the guy. What happened? Is he with them now?"

"Yes," Ky said, annoyed that Minnie's response spelled out her priorities. She found some satisfaction in saying the next part, in knowing she could still hurt her friend: "They found him this morning. He OD'd."

Minnie's physical response was immediate—her eyes became pools, her voice wobbled. "Where did they find—"

"He overdosed at his auntie's house and the police found him dead," Ky said.

She watched Minnie blink, an enormous tear rolling down her cheek, the way her mouth went small, the way her chin wrinkled.

"It was your Thien, wasn't it?"

When Minnie didn't say anything, all but confirming that her boyfriend was Denny's killer, Ky pressed her fists together.

"So you cry when that piece of shit overdoses, but you don't even do anything when Denny is beaten to death," Ky said, her own voice starting to shake.

"Oh, give me a break," Minnie said, a flash of anger in her eyes. "What the fuck do you know about what I did?" Her gauntness exaggerated the creases on her forehead, the deep lines that appeared between her eyes, the downward pull of her lips. "*You* weren't there. *You* don't know me. *You* don't—"

"Then why can't you just tell me what happened? Do you know how much *my* family knows? Denny went to his formal, went out to dinner, then Thien Huynh kicks the life out of him. What the hell is that? How the hell does something like that even happen? What did you do?"

"Why would you think I did anything—"

"Because you were there!" Ky said, giving up on trying to

keep her cool. "Because Denny knew you and you knew the guy who killed him! Because—"

"I didn't kill Denny, okay?" Minnie said, uncrossing and crossing her arms before reaching back into her handbag for another cigarette. Her hands trembled as she tried to light it. "Denny came and said hi to me, and it set Thien off."

"Bullshit."

"It's the truth."

"You have no idea how ridiculous that sounds."

"What don't you get?"

"Denny, the least threatening human in the goddamn *world*, says hi to you, and your junkie boyfriend decides to *kill* him for it?"

"He's messed up, okay?"

"No, no. Stop right there. Explain it to me. From the start. What happened?"

"Explain *what*?"

"Don't play dumb. Tell me what happened."

Minnie puffed away at her cigarette, her hands shaking.

"We'd had a fight, okay?"

"You and Thien?"

"Yes, me and Thien."

"About what?"

"Why do *you* care?"

"Because someone here has to care!"

"About everything, okay? About how he wanted me to basically be a housewife. About how he tried to control me. About how much I was using. About how he kept accusing me of cheating even though who even has the fucking time? About every fucking thing."

"Sounds like a great boyfriend."

"Whatever, Ky."

"Whatever yourself."

"He's possessive and fucked up, okay?"

"Was."

"What?"

"He *was* possessive and fucked up," Ky said. "Past tense. Which is how I have to talk about Denny now, because of you."

"*I* didn't do *anything*," Minnie said, waving her cigarette to emphasize each word. "Thien *was* fucked up. He loses his mind sometimes and isn't himself and—"

"Would."

"What?"

"He *would* lose his mind—"

"Did you come here to talk or to fucking correct me?"

Ky swallowed. In the moment, she wanted to do neither. She just wanted to hurt Minnie.

"So we went to Lucky 8," Minnie said, "and he's giving me shit, and I'm ignoring him, and it's pissing him off even more, and then a camera flashes in our faces." Minnie kept sucking on the end of her cigarette, unaware that the tip had gone out. "Friggin' Denny. He had one of those disposable cameras, and he'd taken a photo of me. He lowers the camera and has this big goofy smile on his face, like he's so pleased with himself, like he just surprised me, and then he says hello."

"Were those his exact words?"

"Why does it matter?"

"How can it *not* matter to me, Minnie?"

Minnie, noticing that her cigarette was out, reached for the lighter again, her unsteady hands making it hard for her to light the ultrathin between her fingers.

"He said . . ."—Minnie took a drag, which seemed to calm her hands but worsen the bouncing of her knee—"'How's it going?'"

"That's it?"

"And . . ."—her knee now bounced so hard it shook the fold-out card table—"'I've missed having you around. The house is so quiet now.'"

Ky could feel her own heart thumping.

"It was . . . a super awkward thing to say. But it's also Denny, so—"

"So?"

"So if you knew your brother, you'd know he's just a super awkward kid. I mean, I remember the time when he went in for a hug when he was, like, in year three, but changed his mind midway and decided to do a handshake instead and ended up jabbing me in the chest with his outstretched fish hand."

"You're saying my brother was killed for being awkward."

"I'm saying it was a misunderstanding."

"So Denny said that awkward thing, and this Thien guy thinks—"

"I don't know if he thought Denny was my ex or whatever, which is impossible because I've never even been with anyone else, and it's Denny, for god's sake, but—"

"That's *insane*."

"I know."

"Really fucking insane."

"I know."

"Then what?"

Minnie, body fidgeting, looked away as she described how Thien punched the camera out of Denny's hands, shattering its plastic shell and destroying the film. She described how Thien knocked Denny to the ground. She described how the light in his eyes blacked out as he stomped and stomped and stomped.

"Okay, that's enough," Ky said, feeling like she couldn't breathe. "This guy was your *boyfriend*? What the hell is wrong with you?"

"I'm not making excuses for him. It was inexcusable—"

"No *shit!*"

"But he was fucked up, okay? You and me, we don't remember being refugees. We were too young. But he was old enough to remember things, and you have no idea—"

And now Ky was trembling, too, furious and bewildered that Minnie was defending the person who killed her brother. "*Our* parents were refugees. *They* remember everything. You don't see my parents going around killing anyone. Don't see your parents . . ." An image of Minnie, her bruises, the raw skin that waited to scab, sliced through Ky's thoughts. "It's not a fucking excuse, okay?"

"I'm not saying it is."

"Then what are you saying? That he was worth it? That you would trade Denny's life for—"

"You're not the only person who lost someone!"

"Because your junkie boyfriend's life was so important—"

"I'm talking about Denny!" Minnie said, now pressing both palms against her eyes.

"As if you give a fuck about Denny."

"Oh, fuck you, Ky."

"No, fuck *you!*" Ky shoved the card table so that it dug into Minnie's ribs, nearly knocking her off the rickety fold-out chair.

"You serious?" Minnie said, dusting cigarette ash off her pants.

"What?" Ky said, knowing that pushing a table into Minnie was childish, but not wanting to apologize, either. "What do you expect me to do?"

"What do you expect *me* to do? I just told you what happened. Do you want me to tell you it was my fault? Sure, fine, it was my fault, I was there, and Denny saw me and said hi to me, and it rubbed Thien the wrong way. Fine, Denny's dead because of me. But I didn't *do* anything, okay? I was just there."

"And you just sat back and watched it happen."

"What? No. I tried to pull Thien off and got the shit kicked out of me, too." Minnie pointed to the side of her face, at the yellow discoloring that turned purple and gray near her hairline. "Believe it or not, Ky, I wasn't born fucking bruised. You'd know if you ever asked."

"What's that supposed to mean?" Ky said, her body knowing what Minnie meant before her mind could catch up. She felt it in the tightness of her skin, like her own body was closing in on itself. The oppressiveness of guilt.

"You know what I mean," Minnie said, looking away, a different type of anger moving across her face.

"I thought you didn't want to talk about it."

At this, Minnie looked Ky in the eyes. "No, *you* didn't want to talk about it."

"What was I even supposed to do? I was a kid. It's not like

I could stop your parents from—" Even now, Ky couldn't say it. She felt herself transported to childhood, the sight of Minnie with new marks on her body, under her clothes—marks that were angry and purple and swollen. As a child, whenever she'd try to imagine what Minnie's dad had to do to leave bruises so broad and dark on her skin, she'd be overcome by a fear so great that she'd have to hard-blink the thought away.

"You didn't have to do anything but listen."

"Well," Ky said, flustered, "it's not like I ever told you to *not* talk about it."

"Except you'd see me with a bruised neck or a busted-up brow and never say anything."

"I didn't know if you'd want to be—"

"Heard?"

"What?"

"Ky, you never wanted to know. You wanted to pretend like we had the exact same problems and the exact same parents and the exact same options. You never wanted to be uncomfortable. You never even tried to understand what was going on."

"Well, whatever it is you went through, you're still alive. Denny isn't," Ky said, her mind defaulting to the most hurtful thing within reach because she couldn't stand how Minnie was making her feel.

Minnie's face was a collision of emotions: she glared at Ky, a rage burning under the skin, while a part of her appeared to crumble at the reminder of Denny. They sat in silence, staring at each other. When Ky couldn't bear to look at Minnie's face anymore, she returned her eyes to her hands, which were covered in half-moon impressions.

"Why didn't you go to the police?" Ky said. "Your boyfriend was abusive *and* a murderer. What if he killed someone else? Why didn't you just go to the police and tell them—"

"Are *you* insane?" Minnie said, her eyes never leaving Ky. "Were you born yesterday? Oh, yeah, hey, Mr. Officer, so my boyfriend killed a kid and beat me up, go arrest him, but please leave me alone, I'm innocent, oh, don't search my bag—" Minnie picked up her black handbag and emptied it on the card table. In it were two packs of Marlboros, four lighters, a wallet, an unsealed envelope stuffed with cash, and five narrow pencil-length packets made from shopping catalogues. "And never mind all my Fit Packs . . ."—she grabbed at the catalogue packets and shook them—"and yeah, that's twelve thousand in cash, but don't worry, I just like to carry it with me for fun, and oh, never mind my arrest record, that's not me, that's another Minh Le, ignore all that, I swear I had nothing to do with it."

"Why not just risk it?"

"What?"

Ky leaned forward, tired and angry. "Why not suck it up, go to the police, and deal with the consequences? Your boyfriend *killed* my brother."

"Because what would it change?"

"It would have gotten a killer off the streets!"

"He's off the streets now, isn't he? He can't hurt anyone anymore, can he?"

"It would have meant justice."

"Oh, come on, Ky," Minnie said, reaching for her box of cigarettes again, even though she still had a lit cigarette in her hand. "You don't honestly think people like us get justice, do you?"

"Why do you say things like that?"

"Denny's killer is dead. Do you feel any better?"

Ky didn't. She felt sick.

"Because that's as good as justice gets," Minnie said. "That's about as good as it'll ever feel."

"I hate you," Ky said.

"Welcome to the club." Minnie snuffed out her unfinished cigarette and lit another. It seemed to Ky like an impulse, like she couldn't sit still. "Did *anyone else* talk to the police?" she said, blowing smoke away from Ky's face. "I'll put money on it. I bet they didn't."

"Thien's auntie."

"And when did she do it? While he was alive? Or did she wait until he was dead and she had nothing to lose?"

When Ky didn't say anything, her tongue feeling too heavy, Minnie continued.

"Yeah, we're all selfish, but we gotta be. You think the police give a shit about Denny? You think they care about us? People won't talk because they know it's pointless, because this whole system is rigged against us."

"You've just got a chip on your shoulder. You always have."

"You *know* what I'm talking about! Stop pretending like you haven't seen it or felt it for yourself. They're all fair dinkum this and everyone gets a fair go that. This is the luckiest country in the world, right? The weather's beautiful and there's so much land and look at our beaches and everyone can get a decent-paying job and we're *so* lucky to have all of that, right? We should be *so* grateful to be here. But they don't tell us that the luck doesn't extend to us. That's the big lie. They've been shoving it down our throats since we were kids. You're a fool if you believe it. Not only are they not gonna look out for us, they're gonna turn on us the moment they think we're a threat. You *know* this. We have to look out for ourselves."

"Who's looking out for Denny, then?"

Minnie looked away, an admission that she had no good answer. "I'm sorry, okay?" Minnie said.

It had been so much easier when they were children. Knowing how hard it was to apologize, whenever one of them volunteered a sorry, the other had to forgive. Ky now felt stuck. How could she possibly forgive Minnie?

"You're not anyone else," Ky said, after another long pause during which her head started to hurt from being enveloped in Minnie's cigarette smoke.

"What?"

"You asked if *anyone else* talked to the police. If *anyone else* helped. They didn't. But you're not anyone else."

Ky could see that Minnie was chewing her tongue again.

"You grew up with us. You knew Denny. We loved you. I'm . . . I'm just so . . ." Ky was overwhelmed with everything she was feeling. What had been white rage had morphed into guilt, incredulity, confusion, and now it was taking on a form that hurt the most. "I'm so disappointed."

Another quiet pause stretched between them. They looked at everything but each other. Disappointment sat like a stone in Ky's gut. She felt like the whole world had let her down.

When Minnie's cigarette had burned out, leaving another

pile of ash between them, Ky stood up and dusted off her pants. "Get up," she said.

Minnie looked up at her.

"I said get up. You're coming with me."

"Fuck no," Minnie said.

"I'm not taking you to the police."

"Then what do you want—"

"I'm taking you to Denny. So you can apologize to him."

Ky could see the gears in Minnie's head turn, her big eyes searching Ky's face for any signs that this could be a trap. Ky cocked her head—*Come the fuck on.*

"I'm not leaving here without you," Ky said. "Get the fuck up."

After another pause, Minnie rose to her feet, scooped the sprawled contents of the table back into her handbag, and followed Ky out the door.

They drove through the center of Cabramatta with Minnie sunken into the passenger's seat, her hair falling over her face.

"So what do you do?" Ky said.

"Ha!"

When Ky didn't laugh, Minnie looked at her. "Seriously?"

"I dunno," Ky said. Every question felt inadequate and dumb. But she found herself genuinely curious.

"Awkwardness clearly runs in the family."

Ky shot Minnie a hurt look. Minnie shrugged, apologetic.

"What do *you* do?" Minnie said.

"I'm a journalist."

The words felt good rolling off her tongue, like she could sit taller, back straighter.

Minnie brought her hand to her forehead like a visor. It wasn't clear to Ky whether she was shielding her face from the sun or if she was worried about being recognized in downtown Cabramatta.

"How's that working out for you?" Minnie said.

"It's great."

If they had still been best friends, Ky would have told Minnie that the greatest part was being able to tell people she was a journalist, but that the work itself was an exhausting emotional roller coaster that she wasn't sure was worth the trouble. Were you meant to wake up every morning heavy with dread? Was the thought of calling strangers meant to make you sweat? Were you meant to constantly fight yourself, repeat *be willing, be willing, be willing,* because that was the cost of feeling like you mattered? That was the kind of honesty you could have in best friendship. She didn't know where things stood with Minnie, though—she'd barely processed the exchange they'd just had, unsure whether she should be angry or forgiving—so she stopped herself from saying more.

"Cool," Minnie said, turning the knob of the air conditioner, which was blasting hot air at both of them.

"How do you spend your days?" Ky asked.

Minnie smirked, lowered her visor hand to cover her eyes. "I do math, assess risk."

"Really?"

"An underground economy is still an economy."

Ky glanced at Minnie, confused. The two briefly looked at each other. Minnie appeared to make a snap calculation in her head as to how much she should say.

"We get the drugs in bulk from people in Strathfield. They get it from Asia. We divide them into caps. We determine market rates, coordinate street sellers. Like any business."

"Is that what those packets were? The ones in your handbag?"

"What? God, no. Girl, do you honestly not know what heroin looks like?"

Ky felt heat rise in her face. She hated feeling dumb.

"Why would I know what heroin looks like?" Ky said. "I mean, I know it's a white powder or something, but I dunno how people sell it on the streets."

"This . . ."—Minnie rummaged through her bag and pulled out one of the shopping catalogue packets—"is a Fit Pack. All the pharmacies in Cabra sell them." She unfolded the top of the pack, shook it in front of Ky's face. "You get one needle, one swab, plastic spoon, sterilized water, and a cotton ball." She refolded the top of the pack, slid it back in her bag. "It's a dollar fifty, everything you need except the heroin itself."

"Is that even legal?"

"Why wouldn't it be?" Minnie said, her hands fidgety again. She played with the zipper on her bag, stuck her hand back in to feel around. "Diabetics use needles for insulin. Cotton balls are just cotton balls. Plastic spoons are just plastic spoons."

"Wouldn't it be cheaper for you to buy that in bulk? Like, go to Woolies and get a party pack of spoons?"

Minnie groaned. "Maybe it would be, but who's even thinking like that?"

"I thought you did math."

Minnie smiled. "Touché."

"And why do you call it a Fit Pack?" Ky asked.

"Because you use it to get fit."

"What?"

"I'm assuming you've never felt withdrawal."

"Like, from caffeine?"

"Sure. You go a day without caffeine, you get a headache, right?"

"Yeah."

"Imagine the worst flu you've ever had in your life. Every symptom under the sun. The wish-you-were-dead kind of flu. Now multiply it by ten. That's what heroin withdrawal feels like."

"Christ."

"Now, imagine if someone told you that a tiny little injection with this . . ."—Minnie dangled the Fit Pack from her fingers—"would make you better right away. Not later today, not tomorrow or a few days from now—immediately."

"Right," Ky said, trying to keep her eyes on the road but also wanting to get a better look at the Fit Pack. "So you're a drug dealer."

"Not exactly."

They were now on Cabramatta Road, passing their old high school. Minnie glanced at the gates to the school's entrance before casting her eyes back to her handbag.

"More of a middleman," Minnie said. "I don't sell to users. You won't see me at Cabra Station or anything."

"That still sounds like being a drug dealer."

"Dealer, entrepreneur. Whatever makes you happy."

They returned to silence. Ky stayed below the speed limit, worried that if she was pulled over, Minnie would be a liability.

She kept glancing over, anticipating that Minnie would complain about Ky's driving like somebody's grandmother—it was something she was used to hearing, people her own age complaining about how she followed the road rules that no one else followed—but it never came. Minnie continued staring out the window, at the houses that got bigger and nicer the closer they got to the Mingyue Lay Buddhist Temple.

On previous trips to the temple, they'd picked out the houses they wanted. Ky liked the two-story ones. Minnie preferred the homes with the remote-controlled gates. Denny liked the house with the arch-shaped entrance and arched double garage—the McDonald's house, he called it. The train line didn't stretch this far, which meant less foot traffic, less heroin. But also less color, less life. Even as children, they never wanted to live in this area. They imagined picking out their big homes and teleporting the structures back into Cabramatta, where things were rougher, sure, but also livelier, more vibrant. Because that was the paradox of Cabramatta—it wasn't like other crime-ridden suburbs where drugs and gangs depressed the local economy and bled the town gray. Cabramatta still had the best phở and the best bánh mì; noisy, colorful, crowded markets; and everywhere you looked, chatty, opinionated old women in visors whose laughs and complaints filled the air with an energetic buzz. Cabramatta proved that a town could be gorgeous and sick, comforting and dangerous, imperfect but home. Ky had wanted so badly to get away from it, all while missing it every day she was gone.

"So are you 5T?" Ky asked as she turned the car into the quiet temple parking lot.

Minnie pushed herself back into a proper seated position so she could better see the temple. "Haven't been here in ages," she said, craning her neck to see the tops of the colorful pagodas.

"Yeah?"

"Yeah, not since Tomb Sweeping Day when we were, like, in high school. What do you know about 5T?"

Ky pulled the car into an empty parking spot.

"Um," she said, trying to remember what Eddie had said the five Ts stood for. "Love, money, prison, punishment, suicide?"

Minnie let out a laugh that surprised her. "Which blowhard did you learn that from?"

"What?" Ky said, defensive, undoing her seat belt. "Is it wrong?"

"Well, technically, those five words do start with T, so, bravo."

"Okay," Ky said, crossing her arms. "Whatever. It's a dumb name anyway. Sounds like a gang for try-hard losers."

"Tuổi trẻ thiếu tình thương," Minnie said.

It was jarring for Ky to hear Minnie speak Vietnamese. Neither of them had ever been good at it. Even at the height of their fluency when they were children, their vocabularies had been about as complex as the subjects they discussed, which were not complex at all. But Ky understood what Minnie said. Five words. Each beginning with T. Tuổi trẻ thiếu tình thương. *Childhood without love.*

Ky understood that she should feel sympathy for the gangsters of Cabramatta. She understood that she should feel bad for Minnie. She even understood that no one would choose that life unless they felt like they had no other choice. But what about

Denny's choice? What choice did he have in getting killed? What choice did Ky have in losing her brother?

"I'm not going to feel bad for them," Ky said.

"No one expects you to."

"Even if it sucks to have shitty parents, it doesn't mean you can just go around killing people."

"I know."

"I hate this."

"Me too."

"I really do."

"Me too."

Outside the columbarium, Ky grabbed Minnie by the elbow. "You're not allowed to say shit when we're in there," Ky said.

"Huh?"

Ky tilted her head in the direction of the entrance. "Once we get into the room with all the dead people's ashes. There'll be photos. Don't say anything good or bad about any of them."

Minnie raised a brow. "You worried ghosts will follow you home?"

"No," Ky lied. "It's just—"

"Give me a bit more credit than that. What do you think I am, some dumb kid?"

"Well, it's just you always . . ." Ky began before Minnie gave her a look that reminded her that any information she was going off was old and probably outdated. Maybe Minnie had changed.

They walked single file into the long dark room, the air thick with burnt incense. They passed the unsmiling photographs of the old, the young, the deceased couples whose urns shared a cubby.

Ky stopped when she got to Denny's photo. Minnie, handbag pressed tight against her side, eyed every cubby until she got to his. She froze.

"Wow."

"Wow?"

"Not wow-wow. It's just . . . this isn't what I'd expected."

"What did you expect?"

Minnie took a step closer, brought her face nearer to Denny's photo.

"Well, for one, whoever was here last put old Happy Meal toys next to his photo," she said, pointing at the hamburger Transformers that Ky's mother had taken from the top of the family's VCR and placed in Denny's cubby.

"My mum still thinks of Denny as a kid."

"Well, he was."

"But not a Happy Meal kid."

"I guess not," Minnie said. "Some people just won't let others change. Right?"

Ky stared at Minnie. Was she talking about her? She waited for Minnie to elaborate, to accuse Ky of doing to Minnie what her mother was doing to Denny. But it never came.

"Well . . ." Minnie said, eyes still on Denny's photo. "Fuck."

"Yeah."

"How was he?" Minnie asked. "Before he died. Last time I saw him—and I mean saw him proper, not at Lucky 8—he'd just started high school."

Ky tried to remember the last time she spent time with her

brother. It blurred with the time when she came home for Tết, the two of them scrubbing windows, Denny calling her out for still throwing tantrums at twenty-two. She remembered going to the Lunar New Year festival in the heart of Cabramatta with Denny and Eddie, treating them to phở and fairy floss, compulsively checking her pager. Once they'd stuffed themselves, they walked up and down John Street between the festive market stalls, pinching the backs of one another's shirts so they wouldn't get lost in the crowd, stopping to watch lion dancing troupes. Every now and again, a white heroin addict who'd ridden the train to Cabramatta for drugs would stand alongside them, face initially lit with confusion, changing to delight, at the way the puppet lion heads batted their enormous eyelids, as though flirting with the crowd. The addicts, normally oscillating between agitation and drowsiness, hollered and applauded when the men and women in the lion costumes got onto one another's shoulders, raised the lion head into the air, and pretended to gobble pieces of lettuce that shopkeepers had hung outside their stores.

"I think he was struggling," Ky said. It was a hard thing for her to admit; she allowed the guilt and shame to wash over her.

"Yeah?"

"Yeah. I think he was under too much pressure. No one should have to be perfect to be accepted, you know? And I think we lost sight of that. *I* lost sight of that."

Minnie reached for the McDonald's Happy Meal toy, held the tiny plastic Big Mac in her palm. She fiddled with it, clicking the plastic arms, legs, and head into place so that the burger transformed into a robot. She returned it to the cubby, gently

323

positioned it so it appeared to stand guard over Denny's photo. Ky had never seen Minnie be so precious about anything.

"I wasn't there for him in the end," Ky said.

"How so?"

"Well, I told my parents to let him go to Lucky 8 after his formal. I told them it'd be fine. I told them everything would be fine, like I knew everything, even though I was in Melbourne."

"You couldn't have known," Minnie said, still looking at Denny's photo. "Even I didn't know what would happen, and I lived with Thien."

"But I just can't help but feel . . . like, if I had done something differently, if I hadn't left in the first place, maybe that would have changed something. Like, if I'd stayed, maybe I could have arranged an after-party for him, or I could have gone to Lucky 8 with him, or I could have just been a better sister and supported him instead of pressuring him into—"

"Ky," Minnie said, meeting Ky's eyes. Her face was soft, sad. "You were just living your own life, like Denny was living his."

"But—"

"You can't be there for everyone. You can't be everything to everyone. People will make their own choices, no matter what you do."

"I wasn't there for you, either," Ky said, surprising herself. She wanted to stay angry at Minnie; she wanted to stay focused on all the ways Minnie had let her down. But standing in front of Denny's smiling photo, she couldn't help but see the connection between her treatment of her brother and her former best friend, how unfair she'd been, how she'd let them both down, too.

Minnie shrugged. She looked at the ceiling, then at the floor. "Even if you'd tried," Minnie said, looking back at Denny's smiling photo, "I don't think it would have been enough."

The words stung, and again Ky found herself wrestling the urge to be combative, to rain down her anger on Minnie, all while pangs of sympathy elbowed their way through. Because Minnie was right. As much as she had wanted to be enough for Minnie, how could she have been? Where Denny and Ky had always had each other, lived under the same roof, shared parents who offered stability, Minnie was only ever a visitor. No matter how much she ate, studied, or played with them, Minnie always had to go home—to what, Ky never fully understood. Of course Minnie had wanted—needed—more.

Ky studied the profile of Minnie's face, recognized the contours of the friend she'd loved the most—the friend who had once been everything to her. But she also saw things she didn't recognize—changes that hadn't so much grown over and concealed the Minnie that Ky knew so much as fused with and fundamentally changed what was there. The woman standing beside her was both Minnie and not Minnie. A sister and a stranger. Someone in need of saving and someone worth condemning. Someone who fought for Denny and still watched him die. Ky felt angry toward Minnie. She felt sorry. She couldn't bridge the two. Not yet. Maybe not ever.

"Don't people burn stuff for the dead?" Minnie said, changing the subject. "Can we do that?"

"There are metal trash cans outside for burning," Ky said.

"But you need to bring your own joss paper. I wanted to bring a Woolies catalogue or something, burn all the chips and chocolates for him."

"Does that work?"

"I dunno. Does Monkey Magic work?"

The corners of Minnie's mouth curled upward, even as her eyes remained sad and heavy. Observing Minnie's face, Ky realized that sometimes you could be too sad to even cry.

"Hey, I've got an idea." Minnie felt around in her handbag, pulled out the Fit Packs. "Look at all the stuff on these wrappers." She examined the packs, turning them in her hands to make out the various deals. "We could burn him some mangoes, rainbow-flavored Paddle Pops, Dove bar soap. *Oooh,* Ferrero Rocher!"

"Come on, I wasn't being serious," Ky said.

"Why not?" Minnie said, a manic quality creeping into her voice. "We can even put it in front of the Buddha for blessing or whatever, make it all temple official. I mean, look, Ky, a forty-eight-pack of Ferrero Rocher. Denny *loves* Ferrero Rocher."

Ky fetched one of the temple-issued poker sticks and trash cans while Minnie dashed into the main hall to wave her Fit Packs in front of the Buddha statues. When she came back, she spilled the contents of the packs into her handbag—Ky winced at the sight of hypodermic needles—and, hands shaking, peeled apart the glued edges and began lighting one catalogue sheet after another, dropping them into the trash can as they blackened and curled. She pulled out a cigarette, dropped that into the trash can, too.

"What the hell!" Ky said as the flames caught and sent ciga-rette smoke into the air.

"He can't die twice," Minnie said. "Besides, think of how cool he'll look! All the ghost girls will be lining up for him."

"You're unbelievable."

"And I'm sorry."

The sudden sincerity in Minnie's voice caught Ky off guard. Minnie grabbed ahold of Ky's free hand. Looking down, Ky noticed that Minnie had a broken fingernail, what looked like bruising and scabs and superficial burns. When she looked back up, Minnie's eyes were so open, vulnerable—she reminded Ky of the friend she'd first made in kindergarten, the one who stuck by her for the next decade.

"I mean it," Minnie said. "I'm sorry for what I said, and the way I left. I was just so . . . I don't know. So angry. Angry and jealous. Angry about being jealous. I'm sorry if I ever made you feel like you weren't enough. I'm sorry I wasn't a better friend. I just . . ." She tapped her chest with a closed fist. "Something felt split open, and I didn't know how to fix it."

"It's okay," Ky said, feeling like she meant it. For years, she'd stewed. For years, she'd sworn that it would never be okay, that the wounds they'd inflicted on each other would never heal. But now that part of their lives didn't seem to matter so much. Things were different. Life was bigger for some, over for others. Denny was dead. Minnie was sorry.

"I'm sorry, too," Ky said. "About what I said and the things I did."

"And I'm sorry about Denny," Minnie added, giving Ky's hand a squeeze. They were both clammy. "I don't know what

I can do to make this right. I know there's nothing that will bring him back, but I can go see your parents, if you think that'll help. I can say sorry to them. I can get on my knees and let them know how I never meant for anything bad to happen."

"I don't think that's necessary."

"I'll even go to the police if you want me to. I can go—"

"Minnie," Ky said, cutting her off before she could speak any faster. "You said it yourself—what would it change?"

Minnie stared into the smoke that drifted from the metal can. "Yeah," she said, her voice a whisper. "I wish I could fix this."

"You can't."

"I know, but . . ." For a moment, she appeared to be lost in thought. "I know we can't go back," she finally said. "But I wish we could."

It was the fantasy that had consumed Ky's daydreams—the fantasy of their friendship never ending, of the different lives they could have lived. But it was just that, a fantasy. The lost look in Minnie's eyes suggested the same.

"I miss you sometimes," Ky said. "Actually I miss you all the time, when I'm not pissed off with you. And even then I still kind of miss you."

Minnie smiled, but her eyes still betrayed a pain that Ky recognized—it was what Ky saw when she looked at herself in the mirror, her attempts to smile that were dampened by the pervasive loss of someone she loved. Minnie let go of Ky's hand, wiped her running nose with the back of her own hand, then wiped it against her pants.

"I miss you, too. And I miss Denny. I even miss your parents."

They stared at the final wisps of cigarette and catalogue

smoke as it emerged from the can and was whisked away by the wind. Ky suddenly felt exhausted, like she hadn't slept in days. Minnie closed her eyes.

"What now?" Ky said.

"Well," Minnie said, squinting at the sun. "We're already here. Might as well ask Buddha for stuff, right?"

They were the only people in the temple's main hall. The three giant buddhas loomed, the Quan Âm to the right, the gold-leaf statuettes of laughing old men surrounding them.

They knelt side by side, knees against cold tiles. Ky pressed her palms together, closed her eyes, curled her body forward, and wished. She felt Minnie do the same.

Chapter 13

I kneel beside her in front of the Buddha, air but not air, existing but not here, and wish. She's much older now. The first gray hairs have emerged on her head. Crow's-feet appear around her eyes. She's traded her rimless eyeglasses for a pair framed by plastic tortoiseshell.

She kneels beside our mother, who has now fully grayed, whose fingers are bony, whose spirit is willful as ever. She offers her a cushion for her knees, but our mother waves her away.

"I can ask for anything I want, right?" she says.

"What you mean?"

"You always told us to ask the Buddha for good grades, but that doesn't really make sense anymore."

Our mother examines her face, taking in the grown woman her daughter has become. When she was the age her daughter is now, she'd already married, had two children, left her first home, struggled to make sense of her second. She tries to see her daughter for the adult that she is, but no matter how tall, freckled, or gray her daughter becomes, she still sees the little girl who used to reach for her, who cried when she was stung by a bee, who hollowed out bread rolls when no one was looking, stuffed the fluffy white insides in her mouth, and left behind crusts for everyone else.

"Ask for anything you want," our mother says.

They make their wishes, they burn their offerings, they drive into town.

Ky hasn't seen the heart of Cabramatta in more than fifteen years. Not since the funeral, not since she tracked down those witnesses. When she does visit, she stays in her childhood home, refusing to venture out. She'd thought, after praying beside Minnie all those years ago, that she might move back to Sydney, work on forgiveness, forgiveness of herself, forgiveness of Minnie, work things out with her former best friend, help our parents navigate their grief. But her own grief—and her own guilt—was so enormous that she returned to Melbourne shortly after. Cabramatta was too stark a reminder of the brother she lost, the fault she bore, the guilt she couldn't shake.

What's changed?

The grief is still there, thick as ever. But she's older, tougher. And she's curious. She wants to know how it might feel to leave her family home, to walk down John Street, to pass Lucky 8. She's terrified. There are moments when she wants to hold our mother's hand. Our mother senses this, of course. Ky thinks our mother moves through the world like a blunt instrument—loud and single-minded and insensitive—but daughters can be wrong, so wrong. The mother senses, and the mother knows. It's just hard for her to be who her daughter wants her to be; hard to undo what she's learned; hard to overcome the blunt pain she's experienced herself, the blunt pain she carries, that makes her both turn inward and lash out, never fully in control of herself. The mother takes her daughter's elbow, hooks her arm through—her way of saying *I'm here, I'm here, I was always here.*

They drop into the Commonwealth Bank, which has gotten new carpet and shinier ATMs, to meet our father for lunch. His hair is a shock of white, his clothes still don't fit, and he's picked out a new phở restaurant, this one the closest to soldier helmet phở he's ever tried.

After years of avoiding each other, father and daughter can finally look each other in the eyes when they speak. He does it because he wants his daughter to know him; she does it because when she told him what had happened to his son, when she revealed everything she'd learned about Minnie and Thien and the lies that were shared by everyone who was there, he'd apologized for all the ways he'd come up short as a father. He'd told her he was proud of her. He'd told her he loved her. He'd never said it again, embarrassed by his own vulnerability, embarrassed by his break from tradition, embarrassed by his honesty. But it was enough. For her, it was enough.

Seated across from her parents at the phở restaurant, Ky wonders aloud about Minnie.

"Maybe you wouldn't even recognize her if you saw her today," our mother says in Vietnamese.

"Maybe," Ky says in English.

"I mean, look at you. You don't look like you did when you were a young girl."

"What's that supposed to mean?"

"I mean you are getting old and if you wait any longer to

get married and have children, the boat will sail without you! And if you don't visit home more often, the next time you come back, your father and I will be dead!"

"I call every week."

"You can call a dead person!"

Ky wants to argue, but instead she tries to savor a moment that feels normal: a moment when together they don't feel especially broken or wounded—just foolish, like everyone else.

Turning the conversation back to her friend, Ky imagines a parallel world where they remained friends. The images are fuzzy, unstable. It doesn't work.

"Maybe she has moved away," our mother says. "Maybe she married rich. Maybe she lives in Perth."

Ky hopes that this is true, even though her heart tells her it isn't.

"I don't see as many junkies around town," she says.

Our mother stares at her, incomprehension on her face. "What you mean?"

"Junkies," Ky says in Vietnamese before immediately switching back to English. "Don't see many."

"They all dead."

"Seriously?"

"Yes. Take too much drug, die too much death."

"No way," Ky says, because how could thousands of people drop dead in Cabramatta without her hearing about it?

"You don't live here; you don't know."

"And you've personally seen thousands of junkies die?"

Our mother shrugs.

"They're all in Redfern," our father says.

"Yeah?"

"They opened injecting rooms in Redfern, so the junkies went there."

"And all dead."

Other things change.

The news no longer talks about Cabramatta. Heroin shipments get cut off. Children who watched their parents and uncles and aunts and big brothers and big sisters lose themselves to drugs choose a different path. Senators who once griped about Asians now turn their attention to Arabs and Africans. The shiny red benches in Freedom Plaza are replaced with shiny gray stone. For a hundred dollars, a local will take white tourists on a food tour. The train station gets an elevator. The Red Lea Chicken shop that sold the best hot chips increases the price of every item.

But some things don't change.

The Red Lea Chicken shop still sells the best hot chips. The Asian women are still loud, opinionated, and wear sun visors. Our mother still doesn't get paid leave or sick leave from her job at the fabric store. The Lunar New Year and Moon Festival are as colorful as they've ever been, with lion dancers mesmerizing adults and children alike. The senators who tear down Arabs and Africans carry the same hate in their hearts that was once reserved for Cabramatta. Memory doesn't fade. It's the same, it's the same, it's all the same.

As Ky waits for their bowls of phở to arrive, she observes our mother straightening the collar of our father's work shirt. She notices our father picking up a lemon wedge from the herb platter—two seeds appearing as eyes, the curl of the lemon's skin a big smile—and making it dance for them. She smiles. But still, here, back home, she can't help but measure the years we've lost.

There is no way for me to tell her that we've lost so much more—more than time with our parents, more than time with each other. There is no way for me to tell her that the loss began well before we were born, that our parents had loss, and their parents had loss, and our ancestors had loss—loss of home, loss of place, loss of self, loss of life—and we were born with that loss, carried it, burdened by it, part of it.

I want to tell her it's not her fault. It was never her fault. I want to tell her that if she wants to do right by us, she has to live the life she wants for herself—without fear, without compromise, without second-guessing whether she belongs. I want to tell her that sometimes you can't go quietly. Sometimes you can't just be good. Sometimes you have to fight—and it's not fair, and it's not right, but what other choice do we have? I want to tell her this, and so much more, but I don't have words, don't have air, don't exist, my light switched off, and yet I'm here, I'm still here, knowing, knowing, burdening, making her carry me, as I carried others, because what do the living do but carry the weight of the dead?

So I kneel beside her, to lighten the load. I kneel beside her, to let her know she's not alone. I kneel beside her because she's my sister. And as she makes her wishes—at the temple, in Cabra, tasting soldier helmet phở—I wish alongside her, with her, for her, because I know how much she wants it, how scared she is that it might never be within reach. Together we wish. We wish for good health and long life and best luck for our parents. We extend that wish to everyone we've ever loved. We wish great things for Minnie—happiness, safety, satisfaction—that she finds what she's looking for, whatever that may be. And then for my sister, for Cabramatta, for everyone who ever came or went or stayed—a wish for comfort. A wish for presence. A wish for power. A wish for dignity. A wish for all the strength in the world to endure, to survive, to finally, finally, *finally* conquer this place we call home.

Acknowledgments

This book is a work of fiction and the characters are my own, but Cabramatta is a real place that did throughout the 1990s experience a heroin epidemic. I grew up in the Cabramatta area, and although I have memories of the epidemic, I was only a child at the time. The work of Dr. Mandy Thomas, particularly her book *Dreams in the Shadows: Vietnamese-Australian Lives in Transition* (Allen & Unwin, 1999), and the comprehensive ethnographic research of Dr. Lisa Maher were invaluable in helping me piece together the sides of Cabramatta I didn't see or, as a child, understand.

The following people helped me bring this novel into the world and to them I give my sincerest thanks:

My agent, Hillary Jacobson, has been a fierce advocate for me and this novel since our first correspondence—I am grateful to have her in my corner. Emily Krump and Manpreet Grewal guided revisions of this novel with great thoughtfulness and care—I couldn't have asked for better editors. The kind souls at William Morrow/HarperCollins and HQ/HarperCollins UK helped usher this manuscript into print, and I am thankful for every designer, copy editor, associate editor, publicist, sales rep, marketer, and intern who gave this novel the time of day. And the lovely Emma Finn at C&W and Sophie Baker at Curtis Brown UK found homes for this novel around the world.

Laura Moriarty is the advisor of dreams who read multiple drafts of this novel, gave incisive feedback, and believed in me enough to demand more of me.

Cote Smith is my writing buddy. Knowing that an author of his caliber would read my earliest drafts made me more determined than ever to improve my craft.

Alexandra Kostoulas taught with unlimited patience and encouragement the first creative writing class I ever took.

Nita Yun suggested that I quit my job to get an MFA. Russ Mitchell cosigned that suggestion with great enthusiasm. It was wonderful advice.

The late Ian Hale taught me to play to my strengths, to never accept mediocrity, and to take pride in coming from southwest Sydney. Thanks, sir.

The late James Morgan set a high bar for friendship. I can't say for sure that he had a direct influence on this book being written, but I just wanted to say, in print, that I love and miss him.

My parents—much has been left unsaid, but I will say this: 妈妈 爸爸, 非常感激你们.

My big brother, Sid, dropped math in year ten, which paved the way for me to drop math in year ten. Life = forever changed. Thanks, bro.

Humphrey and Isabelle are good dogs.

The following friends were sources of encouragement and support during the years when I worked on this novel: Sadia Latifi, Korbin Jones, Rao Li, and Lena Rutkowski. I am also grateful for Movie Club (Alison Grasso, Chelsea Rickling, John Skidmore, Bethany Reis, Zack Akers, John Pels, Colin Miller, Michelle Patches, Matt Patches)—the silver lining of the pandemic.

Finally, Skip Bronkie—my dearest, wisest, worthiest friend. It is a miracle to have found you.

ONE PLACE. MANY STORIES

Bold, innovative and
empowering publishing.

FOLLOW US ON:

@HQStories